A PLACE CALLED JUBILEE

TIMOTHY J. GARRETT

DEDICATED TO CYNTHIA:
FOR ALWAYS LOVING AND BELIEVING IN ME,
FOR SOMETIMES PUSHING ME, AND
FOR NEVER ALLOWING ME TO SETTLE FOR LESS.

CHAPTER 1

WASHINGTON, D.C.

The steamy summer of 1961, a long southern summer lumbering along from April to September. That was the summer that destroyed his life. Like a twister ripping through an old building and the brick façade tumbling down to the street. The dust rising up and the rats scurrying out. After it blows by, there's nothing but rubble.

His name was Coleman Hightower and he had of late begun a new life as a servant of God. His simple room in the rectory, furnished with a single bed and an old wooden chest of drawers, was like a palace compared to the shacks of some of his childhood neighbors. His mornings were spent visiting the shut-ins and other elderly members of the venerated Lamb of God Presbyterian Church. Most evenings, he soaked up the knowledge – both Biblical and temporal – of the Reverend Doctor A. H. Browning.

The beginnings of that summer appeared early in the year. It was a snowy Thursday, the kind of day that crippled the city. He did not hear the bus run by his block all day and cars were strewn about, making the streets look like a giant child's unkempt playroom. Thursday night, he could not sleep. As shadows from trees danced across the ceiling, snatches of Dr. Browning's conversations and sermons came to him. The words stirred his soul, fanning his desire to make something of his life, to be someone of consequence.

A few days before, Dr. Browning said, "Coleman, I am made of different material than those I see around me. God has touched me and called me to lead this mighty church of His. I can do naught else but lead it."

They sat in Dr. Browning's study, a tall-ceilinged cavern of stone containing several centuries worth of bound treatises and sermons, the collected wisdom of many generations of God's appointed shepherds. Dr.

Browning had spoken these words into the dust-flecked air of the study, his hands tented in front of him, a professorial look on his face.

He turned to his young protégé.

"Coleman, I see the same type of call on your life."

Coleman's heart suddenly felt fluttery and muffled, like a bird trapped in a cloth bag.

Dr. Browning opened his palms to Coleman.

"I cannot promise to what height God will see fit to elevate you." A kind fatherly expression spread across the old minister's face. "But, I feel certain He will bless you."

An intense, almost desperate longing, formless yet deeply lodged, stayed with Coleman as he fell asleep.

The snow of Thursday gave way to a brilliantly clear Friday. Workers had toiled through the night and at least the main streets had been cleared of abandoned vehicles.

The sense of excitement in the air was not hard to perceive. People smiled and whistled. Birds chirped. The engine sounds of the taxis that braved the still slushy streets seemed more immediate, more urgent. The change in atmosphere was even expressed by the snow, changing its form from white stillness to fluid, transparent, rushing little rivulets.

He found a spot in the crowd and waited, hands in the pockets of his overcoat. The gleaming white dome soared over the sea of heads. He could see the top of the grandstand on the steps of the Capitol building though the stage was not visible from his location. The mood of the crowd was friendly, the bonds of fellow nationality drawing hearts together on this most American of days. Smiles and good wishes rippled among the throng.

He stamped the numbness out of his feet and shoved his hands deeper into his pockets but he was unable to escape the cold. The heat of thousands of bodies was quickly absorbed by the sky above, dissipating the meager warmth into the atmosphere. A flock of birds flew overhead, black spots swirling across a blue canvas. Though the cold dulled his sense of touch, making him unable to feel his nose or toes, it sharpened his vision and hearing. He glanced behind him and saw the Washington Monument. The starkness of the brilliant spire piercing the blueness was breathtaking. The winter air magnified the obelisk, making it seem as if he could reach out his hand and pluck it from the sky and place it in his pocket. Policemen's whistles, voices on the other side of the Mall, even the squeak of cars' suspension springs as they navigated the rough Washington streets were clearly audible on this January morning.

The crowd began to get restless. Murmurs of conversation grew louder and then faded away. Sighs erupted nearby. An unseen woman broke into a beautiful rendition of God Bless America. Other people joined in and applause erupted at the conclusion of the song. Another interlude of quiet followed. A wave of murmurs rushed back from the front of the crowd, accompanied by pointing fingers. He looked toward the grandstand. Dark-suited dignitaries were beginning to file in and fill the seats at the top. The crowd clapped their hands. The applause swelled.

After a long while, quietness flowed back. Music from a military band blared out. He heard a man's voice coming from a loudspeaker but he could not make out the words.

And then, "You, John Fitzgerald Kennedy, do solemnly swear..."

Another voice repeated the words, "I, John Fitzgerald Kennedy, do solemnly swear..."

The seesaw cadence of the oath of office soon concluded and was punctuated by wild cheering. A woman beside him was standing on her tiptoes, craning her neck to see, tears streaming down her face. Someone farther away could see the stage and said, "Nixon is shakin his hand and grinnin like a damn possum!"

The cheering continued and again a hush swept back. The new president had stepped to the podium.

Coleman turned his head slightly, angling his ear toward the loudspeaker, and closed his eyes. The sensation of people around him fled. The crushed grass beneath his feet, the frigid sky over his head, the city around him, the thoughts of the old life within him - they all rolled away, a withered parchment crumbling into scraps.

The words coming from the speaker poured into his mind like liquid light. The words united him to the man at the podium. The address raised Coleman up from the cold ground, sent him soaring through golden landscapes, set his trajectory toward the brilliant sunrise of a new world and a new way of living. These words, strung together into noble phrases and sentences by a vibrant leader, promised an end to poverty, an end to war, an end to enslavement of all kinds. Coleman stood on the soil of America, the shining beacon of justice for all the world to see. This new man in the White House was the herald of a new form of liberty, an enlightened freedom that would take hold and spread around the globe. How could it not, in light of the eloquence of the speech bursting forth from the loudspeakers?

Fifteen minutes. That was how long the inaugural address lasted. As the New England-tinged voice faded and was replaced by the roaring of the crowd, Coleman was brought back to the present. As if observing from afar, he saw himself joining the cries of approval and the clapping and the whistles. More tear-streaked faces surrounded him. He touched his own face and found it moist.

The crowd lingered after the ceremony, after the retreat of the dignitaries to the warmth of the Capitol building, as if the people wished to savor the moment. Eventually, the throng began to disperse.

He headed toward the side of the Mall, facing a long walk back to the rectory. By the time he was two blocks off the Mall, the smiling faces of the inaugural audience had morphed into the severe determined faces of Washingtonians intent on the business of a cold January morning. Because of street closings related to the ceremony and parade, he had to take an alternate walking route, a path he had not traveled before. After a few blocks, he began to encounter shuttered storefronts and vacant lots. A stray dog barked, peering at him from under a fire escape as he passed. There were no cars moving on these streets still snow-laden from the storm and far down the priority list of the snowplows. He saw a corner ahead with the cross street seeming to be a little wider. He decided to turn to the right.

As he rounded the corner, he saw three men on the sidewalk talking, one of them offering a cigarette to one of the others. For a split second, he paused, a hitch appearing in his step. He continued walking, changing course to pass between the group and the street.

The taller one stepped in front of him, flipped his cigarette to the sidewalk, crushed it out with his foot, and asked, "Where are you going?" Coleman changed course again, intending an even wider berth.

"I said, where are you going?" By this time, the other two had scooted behind him, cutting off his only avenue of escape.

Coleman managed to get some words out.

"Just going home. Been at the inauguration."

The tall one sneered at the others. "Inauguration?" They laughed. "That's just a white man's party. And you shoulda stayed in the white man's part of town."

He addressed the other two the way a teacher would address his class.

"What we got here is a white boy who's lost his way, that's what we got here."

To Coleman, he said, "This is my street and you can't walk down it unless I say so. And I don't say so."

More laughs. Coleman tried to walk between them, head and eyes down. They closed ranks to prevent his passing and shoved him back to the tightening space between them.

Coleman said, "I am a pastor at..."

"I don't give a goddamn who you are. And I don't give a goddamn where you work. And I don't give a goddamn how much money you got except what you got on you."

As if on signal the other two patted Coleman's coat and back pocket. They fished out a few coins and some folded one-dollar bills.

A shaky voice, straight out of the Blue Ridge Mountains. "If y'all will just let me go back, I'll get off this here street."

The tall one laughed.

"Where the hell you from, peckerwood?" He put his hand to his chin

4

and said, "You got a good suggestion, but I'm afraid I can't let you get off my street. You see, you're already on my street and to get off it, you just have to use my street even more. The only way out of this is for us to take care of you."

To the other two, he said, "Y'all want to do what we did to the last cracker that come around here?" They nodded. The tall one looked back at Coleman.

"Boy, what's your name?"

"Coleman," he said.

The tall one chuckled. "Well, Coleman," he said, "I hope you can swim."

Coleman sprang and pushed hard against the smallest of the three and bolted around the corner. After a second or two, he could hear footsteps coming up quickly behind him and he knew he would not be able to outrun them. At that second, he felt two forearms strike his upper back and then the full weight of one of the three force him to the ground. Before he could react, two of them lifted him with their arms under his and spun him around. The tall one punched him in the abdomen. Coleman's breath rushed out and intense pain shot through to his back.

"That's for running. And now, you're going to get wet." He punched him again. "And if you can't swim, you're going to die."

The two dragged Coleman for a block. There, the street passed over an old iron bridge that spanned a canal of fast-moving filthy water. The tall one tapped a bony finger on his chest.

"If you make it out of the water, I better not ever see your white ass around here again."

The other two quickly lifted him over the low edge of the bridge and shoved.

Coleman faced skyward and he clearly saw the three men peering over the side of bridge as he fell. Their laughing faces moved in a slow pantomime. Behind them, he saw sunlight glint off the windows of the run-down brick factory buildings that bordered the old canal. The distorted time allowed him to guess that the canal carried the waste of factories and the filth of the homes of the factories' workers to the Potomac River and thus to the sea. As he descended toward the surface, the bottom of the bridge came into view and he saw that every square inch of the iron trusses was filled with graffiti left by generations of young people for whom the city provided no relief, no hope, no escape. His body twisted slightly and he saw the rock-lined steep banks of the ditch, the bodies of large rats in varying stages of decay stuffed into the dark spaces between the chunks of stone.

His slow fall was vaguely graceful and was accompanied by a numbness that occurred to him must be the sensation that routinely precedes death, else why would not everyone kick and scream their way out of this world and into the next instead of peacefully fading away on a deathbed. As this thought ran through his mind, his body struck the water symmetrically, with feet and buttocks and head entering the water at the exact same split-second. He was plunged into watery darkness. The numbness immediately disappeared and was replaced by the pain of thousands of needles piercing his skin. His face burst back to the surface and he saw the three on the bridge laughing and suddenly turning to run to the other side to watch him float by.

As Coleman was swept under the bridge, he took a deep breath. The air just above the surface of the water was very cold but it quickly warmed as it traveled through his mouth and into his windpipe. This warm, humid, oxygen-rich air rushed into his lungs, the passageways getting smaller and smaller with each fork, hurrying its load of life-giving gas to the tiniest compartments of his lungs before performing an abrupt about-face and carrying suffocating carbon dioxide out and expelling it back into the same atmosphere that provided the oxygen. Coleman's lungs had done this same operation over and over, many times per minute since the day the doctor started their employment with a slap on Coleman's bottom twenty-two years before. However, with the next breath and for the first time since the day of his birth, no air would be travelling down, only water.

Ice cold water.

CHAPTER 2

A SMALL ALABAMA TOWN, 1921

The big man said, "Begin," and gave an almost imperceptible nod to the other man behind her. She could do nothing except stand. The ropes on her wrists drew the blood close to the surface of her thin skin, the selfsame blood that would soon be dripping onto the dusty street. The sun was bright. She looked through slit lids at the men standing in front of her. They looked away, all of them except for the big man.

The crack of the whip was followed within a half second by soft gasps coming from a hundred mouths, a sound that was cut short by the sweeping glower of the big man.

She was surprised. She thought that it might not hurt. She was wrong. It hurt like hell.

The cadence of the whip was slow, like the rhythm of a tired farm hand chopping wood at the end of a long day. The look on the face of the man wielding the whip was not like that. Instead of fatigue, his countenance was one of anger, deep burning rage. The anger came out of his heart, down his arm, into the worn ancient handle of the whip, out its long tendrils. It sparked from the tips and flamed into the flesh of her back. After a couple of slashes, her thin worn blouse started to turn to ribbon and long red lines formed on the wrinkled brown of her back. After a couple more whistles of the whip, the neat lines dissolved into crimson cascades that saturated the clinging strips of cloth and dripped to the street, creating small red beads balancing on the top layer before dissolving into the dirt below. Ashes to ashes, dust to dust.

She could hear a few gasps still coming from behind her and a few whimpers. However, most everyone had become silent. There was no other sound except for the singing percussion of the whip. It did not hurt much at all now. Her shoulders that had been tensed up as the rope held her arms above her head now relaxed.

Everything was getting hazy. She dozed off a few times. The light and the sounds faded, a quilt of comfortable darkness draping around her. Then she heard the whip like it was a sound far away.

What is that? It sounds like they're running the old cane press. Oh, let's run and see if he will let us have one of the cut ends to chew.

But when she tried to run, she found her feet would not move. Her childhood friends dissolved in a jumble of visions. Instead of sweet cane juice in her mouth, she only tasted the salt of sweat and felt the grit of the dusty street in her teeth. Reality slowly drew her back.

Oh yes. That man is whipping me.

Time came to mean nothing to her. A minute could just as well be a millennium. Her eyes were closed. When she finally lifted her head and opened them, she was not surprised to see the big man still standing there. However, she also would not have been surprised if he was not there, if there were no buildings, if the entire town had crumbled centuries ago and had left only her and the ropes around her wrists and the whip striking her back, providing the ticking clock that marked off the eons.

But there he was. He was not looking at her but was inspecting the people behind her, like a drill sergeant scanning for a less-than-erect rifle or an unpolished button. When his eye caught the movement of her face tilting up toward his, he slowly met her gaze.

She gave him a faint smile for which he returned a stony stare. She craned her head higher, miraculously moving against gravity even though almost all of her blood puddled at her feet. The last ounce of blood in her brain drained down the vessels in her neck as her vision, though it should be darkening, grew brighter and brighter. Blinding light flooded down on her and enveloped her in its warmth and consumed her.

She never saw the big man again.

CHAPTER 3

WASHINGTON, D.C., 1961

The stream made a right turn at the foundation of a building just out of sight of the bridge, an architectural feature decided on decades before that saved Coleman's life. As his flailing arms and legs struck the rock bank, they instinctively began to climb, pulling his wet hypothermic body out of the water. He lay draped on the rocks for a few seconds, spewing water and gasping for air, before his body of its own volition began to clamber up the bank.

He emerged on a side street, no traffic visible. His barely conscious brain pushed his body to walk resulting in a shambling gait toward the busier street. He bounced off the brick wall beside him. Another bounce off the opposite wall, a pinball in a hellish slanted world. He reached the main street, stumbled and fell. He rose to his knee, head down, gasping for air, kneeling in a patch of winter sunlight.

A young woman was walking down the street, heading home. When she saw him, she stopped. No one else was in view.

"Hey, you. What's wrong?"

Coleman gave a brief glance and dropped his head again.

The woman said, "Why are you all wet?" He did not answer.

"You're gonna have to stand up. I'm going to take you to Mrs. Rucker's. You're going to have to walk 'cause I can't carry you. I'll hold onto your arm."

Coleman was unable to speak. He rose on wobbly legs and she clasped his arm. They began to slowly walk. She led him past the next block to a tidy wooden row house with blue shutters and a sign in front that read RUCKER'S BOARDING HOME. As she helped him onto the small front porch, a woman emerged.

"Rosalee, you can't bring that white boy in here!"

9

The woman, Mrs. Rucker, saw that the young man was drenched and incoherent, and said, "Put him on the couch."

The young woman led him inside to the plaid woven sofa in the front room. Mrs. Rucker returned with a patchwork quilt. A towel, flannel shirt and work pants were folded under her arm.

"Rosalee, you go on and heat up some of those peas on the stove. Don't come back in here until I say."

As Rosalee hurried to the kitchen, the woman held up the quilt, screening the boy from her vision.

"Son, you're going to have to get them wet clothes off'n you. I got some dry ones for you. You go ahead and change out your clothes and we'll get you warmed up."

Coleman was only partly lucid but he wordlessly obeyed his new caretaker. He let the wet clothes fall to the floor and dried himself with the towel. The dry clothes were oversized and warm. The woman wrapped the quilt around him. Coleman could feel life beginning to course through his body once again.

He only vaguely remembered getting out of the water and walking to the house. At first, he thought the woman was his own Granny Mae and that he had been transported back in time and space to the tiny shack in the mountains.

Granny Mae, I don't want any of that healing potion! It tastes like rotten corn!

Delirium scrolled confusing images and thoughts past his mind's eye as Mrs. Rucker said, "I'll go hang up your clothes in the kitchen where they'll dry out faster. Rosalee is getting you somethin to eat." As she turned to leave, she glanced out of the front window. "Don't you get off that couch. Don't want nobody seein you."

When Coleman woke, the setting sun was casting golden-orange light into the room. He sat up, his muscles protesting. His mouth was dry. He picked up a glass of water from the end table and drained it. A voice came from the kitchen in the back of the house. "You awake?"

It's not the woman, must be her boarder, the girl who rescued me. What was her name?

He saw a figure coming through the door. When the gold-infused light illuminated her face, Coleman's breath caught.

He first noticed her eyes, brown with hints of green. There was a look of intelligence and determination behind them. Her smooth face was crowned by dark hair pulled back by a band of pink and white cloth. The sunlight ignited the outline of her head, creating a halo that dazzled and burned into Coleman's mind and memory.

He did not speak, could not speak. In years to come, he would say that she was the most beautiful woman he had ever seen.

"Bout time you woke up. Here's some black-eyed peas and cornbread."

10

She brought a tray holding the steaming bowl to the coffee table beside the sofa. "After that, you gotta get out of here. Mrs. Rucker don't need trouble."

Coleman remained silent. He put a spoonful of the peas into his mouth. A rich homey taste flooded his mouth. Within a couple of minutes, he had eaten all of the peas.

"Damn, you about swallowed the bowl." She took the tray and started to stand.

"Thank you. That was very good." His voice was hoarse. He turned to her. "Did you have some?"

She scowled and said, "Hell no. I don't eat black-eyed peas. Haven't for years."

He coughed, clearing his throat.

"Well, thanks anyway. Rosalee."

Rosalee's head jerked toward him. She said, "Yeah, great, you know my name. Now, we gotta get you gone."

Mrs. Rucker walked into the room and said, "I see you're up. Did Rosalee feed you?"

Rosalee nodded and said, "Yes. And like I just told him, he's gotta go."

Coleman said, "I really appreciate your helping me." He glanced at Rosalee. "Both of you."

Mrs. Rucker gave a strained smile. She said, "Well, we couldn't very well let you freeze to death. Now, how we going to get you home? Where do you stay?"

Coleman said, "Ma'am, if you will point me to a bus stop, I can make my way back to the Lamb of God Church. I live in the rectory there."

Mrs. Rucker's face brightened. She said, "Oh, you're a man of God. Praise the Lord!"

Rosalee said, "I'm not sure I can believe in a God who would put us on this wet rock and fling us into the darkness and say, 'Good luck. I hope y'all can get along with each other.'"

Mrs. Rucker swatted Rosalee on her bottom and said, "Now listen here, young lady! I won't have you being rude and I shore won't have you disrespectin the Lord in this house!" Mrs. Rucker turned back to Coleman. "There's a bus stop just down the street. We'll walk with you so's we can make sure you get there."

As Mrs. Rucker retrieved his clothes from the kitchen, Coleman said to Rosalee, "I want to thank you. You didn't have to stop to help me, but you did."

Rosalee said, "Like Mrs. Rucker said, we couldn't just leave you there. You probably would've died." Her eyebrows rose. "I still don't know how you ended up all wet in the middle of this neighborhood."

Before Coleman had to respond, Mrs. Rucker returned with his dry clothes and pointed toward a small door. She said, "You can go into the little room there and change into your clothes."

Within a few minutes, Coleman was walking with the two women. Their pace quickened in the cold evening air.

Rosalee said, "Hey, Mrs. Rucker. Here is that meeting I've been going to that I told you about."

Rosalee motioned toward a flyer tacked onto a telephone pole. Coleman saw that it read: *C.O.R.E. MEETING January 28 7 o'clock in Eve. Columbia Heights Community Center (Basement).*

Mrs. Rucker said, "Child, I know you told me about it, and I told you that you didn't have no business going."

Coleman asked, "What is C.O.R.E.?"

Rosalee shot a glaring look at Coleman and said, "I wasn't talking to you."

Mrs. Rucker said, "Rosalee, hush." She turned to Coleman. "It's a group of troublemakers that I don't want Rosalee gettin mixed up with. I'm kindly serving as her Washington mamma since her real mamma ain't around no more. The world's already got enough worry as it is."

The bus stop loomed. As they reached it, Coleman glanced down the street and saw the bus already approaching. He turned to the women and said, "Again, I want to thank you. You have been very kind."

He shook hands with each of the women. The sound and smell of the diesel engine swelled. As the door opened, Coleman stepped on board. He turned once more, gave a small wave, and collapsed into the front seat. The bus started away and the two women on the curb were gone.

His eyes blurred. The rumble of the bus lulled him. The deepening dusk hid many of the features of the city through which the bus rolled. Illumination pooled at the bottom of streetlights and revealed trashcans and mailboxes. Sometimes, the light reached as far as the clinker brick walls of run-down buildings.

As the scenery of the cold dirty town rolled by, his mind wandered through the day. The inauguration seemed like a lifetime ago. He struggled to recall the inspiration he had felt but it would not come. The terror of the assault and his fall from the bridge was easily brought up, like a raw wound that begins to bleed afresh when the bandage is removed. He pushed the memory deep into his mind. He realized what was left.

The memory of a soft hand on his shoulder. Warm sustenance that resuscitated him. An angelic face whose beauty made his heart soar.

A pang when he realized he may never see her again.

CHAPTER 4

TOWN HALL, A SMALL ALABAMA TOWN, 1961

The mayor walked down the empty street. Above her, the moon pushed its dim light through thin high clouds but only barely. She pulled her collar up. She could only see at the periphery of her vision. Objects in the focal point of her gaze disappeared only to reappear when she looked away, a strange and cruel magician's trick. More than once, she was startled by an inanimate object that materialized just before she passed it, a trashcan that she mistook for a dog in the dimness, a street sign that resembled a man.

The phone call had come earlier in the day and had awakened in the small town long-forgotten fears and raised long-buried questions. She realized that it was her responsibility to calm the fears and answer the questions.

Her footsteps echoed off the stone and brick buildings, bouncing from one side of the street to the other, heralding her approach to the other end of the street. But, there was no one there to hear it. They were already inside the castle-like building, seated around a conference table.

She wondered about the conversations that were now taking place, before her arrival. Were they calming each other's fears or merely whipping them to even higher levels, like hurricane winds across the surface of the sea?

She entered the front door and walked to the conference room. As she entered the room, the quiet voices around the long table stopped. The older faces were distraught, some of the younger ones angry, defiant.

She said, "I know you're all worried about this, but I want to assure you that everything will be all right. It was a long time ago, really a completely different age." Her words did not change the faces.

"That's easy for you to say. Nothing will happen to you. You weren't even there," said a hard-chiseled older man. He counted some of the others seated at the table.

"Three of us at this table were. We can't let them come." Several others shook their heads in agreement.

Another said, "Galen's right. We have to tell them they're not welcome. Give 'em some kind of excuse. And if they come anyway, we'll just have to do whatever is necessary."

The ominous words hung in the air and no one in the room batted them down.

She said, "I don't think that is the right thing to do. We want to do away with any suspicion. If we stonewall them, they will wonder what we are hiding."

Galen shook his head even more forcefully and said, "But if they come and start digging, they will know exactly what we're hiding!"

She tried to keep her voice even. She said, "There are plenty of explanations for what they might find. And they might not find anything. We can limit how far this project is able to go." Some of the faces seem to be less sure now. "Let me talk to them. I believe I can handle this so that no secrets are divulged and so that we don't raise questions. Are you willing to give me a chance?"

Several nods broke through the traces of anger and defiance that remained around the table.

The mayor said, "Fine, then. I'll try to get them on the telephone tomorrow and make sure they know we don't want a lot of disruption to the town from their research here."

The group dispersed into the night.

When out of earshot of the mayor, Galen said, "I'll give her a chance, but only one. Not half a chance more."

CHAPTER 5

WASHINGTON, D.C., 1961

The next morning, his head pounded as he opened his eyes. He was so sore that he could barely move but he made it to the bathroom and got dressed. Someone had already brewed a pot of coffee by the time he made it to the small kitchen in the common area of the rectory. He carried a large steaming mug to the bench by the windows overlooking the courtyard and tried to clear the haziness from his eyes and his mind. Snow blanketed the space. Bare branches from scattered bushes poked through the snow like skeletal fingers reaching up from a grave. A dull red bird flew in, flitting around in a vain search for crumbs of food before struggling out of the high-walled stone enclosure.

What am I going to tell Dr. Browning?

He had never before considered keeping anything from his mentor. Dr. Browning's words and opinions had become a touchstone to him, something by which he could judge his own life and toward which he could strive.

However, in the night, when sleep had not come to him despite his fatigue, his soul had whispered to his intellect, *Don't tell him.* Coleman was not sure why the thought came to him unbidden. Dr. Browning should be told what had happened to him, how he had almost died. But then the questions came.

Why were you in that section of town? Dr. Browning told you a long time ago not go to those places. Why didn't you come back the way you went? Weren't you thinking?

He did not want to lessen in Dr. Browning's eyes. Plus, there was the other matter. The girl, Rosalee.

Would Dr. Browning see the spark? Would he be able to discern the curiosity? The desire?

Coleman heard the click-clack of shoes on the slate tile of the hallway.

Dr. Browning.

"Good morning, Coleman!" After glancing at the young man, he said, "My, you don't look as if you are feeling well this morning! Are you ill? Do you have a fever? I am sure that Mrs. Brewer has some aspirin in her desk that you can take."

Coleman said, "No, I'm all right, Dr. Browning. I went to the inauguration yesterday and fell. That and the cold really got to me. I just need some coffee and some rest."

Dr. Browning said, "I suppose that your duties can wait. But please let me know if you need anything else." The clergyman smiled and glanced down the hall toward the kitchen, eager for his own cup waiting there. "I will return with my coffee and you can tell me about your day yesterday." Within a couple of minutes, Dr. Browning returned and sat beside Coleman.

The pastor patted Coleman's knee and said, "Today is a good day to stay inside and get ready for tomorrow. It is strange that Sunday is a day of rest for everyone except for those of us in the service of the Lord. For us, it is the busiest day of the week. We have to take our Sabbath rest on Saturday along with the Jews." He chuckled at the irony. "So tell me, was the inauguration good?"

Coleman tried to recall the spirit of the inaugural scene, the inspiring words, the feeling in his heart at the time. He had a vague recollection that he had indeed been inspired. However, the trauma of the day suppressed the thrill. He said, "It was very good. Historic."

Dr. Browning said, "Yes, I'm sure it was."

They each sipped and contemplated the steam coming from their respective cups. For several moments, neither said anything. Dr. Browning glanced at his watch and started to stand.

Coleman asked, "Dr. Browning, have you heard of C.O.R.E.?"

Dr. Browning settled back onto the bench. "Core? What do you mean? Like an apple core?"

"No, it's an organization." Coleman spelled it out, "C, O, R, E. C.O.R.E."

"Oh, yes." Dr. Browning's forehead furrowed. "Well, I do seem to recall an article in the paper about a group that may have used those initials. What do the letters stand for?"

Coleman said, "I'm not sure."

Dr. Browning said, "If my memory serves me, the article said that the group was made up of radical Negroes who promoted public disruptions as a way to influence the sentiment of the populace. An unsavory bunch of troublemakers, they sound to me." He frowned, looking like he just eaten a particularly sour cherry and was trying to get the taste out of his mouth. "Why do you ask?"

"No real reason. I happened to see a poster for one of their meetings on the way home from the inauguration and I was just curious."

"Well, Coleman, I would not be so curious that you would be tempted to actually go to one of those meetings. Anything could happen. A riot. A police raid. No, that sort of meeting is no place for a rising pastor."

Coleman said, "No, of course not."

Coleman returned to his coffee. A silent battle raged inside him. His heart, his soul, his mind struggled for control of his tongue. He had almost resolved to remain quiet, to allow the clergyman to excuse himself, to keep his feelings private, when he heard himself say, "Dr. Browning, you know that I said that I fell yesterday." The pastor nodded. "Well, it was not just a simple fall. I actually fell into a canal."

"My goodness, Coleman! And it was cold yesterday!" Dr. Browning had spun and faced Coleman, looking at him more carefully, scanning for signs of injury. "Are you really all right?"

"Yes sir, I am fine. I just slipped and fell in. Lucky for me, there was a young lady walking by and she helped me. She took me to her boarding house and warmed me up and dried my clothes."

Dr. Browning's face changed. The fatherly concern flew away to be replaced with suspicion.

"Who is this young lady and where did this accident take place?"

Coleman cleared his throat.

"Her name is Rosalee and it happened over close to H street."

"And, when you say that this Rosalee warmed you and dried your clothes, just what do you mean?" Dr. Browning talked very slowly, distinctly, and evenly as he questioned Coleman.

Coleman flushed. "She took me to her boarding house and the woman who owns the house gave me food, covered me with a blanket, and dried my clothes. Then they both helped me to the bus stop. They were both very kind."

"Can I assume that these two women were colored?"

Coleman heard roaring in his ears and felt tightness in his chest.

"Yes sir." He held his breath and felt his mouth go dry. "Does it matter?"

Dr. Browning sat back. He looked at the ceiling, as if to receive his next words from the Father Himself – words that were so authoritative, so wise, so eloquent that no human intellect or construct could withstand their force. Silence stretched. When he spoke again, it was in a low even tone.

"It does indeed matter. It matters because you reflect on this church. Your actions reflect on me. It is fine for you to enter the house of someone less fortunate than yourself in order to provide comfort or succor. However, it is unthinkable to enter the house of someone to receive comfort from them, especially if that person is of the colored race and especially if you are – do I dare even speak it – naked in that house. What if someone had passed by that house while you were there? What if someone had seen you in the company of a colored woman in that part of town, strolling down the street? Might they not assume the worst, that you were partaking not only of the food and blankets offered up but also of the more carnal things available in that house? You must never associate with those people again on that level. Confine your interactions to the vagrants at the mission union and the odd Negro who finds their way to our sanctuary on Sundays."

Coleman managed to say, "Sir, it was nothing like that. In fact, I believe they may have saved my life, as cold as it was." He returned to a stunned silence.

"I'm sure it is as you say. However, you must remember that lapses like this can have grave repercussions. You must be careful and must concentrate on important things. You cannot get distracted nor stray to the right or to the left."

Coleman nodded. His head pounded anew.

Even as the echo of Dr. Browning's words rang in his throbbing brain, a kaleidoscope of images swirled through his mind. The Capitol building, the attack, the murky water, Mrs. Rucker's front room, Rosalee's face. But one image rose to prominence and his consciousness focused on it.

A flyer and with it, a date and time and place.

CHAPTER 6

A SMALL ALABAMA TOWN, 1921

As the big man walked into his office and closed the huge oak door behind him, the sunlight from the floor-to-ceiling windows momentarily blinded him. Before he pulled the long string that drew down the shade, he surveyed the street. The only people left were a few of his men, just arrived back from disposing of the body. Everyone else was gone. Good.

With the shade down, the room was cast into twilight. The air spilling from the ceiling fan above already seemed a little cooler. He walked to the other wall, an expanse of ornately carved cherry bookshelves interrupted by a patch of plaster in the middle of which hung a painting. He stood before the painting and gazed like a petitioner praying before the shrine of a venerated saint.

The canvas was an old one, covered with thick oils. Swirls of indigo and teal crested with flecks of white. A sea, not angry but not calm and on the sea, a ship. A majestic vessel, its sails hoisted true and sure, no spillage of wind, the Stars and Stripes fluttering regally over the quarterdeck, over the heads of the sailor at the wheel and the two officers standing behind him. The images of the sailing-men were tiny but over the years of his possession of the painting, the man never doubted that he could clearly discern the visage of the captain, the man who – from under a white plumed hat worn fore-and-aft – serenely examined the bobbing horizon for the sails of Barbary pirates.

The features of the captain were familiar, the large nose and deep-set eyes similar to the ones that he encountered in the mirror each morning, and were thus easy for him to pick out of the infinitesimal peaks and valleys of pigment. The tiny ship's commander, forever frozen on the once pitching deck of the vessel that was soon to be the flagship of the squadron he would command, was his grandfather.

19

The big man's being was stirred by a strange swirl of feelings, though if asked he would say that emotion played no part in his life. Emotions were the shifting winds that drove the weak. He was proud that will and intellect and the sheer force of personality were the engines of his life.

Today was a day in which his wisdom came to bear on problems that no one but he could face and face them he did. He felt a sense of slight fatigue, the tiredness of those who wear the mantle of responsibility, who shoulder the weight of societies. The Caesars of old no doubt felt the same weariness as they guided the empire to higher and higher strata of greatness. At the same time, he felt the deep satisfaction that his actions today, the hard decisions that were made and carried out by his loyal workers, would lead to ever increasing peace and prosperity of the tiny town that represented the most precious inheritance of his revered grandfather. If he was honest with himself, he would also recognize a deeper emotion, a guttural feeling of excitement, even arousal, that was kindled to a brighter glow at the sight of blood and violence and death, as the flesh of the old woman almost incomprehensibly dissolved and her human form changed to a pile of bloody refuse, something to be detested and discarded.

The big man did not turn when the door opened behind him. He continued to face the painting, hands clasped behind him. Footsteps approached. He held up a hand and gestured toward the wall. A much smaller and younger man stepped forward. The whip was placed in its customary spot, a cast iron hook beside the painting on which the small man draped a loop of cord threaded through a hole in the smooth wooden handle of the whip. The nine strands of the whip hung below, a sated and slumbering hydra waiting for its next blood meal.

The big man said, "You buried her down through the woods and across the field?"

The young man turned but did not look him in the face.

"Yessir."

He fidgeted. He was a head shorter than the big man. Whereas the big man was tall and broad of shoulder and smooth of face, the young man was scrawny with a pockmarked face. His grey eyes were like small dull pebbles partly buried in red clay. Strings of oily black hair spilled over a shallow forehead.

In a squeaky voice, he said, "Nobody'll find her. We covered it up good."

Frustration drifted across the big man's face.

He allowed it to pass and in a few seconds said, "Before you go, tell me – are you and the men prepared for tonight?"

His voice remained even, aristocratic. He did not look at the young man but continued to peer at the painting. One of his grandfather's sailors who happened to see the big man now would say they had seen the same expression on the old commodore's face when the squadron was chasing a prize, his gaze fixed on the merger of sea and sky, seeking with his entire body and mind that flash of white or red or black that was felt more than seen and that would give away the enemy's position and course.

"Yessir. We got everything all gathered. We can go soon as it's dark. You wantin to ride the horses?"

The big man nodded and continued to stare. The young man scratched his head.

The big man said, "That is all. You may go."

The young man walked to the door, opened it, and started to leave. As he turned to ease the door shut, he said, "I'll see you after supper, Daddy."

Without turning, the big man said, "Yes son."

CHAPTER 7

WASHINGTON, D.C., 1961

Most Saturday mornings at the Lamb of God were a strange combination of busy and quiet. The workmen, gardener, handyman and cleaning woman were noticeably absent. No harsh hum of lawnmowers or vacuum cleaners disturbed the peace around the old building. The church secretary was off on Saturdays and thus no official visitors came to the office. However, while the exterior of the church appeared sedate, there was a flurry of unseen activity inside.

Dr. Browning used Saturday mornings to finish the polishing of his sermon for the next day. He also expected the rest of the ministerial staff to make their final preparations for Sunday. His roving eye was well aware of the young cleric who did not rise to the desired level of industriousness. Coleman did not want to risk being called to the pastor's office to answer accusations of assumed laziness. Thus, he worked – or at least remained in motion or appeared studious.

On this particular Saturday morning, Coleman hovered around the sanctuary. To Dr. Browning or the casual observer, it would appear that Coleman was ensuring there were no unwanted papers on the pews or that he was verifying that the newly installed electric heaters would be sufficient to warm the sanctuary. However, though he moved from pew to pew and glanced at the heaters, his mind was far beyond the stone and oak-beamed space.

He sat on the front pew, staring at the altar. A huge oaken cross stretched toward the ceiling. Sunlight cast multicolored shapes onto Coleman's upturned face.

His emotions swirled as they had done for the week since he had been thrown into the canal. As soon as he came to a supposed conclusion – *I am not going to the meeting* – his heart and gut plummeted into a dark pit, causing him to gasp. He could not bear not seeing her again. His vision dimmed and only when he reversed his decision did his mind and body slowly return to their steady state. But then, doubt crept into his mind.

What if Dr. Browning finds out? What if he expels me from the church? Will I have to go back home?

He gradually talked himself out of going to the meeting and then he fell again, beginning the cycle anew.

He took a deep breath, trying to calm the queasiness, and rested his head on the back of the pew with his face toward the ceiling. Dark-stained oak spider-webbed far above him. Shadows collected there, like dark souls trying to slip through wooden bars and thus escape their stone and stained glass prison. Alternate realities continued to race through his mind, but he already knew what he must do.

He ate a simple lunch in the solitude of the parish kitchen. He spent the afternoon praying. Praying for strength, praying for clarity. Praying that Dr. Browning would not see him leave.

He managed to slip away without having to lie. Two busses later, he was walking up the street to the Columbia Heights Community Center. A small group gathered outside the door, male and female, black and white. He scanned the faces and did not see Rosalee. He approached them.

"Hello. I'm here for the C.O.R.E. meeting." After greetings and handshakes, he went inside.

The large room was filled with folding chairs and a table situated at the front. Several of the chairs were occupied. He took a seat a couple of rows from the front. Over the next few minutes, stragglers drifted in. As each person entered the door, Coleman glanced back to try to spot Rosalee. She did not enter.

When the clock hanging on the far wall indicated five minutes after seven, three men strode through the door near the front of the room, two black, one white. They were dressed in trim black suits and held clipboards under their arms. The youngest of the black men walked to the other side of the table, placed his clipboard on it, and faced the audience. The other two men took seats on the front row. The assembly silenced.

"Welcome everyone. I am glad you came to this meeting of C.O.R.E. I see a lot of new faces." He glanced at one of the men in the front row. "I guess those flyers really worked." A few chuckles from the crowd. "Tonight, we will continue to discuss the bus trips we plan to take this spring. We will begin with a report from Davis who is heading up that committee."

A tall thin black man wearing a tan wool cardigan and skinny black tie rose and started to the front. Coleman glanced around and saw there were about 30 people in the room. About half were men, half women. Most appeared to be in their twenties or possibly early thirties.

"Good evening. Like James said, I am Davis and I have some information about the bus routes."

As Davis began to tell about different bus companies and the routes they take from Washington to the south, Coleman felt a touch on his arm. He turned to face Rosalee. His heart swelled.

"What the hell are you doing here?" she whispered as she slid past him to take the seat beside Coleman.

A scent of lavender filled his nose. Her arm was pressed against his and the warmth radiated inward. He felt heat rise to his face.

Coleman said, "Just interested."

One of the young men on the front row shot a glance at the pair. Rosalee returned it.

"And so," Davis continued, "depending on how many people decide to go, we could take two or even three different buses. We'll just have to decide which towns we want to be sure to pass through on our way to New Orleans. James, I'll turn it back over to you."

The remainder of the meeting was comprised of James and a few other speakers leading discussion. Coleman was not able to make complete sense out of the talk. Questions about the goals of this group came to his mind but were quickly ignored as he noticed every sound or shift that Rosalee made. She seemed to be completely absorbed in the talk emanating from the group, giving him a chance to look at her out of the corner of his vision.

He noticed her lovely neck rising up from a thick sweater. Her ears were tiny, like a baby's ears, each perfectly formed and adorned with a small pearl stud. The skin of her face was utterly smooth, with a faint hint of redness at her high cheekbones, no doubt painted there by the frigid evening air. Her eyes burned as she intently listened to the plans of the coming campaign. Her lips occasionally mouthed words that he did not hear. It was only when she raised her hand that his reverie was broken.

Rosalee said, "What're you looking at?" Coleman seemed puzzled. He looked toward the speaker.

Coleman looked around and saw that most of the people in the room had raised their hands. He turned to Rosalee and whispered, "What was the question?"

Rosalee gave an angry glare. "Weren't you even listening? He asked who is going on the bus ride down south." She leaned toward him. "Don't you dare raise your hand. You don't know anything about this."

James said from the front, "That is very good. A good start."

He glanced at the two men in the front row who both nodded as they finished writing notes on their clipboards.

"Very well. We will plan to meet again next week. Same place, same time."

Murmurs erupted in the group and people began to rise from their seats and start toward the door. Rosalee turned toward Coleman.

"I'm not sure what you think you're doing, but this isn't the place for you."

"Like I said, I just wanted to learn more about C.O.R.E." Coleman met Rosalee's stare. "The flyer seemed like it was saying that anyone could come."

"Yeah, maybe. But still, you don't have any business with this," Rosalee said. "Listen, I've got to go. I don't want to see you here again. You understand me?"

Before Coleman could answer, Rosalee muttered, "Shit! Here he comes." Coleman looked behind him and saw James approaching.

"Rosalee, you must introduce me to your friend." James was all smiles.

"He ain't *my* friend. He might be yours but he sure as hell ain't mine."

James grasped Coleman's hand in a firm grip. "I have learned to ignore her when needed. I suggest you do the same." Coleman smiled. "My name is James."

"Hey, I'm Coleman. I saw the flyer and thought I'd come to see what this is all about."

James beamed. "That is exactly the purpose of those flyers."

Before James could continue, Rosalee cut in.

"He don't need to know any more. I told him there was no need for him to come back." Rosalee crossed her arms, a hard finality in her words and gestures.

James's eyes went wide. "Rosalee! I can't believe you could be so rude!" He turned to Coleman. "Again, please ignore her." Coleman gave a tentative smile.

Rosalee turned to James and said, "James, I'm telling you, he don't need to be here. He lives in a whole other world."

James shook his head. "Last time I checked, we were all in the same world. Coleman here is welcome."

Rosalee scowled and said, "But, he don't know nothing about us. He's here for the wrong reasons."

James said, "It is not ours to question the reasons one has for getting involved, as long as they are not destructive reasons." He considered Coleman for a second or two. "And I don't think we have to worry about that."

Coleman said, "No. I'm only here to learn more and to see if I can help."

James turned to Rosalee. "See? What did I tell you?"

Rosalee's scowl only deepened.

James said, "As far as his not knowing anything about us, I think we can help with that." He gave Coleman a sly sideways smile.

25

"Rosalee, I'd like you to meet with Coleman tomorrow and tell him all about C.O.R.E."

Rosalee gave a violent shake of her head. "Hell no! There ain't no way I'm going to spoon-feed this one. He can come to the meetings if he wants to but I ain't going to waste my own precious time!"

The smile disappeared from James's face.

"Rosalee, I'm not asking."

She stopped shaking her head.

James said, "This is for the good of C.O.R.E. The more different kinds of people we have, the better. If I can't trust you with this task, how can I trust you with anything bigger? O.K.?"

She did not look up. "O.K."

"Good. I'll leave it to the two of you to set up the time and place." James shook Coleman's hand again. "And I hope to see you again next week." James walked to the next cluster of people waiting for him.

Coleman had not expected this, did not know how things would work out. He smiled at her.

Rosalee said, "There's a little park on Georgia Avenue. You be there tomorrow at three o'clock." He nodded.

Before walking out the door, she tapped her finger on his chest and said, "You better not be late or I will leave your ass sitting in the cold."

CHAPTER 8

THE FIVE AND DIME, A SMALL ALABAMA TOWN, 1961

The men trickled in from the dark street one by one, arriving about every minute or so. Each picked his way through the tables and counters piled high with boxes and bottles to a small door at the rear of the store, looking like black knights riding through a labyrinth in the approaches to some medieval fortress. Only after the last one had entered the storeroom and closed the door did Galen turn on the small electric lamp on the table.

The amber light lit the black and white faces from below and cast improbable shadows on the shelves stacked with jars of Brylcreem and boxes of washing powder.

"All right, boys, what do we think?" Galen said. "Are we O.K. with what she said?"

A man in a short white coat stomped his foot. "Hell, no, we ain't O.K.! If it's up to her, we're just going to sit here and do nothing until they find out everything! We just can't let that happen! Not after we've made it this long."

"Ephraim's right." A man in a straw hat placed his hands on the table and gazed into the faces around the room. "If we can hold people off a few more years then it won't mean nothing. But now is still too soon." Nods appeared all around.

Galen turned to a dark man standing in the corner. "Martelle, what do you say?"

The man's dark skin made him melt into the shadows of the room but his eyes were strikingly bright, as if they had been painted with light blue watercolor and then diluted even more with a wet brush. He stared straight ahead, his sight going beyond the cave-like storeroom out across the fields and into the ancient woods. His vision penetrated soil and rock, time and meaning.

After a long while, moments filled with fidgeting of the other men in the room, the man said, "I can't see anything clearly. I ain't as strong as those who came before. But I can see a stranger who asks questions. Danger follows him." His words swirled in the room like steam from a cauldron.

Galen broke the spell. "What do we need to do?"

Ephraim cleared his throat. "This is what I say. We welcome them here, however many that is, hopefully just one. We make'em feel at home. At the same time, one of us is always watching. And one of us is in the woods with a thirty-aught-six and a scope."

The men were silent, their faces now masked in shadow. Ephraim eyed Galen and said, "It's been done before. And, if we have to, we can do it again."

Galen said, "What do you say?"

One by one, each man nodded or gave a soft "Yep". Galen stood.

"It's settled. We'll do whatever it takes to keep the secret where it belongs." As he switched off the lamp, he said, "We'll save this town from itself - again."

CHAPTER 9

WASHINGTON, D.C., 1961

"Damn!"

Sundays were the days she had to herself. The only day of the week for sleeping a little later, for not working. Sometimes Mrs. Rucker would drag her to church but even that was all right, hearing the old hymns her mother used to sing. On Sundays, her mother seemed a little closer. Memories of fried chicken dinners and sweet potato pies floated through many of her Sunday afternoons. Rosalee would sometimes just sit on Mrs. Rucker's front porch. The shady space surrounded by the low energy thrum of a drowsy city brought back the Baltimore of her childhood, one in which her mother took care of her and her father was the breadwinner. Security, peace. Those were the things that colored her Sundays.

But not today, she thought as she walked to the park. *I have to baby talk and pat the head of that stupid boy.*

He was the kind she particularly loathed. The white do-gooders who think they can barge right in, acting like they own the world. Weak people who are in it for the excitement and the proud feeling that they're helping the poor pitiful colored people but who fade away when the hard parts come, when the real work begins.

Who does he think he is?

Not that white people did not have a part in all of this. Rosalee knew some very good white people and admitted that they would be needed to talk to other white people and help them understand what freedom for black people really meant. However, when it came to the actual fight, Rosalee knew that would fall to her kind, to people who had been oppressed themselves, who had felt the hatred that rose out of a prejudiced ignorant heart.

Does that white boy know how it feels to not be let in a restaurant because of the skin he was born with? To be stared and pointed at when you're walking in a part of town where most of the people don't look like you? To be like our brothers and sisters in some parts of the country that can't vote or own property? No, he don't know. To fight that kind of injustice, you got to have the fire in your heart, deep down in your soul. The fire don't come secondhand.

She made it to the park early and sat on a bench facing the sidewalk. She pulled a cigarette out of her purse and lit it. As she blew smoke toward the cold sky, she decided to purposely suppress the discontent that had descended on her during the walk.

She thought back to another Sunday, a bright day spent sitting on a Baltimore sidewalk. She had some chalk her teacher had given her and she was drawing on the concrete. Pictures of flowers and clouds and rainbows. One of the stick figures was she and other chalk lines outlined the form of the little house in which she and her chalk family lived. A curl of white smoke came out of the chimney of the house, a dwelling that was surrounded by a meadow and flanked by trees with corkscrew limbs stretching up to a cement-colored sky. They were happy there, she and her mother and her father, all of them living as chalk-people in a chalk world with no other people around but even if there had been, they would be chalk-people too. She gave each of the stick figures voice.

"Rosalee, get ready. Your daddy will be home soon."

"My hands are all clean. Mommy, he's here!"

"How's my little girl? Hey sweetie, what smells so good?"

The chalk family went inside their little house to share dinner.

She remembered her Daddy. He came walking up the sidewalk from the bus stop, walking slowly, the fatigue of the long day showing. He swerved to avoid the chalk house as Rosalee gave a little warning squeal. He dropped his lunch pail and spread wide his arms. She flung herself, nestling into the warmth, smelling his sweat-soaked shirt that had dried during the bus ride, feeling at home and safe as she kissed his rough cheek and lay her head on his coat.

The coat. Her heart fell. Darkness took all of the pleasant images.

At that very second, she heard Coleman. "Hey Rosalee. I'm not late, am I?"

The frustration and discontent dropped on her like a bucket of cold water.

"I don't know. What time is it?" As he fumbled for his watch, she said, "Never mind. Just come and sit here." She motioned to the other end of the bench. Coleman sat, a sheepish look on his face.

"Listen, I'm not sitting out here all day. I am supposed to tell you all about C.O.R.E. and what we are planning. After that, we're through."

Coleman nodded. "I understand. But I already know that I want to be involved."

"Yeah fine. But you just wait until after we talk and we'll see how all fired up you are about gettin involved." Rosalee threw her cigarette to the sidewalk and crushed it out with her toe.

Rosalee saw Coleman's frown and said, "What, you don't approve of smoking?"

Coleman said, "It can't be good for you."

Rosalee said, "Smoking helps clear my mind. When you've seen all the shit I've seen, your mind needs about two packs worth of clearing a day."

She had thought about what she would say but now she was not sure. Bare limbs stretched into the deep blue sky. Her breath appeared in front of her and instantly dissolved into nothingness. She inhaled a long breath of cold air. "What do you know about us?"

Coleman seemed confused. "I thought that was why James wanted me to come. For you to tell me about C.O.R.E."

Rosalee said, "I don't mean C.O.R.E. What do you know about colored people?"

Coleman said, "I mean, I guess I know a good bit. I've learned more since moving to Washington."

Rosalee stared at him. "How many colored people did you know growing up?"

Despite the cold, Coleman's face flushed. "Not many." She saw sweat on his upper lip. "I talked to some when I went to Chattanooga one time."

Rosalee continued to stare. "Nobody else? Nobody from school or a neighbor?"

Coleman said, "But, Rosalee, that's not fair. Just because I grew up in a place where there aren't many colored people, it doesn't mean that I'm not interested in the rights of colored people."

"No, you have every right to be interested. I just find myself wondering why you are interested."

Rosalee saw Coleman squirm. His face reddened and his jaw flexed. A hint of anger flared in his eyes. She had not expected to see that. He pointed his finger at her.

Coleman said, "I was singled out because of the color of *my* skin. I was thrown into a canal to drown by people who had nothing against me except that I was white and was in their neighborhood. I got a little taste of what colored people feel and I want to do something about it."

Rosalee's countenance softened a trace. "I know that's what you think." Coleman sat back. Rosalee gathered her thoughts again, remembering what she had wanted to say, the message she wanted this person to hear.

"I want you to know this is not some club or social organization. C.O.R.E. is on a mission to bring about justice and it's going to be hard work and I don't think you got it in you."

The anger flared in Coleman's eyes again. "You don't have any right to say that. You don't know me."

Rosalee said, "No, I don't know you but I seen lots of people like you. White people who want to change the world." Coleman started to speak but Rosalee held up a hand.

"Listen, I asked you if you had been around many colored people growing up and you said no. Well, I have been around lots of white people."

She faced straight ahead but did not see the drab building across the street. Instead, she gazed into the past and saw a street in Baltimore. Her mother sat on the stoop waiting for her to come home from school.

"My mother taught me about white people." She spoke in a low voice, as if she was speaking from a great distance. "She told me to be quiet when a white person was around. She told me to step aside on the sidewalk and let a white person pass if they came up behind me. She told me to stay away from policemen because you never know when you might be arrested or beaten or even shot. You know, my mother was right. If you're colored, you just might end up dead if a policeman doesn't like who you are or what you're doing."

Coleman said, "Rosalee, a policeman isn't just going to shoot somebody for no reason. You don't have to worry about that."

The fire reappeared in Rosalee's eyes. "No, *you* don't have to worry about that. On the other hand, I do have to worry about that. Colored people ain't safe from policemen's bullets just because they are innocent. Even innocent colored people are liable to get shot."

People in long coats and scarves hurried past the two sitting on the bench. Some glanced at them, most simply walked past hurrying along on their chores of the day.

Coleman cleared his throat and said, "What you say is right. Somebody needs to stand up for the colored people whose rights are being denied and especially for those who are being killed. But, you have to remember that the people down south have been living like this for more than two hundred years. Their great-grandfathers actually owned slaves. It will take a while for their mindset to change."

Rosalee turned on the bench to face Coleman. "So, you're saying that we can't expect them to know better?"

Even in the chilly air, redness rose to Coleman's face. His blush was not lost on Rosalee.

Coleman said, "No, what I'm saying is that those people were raised in a different culture. They are a product of their times. We can't blame them for not knowing better." Rosalee continued to stare. "Of course, now that they know, they should be expected to change."

Rosalee fell back in the seat. "I don't accept that. I can't accept that."

She once again turned to Coleman. "You don't have to be told that it is wrong to make an old lady get up out of her seat on the bus to let a perfectly healthy man sit down just because her skin is dark. You don't have to be told it is wrong to keep a man from voting when the Constitution says that he has every right to do so. You don't have to be told that it's wrong to beat a little boy to death for whistling."

Her voice rose. "No, I don't accept that. They should have known. Nobody has to tell you when something is wrong." She placed her hand on her chest. "You know it right here. If you know something is wrong and you don't change it, you either don't want it to change or you don't have the courage to change it. What I want to do is fight against those who don't want it to change and help to give strength to those who don't have the courage."

"But how is that going to happen? What can be done?" Coleman asked.

Rosalee said, "That is exactly what C.O.R.E. is deciding. And that is why what we are doing is so important. What you have to do is look into your own heart and ask if this is what you want to get involved in. Do you have the desire? Do you have the courage?" He opened his mouth to speak, but she stopped him with a wave of her hand. "Don't answer now. This is something you need some time to think about. If you are ready to commit to do whatever is in your power to make change happen, then come to the next C.O.R.E. meeting. If not, forget all about C.O.R.E. and go and live your life in your white world and leave the hard work to us."

Coleman was silent. Rosalee rose from the bench as a bus approached and said, "I don't expect to see you again."

She stepped to the sidewalk and climbed the steps of the bus and took a seat. She saw Coleman standing there waiting for the next cross-town bus. Great puffs of white smoke wreathed him. Their eyes locked.

In his eyes, she saw despair.

CHAPTER 10

ALEXANDRIA, VIRGINIA, 1961

As the train slowed, Dr. Browning was stirred from his thoughts. He was surprised to see the station platform appear and slowly creep by his window. He did not remember the train crossing the river, did not notice the Virginia tidewater passing by. His mind had been occupied, trying to further understand the feelings stirred by his protégé's words. The conversation with Coleman had left Dr. Browning uneasy, had brought to the fore actions that had been too long postponed.

He gathered his belongings and exited. He cinched his wool scarf against the cold and made his way into the peaceful town. Ocher light spilled onto the sidewalk, hinting at warm hearths and comfort within the colonial brick homes and quaint offices that lined the street.

The lawyer's office was only a couple of blocks from the station. He shook off the cold as he entered and closed the door behind him. There was no one sitting at the small receptionist's desk and the attorney himself seemed to be away as well. Dr. Browning checked the time on his watch and realized they had likely stepped out for lunch. He sat in the wooden chair by the door to wait.

The errand he assigned to Coleman that morning would take the young intern in the opposite direction, the better to prevent uncomfortable questions.

Of course, Dr. Browning would protest that he had nothing about which to be uncomfortable, He was here on a mission of generosity, of mercy. He was not required to come, not obligated to give, but he came and gave just the same.

I care deeply about all of God's children, no matter the color of their skin. God our Father created all humans each after their kind.

A clock from within the lawyer's private office ticked loudly. The sound echoed within the small suite of rooms. A sense of satisfaction began to lodge itself within Dr. Browning's breast. It was deeply gratifying to turn a good deed. Driven out were any twinges of doubt, any inkling that shame should be attached to a past forgotten act.

Charity. It is the greatest of these. He knew that. At the same time, he knew the reality of the world in which he and Coleman lived, the expectations of the throngs that looked to men of the cloth for guidance.

Perhaps it is acceptable for some white men to become involved with colored women. He had heard of some white men in California who became involved with and even married colored women. Of course, the women were mulatto and also, of course, that was California. He was not sure whether God led those men to some purpose, the way he led men and women to minister in leper colonies or to give their lives to spread the Gospel in darkest Africa, or whether those men were simply following their lustful cravings for strange flesh. But, whether or not he acknowledged that some men might rightly join themselves to women of another race, he knew that was not the proper path for anyone associated with the Lamb of God Presbyterian Church.

It is good that Coleman has me to guide him.

Dr. Browning felt a sense of duty, of fatherly responsibility toward the young man.

Coleman speaks very little of his earthly father. I know he yet lives but it seems that Coleman does not think highly of him.

Dr. Browning also recognized that Coleman filled a void in his own life. As an apprentice cleric, a young Alphie Browning had vowed to follow Saint Paul's admonition to abide even as he and to remain unmarried. He had thus forsaken a potential family for a life completely devoted to service of the Lord and His church. Coleman seemed a kindred spirit, a facsimile son, one into whom Dr. Browning could pour his wisdom, hopes, dreams. Like a painter laboring on a self-portrait, it was rewarding to see Coleman respond to his advice and to grow more and more like him.

As Dr. Browning glanced at his watch again, the door opened beside him and the attorney entered.

"Reverend! It has been quite some time." He closed the door behind him and stepped back to view the pastor, a surprised, even bewildered look on his face. "I hope nothing is wrong."

Dr. Browning stood and held out his hand, giving the attorney a firm handshake.

"No, no, nothing at all. I am here to make a donation, as I have done before."

His words were met with more puzzlement on the attorney's face. The attorney moved toward his private office.

"Very well. Allow me to clear part of my desk and then you may sit in here." The attorney looked back into the waiting area of the office from his desk and said, "I wish you had told me you were coming and I could have had Joyce find the file."

Dr. Browning said, "I only decided to make the jaunt from Washington this morning and, regardless, I would not want you to go to any trouble for this small gesture of mine."

The attorney said, "Come on in, Reverend."

Dr. Browning shouldered his way into the tiny space and alighted on a chair on the other side of the desk.

The attorney considered him for a long second and said, "I can't decide which I am more surprised about, whether it's that you're here or that I haven't seen you for so long until now."

Dr. Browning straightened in his chair and held up an index finger.

"You will recall that I did everything that was required by me. I gave the money requested by –," he paused and spat out, " – the other party." He shifted in the hard chair. "And I contributed to the school fund as privately requested by the judge."

The attorney's gaze hardened.

"Reverend, *you* will recall that it wasn't a request by the judge. It was an order of the probate court, an order that was kept sealed along with the proceedings only because of my good relationship with Judge Hammond."

The attorney spun the desk chair to face an old metal cabinet and extracted a thick file from the bottom drawer. He flopped the file heavily onto the desk.

"And, you will recall that you promised to make additional donations to the fund."

Dr. Browning cleared his throat. "Yes." He nodded, a sheepish look on his face. "That is why I am here."

The attorney flipped open the file. The sight of the filings flooded Dr. Browning's mind with memories, all of them depressing. He looked away, trying to rid himself of the guilt that had suddenly descended on him. He wondered why he had come. The lawyer seemed to sense the emotion under the surface of Dr. Browning's façade but continued.

"The problem is that the black school has already been completed. That fund hasn't been active for a while now."

Dr. Browning's face fell, the façade disintegrated.

The attorney said, "But I suppose they could always use some money for supplies and such."

Dr. Browning brightened. He withdrew a checkbook from his inner coat pocket and wrote a substantial sum on the amount line. On the for line, he wrote Parker-Gray High School. He handed the check over to the attorney and stood.

"Thank you very much for your help." Dr. Browning extended his hand to the attorney, who was gazing at the check with astonishment. He took the pastor's hand.

"I don't know what caused you to do this, but I'm sure the school will be grateful." The attorney followed the pastor as he walked to the door. "I suppose you want to keep this anonymous just like before."

Dr. Browning said, "Obviously." He replaced his hat, touched the brim, and started back to the station.

By the time he had completed the short walk, the warm feelings accompanying a good deed had returned to his heart and mind. The unpleasantness of previous stumblings faded away. He felt lighter, healthier, more vibrant. Exuberant.

His thoughts turned toward Coleman. He was confident that his plan to arrive at the church before Coleman's return was still on course. He felt sure that taking care of this matter today would help him to remain undistracted in the advisement of his pupil. As he settled into the seat of the return express, he prayed.

I thank Thee God that You have granted me this position. I thank Thee that I am not like some others, unjust publicans, all the rest. I thank Thee that You have given me a young man with a mind and heart to aid You in shaping. Your humble servant stands ready to do as You will.

Amen.

SILVER SPRING, MARYLAND, 1961

As Dr. Browning prayed, Coleman sat in the seat of another train, this one rumbling north, away from Washington. Coleman was glad to be leaving the city, even if on a short errand involving picking up a case of new hymnals from a music store. He had momentarily wondered at Dr. Browning's careful explanation that the hymnals were not available at the local store and thus must be obtained in Silver Spring. However, his mind quickly moved to a nagging uncertainty that had dug at him for weeks, like a small pebble caught in the sole of his shoe.

In a deep part of his heart, a speck of a thought had begun to germinate, drawing fragments of doubt and misgiving and fear to itself, growing in the shadows out of view of his conscious mind. He felt it there but was not yet ready to acknowledge it because he knew that when he recognized it for what it was, everything would change. His mind's eye shied away.

Coleman's thoughts were jumbled, his emotions erratic like the leaves blown around by the passing train. His view of vacant fields and moving water and floating clouds outside the train window helped him focus.

He knew that Rosalee was right. He had not known many black people in his mountain home. Being perfectly honest, he had to admit that he had not known any. Newspapers and magazines and television had brought

37

their images into his sheltered life but he had no black friends or acquaintances. Was his growing awareness of racial inequality enough to overcome the ignorance of his life up until now? He was not sure.

A Farmall tractor sat idle in a field, glowing scarlet against the fallow brownness. He was immediately transported to another field, one whose soil had never collapsed under the weight of machinery, one that had only ever been plowed by a mule dragging rusty metal through its rocky skin. His father toiled countless days every March to November wringing a pathetic amount of sustenance from the organic-poor soil and cursing the boulders that God had seen fit to deposit in the Hightower's ancestral plot. Coleman remembered his father coming in, exhausted and defeated by the field. He saw him come home with the same look of desolation after working at some odd job on rainy days and during the winter between planting seasons. His father's life was a constant struggle, a never-ending slog through all of the misery the world could muster.

Coleman did not remember his mother. His father never spoke of her. Granny Mae held the only memories of her that were communicated to him.

"My Susie, she was something else. Always smiling, humming. I can see her light in your eyes sometimes, Coleman. I'd like to say that your mama's dying sucked the life out of your daddy. But, I'd be lying. Truth is, he never had much life in him to start with. His heart is like them rocks in the field that he hates so much. Hard and flinty."

The train arced around a curve and Coleman could see the engine, its passenger cars stretched out behind. The engine belched a thick cloud of black diesel smoke that for a second, through a trick of the wind, floated motionless in the interior of the track's curve before slamming directly into the windows of Coleman's car causing him to flinch backwards.

He put his head against the seat and closed his eyes. He could see his father gathering corn stalks in the fall and setting them alight. The flames climbed into the sky, turning from bright yellow at the base to deep orange and sooty black at the tips before giving rise to a tall column of black smoke that only became tattered at a great height where the wind blowing over the crest of the hill was finally able to reach it. One such fall not that many years ago, he had stood with his father, both of them mesmerized by the luminance and heat of the fire. Coleman said in a trance-tinged voice, "I want to do something big with my life. Granny Mae is teaching me to be a healer like her. I might do that or I might be some kind of leader or boss of a big company or something."

Coleman peeled his gaze away from the fire and saw his father's tired eyes considering him for a long moment. His father turned back to the fire, coughed up a thick wad of phlegm, and spat it into the flame.

"I reckon dreaming is fine for some folks. But, hard work is the only thing that puts food in your belly. That don't leave much time for dreaming. When it comes down to it, you just got to get up everyday and do what you have to do. Do that long enough and the dreams will stop coming and bothering you."

The train passed over a small river. Fog rose from the surface of the water creating a milky aqueduct in the brown winter landscape. Coleman recalled clouds that rolled over the mountains on the other side of the valley from Granny Mae's little shack. Their mist and droplets had leapt up from the ocean and rushed across the land, piling up in great masses to dump their nourishing load on crops and trees, to replenish streams and lakes, to sustain people and animals. The clouds' duty was solemn and accompanied by darkened skies and rumbles of thunder. Coleman sat on Granny Mae's front porch watching, content to let the clouds do their important work. On that day, he felt no duty, no urge to action, no thirst for something better. What he had was good enough.

Granny Mae came out and sat in the creaky rocking chair beside him, a pan of string beans in her lap and a paper sack on the floor beside her. The pungent smell of the beans met Coleman's nose as she strung and snapped them, throwing the strings in the sack and letting the fat segments of bean fall back in the pan. It smelled like summer.

"It shore is pretty, a storm coming over the mountain." Coleman nodded. Granny Mae said, "Remember these times, this place, Coleman. You ain't gonna be here forever."

Coleman said, "Yes, ma'am. I know we're all gonna die someday."

The old woman said, "That ain't what I'm a-talking about."

Her gaze swept over the valley, a place she had lived all her life. She had rarely left the valley and had never been more than thirty miles in any direction from the front porch on which they sat. She said, "Coleman, this ain't the place for you to stay."

He sat forward in his chair, a look of concern clothing his face. "What d'ya mean, Granny Mae?"

She smiled and rocked, her hands working mindlessly on the beans. "I mean that you're meant for somethin more. Just like my Susie."

"A healer like you, Granny Mae?"

"I'm a-gonna teach you all I can about conjurin. But, the Lord might have somethin else in mind for you. Somethin outside this little valley. You're gonna get some schoolin and then we'll see what happens."

A couple pushed by Coleman's seat, making their way to the passenger car's door in preparation for the next stop, a pretty girl and a lanky boy with a red M emblazoned on his sweater. The train stopped and they exited. Coleman's eyes followed them until they disappeared down the stairs. The train paused for only a moment and lurched into motion again.

He went to college like Granny Mae had wished, though her body rested beneath the impossibly green grass of the Liberty Hill Baptist Church cemetery before he received that piece of parchment, the first Hightower to ever get a degree. All the rest of his kin got a little schooling – maybe eighth grade, some even getting a diploma – before melting into the red clay fields and garages and sewing factories that dotted the valleys of his homeland.

Bethsaida College's venerable dean of students developed a fondness for the quiet boy, someone in whom he saw potential and determination veiled with shyness. He took him under his wing and spoke lofty dreams into Coleman's heart. Coleman's first glimmer of a life in the church came in the dean's office during their advisement sessions.

"Coleman, a life serving God and His people is an admirable life. Of course, taking care of temporal things is fine. We need physicians to care for our earthly bodies and lawyers to help us with our worldly possessions and we need other professionals. But, a minister of the Lord cares for the eternal souls of the people in his charge. What could be more important than that?" As graduation neared, it was the dean who had arranged Coleman's introduction to an old classmate, Dr. Alphie Browning.

The slowing of the train brought Coleman's mind back. He checked his pocket and found the slip of paper containing the address of the bookstore. The air was chilly as he stepped from the train and walked across the platform, the sun not yet providing even its paltry winter warmth to this part of the station. He stepped into the street and a car horn blared in his ear as a shiny blue Rambler swerved and zoomed past him, the driver gesturing as he passed. Coleman collected himself and began walking.

The store was a few blocks away. He quickly made the purchase and was soon walking back to the station carrying a case of hymnals. The smell of fresh ink and newly bound leatherette covers permeated the box and was faintly nauseating. Coleman shifted the box to his other arm. Elvis crooned from behind the plate glass of the record store. *It's now or never...*

He saw the train station ahead and mentally checked the schedule. *Good, I'll be able to catch the three thirty.*

As he crossed the curb and stepped under the station's awning, he heard a loud voice. He turned and saw two policemen. Pistols were holstered on their hips and gleaming black billy clubs swung from loops on their belts. One of the officers yelled at a young black man who had just exited a train and now walked at a steady clip toward the street. He carried a sign under his left arm. The young man tried to ignore the officers, to pretend as if they were talking to someone else. However, it was clear that he was the target of the cry as there was no other person near him. He halted and turned to face the two men, though his eyes did not meet them.

"Boy, whatcha got there?" One of the officers pointed at the sign as they stopped in front of the young man, their hands on their belts. The young man looked down at the pasteboard tucked under his arm and seemed surprised to see it there. He turned back to the men, still averting his eyes.

"A sign."

One of the officers scowled and put his hand on the handle of his billy club. "Are you getting smart with me?"

"No sir."

The officer said, "Where've you been with that sign?"

"Over to Bethesda. Just heading home now."

"Let me see that." The other officer snatched the sign from under the young man's arm and held it up for both of the officers to see. "Glen Echo Park For All," he slowly read. "Jimmy, looks like this is a protest sign."

The first officer nodded gravely. The young man's mouth dropped open a little, sweat appearing on his forehead and his breath coming more quickly. The first officer leaned toward him. "Do you have a permit to carry this sign?" The young man's gaze went back and forth between the two officers' faces. Coleman stood twenty feet away, paralyzed with apprehension, not sure whether to keep walking or to say something. Instead, he stood, watching and witnessing. The second officer took a half step closer to the young man, his hand on the butt of his pistol.

"I believe Officer Samuels asked you a question."

The young man stammered. "I'm n-n-not protesting here. I was over to Bethesda."

Officer Samuels pulled the billy stick out of the loop. His knuckles whitened on the grip, the menacing shaft of the stick lying in wait in the palm of his other hand. He said, "That's not what I asked. Do you have a permit?"

The black man slowly shook his head, eyes on the cement. Officer Samuels's partner ripped the sign into two jagged pieces and pivoted, throwing the fragments into a trashcan. When the officer pivoted back, he swept a foot behind the black man's ankle. The young man crumpled to the ground. Coleman took a step forward and froze as the second officer turned to him, hands on his billy club.

Coleman was close enough to hear Officer Samuels bend over the young man sitting bewildered on the ground and say in a low voice, "You get your black ass out of here and I don't have to tell you to keep your radical nigger shit out of my station."

The two officers walked past Coleman, their glares telling him to mind his own business. Coleman waited for them to turn the corner around the building and approached the young man on the ground. The black man sat with his forearms perched on his raised knees. He breathed deeply, head down.

"Are you all right?" The black man's head jerked to face Coleman and a protective arm sprang up.

"Man, just leave me alone!"

Coleman took a half step back. "I just wanted to let you know I can help if you need it."

The black man began to stand. "I don't need your help. I don't need nobody's help. I'm just trying to make it along and I want y'all to just let me be and get out of my way." He pushed by Coleman and disappeared in the opposite direction from the policemen.

Coleman watched him as he left. He turned to walk toward the platform, still clutching the case of hymnals, his pace slow and shuffling, matching the despondency that overspread his heart.

What good am I? What can I do?

These questions seemed to draw the deep hidden thought out, like one of Granny Mae's poultices drawing an abscess to a head so that it would drain, bringing relief, causing an end to suffering and dread. The deep hidden thought crept out of the shadows. He felt it rising, still not conscious of its meaning, not knowing until it was spoken, with Coleman watching and listening like it was a pronouncement from the oracle.

"I don't want to be a pastor."

He said it quietly, though someone standing on the train platform with him would have heard it. However, no one was there. He was alone with the revelation. He felt relief. Not disappointment. Not grief or sorrow or embarrassment. Relief. He said it louder.

"I don't want to be a pastor."

A smile spread across his face. He yelled, "I DON"T WANT TO BE A PASTOR!" An old man arrived at the platform a second later and glanced around to find the source of the shouting. He shot a suspicious glance at Coleman. Coleman chuckled and turned away.

After taking his seat and beginning the ride back to Washington, Coleman felt that the whole world was open to him. He felt freedom, maybe for the first time in his life. There were no expectations of others to consider. He could choose his own path. After a few miles of Maryland brownness had passed by his window, he realized that he had chosen this path away from traditional clergydom many weeks ago.

He imagined himself at the podium in front of a great crowd, a sea of people stretching to the horizon. His voice was picked up by a tiny microphone and boomed into the audience. His words lifted them, carried them. He spoke of justice and liberty and law and peace. The crowd rippled as if his words were skillful fingers and the throng was a harp. They threw back applause and cheers in exchange for wisdom and inspiration.

The crowd dissolved and he was at a table facing a row of serious men, men with names like Byrd and Muskie and Goldwater. He spoke with eloquence and felt a part of the great men but also above them. He imagined invitations to universities to speak about the great civil rights movement, biddings by presidents and kings and potentates to dine with them and share his stories of the fight for freedom, the second American Revolution. He was a father of a new kind of nation.

As the miles passed, the glow faded. He realized he would have to tell Dr. Browning but knew there was no rush. His mind turned to other things. Actually one thing – one person.

He smelled her scent in his memory. He felt her warm touch. He saw her lovely shape, the way she moved. He longed for her.

He would have her.

CHAPTER 11

WASHINGTON, D.C., 1961

Rosalee walked from the bus stop through the gathering gloom of a cold Saturday evening. The bus had been almost empty, most people preferring to stay inside, gathered around supper tables and drawing warmth from family or whomever else they had. The only family Rosalee had – other than her surrogate mother, Mrs. Rucker – was starting to congregate in a meeting room just ahead, a disparate family of different temperaments and talents but with the same conviction. She was grateful to have someone to be with tonight. She felt particularly alone that frigid Saturday, the icy wind piercing her body when she stepped outside in the early morning hours and causing her to have an acute awareness of her lack of real friends.

Earlier, as she stared out of the window in her little room at Mrs. Rucker's, she pommelled herself with questions and indictments.

Why do you always push people away? You don't ever let anybody get close. Just because Mama and Daddy died, it don't mean that you can't ever have feelings for somebody else.

She pushed back at her inner accuser.

I let people in. Look at the people in C.O.R.E.

The accuser shot back, *What about Coleman?*

She immediately objected.

Now wait a minute! That boy ain't got nothing to do with it. He don't belong!

She dismissed Coleman and any further thought of him and spent the day in melancholy, missing her father and mother and wishing for a home.

Her gloominess abated as she arrived at the meeting and took her customary seat near the front of the room while other people straggled in. She nodded and smiled at a girl who entered, an acquaintance who sat on the opposite end of her row. As she moved to rise and greet the new arrival, Rosalee felt a hand on her shoulder. She turned and saw Coleman standing there.

He pointed at the chair on the other side of Rosalee's and said, "Is that seat taken?"

She stared at him, blank-faced, and moved back slightly so he could pass.

He smiled at her and plopped heavily into the chair before he turned to her and said, "Thanks. How are you?" She fixed him with a glare for a long moment.

"What the hell are you doing here?" She dropped her chin. "Like I told you before, this ain't the place for you."

Coleman's smile melted.

Rosalee said, "You think you can use us to become some kind of big man? You think we're going to thank you?" A sneer appeared on her face. "Thank you Massa Coleman. We po' black folk thank you." Disgust was in her face. "I tell you what, I ain't going to be licking your shoes."

Rosalee watched him, expecting him to wordlessly stand and slink out of the room. He did not. Steely determination spread across his face. Now, it was Coleman's head that slowly shook from side to side.

He said, "You're not going to be able to push me away."

Rosalee opened her mouth to speak but Coleman held up a hand.

He said, "I am here to help. I have just as much right to want to be a part of this movement as anyone. You don't have to like it and you don't have to like me. But, I'm not going anywhere."

Fire rose from Rosalee's gut. She felt a torrent of words approach her mouth, a flood of such vehemence as to completely consume this arrogant little white boy. Her heart screamed that this little piss ant most certainly did not have as much right as she. But instead of unleashing her fury, she merely shot a look of repugnance and slid past Coleman to sit beside the girl at the other end of the row.

Within a moment, James stood at the front of the room and said, "Tonight, we are honored to have three people from Nashville who are going to help us prepare for what we may face along the way to New Orleans. These gentlemen and this lady have had experience in various types of civil disobedience including marches and sit-ins. Ed, I will turn it over to you." A tall white man rose and turned to face the group.

"Hello, my name is Ed. This is John and Em."

He spoke in a soft voice that nevertheless carried to the back of the room. Rosalee thought that he seemed nervous or embarrassed.

"John, why don't you come up and tell the folks what we are going to do."

A short but powerfully built black man came. When he spoke, the cadence of a minister was in his voice.

"People, you are about to embark on an important campaign, a campaign to rid our nation of hate and fear. To get to that goal, however, you are going to have to face your own fear, you are going to have to pass through a valley of hate like many of you have never experienced." He motioned toward Ed and the petite black woman still sitting. "We are here to help you get ready." The woman rose and came to stand beside the two men. John continued, "We're going to start off with a little exercise. It will help you to see what you are up against and how you might respond."

The three of them moved to the other side of the table. The woman, Em, said, "We're going to need three volunteers." Her eyes came to rest on a young black man toward the back of the room. She pointed.

"How about you? Will you come and sit here?" The young man rose and took the seat. She pointed at Coleman. "And you. Will you take this seat?"

Rosalee's head jerked toward Coleman. Her expression revealed a frenzy of indignation. She wanted to jump to her feet, to scream at the stupid people from Nashville. Don't they know what they're doing? Coleman slowly stood and walked to the front.

Em completed the trio by choosing a black girl sitting toward the front. Em turned toward the audience, patted on the table, and said, "This is a lunch counter in Alabama. These three have just exited the bus and have taken a seat at the counter. I am the white waitress who is working. John and Ed are a couple of people from the Alabama town."

She turned to the three seated at the table and spoke in a low voice. "I want you to order just like you would at any lunch counter. No matter what John, Ed, and I say, just pretend we are people from that Alabama town and say what you would to them. Are you ready?" The three of them nodded.

John, Ed, and Em walked to the side of the room and spoke quietly to each other. Em walked back. She walked straight to Coleman and spoke only to him.

"Hey mister. What can I get you?"

Coleman blushed. Several people smiled at him and nodded. Rosalee glared at him. Coleman said, "So you want me to just pretend like I'm ordering something?"

Em flashed a smile and said in a southern accent dripping with sweetness, "Honey, you don't have to pretend. Tell me what you want and I'll get it for you."

Coleman said, "I guess I'll just take a cup of coffee."

Em started to walk away. The young man seated at the other end of the table, Roger, spoke.

"Miss, I'll take a cup of coffee also. And this lady here needs to order." He motioned toward Mary, the seated woman.

A sneer came to Em's face. She gave a little snort and turned with a flip of her head and walked away.

Roger said, "Miss, are you going to take our order?"

Em did not turn back. Instead, Ed and John came walking to the table. They stood behind Roger.

Roger turned to Ed. Ed snarled. "What are you looking at, boy?"

Roger's eyes widened. Mary, sitting in the middle seat, also turned. John, standing beside Ed, whipped around to face Mary.

"Nobody said anything to you!" John's furious eyes burned into Mary. "Why don't you get on up from this counter? This is for white folks only." Mary continued to stare. John slapped her on the face. Gasps rose from the audience.

Coleman started to rise from his seat. He said, "Hey, that's enough."

Coleman said it in a low voice, meant to only be heard by John but Rosalee heard it also and her fiery disgust for Coleman cooled a little. She saw a protective look in Coleman's eyes, the look of a father protecting his children or a husband standing up for his wife.

An unbidden pang of sympathy shot through her loathing of Coleman. But it was more than sympathy. It was…longing. She quickly suppressed it, dowsed all emotion with the smothering blanket of duty.

I'm here to learn, to get ready for the ride.

She saw John turn toward Coleman.

John said, "And what've we got here? A nigger lover? Is this here your girlfriend?" John shoved a finger into Mary's back. "Afraid I'm going to mess up your property?" A cruel smile spread across John's face. John slapped the back of Mary's head.

Rosalee gasped. She felt an instinct to jump up, to rush to Mary. Others in the room shifted forward in their seats.

Coleman started to stand. However, his feet became tangled in the legs of Mary's chair and he fell. He landed at the feet of John. John's arms flew into the air. He jerked his head toward Ed and said, "Did you see this nigger lover? He tried to attack me!"

John began to kick Coleman in the back. The first kick led to a muffled whoof. Two more followed.

The room erupted. Chairs flipped as people rushed forward. Rosalee was on the advance edge of the throng that surged toward these strangers. Her hands were clenched into fists and the crimson hue of combat colored her vision.

Ed threw up his hands and stepped in front of Rosalee, shielding John and Em from the rushing crowd. He shouted, "All right. That's enough. That's enough. Everything's O.K. This is just an exercise."

John immediately bent over and grabbed Coleman's hand. Rosalee saw that Coleman started to fight back.

John said, "Whoa! It's all over. Let me help you up."

Coleman grabbed John's wrist and allowed him to pull him to his feet. John patted his back and said, "Sorry about that. I had to make it look real." Coleman gave a single wordless nod.

Em moved to the center of the crowd, a pack still humming with slowly receding wrath. She said, "This is just a little taste of what you will encounter in the South," Em said as her gaze slowly swept the faces. "You notice I did not say that you might encounter this. Oh no. This kind of thing will happen."

Em's gaze paused at each face in the front ranks of the audience. Rosalee felt Em's eyes penetrate hers.

Em said, "You have to be ready. You have to know what you're going to say, what you're going to do."

Rosalee glanced at Coleman. He stood apart from the crowd, rubbing the back of his neck. His head was down. He seemed to feel Rosalee's gaze and met her eyes with his. Rosalee saw defeat and embarrassment. He turned away.

A voice from inside her said, *He tried to protect her. He stepped up.* Something in Rosalee softened. She moved to his side while James stepped back to the front of the room.

After covering some other business, James said, "O.K. everyone. That is our meeting for tonight. Thank you Ed and John and Em. As we have seen, we have a lot to learn."

As a murmur from the crowd swelled and the group began to disperse, James added, "Please remember the rally at Justice Park this Thursday. See you then."

Rosalee turned to Coleman. "What you did up there was good."

Coleman shook his head, his eyes downcast.

He said, "I was stupid. Didn't know what to do. Looked like a fool." He glanced toward the door. "I have to go." He started to move toward the exit.

Rosalee put her hand on his arm and said, "What you did was brave, it was right." She gave his arm a squeeze. "Come back and you can learn what to do, how to do it better."

Coleman said, "No, you were right the first time. I don't belong here." He shrugged off her hand and started toward the door.

Over his shoulder, Coleman said, "No need to worry. You'll never see me again."

CHAPTER 12

WASHINGTON, D.C., 1961

Coleman was weary. He had heard others use that word – his father, Granny Mae, even Dr. Browning – but he had not actually felt weariness himself before these last few days after the C.O.R.E. meeting. He had the sensation that every movement was hampered, like he was walking upstream in a swift flowing mountain creek. His ability to think was hazy, he did not feel like talking, and he avoided human contact as much as possible. Dr. Browning's questions of the past week had been answered with monosyllabic utterances or sometimes with a simple tired nod of the head, leaving Dr. Browning to stare after his protégé and wonder what was the matter.

On the train back from Silver Spring the week before, a flurry of emotions and thoughts had filled Coleman's head. It had been a moment of clarity. He could almost see different life routes stretching out, each one trailing sparks and spiraling off into the future. The path of the one he chose would not soon cross any of the others, if ever. The decision to simply say yes or no would have consequences, would carve a furrow he may find difficult to leave. Even with this heavy weight accompanying the decision, the conclusion to abandon the plan to become a minister had seemed to come easily, almost subconsciously.

After the C.O.R.E. meeting, Coleman's future had gone dark. The bright path of a life as a civil rights leader that had glowed golden had tarnished into ashen gray and then crumbled away all together after he carried his shame out of the meeting room. The embarrassment had stayed with him and it brought to the surface the self-conscious feelings that had first plagued him in his early days in Washington.

Coleman had long ago put aside the Pointer overalls and brogans of his early youth. The singsong drawl and mountain perspective on things were harder to shed. Though he was able to mostly suppress it, his accent still clung to him like red clay under his fingernails. In unguarded moments, phrases like "I'd shore be willing to holp y'all" slipped out of his mouth. The snickers from people who first heard the mountain twang in his voice and the even more impolite calls of "damn ignorant hillbilly" had pierced him deeply in the first few months in the city. But the hard edges of his accent had been chipped away and he had not faced the humiliation of an outsider for quite a long time.

Until now.

Coleman dragged himself into his little room at the rectory. He found it difficult to sleep. He undressed and prayed for at least a few hours of sleep, of unconsciousness in which he could leave his cares, to forget that he was drifting aimlessly in a vast leaden sea.

When Coleman pulled back the blanket tucked around the corners of his bed, a small red bundle fell to the floor. He retrieved it and shoved it back into its place under the pillow. *I hope that Dr. Browning never sees that*, he thought as he laid his head on the pillow and stared at the ceiling.

The room gradually faded and then dissolved completely. Granny Mae and he were in his old room. He was packing to go to college. His weathered tan suitcase lay open on his bed. He had placed into the suitcase stacks of underwear, socks, a couple of new pairs of stiff twill pants, some shirts, and a jacket. From her apron, Granny Mae pulled out a handful of items and laid them on the bed. She brandished a pair of black-handled scissors.

"Come over here, Coleman. I need to get a lock of your hair." Coleman started to protest.

Granny Mae held up a hand and said, "I ain't gonna hear it, young'un, I ain't about to let you go all the way off to college without you having some kind of protection. You never know what kind of people might be at that place."

Coleman relented and she snipped a thick bunch of hair. To the hair she gathered the other items on the bed – a short tree branch and some fingernail clippings. These she wrapped in a scrap of red cloth and tied it with a bit of red thread. She placed the bundle in the suitcase.

She said, "Them is my fingernails and that's a stick from down near the creek. I want you to promise me that you'll carry that little pouch everywhere you go."

"Yes, ma'am."

Granny Mae said, "I want you to make me an oath, Coleman."

"Yes, Granny Mae. I promise you that I'll keep it with me."

He woke with a start and slid a hand under the pillow, cupping the tiny packet in his palm. Did that little bundle really protect him from curses?

He was not sure. He felt cursed, bedeviled with doubts, with complications.

But where would I be without it? Maybe dead, my body floating down the Potomac and then out to sea, feeding the fish of the Atlantic by now. Or maybe I wouldn't have made it to Washington at all. Maybe I would be plowing the field with Papa, my joints being torn and my bones being broken a little bit more every day until finally I died from despair more than anything else.

Coleman knew that it did not matter if he believed in the power of the talisman or not. He had made a promise to Granny Mae and he would keep it.

Promises. What other promises have I made? Promises to myself, to make something of my life, something of substance, of value. Promises to Papa — even if he didn't hear them — to do something to make him proud.

Promises to Rosalee.

He told her that he would not leave. Coleman did not know everything about Rosalee's past, but he knew that she no longer had either one of her parents. They had both left her.

I can't be the next one to leave, another disappointment in her life.

But, I can't go back to C.O.R.E.

As he practically ran out of the last meeting, his mind had reeled. He heard a voice screaming, *Get out of this place! These are not your people!*

He realized the voice was his and immediately felt shame. He could not bear the thought of harsh words, physical blows, hatred poured on him like red hot coals being heaped upon his head.

He lay in his dark room, spirits swirling through the blackness, brushing by his heart and mind. Gradually, the voice of Granny Mae rose to prominence, drowning out the rest of the cacophony.

Coleman's mind went back to the last time he saw Granny Mae alive. He had been home from college on break and was waiting for a friend to take him back to campus, his packed suitcase beside him on the front porch as Granny Mae slowly rocked. The creaking of the chair was like the heartbeat of the mountains, a slow sleepy rhythm, the same rhythm that had marked the lives of many generations. The rhythm was mimicked by the flagging heart within the chest of the old woman, a heart that would push its last bit of blood in a scant three months.

"Coleman, you're a-doing real good at college." She paused to spit a dollop of tobacco stained saliva into an old Dinty Moore stew can. "Me and your Papa are proud."

Coleman said, "Granny Mae, I know you're proud, but I don't know about Papa."

Granny Mae smiled, the brown stain on her lower lip widening. "You know your Papa don't talk a lot and when he does, he ain't gonna waste any breath on his feelings. But, he shore has some, way down deep. He's a-proud of you in his own way."

51

She reached a bony hand over and patted his leg. Her skin was transparent, like thin butcher's paper saturated with grease. It appeared that the blood vessels and bones and tendons could pop out of their gossamer casing at any second. She craned her neck up to look at Coleman and she resembled an ancient bird, some prehistoric creature that had spent its life snatching scraps of food from the prey of dinosaurs before lying down to a long sleep and being covered with dirt and stone and water and eons later being freed by a pick and seeing the light of a new era, light that was dim and filtered down from high museum windows. Granny Mae seemed to know that she was about to enter that sleep and she expected to wake to the permeating light of glory, light that emanated from the Lamb and was reflected up to her by streets of gold. Before she left, she aimed to fortify her only grandchild with the things that his dead mother could not and his barely alive father would not.

She said, "Coleman, you are the sparkling jewel of this here family, the precious one that is going to leave this valley and do great things. All you gotta do is believe. You gotta believe in the Lord our God and in His Son Jesus. But there's something else you gotta believe in."

She pressed one of her bony fingers into Coleman's chest. It felt no heavier than a butterfly wing.

"You gotta believe in you. I do."

She sat back and started rocking again, the creaking serving as punctuation to her pronouncement.

She said, "You promise me that you'll always believe in yourself."

That Coleman, the Coleman of three years ago, nodded.

"Yes, ma'am."

The Coleman that lay in the bed of the rectory of the Lamb of God Presbyterian Church was not as confident, not as sure, not as unquestioning of the wisdom of his grandmother as that earlier version of himself. However, he remembered his promise.

He would believe. He would keep his promise to Rosalee. He would return to C.O.R.E.

On Thursday, Coleman took the bus back to Columbia Heights. He did not have to try to avoid Dr. Browning because the pastor was in Virginia visiting his sister.

Coleman walked the two blocks from the bus stop to the park. The day had warmed and blue sky was visible between the buildings. The uneasiness of coming back to a C.O.R.E. event was pushed away by Coleman's anticipation of seeing Rosalee. As he neared the park, he saw a few knots of people standing and talking. Cardboard signs on sticks were piled beside one of the benches. He walked through the arched entrance and saw Rosalee. She walked toward him.

She said, "I didn't know if you was going to come. In fact, I didn't think you would after the way you left the meeting the other night." She crossed her arms. "You know, I was trying to be nice, trying to change my mind about you. But I just don't know."

Coleman noticed that she wore the pink and white scarf that he had seen the first day he met her, when she had saved his life. He had thought then that she resembled an angel. He still saw heaven in her face.

"Yeah, I know." He kicked the ground. "I guess I was feeling pretty bad about that lunch counter exercise."

Rosalee continued to stare at him.

"Well, like I said, we all got a lot to learn." She let her arms fall to her side. "I'm glad to see you here, giving it another chance." Coleman saw a sly smile appear.

She said, "You did look pretty silly falling down like that."

Coleman smiled and said, "I never was very graceful." She chuckled.

Coleman said, "Where is everyone? I thought there'd be more people than this."

Rosalee frowned. "Yeah, me too. A lot of people weren't able to get off work early." She looked at her wristwatch. "We had to have it this early because this was the only time the reporter could come."

He said, "There's going to be a reporter here?"

Rosalee said, "Yeah, James knows someone who is friends with this reporter. He's coming so that we can spread the word about what's going on down in South Carolina. The newspapers here aren't printing anything about it. James says sometimes you got to shake up things to get noticed. That's why we're going to do this protest."

Coleman noticed the signs on the ground. The top one read, *Free the Friendship Nine*. Coleman turned to Rosalee and said, "You'll have to forgive me, but what is this about?"

A small burst of anger appeared in Rosalee's eyes but then she nodded. "Like I said, the newspapers here haven't been telling about it." She pointed at the sign. "The Friendship Nine are nine people who were arrested in South Carolina just for sitting at a lunch counter."

Coleman's hand involuntarily went to the back of his neck and rubbed.

James appeared. He pointed at the signs and said, "Everyone grab one. The man from the newspaper should be here anytime. We have to be ready. He won't wait long if nothing's going on."

Rosalee and Coleman stooped to take a sign. Coleman saw that his read, *Desegregate Now!* They took their place in front of a concrete dais on top of which James stood.

James said, "Here he comes." To the small crowd. he said, "Let's hear it!"

Someone at the back started to chant. "Free the nine! Free the nine!" Others took up the chant. As the reporter neared, the crowd got louder.

"FREE THE NINE!"

Their voices rang in Coleman's ears. He felt excitement rise. A burning ignited in his belly and spread upwards. His arms began pumping the sign up and down. He heard himself screaming. "FREE THE NINE!"

The reporter stopped at the entrance of the park and raised his camera, its clicks made inaudible by the chants. A joy permeated Coleman. He felt a part of something important, something of substance. This was not some inconsequential grievance, like the changing of the dining hall menu he had protested at school. By God, people were in jail! Flesh-and-blood people in a stone-and-iron jail! This was real!

James started to gesture wildly from atop the concrete stage. Shushes erupted among the crowd. The chants faded away. The reporter let the camera fall to his chest and pulled out a small notepad, flipping it open and wetting a pencil tip with his tongue.

James said, "Brothers and sisters!"

His words were like a peal of thunder, rolling across the park, bouncing off the buildings.

"I thank you for gathering here in this place, under God's sky, to bring to light a grave injustice."

His pause was filled with yeses and even some amens. Coleman could tell that the man from Nashville, John, had influenced James. His speech sounded like a sermon preached from the pulpit on a hot summer Sunday.

"Nine brothers, one of them our very own Thomas, were brutally and unfairly removed from a public place of business in Rock Hill, South Carolina. They were dragged to the street and then thrown into jail."

The crowd erupted with cries of "No, no!" and "Free them!"

James raised his arms again. "Yes, they were thrown into jail for sitting at a lunch counter – for sitting at a lunch counter!"

"Why, why?" the crowd called.

"Why, do you ask? Why? You know very well why. Because they are black!"

"FREE THE NINE! FREE THE NINE!"

The crowd chanted for a full minute. James stood with his arms crossed. Coleman saw that the reporter was putting his notebook back in his coat pocket. James raised his hands to quiet the throng.

James said, "Their skin is black. That was the reason. If they had white skin, they would have been served."

His voice was low. His eyes scanned the crowd. The reporter flipped his notebook open again.

James said, "You know, I bet that if you looked in their wallets, their money was just as green as anybody's."

Laughs erupted. The crowd took up a different chant.

"Black skin, green money! Black skin, green money!"

The chant got a little louder and some of the people in the crowd started to pump their signs up and down with the chant. Coleman began to feel uncomfortable. He could not bring himself to join in. He saw the reporter chuckle to himself. James waved his arms again to get the crowd's attention.

He said, "Brothers and sisters!"

The crowd quieted. The reporter listened. James spoke quietly. There was power in his voice.

"We aren't looking for a free handout. No." He shook his head. "We aren't asking for a free ride. No." The crowd shook their heads and echoed back the no.

"We aren't begging for a free seat at the table. No."

James looked over the crowd. The silence stretched. The faces craned in anticipation. Even the reporter waited motionlessly, his pencil poised above the page. James's voice boomed across the park.

He said, "WE ARE DEMANDING FREEDOM!" The crowd erupted in wild cheering.

James said, "WE ARE INSISTING ON JUSTICE!" Voices bounced off the walls of the surrounding buildings. Passersby had gathered at the entrance to the park, peering in at the cacophonous assembly.

"WE ARE CLAIMING THE VERY RIGHT TO LIFE, LIBERTY, AND THE PURSUIT OF HAPPINESS!"

Some of the members of the crowd had their hands in the air, like they were at a church service and the spirit had taken them. Coleman moved toward the periphery of the group, not comfortable in joining in the ecstasy, not knowing what to do. He glanced at the reporter, who was apparently having the same thought. The reporter once again moved to put his notebook in his pocket. James jumped down from the platform and approached the reporter, speaking words unheard by Coleman over the cries still coming from the crowd.

Coleman saw a pair of tall black men break away from the crowd and rush to the other side of the reporter, blocking the way to the park's exit. A frightened look appeared on the reporter's face. He tried to push between the men, but they did not budge. James attempted to intervene, but he was swept up in the flow of people from the crowd. Coleman had a clear path to the reporter and thus hurried to his side and motioned for the two men to step aside. The two men started to yell.

"He ain't going nowhere! We ain't finished! I want him to write down everything everybody says!" The man punctuated his statement with a finger jabbed in Coleman's direction. The other man was yelling also.

"Put it in the paper! Free the nine!"

Coleman positioned himself between the reporter and the two men. They continued to yell. He said over his shoulder to the reporter, "Just wait a minute and James will be here."

The reporter was wide-eyed, his gaze flitting around, searching for a way of escape.

The reporter said, "Buddy, this is getting a little out of hand. I'm leaving."

At that moment, James ran up and turned to the two men and said, "Men, thank you for your input. Let's now let this fine man go and do his job." The two men stepped aside. James accompanied the reporter to the street.

Rosalee came up behind Coleman. He jumped at her touch and said, "Whoa, those two really let that reporter have it." He motioned at the backs of the pair walking deeper into the park now. "I thought it was going to get physical."

Coleman turned to Rosalee. "Why are they so angry?"

Rosalee seemed speechless, her mouth hanging open. "Haven't you been listening?"

Coleman said, "There was no reason for them to take it out on that reporter. He didn't lock up those people in South Carolina."

Rosalee said, "Of course not. But that's not the issue. The problem is that no one is listening. No one cares. Everybody's content to just live their own lives, to hell with what is happening with anyone else."

Coleman said, "But you don't think that treating the reporter like that is the best way to get him to write a positive story about this group, do you? Threatening him and scaring him half to death is no way to make a good impression."

Rosalee said, "Of course not. That's why James came over and smoothed things out. Horace and Coop carried it too far. But, still, they have a right to be angry. Things have gone on too long."

Coleman said, "I agree that things are bad in some places, but that's just change happening. You've got to expect that there will be resistance to change."

"Simple resistance to change is not what this is," Rosalee said, shaking her head. "Resistance to change is what happens when people complain about an old building being torn down to make way for a supermarket. Coleman, people're being killed. People're being thrown into jail. Being beaten. No, this ain't just resistance to change."

She looked at Coleman's face and said, "The trouble going on right now is due to fear and hate. And, of course, hate's just a type of fear. Hate happens when you're so afraid of something that you're willing to do anything to make it go away, even kill it." She swung her arm to encompass the entire park with all of the members of C.O.R.E. in it.

She said, "We're fighting that fear. We're fighting it by speaking the truth. We're fighting it with non-violent protest, just by being present in places where it is difficult to be." She put her hand over her chest.

She said, "We're fighting it with love. The opposite of fear is love. Love is the cure of fear and hate."

Coleman felt hope and despair in her words. Hope that there was good in the world, kind-hearted courageous people who would stand up for what is right, no matter the cost. Despair because, deep down in places he dared not glimpse, he doubted that he was one of those people.

The sky above them was now a deep purple with pink edged clouds being illuminated by the sun from below the horizon. The chill that had been pushed into the shadows by the warmth of the sun's rays now crept back, at first sending its tendrils around their ankles but now climbing up their bodies. The crowd had started to disperse into the evening. Hoarse voices bid farewell to others.

Coleman turned toward Rosalee. She seemed to be examining his face, trying to read it to see if her words had an effect.

Rosalee said, "So, what do you think?" She waited for a reaction. Nothing. "Listen, I don't think this is going to work."

Coleman turned to protest. "What do you mean? Are you talking about us? Or are you talking about this?" He swept his arm around the park.

She said, "All of it!" Her eyes flared. "First off, there is no 'us'. There's only you and there's only me." She stamped her foot. "And yes, all of this. You don't belong in C.O.R.E. I thought you might but you don't have any clue what we're about. You're just standing on the edges, watching things happen. You don't have the passion the rest of us have. You need to just go on back to your big old church and your pastor hero and leave this fight to us."

Even in the deepening dusk, Coleman could see her eyes filled with anger like white-hot coals.

He said, "That's not fair." Coleman felt his own anger rising. "And my church and Dr. Browning don't have anything to do with this."

Rosalee gave a laugh. "I hear the way you talk about Dr. Browning. I can see the pride inside you when you tell people that you work for Dr. Browning at the great Lamb of God. You think that Dr. Browning is perfect, that nothing can touch him. You think he is like one of those marble statues in a museum, lovely, unchanging. And you want to be just like him. You want to be up in a golden pulpit, with everybody looking up to you. But that's not the way it is. People are not like that, not Dr. Browning, not you. He's human just like you and me. We're not made of smooth stone, cold and dry, sitting in a pretty room. We are out here in the world, where there's wind and rain and trouble. We're soft, fragile, warm, and wet. Hate can kill us just as well as a freight train."

Coleman threw his hands up at the sky and said, "I don't know how to convince you that I want to help. I feel bad about all of the injustice toward people because of the color of their skin. Maybe I don't have the same passion about it that you do and that some of the C.O.R.E. members do because I haven't been living it like you have. But that doesn't mean I don't have any part in this. What can I do or say to make you see that?"

Rosalee said, "You haven't committed to going on the bus down south. When are you going to decide?"

Coleman's heart sank. The fire he had felt moments before dwindled as if her words were a bucket of water poured over him. The conflict within him had not been resolved. She saw his hesitation.

Rosalee pointed at him and said, "That's what I'm talking about. You don't know. You like being caught up in all of the excitement of the meetings and the protests, the speeches and the rallies. But when it comes down to it, you don't want to risk anything. You don't want to get your hands dirty." She pulled her coat around her and glanced toward the entrance, preparing to leave.

She said, "That's what you have to decide. Now that you know what C.O.R.E. is all about, are you willing to risk everything? If you're not, you're just wasting your time, my time, and everyone else's time." She turned and walked through the gate, leaving him standing alone in the darkening park.

Anger, embarrassment, fear returned, blowing inside him like debris swirling in the wind. His path forward was not clear. The call of greatness was on his life. But what greatness?

CHAPTER 13

WASHINGTON, D.C., 1961

The article came out in the morning paper. Coleman had expected it but nevertheless felt a sudden fall of his stomach when he first saw his own face staring up from page five. He thought, Page five. Maybe he won't see it. But he knew that Dr. Browning would see it and was not surprised when the church secretary came to the small inglenook in which his desk was wedged and said, "Dr. Browning would like to speak to you in his office. Immediately, if you please."

When Coleman had decided to leave the path to becoming a minister, he had known that he would have to tell Dr. Browning eventually. But, he had counted on having months, time to see if a relationship with Rosalee developed, time to allow her to return from the bus rides that were scheduled to begin in May, time to see if other opportunities within the civil rights movement revealed themselves. In the meantime, he would have a salary and a place to stay while he researched his next career move. Coleman had recognized in some deep part of his mind that this plan was dishonest, that he was taking advantage of Dr. Browning but he justified it by telling himself that he was simply waiting patiently on the Lord's message to him.

As he walked to Dr. Browning's office, Coleman realized how much he had learned from his time at the Lamb of God and how much he still valued the old clergyman's high opinion. When he first met Dr. Browning, Coleman thought he knew how to behave around great men, thought he had learned how to move in that world during the time he spent around Dean Simpson at college. When he first arrived on campus as a freshman, he was ignorant and naïve, a real rustic. He had coped by simply remaining silent, by blending into the scenery. Dean Simpson had drawn him out a little.

However, it was Dr. Browning who had taught him, mostly by example instead of through words, how to have an intellectual bearing, how to project an air of confidence and saintliness. Dr. Browning had recently remarked on the incredible progress that Coleman had made. Coleman did not want to diminish in the pastor's view.

Coleman closed the door behind him as he entered the clergyman's office. Though the office was only sparsely furnished, it was nonetheless befitting the senior pastor of a large church like the Lamb of God. Granite walls stretched twenty-five feet above the cold tile floor and two large windows faced the courtyard. The pastor's desk was relatively small and modestly faced one of the stone walls. Over the desk hung an arrangement of three black and white photographs of Dr. Browning in his ecumenical robes smiling and grasping the hands of Cardinal Spellman, Clark Gable, and President Truman. Dr. Browning bent over a piece of paper, his pen scratching unseen words. A folded newspaper was on the corner of the desk. He glanced over his shoulder.

Dr. Browning said, "Please take a seat, Coleman." Coleman sat in one of the leather-upholstered armchairs that faced the windows. A bird flitted through the sun-dappled center of the courtyard. Coleman could hear the chirps of birds at the bath just out of view beyond the edge of the window.

The courtyard was meant by the designers of the church to aid in creating a contemplative mood in petitioners as they approached the altar inside but the courtyard was not currently having its intended effect on Coleman. His heart raced, the sound of blood surged through his hearing, and his palms were covered with a sheen of sweat.

Dr. Browning finished his writing with a dramatic flourish of the pen and swiveled his desk chair to face Coleman. He reached behind him and retrieved the newspaper. Holding it up, he said, "I suppose you've seen this."

"Yes sir. I saw it this morning."

"And what is your explanation?" Dr. Browning's face and voice remained steady. The calmness with which he spoke did little to ease Coleman's anxiety.

"Well, sir, a reporter came to last night's rally and was interested in what the group had been doing."

A bird smacked into the closed window and fell to ground. Dr. Browning pivoted toward the loud sound and watched while the bird popped up to its feet, shook its head, and flew off.

Dr. Browning turned back to Coleman and said, "I am aware that a reporter spoke to the group. What I am wondering is the reason for your being at the rally. I thought we had an understanding that you would be severing your relations with this group and with," Dr. Browning pointed, at a figure in the photo, "this young lady."

Coleman felt himself shrinking in the chair. His mouth was dry. One half of his mind urged him to submit, to agree to Dr. Browning's desire, to admit his mistake in taking part in this foolish endeavor, to repent of his pursuit of Rosalee. The other part of his mind screamed at him to profess his heart's passion. That part of his mind wanted to lunge at the smug old man in his swivel chair and fine office and claw his face to a shredded mess, to hear his cries for help, to choke the life out of the stuffy figurehead of a dying faith.

Coleman said, "Sir, I know we spoke of C.O.R.E. and of Rosalee and I remember the opinions you expressed. However, I'm afraid I don't share your views. I believe that C.O.R.E.'s mission is a noble one and that Rosalee is a fine girl who I would like to know better."

As Coleman spoke, Dr. Browning's placid countenance changed. His brow became furrowed, his eyes blazed, his cheeks flushed scarlet. Coleman avoided his gaze by turning his eyes to the window again. However, the tone of Dr. Browning's voice when he spoke again snapped Coleman's eyes back.

"You believe? YOU BELIEVE? I CARE NOTHING FOR WHAT YOU BELIEVE!" Dr. Browning's voice echoed around the granite walls and shook the glass in the windows.

Dr. Browning said, "My opinion is not my opinion alone." His voice dripped with condescension and spite. "It is the opinion of this parish. In this church, I am the voice of authority." Dr. Browning rose to his feet. "It is my word, my good graces, by which you have a position here. Without my say, you will go nowhere in this religious life you have chosen. You will remain a lowly apprentice or will be cast down to a sleepy parish church with moldy parishioners."

Dr. Browning's voice softened. "Coleman, my son. Please understand. I want what is best for you."

Dr. Browning pulled another of the armchairs and sat facing Coleman, knee to knee. He put one of his slender hands on each of Coleman's thighs.

"Coleman, I see a bright future for you here. You and I were born for this place. I have brought the Lamb of God this far, you can take the helm when I am gone and guide the next generation even further." He patted Coleman's thighs. "Just think. I can continue to train you. You can soak up all of the knowledge I have accumulated and add your own. You can be the pastor of representatives, senators, Supreme Court justices, even presidents. You can be responsible for the spiritual welfare of the most powerful men on earth. You will have their ear, share their deepest secrets, their most fond dreams. Think of the good that you can do, the glory you can bring to God and His church." Coleman again looked out of the window. "So, Coleman, can't you see the folly in associating with this revolutionary group. You cannot expect to be a part of them and to remain here at Lamb of God."

Coleman said, "But what about Rosalee?"

Dr. Browning said, "I'm sure that you can see that it is not at all proper for a man of God to pair himself to someone of another race. We are called to be equally yoked. It is unthinkable that you could have anything other than a pastor-parishioner relationship with a colored girl."

Dr. Browning cleared his voice and stood. His voice changed from that of the warm father figure to that of the busy administrator, making it clear that the meeting was over.

"Coleman, thank you very much for coming to talk to me. You have some things to think over. Please stop by Mrs. Brewer's desk on the way out and make an appointment for tomorrow morning. I must ask you for your decision then. If you decide to break ties with that group and all of its members, we can use tomorrow's meeting to discuss the next phase in your development here at Lamb of God. If you decide otherwise, I am afraid that we will have to use tomorrow morning to make arrangements to end your employment here and make plans for you to vacate the premises by week's end."

Dr. Browning walked to the door, opened it, and said, "That is all. Again, thank you for coming."

CHAPTER 14

ARLINGTON, VIRGINIA, 1961

He hung around the bus station. He usually did that when he first arrived in a town, though he knew this particular city well. The bus station was a place where he could usually find odd jobs to do, loading trucks, sweeping floors, anything to get a little money to buy cigarettes and something to eat.

His life was hard. Nothing came easy. Every day was spent scraping to stay alive. Though his little mind was not capable of great thoughts, he longed for a day here and there in which he could walk barefoot in the grass like he used to.

He hated. He blamed everyone for his life. His teachers who had not taught him to read. His daddy who would not even claim him as a son. And most of all, niggers.

How can any of them think they're better than me, a white man?

A man in an old truck pulled up to the bus station and pointed at him. "Hey, you. Do you want some work? I can pay you five bucks for the day."

He walked toward the truck. "Doing what?"

The man in the truck said, "Do you want the work or not?"

He nodded and climbed into the bed of the truck. The man drove to an old warehouse on the edge of town and stopped. The warehouse was enormous and mostly empty save for a few tall piles of junk scattered about the floor. A large metal container stood in the center of the warehouse.

He jumped down from the bed. The man motioned toward the piles. "I need you to sort through all of this trash. Anything that looks like I should keep it, put it in the corner over there by the door. Everything else goes in the dumpster."

The man walked to the huge door at the other end of the warehouse, turned a key in a padlock and pushed the door open. There was a fence and beyond it was another fence and then a green lawn spotted with row upon row of white stones.

The man said, "It sometimes gets hot in here, even when it's cold outside. I'll leave the door open for you." He walked back to the truck. "I'll be back at about four. If you've done a good job, I'll pay you."

After the truck drove off, he started on the piles. Fragments of wooden pallets made up a large portion of the mounds. He threw these in the dumpster. Sheaves of paper, old catalogs, broken furniture followed the pallets into the container. He found a wicker picnic basket containing a full set of plates, only one of them broken. This he placed in the corner.

He worked steadily for three hours. He walked over to the open door and pulled a hunk of bread and a little slice of hard cheese out of the pocket of his grimy jacket. He leaned against the doorframe and ate as he gazed out at the cemetery. He finished the bread and cheese and noticed a full rain barrel just outside. He cupped his hand and brought some water to his mouth, his eyes remaining on the green grass.

He returned to the trash piles and soon was making noticeable headway. After finishing one pile, he found a broom and swept away the rest of the trash and started on the next pile.

After carrying several loads of trash from the last pile to the dumpster, he saw a strange shape in the remaining trash. He bent down and grabbed the shape. It was a gun.

He brushed the dirt off the pistol. The dull metal felt cold and heavy in his hand. He checked the cylinder. Four bullets. He lifted the gun and peered down the barrel toward the far wall. The broken wooden grip bit into his palm but the gun was well balanced. He felt power surge through him.

He glanced over at the small stack of items near the entrance and thought for a few seconds. He tucked the gun into his belt at the small of his back and pulled down his jacket.

The man returned at four o'clock and said, "This looks real good. Here's your five dollars and a couple of extra." The man handed him the bills and asked, "Do you need a ride back to the bus station or somewhere?"

He squinted at the man for a second and asked, "You got a dime for the phone I can have?" The man fished a dime out of his pocket and drove off.

He stuffed the paper money into his back pocket, walked to the phone booth on the corner, pulled a slip of paper out of another pocket, and dialed the number on the slip.

His voice was loud, a product of his environment, the voice of someone accustomed to having to shout to be heard above the din of humanity scrabbling for the bits of sustenance that fell from the tables of the fortunate.

Someone standing outside the phone booth on that cool Virginia evening would have heard a long pause after the jingle of the dime. They would have heard the man in the booth say in a growling drawl, "Do you know who this is?" Maybe some low garbled muttering would have been heard from the receiver pressed to his ear and then they would have heard him say, "Don't get all bent out o' shape." A pause and then a yelled response to the other's words.

"I AIN'T CALLIN JUST TO CHITTY-CHAT! WE GOT SOME BUSINESS TO DO!"

A low crackle of static and another pause as more words were spoken into his ear.

In a more reasonable voice, he said, "I need a little more money and then I'll try to be out of your hair for good."

As he listened to more talk from the other end of the phone line, he scanned the darkening street, a habit born out of prior muggings, thieves robbing thieves.

He said, "I reckon I could do that for you as long as you pay me. Tell me again who it is and where I can find 'em." More muffled words heard from the receiver.

He said, "You just send the money where you did before and I'll do what you want. Maybe I'll call us even after this, maybe not."

After a click, he pulled the dead receiver away from his ear, chuckled, and slammed it home. As he walked back up the street searching for a dark hole where he might weather the night, he patted his chest and talked to the night.

"Won't be long now. Gonna get you some real money. Gonna get you a place where you can sleep inside every night."

As he crawled into the weeds under a set of old wooden stairs, he pulled his jacket up over his head.

"Won't be long now."

CHAPTER 15

THE LAMB OF GOD CHURCH, 1961

Coleman slowly attended to his duties about the church for the rest of the day. The light of day and Dr. Browning's words had not made his path any clearer. If anything, he was even more confused. He sat over a bowl of soup that was his dinner, his appetite as confused as the rest of him. As evening turned into night, he could not bear the thought of bed. He put on his coat and began to walk.

The windows of storefronts were dark, like black eyes of prone giants watching him as he passed. The sky was clear and in particularly dark spaces, Coleman could see brilliant stars sending their cold light to earth, light that had passed through space that was desolate beyond the comprehension of men, emptiness so complete that no air, no substance, no life was present, only a thin, twinkling sliver of starlight hurrying its way to Coleman's eye, thousands of worlds away. Coleman felt a kinship with that slender beam. He felt alone. There was no one to help him decide his path. All he could do was keep going toward a future that he could not yet see.

His feet took him to the Mall. He walked around the refuse of construction workers, fresh earth and safety barrels, at the unlighted Monument, a great leaden finger pointing at the black velvet above. The Capitol rose in the distance, its illumination made even more spectacular by the dark shadows that enveloped him. The building seemed to shine from within, as if the power and wisdom of its inhabitants were diffusing through the stone and mortar and shooting out into the night. Thoughts flitted through his tumbling mind.

I can be one of those great men. But what about Rosalee?

Coleman walked. Lovely brownstones with warm light and butlers and maids within. Stark cold government buildings festooned with eagles and arrows and cannonballs. Corrugated tin covering dilapidated garages and sheds. They all filed past him in the night. He met almost no one and did not speak to the few he met. An old man with a paper-bag-wrapped bottle lifted his chin as he passed. A mother glanced at him through a window and quickly drew the curtains against the stranger and returned with the bottle to her baby.

The quietness of the city and the calmness of his demeanor belied the turmoil in his mind. During his night walk, he made many definitive decisions only to completely reverse them moments later. He could feel the slow steady progression of the earth beneath his feet. The globe spun, bringing him ever closer to the meeting with Dr. Browning.

As the world's rotation pointed Coleman toward the brightening of the coming day, Coleman found himself back at the Lamb of God. He stood in front of the great oaken front doors. Sturdy ancient granite supported his feet. The stone spire soared into the lightening sky, the last few stars forming a crown around its tip and silently winking out.

As he watched, the sun peeked over the horizon and painted gold the granite ball perched two hundred feet above him. Golden light crept down the spire. Indistinct details leapt to crystal clear resolution. Stone flowers bloomed to life. Carved flourishes cascaded down as chiseled trees reached toward heaven. Coleman's breath caught in his chest. As the sun lit and warmed the stone high above, he felt his heart and mind melt and coalesce around one thought.

His decision was made. He knew what he must do. He called and left a message asking Rosalee to meet him later in the day. After that, he walked to Dr. Browning's office.

WASHINGTON, D.C., ACROSS TOWN

Rosalee was surprised when Mrs. Rucker gave her Coleman's message. On the way by bus to the Lamb of God, she tried to predict what he might say. Arguments rose in her mind.

What the hell does he want? Maybe he has changed his mind, changed his heart. Maybe he really is beginning to understand the struggle. But what difference does that make?

The bus pulled up to the stop. He was waiting as the door opened.

Rosalee said, "What's the big secret?"

Coleman said, "I asked you to meet because I need to discuss something with you."

Rosalee stared, waiting. "What is it?"

Coleman said, "I don't want to talk about it here." Rosalee glared at him for a second and started to walk toward the church. "No wait." Coleman tried to take her hand but she recoiled from his touch. "We're going to go somewhere quiet where we can talk in private."

Rosalee said, "Where?"

Coleman glanced toward the bus schedule to make sure he had read it correctly. He nodded.

"Arlington Cemetery."

CHAPTER 16

ARLINGTON, VIRGINIA, 1961

By the time they made it to the cemetery, the land all around them spoke of the setting sun. Washington's white buildings, visible across the Potomac, robed themselves in glowing orange. The trees donned golden tips and edges on their leaves and limbs. Even the darkening eastern sky paid tribute with a distinct pink blush at its horizon. Coleman and Rosalee sat silently on the bench, the brilliant scene stealing their words, words that nevertheless needed to be said.

As the gilded landscape slowly faded, Rosalee broke the silence.

She said, "Mama was cooking black-eyed peas on the stove on the night it happened. There was a knock on the door and Mama told me to stir the peas while she went to answer it. I took the spoon and stirred but I stepped over to where I could see the door. There was a policeman standing there, holding my daddy's coat, the one Mama had given him for Christmas. The policeman said, 'Does this belong to your husband?' Even I could see the bullet holes in the back of the coat and the blood and Mama knew what had happened. She fell in the floor crying. She didn't answer. Of course, she didn't have to."

Rosalee kicked her foot on the ground and said, "My daddy was shot dead by a policeman. My daddy had just robbed a grocer on the other side of town. He had lost his job at the train yard two weeks before and hadn't told my mother. We guess he was trying to get some money so that he wouldn't have to tell her, at least not yet. I have wondered hundreds of times whether the police would have shot him if he was white. They shot him in the back. He didn't have a chance."

Coleman could not meet her eyes. Her pain pierced him. What could he say? The silence crowded.

He said, "I'm sorry."

"Yeah," Rosalee said. "Everybody's sorry. Poor little orphan girl."

"But your mother..."

"She laid right there on the floor all night. I made some breakfast for her the next morning and finally got her to eat. I went to school. I asked the old lady who lived next door to check on her. When I got home, Mama was in the bed. There was an empty liquor bottle in the floor. Mama never drank liquor in her life until that day. Said she didn't like the taste or the smell. But after Daddy was killed, she started drinking everyday. She did piecework, sewing shirts for a little money. I dropped out of school and got a job and between the two of us, we made just enough to stay in our apartment and to keep from starving. After about a year, she stopped sewing because she was too drunk all the time."

Rosalee crossed her hands and gazed across the rows of headstones. She took a deep breath and exhaled.

She said, "I found Mama dead at home when I was seventeen. I could smell something when I first entered the door. It smelled sort of like when you put a dirty old penny up to your nose. It was minerally. She was in the back room. An empty liquor bottle was on the floor beside her chair. Her back was to me. When I came around the chair, her eyes were open, staring out the back window. She was wearing a red blouse. At least, I thought she was at first. I then saw it was blood. She had vomited so much blood that she bled to death right there in her chair."

Coleman softly said, "I'm so sorry."

Rosalee said, "All of that is not why I do what I do. Sure, my father might not have been killed if he wasn't colored but still he was doing something wrong. I'm concerned about all of the people who are being hurt and even killed when they haven't done anything wrong at all. People like that little boy in Mississippi who was killed. And it's not just physical pain these people are feeling. It's having their rights taken away from them. Like the right to vote. Or even just the right to sit in a bus seat. And this has been going on a long time. Something's got to be done."

She turned to face Coleman. "I had this dream night after night when I was little, before Mama and Daddy died. In the dream, I would get to school and then there would be something that I forgot, like forgetting to bring my lunch or even forgetting to put on clothes. I would wake up with this bad feeling deep inside that I had left something necessary undone."

She smiled, wordlessly remembering better times with her mother and father, simpler times, safer times.

She turned back to Coleman and said, "And now, I've got bigger things to worry about. People are suffering. People are dying."

She shook her head, tears balancing above her lower lids, giving a luminance to her eyes.

She said, "The glory of doing something great is not what keeps me going. It's the grief of leaving something necessary undone."

He turned to her, took her other hand in his, and opened his mouth. Before he could say anything, Rosalee said, "I know what you're about to say." He sat back and let go of her hands.

Coleman said, "How could you know?"

"I know why you brought me out here." She eyed the city, gathering courage from the buildings, now light gray against the deep slate sky of early evening. "You ain't coming back to C.O.R.E."

Coleman said, "You don't know what I've been thinking. You don't know how much I've been thinking. I spent all last night considering everything from all sides. I remembered the words you said. I remembered the words all the C.O.R.E. people said. I remembered what Dr. Browning said. All of these words, swirling around in my head. I saw the sunrise and I decided what I had to do."

Coleman took her chin in his hand, and gently raised her eyes to his.

He said, "No, Rosalee, you don't understand. I choose you."

Her first instinct was to protest, to make it clear that choosing her was not an option, but she stopped. As if a light switch had been flipped, she saw her life differently. She did not have to be alone. She looked around like she was just arriving on earth, like she was seeing for the first time the trees and grass and setting sun and the man sitting beside her. It was all strange and familiar and beautiful and scary.

Inside Rosalee's heart, it was not so much a thawing as a redefining that happened. True, she had walled off her feelings, her deepest desires, anything that would interfere with the fight for the rights of her people. And that's the way she thought of it – my people, my struggle, my war against injustice. In the infinity of the few seconds that she sat there wordlessly, she saw that loving and receiving the love of a man did not mean she would have to give up her fight, even if that man was white. In fact, her love for Coleman would strengthen her resolve. If she can learn to give her heart to a white man, surely white men can learn to give justice to black people. And if they cannot, if racial injustice continued to go unchecked, if the cancer of prejudice spread, she would at least have a partner who would both be at her side and at the same time embody her hope for a future when all people can live in harmony.

My fight will become our fight.

She saw it in his eyes. The love that had shown in her father's eyes. The love that she had wished for even though it had never risen to her conscious mind. The love she had searched for in a thousand different ways but never found until this awkward boy, this caring man came unbidden into her life.

"So what now?" Rosalee said.

He said, "I don't know. Lots of things are stacked against us. Things that other people will throw at us. Things that will well up from inside ourselves."

Coleman reached over and took Rosalee's hand. She saw her hand in his, an amazed expression on her face, as if she was looking at a lost treasure inside an old trunk that had just been opened, a trunk that had sat neglected in the attic for generations. She slowly raised her eyes to his. Though the sun had dipped below the horizon, Rosalee's face glowed with new love, new feelings, a depth of happiness and excitement she had never experienced.

Coleman smiled sweetly and said, "But I do know one thing – I will never leave your side." He squeezed her hand. "Never." She smiled. He said, "And that includes the bus ride. I am going with you."

Her face jerked up toward his and she said, "Coleman, I don't want you doing all of the C.O.R.E. stuff just because of me." She placed her palm on his chest. "I want you to do it because you feel it in here."

He put his hand on hers and said, "I am doing it for you."

She started to protest but he cut her off.

He said, "I'm doing it for you and for Mrs. Rucker and for your father and for your mother and for everyone else I know who has had a rougher life than they should've had just because of the color of their skin." He brushed a tear from her face. "I know my calling and I know that I won't stop until white people and black people can live together as brothers and sisters."

"And more than that?" Rosalee said softly. "As lovers?"

Color rose in Coleman's face. "Yes, even as lovers."

Rosalee leaned forward and kissed him gently on the lips. She breathed in his essence, felt the fire in her chest radiate down. She wanted to drink him in, to dissolve with him, to dance among the trees and never go back to the everyday world. An eternity lived in their kiss.

She smiled and said, "Your work won't be done alone. I'll be there."

Coleman nodded and smiled. He said, "I promise that we will do this side-by-side. Together. Forever."

He leaned back and said, "I don't have a ring or anything to give you."

She said, "That's O.K. It would only cause a bunch of talk that I don't have time to answer."

She carried a small clutch, which she opened. She withdrew a slender silver pen and handed it to Coleman.

"What's this?" he asked.

She said, "It's a pen, silly."

Coleman said, "I know what it is. Why are you giving it to me?"

Rosalee placed the pen in Coleman's hand and said, "It was my father's. Somebody gave it to him, thinking he might use it. I don't know that he ever did."

Rosalee closed Coleman's fingers around the pen. She said, "I want you to have it. Sort of like a token of our commitment. You can remember tonight when you use it."

Coleman opened his hand and ran the finger of his other hand down the shaft. There was a miniscule dent in the side. He looked up at Rosalee and said, "I won't ever need anything to help me remember this night." He slid the pen into his pocket. "I will cherish this pen forever. It's a little piece of your family who I will never know. I will never forget you. I will never forsake you."

They kissed. Long and passionately, they kissed. Whispered words passed back and forth between them as a gentle Virginia dusk descended around them, filling the small valleys of the cemetery with velvety darkness while the polished white marble stones stood in eternal vigilance and faded into the night.

The two new lovers were so caught up in the moment that neither of them saw the dark figure watching them from the shadow of a great oak, a dark figure that had boarded the bus right behind them, melted into the anonymity of homeward bound denizens, and had exited unseen at the Arlington stop.

Rosalee swung Coleman's hand back and forth as they walked toward the bus stop. She smiled and he squeezed her hand. The twilight on her face touched him, made his heart flutter a little. Feelings welled. He was excited, completely satisfied, inspired. Part of his mind took note of the shadow moving behind the big tree but was too occupied with Rosalee to pay any more attention.

"Hey, what's going on here?" The voice was loud in the early evening quiet. Rosalee spun around to face the stranger.

Coleman spoke softly. "Don't say anything. Just keep walking." Coleman did not look directly at the intruder. He moved between Rosalee and the figure and quickened their pace.

The intruder said, "Hey, hey! Not so fast! I just want to talk to y'all. I want to see what's going on here."

Coleman urged Rosalee with his eyes to keep walking. However, the shadowy man moved quickly to cut off their path of escape. Coleman said, "Mister, we don't want trouble. We're just headed back to town."

The dark figure gave a chuckle. "Like I said, I just want to talk to you. So, what y'all doing out here all by yourselves? I hope it wasn't nothing physical."

"We were talking to each other. Just leaving." Coleman could see the

73

man's dirty white face. The man leered at Rosalee.

"You ain't leaving. At least not until we're finished talking." The man gestured toward Rosalee. "And not with her."

Coleman shifted to move toward Rosalee. The man took a step back and reached behind him. Coleman saw that he aimed a pistol directly at Rosalee. Rosalee began to cry.

The man said, "Let's all just calm down now." His words came out in a long drawl.

Coleman said, "Please just let us go."

"I can't let you take that nigger girl with you. It just ain't right." The man raised the pistol and cocked the hammer of the revolver. "Ain't natural."

Coleman felt panic rising through his chest. Pain, darkness, death loomed. He lunged and hit the man's arm. The pistol fell to the ground. Coleman regained his balance, grabbed Rosalee's hand, turned, and ran. They vaulted a low rock wall and sprinted between rows of headstones. Coleman's feet churned toward the street below them. Shouts and footfalls were behind them but Coleman did not look back. They were about fifty yards from the street when he felt a punch in his left upper back, a jolt that threatened to spin him around. However, he kept running. He saw a man with a flashlight running toward him. As they neared him, the policeman's cap became visible.

Coleman shouted, "Help, he's trying to kill us!"

The officer drew his pistol and kept running toward them. Through the sound of panic surging in his ears, Coleman heard a loud sound that resembled a distant rumble of thunder. The policeman stopped in midstride and slumped to the ground.

Coleman still gripped Rosalee's hand. He slung her to the other side of the motionless shape of the officer, pulled her to the ground, and fumbled for the pistol gripped tightly in the policeman's fingers. Another blast reverberated through the cemetery. He heard a scream behind him. He turned and saw Rosalee with her hand on her chest. A deep part of his mind pulled his eyes away from Rosalee and back toward the threat coming down the hill. Coleman raised the pistol. The man stopped, stared at the bodies on the ground for a second, and turned and sprinted back up the hill.

Coleman spun around. Rosalee was lying on her back, her eyes closed, her face visible in the quickly failing twilight.

"Rosalee, are you alright?"

She did not answer. As he positioned himself to check Rosalee's breathing, he saw the lifeless face of the policeman staring at the star-filled sky with wide-open, unseeing eyes. He heard a low sound and felt the gentle puff of Rosalee's breath against his cheek.

"Rosalee, are you awake?" He gently shook her shoulder. "We need to move. He might come back."

She did not respond.

He wanted to stand, to find help, but his legs would not comply. His breath became short.

Rosalee's lips were pale in the low light. He could see the life ebbing away from her.

A ball formed in his gut. It welled up through his body. It drew all life and all thought and all nameless hope to itself as it rose. It rose up until it exited his mouth as a long wail, a mournful sound that the surrounding stones knew well. The same wail had come from soldiers' mothers, from the friends of marines and sailors, and had echoed through these hills.

Coleman fell forward, his face to the ground. He tasted blood. He coughed. Bloody spume fountained from him. He felt pain in his back and chest. His right hand tortuously navigated under his jacket and shirt to his left upper back and withdrew. The hand was wet with blood. The twilight deepened. He saw flashing red lights on the pavement below and, through fading vision, a uniformed man running toward him with gun drawn and held aloft. Then, blackness and cold.

CHAPTER 17

WASHINGTON, D.C., 1961

The days stretched on as Coleman's body healed. The tube in his chest was removed about a week after he was shot. The nurse had told him to take a deep breath and then let it all out and to not breath until she told him. As he exhaled, he felt a tug at his side and it felt as if the entire inside surface of his chest was being ripped out through the small hole. He saw lightning shoot through the room and he almost passed out.

After that day, he waited. The doctor was concerned about the healing of the gunshot wound in his back, saying that it showed signs of infection. Thus, Coleman was given antibiotics that made him queasy and was regularly wheeled on a squeaky gurney to the radiology room to have a chest X-ray to ensure that his lung remained fully inflated and to check for signs of infection inside his chest. For several days, he remained weak, too weak to walk. He ate hospital food that he thought was tasteless at best, disgusting at times.

He was desperate for word of Rosalee but no word came. There were no regular lines of communication between the black hospital and the white and Dr. Browning did not deign to carry any messages.

Late afternoon on his thirteenth day in the hospital, Coleman was rolled back to his room after another X-ray.

"The radiologist said that one looked good, Coleman." The nurse smiled as he shifted his body off the gurney and to the hospital bed. "It won't be long until you'll be going home."

Home. Coleman wondered where that was.

Do I even have a home?

Coleman realized that he did not feel as exhausted after the trip downstairs as usual. He flexed his legs. No pain, no fatigue. He swung his legs around and stood. No dizziness.

76

He moved to the window and stared across the street, over the roofs of building, over the spreading tops of trees, into the distance where Rosalee lay. He stared for a long moment and turned and began to rummage through the drawers of the small chest in his room.

That night, when the nurse came in on her rounds, he kept his eyes closed. The nurse placed a finger on his wrist, counting his pulse. Coleman shifted in the bed but did not acknowledge her. She turned off the light, took his half empty dinner tray, and slipped quietly out of the door.

Coleman waited for a few minutes and heard no sound from the hall. He pulled back the covers and pivoted his fully clothed body to the side of the bed. His toes found the shoes he had hidden under the bed. He slid on the shoes and stood. He had not worn street clothes for a long while. The clothes hung off his frame, his muscles shrunken by the stress of healing and days of inactivity.

He peeked into the hall, saw no one, and headed toward the stairwell at the end of the hall. The stairs deposited him into the lobby and then to the street.

The evening air was warm, a Washington springtime night. Even a light breeze wafting down the street did not reduce the warmth. He saw a taxi at the end of the block and waved.

"The Freedmen's Hospital," Coleman said as he climbed into the back seat.

The driver turned, a grin on his face. "What's a matter? Them nurses ain't treatin you good enough here and so you going over to the nigger hospital?"

"Just drive."

The driver's grin ran away. "Damn! Just trying to be sociable." He mumbled to himself as he turned at the next intersection.

"Wouldn't mind havin one of them nurses give me a sponge bath, no sir." He chuckled and began to hum softly.

The darkening streets rolled by Coleman's unseeing eyes. His mind tried to get a glimpse of what those eyes might encounter when they reached the other hospital. A broken body? A reasonless gaze that looked right through him, no recognition, no feeling? A vegetable? He recoiled from the thought of those warm brown eyes being lifeless and not lit by intelligence.

He knew, though, there was something that he feared even more.

What if she blames me for what happened to her? What if she refuses to see me? What if she hates me?

The hospital appeared in the windshield. The driver said over his shoulder, "I'll drop you off at the front door."

"No, stop here." Coleman handed the driver a folded bill and stepped to the sidewalk. Shadows pooled around a side entrance. Coleman tried the door and found it open. He slipped inside.

The crypt-like hallway was dank and the bare light bulbs in the ceiling shed just enough light for Coleman to make his way to a narrow staircase at the other end of the passage.

This doesn't look like a hospital – more like a prison. Maybe the basement of my hospital is just as bad.

The stairway led up to a metal door. Coleman jiggled the knob and found it locked. He steeled himself and hit his shoulder against the door. Pain bolted from his shoulder to his neck. The door opened.

Coleman could see a small unoccupied desk at the far end of the hall. The light in the hall was not much better than in the basement. Chipped tiles lined the floor and the walls were made of stained plaster. He started to make his way slowly down the hall, pausing to listen for movement, ready to dart toward the stairway if necessary.

Small cards on each of the doors gave the names of their occupants. He scanned them as he crept past the desk. At the far end, he found her room.

Coleman entered and silently closed the door behind him. A small lamp was on the nightstand beside the bed. He saw a shape under the covers, heard the soft sound of breathing. He felt a brief shot of relief.

She's alive.

He moved to the bedside and touched her shoulder. She faced the window, away from him, but at his touch she slowly turned.

Her face was thin, drawn. Her lips and eyes were pale. For a few seconds, no emotion showed on her face.

Coleman's heart dropped. Everything he had planned to say, the future that he had envisioned, all began to crumble.

Her eyes sparkled to life, as if waking from a dream and realizing she was back in the real world. A faint smile curled the edges of her mouth. She struggled to withdraw her hand from the bed sheets and gripped his wrist in a weak featherlike grasp.

"I knew you'd come."

Coleman smiled. His chilled heart began to beat again. He held her hand.

"Sorry it took so long." He leaned closer. "How are you?"

She took a deep breath and slowly sat. Flashes of pain flew across her face.

"I'm getting better. It's been slow."

Coleman said, "I didn't know if…"

"Yeah, when I came to, I didn't know if you were alive either. One of the nurses told me she saw in the newspaper that you were still in the hospital. That's the only way I knew."

Coleman sat on the edge of the bed, careful not to cause her any discomfort, and gazed at her. There was a hint of red on her cheekbones but otherwise her skin seemed washed out, like a photograph that has faded with time. She appeared frail.

"When did you wake up? I mean, after that night."

"I don't know, a couple of days at least. When I first opened my eyes, I thought I might be dead, in heaven."

"I thought the same thing. Like I might see my mother."

"Yeah, me too. And my father."

He grasped both of her hands in his. Peace poured over him. Anxiety about what he would find, harsh emotions toward Dr. Browning, bodily pain – they all flowed away. Here in this dingy room with walls neglected by the city and floors left over from the last century while sparkling new facilities were built for Washington's white citizens, Coleman felt the thrill of spring, the dawn of a new life.

She's alive.

CHAPTER 18

A PHONE BOOTH IN WASHINGTON, D.C., 1961

Coleman woke the next morning with a new feeling in his heart, a different tint to the world. Gone was the gray drudgery of the prospect of a life without love, replaced with the multicolored hues of hope.

He began to make plans in earnest. The nurse was right – he was getting better and would soon be leaving the hospital. The question that remained was where he would go.

He had made arrangements with Rosalee to telephone her later in the day. She would go to the lobby of the Freedmen's Hospital, the only place where she could have easy access to a telephone. Coleman would go to the phone booth on the corner in order to have a modicum of privacy.

As Coleman walked to make the appointed telephone call, his mind raced. *Maybe I can find a boarding house close to Mrs. Rucker's, one that will take men. I can get a job.*

He closed the glass door behind him and dialed the number.

"Hello?" Rosalee's voice was weak.

"Hey. How are you feeling?"

She said, "Maybe a little better. Still hurting pretty bad when I walk or take in a deep breath." She coughed. "Or cough."

"When do they say you can go home?"

"I don't know, Coleman. They haven't said. I still got a lot of healing to do before I'll be ready to leave."

Coleman took a deep breath. Even in the warm evening, he felt a chill. His glass encasing dissolved away. He felt himself on a precipice, ready to take the next step but not knowing what would happen.

"I'll be out of the hospital soon," Coleman said. He heard her breathing on the other end of the line. She said nothing. "I want to be with you."

Coleman waited. She remained silent.

He said, "Did you hear me? I want to be with you."

Rosalee said, "I heard you. I just don't know what you mean."

He said, "What do you think I mean? I want to be with you. When I leave the hospital, I want to come and see you in your hospital until you are ready to go home. Then, I want to live close to Mrs. Rucker's. After that, I want us to get married, like we promised each other."

Silence again stretched from across town.

Coleman said, "Isn't that what you want, what you said that night?"

"I know what I said. It's just that so much has changed. Coleman, we almost died. I'm still a long way from being well."

"Don't you think I know that?" Coleman's voice rose. "Remember that I took a bullet too. The only thing that kept me going was the thought of you. I couldn't rest until I knew you were O.K. Since I found out that you were, the only thing I have been able to think about is being with you, sharing my life with you."

"Coleman, listen. I'm glad we're O.K. An inch or two either way and one or both of us might be dead. Thank goodness that didn't happen."

The air inside the phone booth became stifling. Coleman wanted to throw the receiver down, to bolt into the night, to try to sprint back to the time before the shooting, a time when all seemed possible.

"But, I think we need to take this slowly. It's going to be a while before I leave the hospital. You're welcome to come see me. After I'm released, we can try to pick up where we left off, if it is seems like we should."

The stifling air seemed lighter.

She didn't push me away. At least not completely.

She said, "You need to go back to the Lamb of God – "

His heart crashed again. "Wait a minute! I can't go back there! I want to be close to you. I can get a job and a room somewhere close to Mrs. Ruckers –"

"Coleman, listen to yourself! You just got over a gunshot in your chest! You ain't gonna get a job that will pay for a room!"

"But, Dr. Browning doesn't want us to be together."

"Well, we ain't gonna be together anytime soon anyhow, not til after I'm out of the hospital. After that, what he don't know ain't gonna hurt him any."

Silence stretched the opposite direction.

Rosalee said, "Coleman? What do you say?"

"I guess there's nothing I can say. I'll go back to the Lamb of God."

As much to himself as to Rosalee, he said, "I'm not giving up on us."

CHAPTER 19

A HOSPITAL ROOM IN WASHINGTON, D.C.

Dr. Browning appeared in his room on the last day and said, "Good morning, Coleman. It is very good to see you sitting up. I was afraid at one time that I might never see that again."

The pastor wore his elegant black overcoat. Perfectly trimmed hair peeked from beneath a dignified hat. An air of royalty floated about him.

"Do you feel fit and ready to come home?"

Coleman had secretly wondered what he would say to that question. In the gloomy hours of the nighttime hospital after he and Rosalee had talked, when the cries of hurting people and the rattle of machinery echoed down the tiled hallways, he pondered if he would be able to pretend that he was ready to go back with the clergyman to a place that seemed to be synonymous with betrayal of the love he felt for Rosalee.

"Yes sir, I am ready to leave and, as long as you are comfortable with my coming back, I would be grateful to return to the Lamb of God. I don't want what happened to me to reflect poorly on you or the church." He said it with an aloofness that Dr. Browning did not seem to notice.

Dr. Browning said, "Let us not speak of the incident. As I have said, I lay no blame at your feet."

On the drive back to the church, Coleman tried to push the thoughts of Rosalee out of his mind, to temporarily lay aside his love for the purpose of mere survival.

The next morning, Coleman woke not to the harsh sterility of his hospital room, but to the soft light, the familiar smells, the warm blanket feeling of his room at the rectory. He sat up. He had not realized it until he had walked across the hospital lobby to Dr. Browning's car and from the car to the rectory how very weak he was. He was out of breath after just a few steps, and he occasionally felt dizzy and faint. Dr. Browning had noticed and had urged him to take things slowly. The pastor said that he wanted to talk to Coleman about his duties and had set an appointment for ten o'clock in the morning.

Coleman made his way to the small kitchen and ate a simple breakfast. He got dressed and was at Dr. Browning's door at exactly ten o'clock.

Dr. Browning said, "Come in, Coleman! How was your first night back in familiar surroundings?" Dr. Browning motioned toward a chair. "Please have a seat. I want to talk to you about some ground rules."

Coleman's breath caught. *Ground rules?*

Coleman sat slowly in the chair as Dr. Browning leaned back in his chair and placed his hands together in front of him like he was praying.

"Coleman, I again want to say how glad I am that you survived the Arlington incident. I am very sorry that your former friend was hurt and the poor policeman coming to your aid was killed. I want to assure you as your pastor that any guilt you feel about her injuries and his death will eventually pass. I have already prayed for you and you should know that God forgives you. You must now forgive yourself."

Coleman was speechless. The air was sucked out of his lungs. His mind screamed, *He won't even say her name!*

The pastor said, "Of course, you violated the conditions that I laid out before you at the last meeting we had in this office. However, given the circumstances, I am willing to forget that and let you start anew." Coleman remained silent.

Dr. Browning said, "First off, I want you to curtail your physical activity while you heal. You may limit your hours of work to three per day with no strenuous physical labor whatsoever."

Coleman nodded. "Thank you Dr. Browning." Coleman struggled to control his face. Anger seethed beneath.

"I expect you to resume your ecclesial studies in the rectory or the church library for the remainder of the hours in the day." Dr. Browning motioned toward his bookcases full of volumes. "You are free to use any of the books in my collection."

Dr. Browning fixed Coleman in his gaze and said, "Coleman, I need to give some instructions that may not be needed but that I feel duty-bound to give."

Coleman suddenly felt short of breath. The ceiling – though soaring by any standard – felt close. He tried to breath deeply but a sudden stab of pain in his back kept him from doing so. He felt dizzy again.

"Are you quite all right?" Dr. Browning said.

Coleman managed to take in a gulp of air.

"Yes sir. I'm O.K. Just a little dizzy." Coleman composed himself.

Dr. Browning said, "As I was saying, I need to bring up an important matter."

Dr. Browning leaned forward in his chair, his fingertips now perched on his desk. His hands looked like gigantic spiders, ready to scurry across the desk and latch onto Coleman's neck and suck his life's blood out. Coleman felt as if we were sinking in his chair. Coleman blinked his eyes to clear his head and listened.

Dr. Browning said, "At the hospital, you told me that before the shooting you were planning to end your friendship with the colored girl and that you were going to stop all contact with that militant Negro group." Coleman remained stoic.

Dr. Browning said, "I need to make it clear that I expect you to avoid that girl and that gang of radicals. It is my hope that your recent unpleasant experiences have given you pause and have helped you to understand the value of working diligently in the place where God has positioned you." Coleman was silent.

"Coleman, I must ask you to promise me that you will not go near the girl or that group. If you do, I will again have to ask you to leave. I do not want to go through that disagreeable experience again." Dr. Browning waited and said, "Coleman, I need to hear your answer."

Though Rosalee had said that temporary deception was excusable, Coleman felt the weight of infidelity pushing down on him.

Can I really tell myself that I love her if I tell this man that I don't?

He felt that his words, even if they had no meaning behind them, might set a path that he did not want to walk, a path to unfaithfulness and separation and desolation.

Coleman felt the presence of Rosalee. It was like she was standing right behind him, her hand poised over his shoulder. From across the miles, through the streets of the city, winding around green trees, skimming over the top of gray stagnant water, he could feel her warmth, could sense her radiance. He smelled her scent but not with his nose. It was a much deeper sense, one in the core of his brain, in the heart of his being. It was her essence that diffused through him.

As she flickered around and in him, he heard his own voice, a croaky oboe sound, "I promise." Her spirit left him, like smoke before the north wind.

Dr. Browning released him from the office. Coleman returned to his room and collapsed into bed with a charred and ruined interior in the passageways of his heart and mind.

CHAPTER 20

WASHINGTON, D.C., 1961

A particular block in the wall of the church library for weeks commanded his attention. This block, at first glance, was no different from the hundreds of other blocks that made up the structure of the venerable building. However, Coleman had examined the block for so long and with such scrutiny that he was now intimately acquainted with the stunning uniqueness of this stone. He knew the gradations of gray and black and silver and even a touch of bronze. He knew the smooth area in the left upper corner and the wild rugged region in the center. He came to know the block with such familiarity that its details felt more recognizable to him than those of the home in which he was raised.

He had gazed at the stone while open books sat on the desk in front of him. He preferred the world of the stone block, with its deep valleys and soaring ridges, to the confessions of Augustine. The worlds present in the age-scented pages that had resided on Dr. Browning's shelves felt lifeless to him. It was Luther and Calvin and Whitaker that were cold and insensate and inert. That block was real and sturdy and strong. After all, it was part of the wall that held up the roof.

It was just as well that Coleman's body was not fit for the church's work. His heart and soul were not fit either. It was as if his whole being had faded. He was present at the church but he was not present in the moment. He did not live in the past or the future either. He was outside of time and space, waiting for something else, not willing to go down a less-desired path that might prove difficult to leave.

His existence felt like the space on a record after the record player needle had left the groove of the song. The needle moves to the center of the record and just bounces and scratches and buzzes as the record player keeps spinning the record. One song in Coleman's life had ended and God had not flipped the disc over yet. Coleman was not sure that He ever would.

Coleman had tried to move along his relationship with Rosalee. However, she languished in the hospital, her body not responding to the doctors' prescribed treatments as quickly as his. She remained physically weak, short of breath, a series of infections further depleting her energy.

Coleman slipped away to visit Rosalee when he could. However, their conversations became stilted. He longed to whisk her away, out of the hospital, to start a new life together. However, her body kept her anchored to the bed and her soul did not seem to desire to be joined to his.

Coleman wished he could ask his long-dead Granny Mae to help. Frequent visitors had come to Granny Mae's kitchen, seeking a healing potion. Some had even come asking about the future or desiring to contact someone from the past. Maybe Granny Mae was able to penetrate the barrier of the grave, but Coleman never sensed her presence.

When not sitting in the library, Coleman spent his days shuffling around the church trying to avoid Dr. Browning. When he felt it was safe, he napped in his room. At first, Dr. Browning knew about his daytime sleeping and begrudgingly allowed it in light of Coleman's on-going recovery. However, as March turned to April, it became clear that Dr. Browning was becoming impatient with the rate of Coleman's healing.

"Soon, Coleman," Dr. Browning said on a few occasions, "you will be well enough to resume all of your duties. I have a list of shut-ins that you may begin to visit as well as some other duties around the church."

However, Coleman was successful in eluding the pastor so as to never be the recipient of the to-do list. When he was sure that Dr. Browning was away from the church, Coleman snuck to his room to sleep and to thus escape his prison for a while.

Each Sunday, Coleman sat in the church sanctuary with all of the regular attendees of the service and listened to Dr. Browning's sermons. It was always impressive. An imposing distinguished man in flowing robes standing on an ornate wooden pulpit surrounded by towering stone walls set a most worshipful tone. Dr. Browning's booming voice reverberated among the pillars and rafters. Pious faces never strayed from him as he spoke, seeming to absorb all the knowledge and wisdom of the ages in his words.

However, the reverence of the service and the brilliance of the speaker did not penetrate the hard crust forming around Coleman's heart and mind. During the services, Coleman had taken to counting the people and mentally dividing them into groups of most likely secret sin. The philanderers, the tax cheats, the liars, the gossips – each had his or her own little cohort in Coleman's organizational structure. He rarely listened to the sermon but always maintained a look of placid attention and concurrence.

On the last Sunday in April, Coleman found himself sitting in a church service once again. The preceding week had been a frustrating one. He had been unable to slip away to visit Rosalee and she had not felt well enough to come to the phone when he called. Dr. Browning had stepped up his cajoling and was on the cusp of demanding more activity and productivity from Coleman. However, Coleman managed to stay one step ahead of the pastor. He had shown some ostensible initiative by appearing to take on the job of reorganizing the organ music in the church library. This had been enough to dissuade Dr. Browning from pushing for more and had given Coleman a little more time to consider his stone block.

As Coleman sat in the third pew, his eyes wandered around the cavernous church and lit upon a particular stained glass image. The ark perched on top of a glass mountain and vomited out its cargo of animals. A stern-faced glassy Noah watched over the proceedings from the deck of his boat – staff in hand, long white beard cascading down. Above them all stretched a rainbow. Each end of the arc emerged from an intricately designed billowing cloud.

The colors of the rainbow shone down on Coleman's face, the sun directly behind it. Coleman was dazzled by the beauty. Shafts of colored light shot into his mind, exposing long hidden corners, illuminating dark recesses. Red and yellow light fanned the flames of his heart.

Suddenly, he remembered why he had first come here, what he wanted for his life. He remembered President Kennedy's speech, the great exciting world in which he could have an important place. Most of all, he remembered the thrill of meeting Rosalee, the feeling of adventure when he became involved in C.O.R.E. He shifted and the cooler green and blue did nothing to dampen his feelings.

Coleman felt as if he had just awakened from a long sleep. He felt completely alert, alive.

An organ chord bounced around the rafters far above and faded as Dr. Browning ascended to the pulpit.

"Good morning. Today, my message will come from the ninth chapter of the book of Genesis."

Coleman's heart skipped.

Genesis 9? That's about Noah!

Coleman grabbed his Bible and hurriedly flipped to the passage. As Dr. Browning droned through the verses, Coleman struggled for meaning.

Why is this happening? What am I supposed to get out of this?

"And so, my dear people, you may ask what meaning this has for you in your life today."

Dr. Browning smiled benevolently at his congregation. Coleman waited, barely daring to breath.

"I have learned in my long life as a servant of the most high God that we can depend on God for everything. This passage says that God gave Noah food to eat. God kept him and his family safe. The Bible tells us that God took this promise very seriously, so much so that God placed the rainbow in the sky, a sign for all of us to see."

Coleman tilted his face toward the stained glass. Flashes of color bathed him as Dr. Browning's words shattered the callus around his heart.

"God has placed each one of us here for a purpose. He has given us a place and a way to serve. The rainbow that God placed in the sky serves as a promise that all of us can have a life that is worth living."

As Coleman gazed up, the colored light coalesced into a brilliant white, bathing him in its warmth. He closed his eyes and felt the light diffuse through him, urging him on.

On Monday morning, Coleman managed to evade Dr. Browning and make his way to The Freedmen's Hospital. The nurses had become accustomed to the young white man who came every so often to visit. They returned his smile as he passed the desk on the way to Rosalee's room.

The room was dim. Condensation collected on old plaster and dripped down the walls. Rosalee lay under a sheet simply staring at the celling. When Coleman slipped through the door, Rosalee slowly turned toward him. A tired smile appeared.

"Hey Coleman. I didn't know you was coming today."

Coleman came to the bed and gingerly sat on the edge. He placed a hand on her shoulder, leaned in, and placed a gentle kiss on her forehead.

He said, "I just had to come. It's been so long since I heard your voice and I couldn't wait any longer."

Rosalee withdrew her hand from under the sheet and placed it on Coleman's hand.

She said, "I'm glad you came. I get bored and lonely in here and I'm not well enough to get around much by myself. Getting better, though."

The musty smell in the room assaulted Coleman's nose. He glanced at the peeling paint on the old iron hospital bed and metal side table.

He said, "When will you be getting out of here?"

Rosalee said, "Like I said, I'm getting better but not good enough to leave yet. Maybe in a week or two." She smiled. "Mrs. Rucker will have to take care of me for a while like I'm a little baby – or maybe a little old lady."

She laughed. Coleman's heart soared. He had not heard her laugh in a long time, had rarely heard her laugh like this, an unguarded laugh, a happy sound like the splash of water over a tiny mountain waterfall.

Coleman pulled his hand back and said, "Is that what you're going to do when you get out? Go back to Mrs. Rucker's?"

A confused look appeared on her face. "Yeah, that's the plan. Where else would I go?"

Coleman swallowed. "I was hoping you might come to me."

Her brow wrinkled. "To the rectory?"

Coleman said, "No to somewhere else. Our own place."

Rosalee had started to lean forward, to try to sit. Her head now fell back to the pillow and her eyes closed. After a moment, she said, "Coleman, we already talked about this."

Coleman said, "I know. We said we would take it slow, but that was weeks ago. I am ready. I committed myself to you. You are my destiny."

Rosalee said, "Destiny? That's a big word. Are you saying we was meant for each other, that there ain't nothing we can do but to be together, that I might as well just give up and come to you?"

Coleman said, "No, I'm not saying you don't have a choice, but I thought you already told me that you choose me. That night in the cemetery. You said on the phone that we could pick up where we left off."

Rosalee nodded. "Yeah, I said that, but I also said that lots of things've happened and that whatever is between us has changed." She placed her hand on his. "Listen, Coleman. I care about you. I want good things for you. Maybe the best thing is to count our friendship as just that – friends, nothing more."

He started to draw back his hand, started to protest. She went on before he could speak. "The reason you got shot was because you was with me, a colored girl. I don't want the next bullet to put you in an early grave."

Coleman again felt himself on the brink of a cliff. He pushed away the doubt and said, "Rosalee, I don't care about all of that. I know I could've died. You could've died too. That can happen anytime, even if we're not together. All I know is that I love you and I want to be with you. Don't worry about me. I'll keep myself safe and you too."

The squeak and growl of sluggish cars and trucks struggled up from the street. The whirr of a lawnmower drifted in. Rosalee was silent for so long that Coleman thought she might have drifted off to sleep.

She turned back and said, "I am scared that us being together might get one or both of us hurt. I don't care if I get hurt but I wouldn't be able to forgive myself if you got killed and it was my fault. But, that ain't the only thing making me wonder whether you and me should go on together."

Her eyes drifted to the ceiling, like she was trying to see past the stained plaster to look into a future not yet defined, a path not yet chosen.

She said, "I guess you're talking about the two of us getting married." He nodded.

She said, "I see people all over who is on fire. They see injustice and want to stamp it out, they see prejudice and they want to shine the light of day on it, they see hate and they want to dowse it with truth. Some of these same people, I see them pair up with somebody else. Usually it's somebody who is on fire like them, somebody they been soldiering side-by-side with. These people get married cause they think it's the thing to do. After they get married, it's like the brightness in their eyes gets snuffed out. They was ready to change the world before they was married and then they get a husband or a wife and they seem to get comfortable. The fire goes out. Pretty soon, they just like everybody else, raising their kids in the same shitty neighborhood they grew up in, reading in the newspaper about all of the violence going on someplace else, and saying 'We got it pretty good' just cause they're together."

Coleman sat stone-faced on the bed. Rosalee said, "I don't want that. I can't live like that."

Coleman said, "What happened to standing with each other and fighting for civil rights no matter what happens?" Color had risen to his face. "We made a promise to each other."

Rosalee blinked slowly and said, "That promise was made in the heat of a moment and that moment was ended by a bullet. The promise is dead, just like we could've been, maybe like we should've been."

A coolness came into her eyes. This was someone that Coleman did not know. He had come here to profess love once again, to sweep Rosalee away, to begin a new life, a life hinted at by his vision of the rainbow, a promise that God indeed had a wonderful future for him with Rosalee by his side. Now, he only felt coldness and despair.

Coleman said, "I can't believe this is happening. What can I do to show you that I love you, that I will always protect you, that I share your dreams?"

Rosalee said, "If you want to show me that you care about me and my dreams, get up and walk out that door and leave me alone."

CHAPTER 21

THE RECTORY

Coleman's heart and mind struggled for a foundation in the days after he left Rosalee's hospital room. The clarity that had come with the rainbow vision completely evaporated with Rosalee's words. Coleman was adrift, not sure where this life would take him.

He rose from his cot, dressed, and went to make some coffee and toast for his breakfast. As the coffee began to percolate on the stove, he flipped through the newspaper that he had retrieved from the side stoop of the church. Breakfast was forgotten when he saw the small story on page 5.

Local Group Starts Bus Ride (Thursday, May 4)

The members of the Congress Of Racial Equality will board buses headed for New Orleans, Louisiana this morning in an effort to promote fairness. The members, both white and Negro, hope to show that all races can share the nation's bus lines and stations. The group plans to host a rally in New Orleans at the conclusion of their trip.

Coleman felt a momentary thrill at reading the words followed by anguish. He had planned to be on that bus with Rosalee. Even now, they would have been speeding south, hand-in-hand, not knowing what lay ahead but happy to be at each other's side. He thought of John and James and Em. He wondered where they were by now. Richmond? North Carolina?

Coffee bubbled into the glass knob at the top of pot and filled the small kitchen with a sharp aroma. The smell of burning bread caused Coleman to turn and hit the lever on the toaster.

Whatever duties he would have attended were now abandoned. Coleman found himself back at his desk examining his stone. The black pit over which his life was suspended yawned below him. Only the crevices and shelves of his rock gave him any traction on reality.

Late in the afternoon, Coleman walked outside. The day was hot, the air heavy-laden with moisture. He heard a rumble of thunder in the distance. He walked to the end of the street and a wide vista opened before him. The Potomac curved away in the distance. A thunderstorm was dumping its load of water on the distant Virginia hills. As he stood, the sun broke through a wall of clouds in the west, golden beams piercing the mantel and illuminating the tops of hills like some grand coronation ceremony. His gaze crept up and he was startled.

A brilliant rainbow was there, bridging the clouds in front of him, so distinct and solid that he felt he could walk on it.

What does this mean?

He contemplated the rainbow but got no answer.

In the next day's newspaper, he read that an astronaut was going into space on that very day, the first American to ever do so. The heroism and patriotism wrapped up in that story would have moved him deeply only weeks before. Now, however, he barely thought about it but instead hurriedly scanned the rest of the paper for anything about the C.O.R.E. riders, the Freedom Riders as they called themselves. Nothing.

Late on Friday, he again walked out as he had done the day before and made his way to the end of the street. Another vivid rainbow stretched in front of him. A sign? An omen? He thought back over all that Dr. Browning had spoken of in his sermon. He thought about what he had read. Coleman could not make sense of it all.

Does this mean I am where I should be? Is the rainbow telling me to stay here? Or to leave Washington?

He could not say.

Every day for a week, a rainbow appeared in the southern sky. Every day, Coleman searched for answers. He read. He prayed. No response came.

One week and one day after the Freedom Riders had left Washington, Coleman sat at the breakfast table. He was now fully back in his melancholy state and had spent most of the last two days in bed. He no longer cared if Dr. Browning found him. He almost hoped that Dr. Browning would throw him out into the streets. There, Coleman would fall in with the other homeless men who inhabited the dark alleys and hidden places of the capital. He could be a vagrant without fear of repercussion. He could have an existence reduced to the basics, no more clamoring for success or feeling anxiety about a future career. His sole focus would be in finding food for the day, in fighting for shelter. He would be just above an animal, living in the present, forgetting the past and having no future. As he sat at the table with his strong coffee and dry toast, the newspaper caught his attention. His toast dropped to the floor.

Freedom Riders Attacked in S. Carolina.

He quickly read. John was hurt. Some others also. Horace and Coop were arrested.

What can I do?

Coleman walked outside. A half-hearted sun hung in the hazy morning sky, shedding its paltry light onto the sluggish city. He walked to the end of the street and stood staring across the river, as if he was trying to see past the Virginia hills, over the tobacco fields of North Carolina, all the way to the little town balanced on the border of the Carolinas. He could not see John. He could not see any of the others. Coleman could only see his world, confined by a river, anchored to a stone building behind him.

I can't just go. Where would I be going? Who would I be going to see or to be with? No one knows what is going to happen.

No answers came.

A swirl of confusion swept around him all day. He tried to sleep but could not. His stone in the library was no comfort. Restlessness caused him to pace the corridors of the church and to tread the paths outside. He did not notice an afternoon shower that drenched his hair. He came dripping into the rectory. Dinner did not enter his mind.

Late in the evening, Coleman stood naked in the hall outside his room. He did not know what to do but was certain that he could not go on like this. He thought of the narrow staircase that led up to the belfry. If he jumped tonight, Dr. Browning would likely be the one to find his bloody and broken body in the morning.

Maybe my brains would be splattered all over the front of the church, maybe too messy to get it all cleaned before Sunday morning and the pious parishioners would arrive at church and there would be my brain dripping down on them and a bloody shape would be there under their feet. My blood calling up from the ground to them, telling them to listen and learn from the good Dr. Browning and you too can be a spot on the pavement.

Coleman began to cry. He sobbed in the hall, crying for his loss, his dead mother, his lost career, all of the lost years. Most of all, he cried for Rosalee.

"ROSALEE!"

Tears poured from his eyes. Sobs wracked his chest, causing him to gasp for air. He felt dizzy.

The first part of his mind had already traced out the path to the belfry stairs and was ready to end this pain and confusion. However, the second part of his mind said, *Let's just go.*

Coleman's sobs stopped. He sniffled. He asked aloud, "Go where?"

His inner voice said, *South.*

Coleman was calmer now. "Now?"

Sure, why not? You can catch up with them by New Orleans.

"What will I do?" Coleman asked. He was already starting to feel surer. This felt right.

Whatever is needed to show her that you love her.

Coleman stood motionless. He did not allow himself to doubt, to wonder about Dr. Browning's opinion. He simply said, "Yes."

The confusion melted away. He felt a flicker in his heart. He walked into his room and began to pack his small suitcase.

CHAPTER 22

WASHINGTON, D.C., 1961

As Coleman approached the office door of the Lamb of God, Dr. Browning was coming out.

Dr. Browning said, "Good morning, Coleman. How are you today?"

Coleman gave a waxen smile and said, "I was just coming to see you, sir. I need to talk to you about something."

Dr. Browning said, "That's fine. It will be good to talk. I was just headed toward the churchyard for a brief walk. Perhaps you would like to accompany me."

"Yes sir."

Coleman and Dr. Browning walked around the building and through the ornately carved stone archway of the cemetery. Weathered, crudely etched stones littered the ground near the entrance. Coleman and his mentor walked in silence until they reached newer monuments, only one century old instead of two, bedecked with stony flowers frozen in perpetual bloom. Mossy granite labeled with old and prominent Washington family names, Carroll and Thompson and Beall, served as silent witness to their conference.

"Dr. Browning, sir," Coleman said, "I'm afraid that I have to leave the Lamb of God."

The calmness on Dr. Browning's face did not shift a millimeter. He said, "I see. Go on."

Coleman nodded. "Yes sir. I must finish something that I promised I would finish. I know that it is the right thing to do."

Dr. Browning considered Coleman for a long moment. "Does this have to do with the colored girl?"

Coleman said, "Rosalee."

"Yes. Rosalee."

Coleman said, "Yes sir, it does. I promised her that I would go on the bus ride with her."

Dr. Browning made an uncomfortable grunting sound and said, "Yes, but as I understand it, she is still too ill to travel and you made a promise to break your relationship with her."

Coleman gazed at the ground.

Dr. Browning said, "May I assume that you have broken that promise and have been in contact with her?"

A sense of justice and anger and courage swelled inside Coleman. He faced his mentor and said, "Yes sir. I have seen Rosalee. In fact, I saw her last week."

"I see." Dr. Browning removed his glasses and made a motion of cleaning the lenses. "Am I correct in stating that she has not recovered from her injuries sufficiently to travel?"

Coleman said, "Yes sir, she is still in the hospital. She may be getting out soon but she is not well enough to be on a bus."

Dr. Browning said, "Very well, then. I do not see the point in your contemplation of going on some bus ride. She is not capable of traveling. In addition, those troublemakers have already left for the South and this riding of the buses has become something of a disaster. Riots and martial law and all sorts of things have been reported on the evening news." Dr. Browning replaced his glasses and peered at Coleman over them. "Surely you do not want to get mixed up in that."

"But, you see Dr. Browning, that is just why I must get involved." Dr. Browning gave a quizzical look.

Coleman said, "Rosalee wanted to be there if the rides led to some type of response. It was important for her to be able to see firsthand what happened. With her unable to go, I have to fill that role. To be her eyes and ears."

Dr. Browning gazed at Coleman and said, "Is that what she wants you to do? To put yourself in grave danger just to fulfill her curiosity?"

Coleman said, "No, she didn't ask me to do it. In fact, she wants me to leave her alone. But, that is not what matters. I made a promise to her. I aim to keep that promise. It might be the thing that will open her heart to me."

"Do you hear yourself, son?" Dr. Browning said. "You are considering committing this rebellious act, going against the laws and traditions of this country in conjunction with a gang of miscreants, and doing it all for the love of someone who does not return your love. In addition, this person is not even of your kind – a double sin!"

"Dr. Browning, I don't believe it is a sin, none of it. I have to do this to honor Rosalee, even if she doesn't appreciate it. If I don't, I know that I'll regret it the rest of my life."

Dr. Browning let his hand drop and said, "No Coleman. Throwing away what I have provided for you here is the thing that you will regret."

Coleman said, "Dr. Browning, I just can't believe that you would hold my love for Rosalee against me, even after she saved my life. As for my position at the Lamb of God, if I go south and find nothing for me there and find there is no future with Rosalee, I hope you would consider letting me come back and resume working with you."

Dr. Browning's face remained clouded.

He said, "Coleman, that will not be possible. I must ask you to decide now which path you will take."

Coleman nodded.

"I understand, Dr. Browning."

Dr. Browning said. "Coleman, I am sorry that your time here will end on such a low note. I had such great aspirations for you. I regret that my discipline of you was so lax. When you disobeyed me and saw that girl again on the night of the shooting, I should have punished you. However, your injury led to my leniency."

Coleman stood in stunned silence for a few seconds and said, "Of course, it was more than just a little injury. I almost died."

Dr. Browning said, "Yes, I know. It was not meant to be that way."

The ground rocked under Coleman's feet and the tombstones seemed to shift. He said, "What does that mean?"

Dr. Browning stared up at the church's tall steeple and said, "I felt that I made it clear how much I disapproved of your relationship with her."

Coleman squared his body with Dr. Browning's and said, "Yes, you made that very clear. What does that have to do with what happened?"

Dr. Browning said, "The arrangement was for the man to simply give you and her a scare, to make it clear that it was too dangerous for you to be together. You were supposed to come to your senses."

Coleman began to tremble. His voice shook.

"*You* sent him?"

Dr. Browning said, "I simply did what I knew was best for you. As I have said, God has given me this church to lead and the wisdom to do so."

"You had us *shot*! And you murdered that policeman!"

Dr. Browning held up a finger and said, "No, I most certainly did not. The man shot you and the girl and that policeman, I know not why because those were not my instructions." He pointed the finger at Coleman and said, "If anyone it is you, my young protégé, that are responsible for your injuries and his death. You persisted in pursuing her even in the face of my sage advice. If you had not done so, the policeman would still be alive and you would not been wounded."

The cemetery spun around Coleman. He felt short of breath.

"I'm going to call the police and tell them what you've done."

Dr. Browning smiled and said, "In fact, I had dinner with both the chief of police and the mayor just last night. They have been strong supporters of my charity. They voiced concern that your attacker has not yet been identified. I thanked them for their concern. No, there is no need to call the police. The police chief implicitly trusts me and will believe anything I tell him, even a sordid tale of a lust-filled young man who tried to take advantage of a colored girl's virtue, shot her in a fit of rage, shot and killed a policeman, and then shot himself to cover up the crime."

"That's not what happened!"

"Of course, you and I know that, but the police will believe my account over a Negro girl or the pitiful mumblings of a nobody playing church like he can actually rise above his pathetic family tree." Dr. Browning sneered. "Knowing where you're from, it's more likely a family stump, rife with incest."

Coleman's face flushed. His fists clinched. He said, "I bet they'll believe me when I tell them it was you!"

Dr. Browning smirked. "You forget that I know who the girl is and where she is. Just a snap of my fingers can send someone to silence her if you breathe one incriminating word to the authorities. You don't want that on your conscience, do you?"

Rage surged to Coleman's heart. He pointed a shaking finger at Dr. Browning's face.

"Listen here, you dayum, you dayum – "

"Oh, I know you try to disguise your accent." Dr. Browning smirked. "You try to pretend that you are one of my kind. But there is no hiding that you are a contemptible creature reared in some unkempt hovel. No amount of pretending can hide your uncouth mind and spirit. So you might as well let fly with your 'howdy y'alls' and your 'oo-wees'," Dr. Browning said, as he slapped a thigh in his caricature of an Appalachian native. "No need to pretend anymore. You will never be anything beyond a simple hillbilly. So run along back to your hollow and do not let me ever hear of you again in the land of intellectual people."

Dr. Browning's face floated in front of Coleman's as the young man's fist streaked from his side and connected with the pastor's smug face. Coleman felt the flesh give beneath his knuckles, the crunch of tiny bones. Dr. Browning sank to the lush green turf, his arms held up to protect him from further blows.

Coleman glared down at him with an expression of undiluted hatred.

He said, "You'll never be nothin more than an asshole."

Coleman launched a thick wad of saliva onto the upturned face and walked away from the Lamb of God.

Forever.

CHAPTER 23

U.S. HIGHWAY 1 SOUTH

The hum of the bus's engine lulled him in spite of the adrenaline coursing through his body. He had not slept since deciding to take the bus south. After packing the night before, he had wrestled all night with what to say to Dr. Browning. He now slumped in his seat, a cloth wrapped around his bruised knuckles. Duty lodged in his heart, duty to keep a promise, duty to draw danger away from the one he loved.

As the bus sped through the greenness of Virginia, Coleman dreamed. He is six years old and sits in Granny Mae's threadbare easy chair, her little Franklin stove more than adequate to heat the tiny house. Granny Mae hums to herself in the kitchen while she mixes up biscuit dough. A thick quilt spread over him presses down, a comfortable weight. He drifts off and re-inhabits his adult body on Highway 1 South.

The bus stopped several times during the day, small places that remained nameless to Coleman. He sustained himself with crackers, Pepsi-Colas, and candy bars. Weary passengers shuffled off the bus on road-stiff legs and lined up at station restrooms. Occasionally, ecstatic family members greeted a passenger at the steps of the bus, screaming and laughing as the passenger exited, enfolding them in embraces at the bottom of the steps. Coleman watched them from his seat, his cheek pressed to the window, before slowly standing and shaking the miles out of his limbs and going in search of a toilet and a Milky Way. He passed telephone booths and thought about calling her, knowing that she would say things he could not bear hearing, not now. His resolve to carry out this responsibility was strong but not impervious.

The sun set as the bus reached the North Carolina line. Coleman slid open the window a little as they hurtled through the darkness. The smell of green tobacco filled the interior of the Greyhound. It was an old smell that spoke of the Powhatan and mule-led plows and ramshackle stores lit by kerosene. His sandwich dinner settled uneasily in his stomach. The catnaps of the day held off the night's sleep.

He wondered what this journey would bring. Would it open her heart? Would it lead to even more sorrow?

Since the moment he had decided to go, Coleman had thought of her. He felt her deep inside his head. Her form did not invade his dreams but she was there when he slept just the same. It was comforting. It was what kept him going south.

Before dawn, the bus reached the outskirts of Charlotte. The Greyhound crept through the streets and pulled into the quiet station. The driver announced that there would be a three-hour delay while waiting for another driver. Groans drifted from the passengers. Like many others, Coleman nestled deeper into his seat and closed his eyes.

It was light when he woke. He blinked himself back to reality and unfolded himself from the seat. The pavement felt strangely stationary as his highway-accustomed legs stumbled down the stairs and reached the bus platform. He glimpsed a diner counter inside the station and felt the pull of strong black coffee. He shuffled toward the door along with the other bus occupants. His gaze took in the taxis, the station attendant, the luggage lined up against the wall. His eyes locked onto the man propped near the door. His stomach fell.

The man had the face that he would never forget, a face that brought the terror back, that brought desolation and pain.

The man saw him at the same time and suddenly straightened. Coleman did not know what to do. He saw an open path to the side of the station and started running. The people in front of the station watched him as he ran away. No one called after him or followed him.

The man near the door, the killer, moved in the opposite direction, away from the gaze of the crowd. When he was out of their sight, the killer began running with all of his might.

Frantic sensations of gunshots, blood, darkness, hatred, and death bounded through Coleman's mind. His feet churned and propelled him through the streets. He randomly turned at corners, not knowing where he was or where he was going. The early morning streets were mostly empty, only the occasional garbage man or postman.

Slowly, his panic began to subside. As if emerging from a dream, he wondered, *How long have I been running? Minutes? Hours?*

He saw no one at first. After a minute, he saw the killer walk across an intersection at the far end of the street. Coleman quickly ducked into the doorway of a store and peeked around. The killer stopped and began to scan the streets. Coleman pulled his head back. After a minute or so,

Coleman dared to look again. The street was empty.

What can I do? Find a policeman. And tell him what? There is a man who shot my girlfriend in Washington and he is here. Well, officer, she was not really my girlfriend. She was a colored girl that I had just confessed my love to. I'm sure that would go over really well.

Plus, what if Dr. Browning somehow found out, what if his tentacles stretched to even here? Coleman could not, would not risk it.

Coleman felt the hairs on his neck stand. The killer could be on the opposite block, even now moving to come up from behind. The sun was still low. He had not been running very long. He knew he must get back to the bus station.

Coleman peeked out again and eased from his sheltered position. No movement. He guessed at the direction of the station and started to run. His head swiveled every few seconds as he ran. He tried to feel his way back through the drowsy city, sometimes turning at an intersection, sometimes going straight. He rounded a corner and saw the familiar Greyhound sign. In a place below his conscious mind, another familiar sight was registered, causing his legs to speed toward the security of the corner of a building. The killer was standing at the station.

I have to think. How can I get on the bus?

He was able to ignore his rapidly beating heart, to will the adrenaline to subside. He peered out again. Was there a way to get there unseen? The killer looked away and Coleman did not hesitate. He darted to the next screened spot, behind a parked car. He lay on the sidewalk and peeked under the car. The man was still there but did not move.

Coleman saw a mailbox that was on the corner opposite the bus station. He waited for the killer's feet to shift, turning away from his direction and Coleman ran to the mailbox.

The replacement bus driver strolled to the bus and climbed the stairs. The big diesel engine rumbled to life. Passengers began to exit the station and re-board the bus. Coleman had only moments.

The bus driver shouted, "All aboard! Leaving in one minute!" Several more passengers scurried from the station to the stairs of the bus. An old truck pulled up to the bus station. A man in dirty coveralls slid out of the driver's seat and approached the killer.

"Hey buddy. You looking for some work?"

The killer glanced back into the station and scanned the street. "What d'ya need?"

Coleman saw his chance. With the killer turned away from him, Coleman dashed from behind the mailbox. The bus driver had already begun to close the door but turned toward Coleman and kept the door open. Coleman scampered up the stairs and the door closed.

Through the window of the door, the killer caught sight of Coleman but started to dash toward the bus too late. The driver put the bus into gear and pulled out of the station with a roar.

Coleman ran to the rear windows. He saw the killer standing in the street watching the receding bus, the silver body, the dark windows, the sign at the top that read *NEW ORLEANS*.

CHAPTER 24

ATLANTA, GEORGIA

It had been easy to find a car. One of his cellmates from long ago had taught him how to hot-wire, lessons whispered deep in the night.

The killer had started out within a couple of hours of the bus's leaving Charlotte. All down the highway, he had sped along looking for that big silver bus. Each time he saw one, his heart started to race again. Each time, though, the sign read something different. Tallahassee, Birmingham, Miami. Never New Orleans.

South Carolina fell away and he crossed the bridge into Georgia. Before long, he saw the buildings of Atlanta. The map he had picked up in Charlotte lay in his lap. He found the bus station symbol through glances down while flying along the highway. As he pulled into the station, he saw several buses but none with New Orleans emblazoned on the front. He walked inside and scanned the room full of people. Maybe the bus is around back and he's in here. But his prey was not in the lobby. He walked to the counter.

"Ain't there a bus going to New Orleans that's stopping here?" A girl referred to a schedule taped on the counter in front of her.

"Yes, but you just missed it. They left – " her finger scanned across the schedule and she glanced at the clock on the wall, "fifteen minutes ago." She gave him a smile. "But if you're here to meet someone, they're probably either in the lobby or sitting outside."

Her smile disappeared when she saw his hard eyes. Here was danger.

"OK." He walked away without another word.

He was hurrying back to the stolen car when he noticed an old Dodge in an alley. He glanced around and walked to the car and peered in through dusty windows. The car had obviously been there for a long time. Inside, the dash was stripped and the upholstery lay in ragged strips in the floorboards.

I can still use part of this, he thought. With his penknife, he loosened the screws holding the license plate.

Peach State.

He walked back to his car and replaced the North Carolina tag with the Georgia one. He swerved out of the parking space and headed to the highway.

About thirty minutes to make up.

He glanced at the map he had placed back on his lap. At a stoplight, he ran his finger over the red line of the expressway.

No good places to catch him in Georgia.

His finger continued over the Alabama line and stopped in the middle of the state.

Montgomery.

CHAPTER 25

MONTGOMERY, ALABAMA

Coleman slouched in his seat as the bus pulled into the station. He heard no shouts, no signs of commotion. He peered out of the window. Two soldiers, the butts of their rifles resting on their hips, watched the passengers exit the bus. Coleman craned his neck to look all around the platform. He did not see the killer. He exhaled and stood.

He did not dare to leave the bus in Atlanta nor at any of the stops before or since then. By the time the bus crossed into Alabama, Coleman started to believe that the killer had not followed him.

In another situation, he would have probably felt intimidated by these National Guardsmen, serious-faced and trigger-happy for all he knew. However, the sight of the armed soldiers as he walked down the stairs was actually a comfort. He again scanned for any familiar faces. Nothing.

He knew he should call her but was not sure what he would say. Speaking of the shooter would only bring back the terror for her. Coleman did not want to cause her to worry. However, if Coleman was to die on this trip, to have his life ended at the hands of this man, he wanted to hear her voice one last time.

He headed toward the restroom. The station was quiet, knots of people scattered about it. A janitor idly swept on the other side of the shiny tile floor.

Coleman walked into the restroom and stepped to the urinal. He was alone. Spots swam on the white tile in front of him. The terror of the past day had drained him. Weariness pulled on his shoulders, his legs. He thought of his small room back at the rectory, the metal bunk in the corner. Not for the first time on this journey, he longed for a few hours in that bed.

He heard motion behind him. Glancing over his shoulder, he saw the back of the janitor bending to lock the door behind him, his mop bucket sloshing water onto the floor beside him.

"Sir, I'm in here." Coleman hurriedly zipped his pants and turned. "Let me wash my hands and I'll be out of your way."

The janitor turned and the breath was stolen from Coleman's lungs. The janitor's face was one he had seen in nightmares, a visage that brought back pain and grief and terror.

The killer dropped the mop and pulled a menacing blade from his pocket. Coleman's sluggishness flew away. For the moment, panic remained submerged beneath fear-fueled efficiency of thought and movement. Coleman kicked at the knife, pushing it aside. He kicked again, connecting with the killer's chest. The killer fell against the locked door and crumpled to the floor.

Coleman darted into the toilet stall, a separate tile-walled alcove with its own door. He slid the latch closed.

A wooden-handled plunger stood in the corner. A small opening with fixed glass blocks allowed light into the room. He picked up the plunger and wielded it like a mace. He heard the killer, a moan, a cough, and a shuffle. He would be here in seconds. The door would not hold.

Coleman stood on the toilet and hit the glass blocks with the plunger handle. A cracking sound reverberated in the small room. He hit it again and felt the glass blocks move. One more strike and the grid of blocks collapsed, spilling outwards.

Coleman pulled himself up and slid through the tight opening, sharp flakes of mortar cutting his clothes and scratching the skin of his abdomen and back. He fell, managing to pivot and land on his side and thigh instead of on his head.

As he rose, he heard the toilet door splinter against the foot of the killer.

Coleman ran. At the end of the alley, he heard a single word shouted from the ragged opening in the wall behind him – "Hey!" He did not turn back.

Paradoxically, panic now began to set in as the adrenaline born out of the immediate threat subsided. He felt the loom of the killer behind him though he was not visible. He turned at the street and ran blindly. The coppery taste of fear flooded his mouth. The few people who braved the martial-law-controlled streets saw a young man with blood-stained and torn clothing running with an deranged look in his eyes.

Coleman's pounding heart and struggling lungs finally forced him to slow. He started to become aware of his predicament, the shock ebbing to a lower state. He saw a middle-aged woman crossing the street on the next block over. She did not look his way but hurried to a door and disappeared

inside. He began to walk. Empty stores lined the street. A sign read
CLOSED FOR THE DURATION.

He saw a stately red brick building topped by a cupola at the end of the
street. He stepped into a recess in front of a store.

He peeked out at the brick structure. There was a sign in front but it was
too far away to read. He squinted down the street and his heart leapt again.
The killer crossed the street two blocks from where he stood. He jerked his
head back into the protection of the recess. After a second he saw the killer
disappear down a side street.

He sprang from the cover of the alcove and ran toward the brick
building, his mind fixed on gaining the cover of the shrubs in front of the
building. As he reached them, Coleman dove into the boxwoods, the
branches further scratching his body and tearing his clothes. He wiggled his
way deep into the shrubs and lay motionless. He was able to see the entire
street. He found that he was holding his breath and exhaled. He closed his
eyes and willed his body to relax. When he opened his eyes, he saw the
killer.

The man held the knife as he walked in the middle of the street, glancing
in storefronts. When he reached the end of the street, he stopped. He tilted
his head back, gazing at the cupola. Coleman remained motionless but with
his muscles tensed, ready to spring. The killer's vision followed the lines of
the building down until he was facing the shrubs. Coleman was sure that
the killer was looking right at him. Inside him, a scream. *Run!* Just before his
taut legs of their own volition caused him to dart from the shrubs, the killer
turned and began walking away. Coleman exhaled and almost fainted.

He waited for a long while before daring to move. He crept from the
shrubs and moved to the other side of the building, keeping his head turned
over his shoulder as he went. He rounded the corner and saw that the large
building formed one side of a grass-filled quad. He dashed to the other side
of the lawn and tried the door. It was locked. He ran to the next building
and found the door open. After seeing no sign of the killer or anyone else,
he entered the building.

Inside was cool and dark. The scent of chalk and abandonment floated
in the air. Coleman heard no sound other than that of his feet striking
speckled green linoleum. He walked slowly around the halls that encircled
the first floor of the building, passing closed doors pierced with tall thin
windows behind which he could see rows of empty desks. A mop bucket
had been left in the hall, a musty smelling damp mop still sitting in it.
Coleman reached another external door opening onto a narrow street. He
exited the building, peeking down the street before doing so. He found an
unlocked door and entered a long red brick building on the other side of
the street.

Light fixtures shone in the ceiling of the hall that he entered. Coleman involuntarily tensed. He walked down the hall and stopped. He sensed something at the back of his brain, not sound but the feeling that comes just before sound, an intimation that something is about to become audible. He waited. His ears strained but did not detect anything. After a few moments, he walked on. After a few more feet, the feeling came back. Are those voices? He put his ear to the wall. As if from far away, he heard a murmur. He was still not sure it was talking that he heard. Then he heard the distinctive trill of a high-pitched laugh. He stepped back from the wall and heard it again. Above him.

He walked farther down the hall and encountered a stairwell angled perpendicular to the hall. He climbed a few steps and again paused. He could hear the indistinct sounds of a conversation. He continued to climb. At the top, he steeled his nerve and peeked into the hall. No one was there.

He saw light emerging from a room about halfway to the end of the passage. He sidled to the door. Young voices came from within. He glanced through the window and saw a group of people, the ones near him with their backs to the door. Coleman had no choice. He knocked.

A girl's voice whispered. "Shh! Shh! Someone's at the door!"

Chairs slid and bodies shuffled. Then quiet.

"Who's out there?" a shaky male voice said.

Coleman took a deep breath, reached for the doorknob, and slowly turned it. He opened the door and stepped into the opening. He encountered a group of fifteen people, most huddled behind three young men who crouched with improvised weapons in their hands – a monkey wrench, a broken broom handle, and a wire coat hanger. Coleman saw their eyes get wider as they scanned him. Coleman realized he must appear a fright with torn bloody clothes and the look of the hunted hanging about him. The one with the monkey wrench spoke.

"How the hell did you get in here?" He was a muscular black man, in his early twenties like all of the other people in the room. He shifted the monkey wrench in his hand, getting a better purchase on the handle in preparation for a fight. The rest of the crowd – a collection of neatly dressed young people, both white and black – scooted closer together like they were trying to hide from the intruder behind the three protectors up front.

Coleman held his hands in front of him, palms to Monkey Wrench.

Coleman said, "The door was unlocked and I came in. I heard you up here."

Coleman saw one of the young men in the crowd behind turn to another boy, scowl, and say, "I thought you said you locked it!"

The other boy said, "I did! Or at least, I thought I did."

Monkey Wrench's face darkened and he slapped the wrench with his other hand.

He said, "Who are you? What are you doing here?" He again glanced down at Coleman's torn shirt.

Coleman swallowed. His hands shook. He could not go back outside.

"My name is Coleman. I just got here. I'm in trouble."

"What kind of trouble?" Broom Stick asked.

Coleman turned his face to him. He was also black and appeared younger than the other two. He spoke in a soft voice and somehow seemed more serious, more earnest.

"A man is chasing me. He wants to kill me."

Monkey Wrench said, "This is crazy!" He took a half step toward Coleman and said, "Just turn around and get out of here! Or I might just kill you myself!"

Coleman stepped back and placed his hand on the doorknob. He thought about simply walking away. But he knew that was not an option. Coleman moved away from the door. Monkey Wrench did not flinch.

Coat Hanger said, "Joe, let's hear what he has to say. Maybe he really is in trouble. Lot of that going around lately."

Other soft voices from behind rose.

"Yeah, let him talk."

"He looks hurt."

Joe stood taller and said, "O.K. But, I'm telling you, if he makes a move, I'm going right up side his head!" He patted the red monkey wrench in his hand.

The three protectors backed into the room, the crowd parting a little to let them rejoin. Coleman eased into the room. Coat Hanger slid a chair and situated it so that it faced the group. He patted the chair, indicating that Coleman should sit. As he took a seat, Coleman felt the weariness that had permeated his body, fatigue born of terror even more than exertion.

Joe crossed his arms, the wrench sticking up like a scepter. "All right. You're here. Tell us your story. If it's good enough, I might let you stay."

Coleman heard sighing and a voice from behind.

"Shut up, Joe, and let him talk."

Coleman breathed deeply. Pain shot through his chest. He saw concerned faces, frightened faces.

He said, "The man who shot me and my girlfriend and killed a policeman is here in Montgomery. He saw me at the bus station and tried to stab me. I escaped and made it here. I've got to get out of Montgomery without him finding me."

Shock replaced fright on the faces. Girls put hands over open mouths. Joe said, "Wait a minute. You're going to have to give us more than that. Why did somebody shoot you?"

Coleman told them everything. He relived it all. By the end, most of the people in the room dabbed at tears. One of the girls spoke.

"We have to help him. We can't just send him back out there. That man might find him and kill him."

Joe said, "Coleman, if you're trying to hide out, this is the last place you should've come. Ever since the Freedom Riders came and we supported them, the police and everyone else has really cracked down. They pulled the accreditation of the college yesterday. Police have been walking around here everyday."

A white girl said, "No offense, Joe, and we're very grateful that you here at Alabama State have given us a place to stay, but the police are not what should worry Coleman. It's that man looking for him. And with the police here so much, the killer will probably stay away." A few of the other people in the cluster nodded agreement.

Joe stared at the girl and said, "And so, Emily, what do you suggest?"

Emily turned to Coleman and said, "You have a place to stay here with us." She turned back to Joe. "If that is O.K. with you."

Joe closed his eyes and gave a single nod.

Coleman stretched his hand out to his new protectors and shook several hands.

"Thank you." He looked around the room and said, "Do you have a telephone I can use?"

CHAPTER 26

MONTGOMERY, ALABAMA

The phone call was a short one. Coleman called the switchboard and was connected to the nurses' desk. A nurse fetched Rosalee to the phone. Coleman told her where he was and what had happened during the bus ride.

Rosalee said, "Why would you go there without even talking to me?"

Coleman said, "You told me to leave you alone. I didn't want to worry you."

She said, "I meant to leave me alone and go live your own life, not try and live mine for me."

Coleman said nothing.

Rosalee said, "Listen, I can't talk anymore. The only promise I want you to make and keep now is to get on a bus and get out of there. Stop trying to do something for me. I don't need it."

That night, Coleman's emotions swirled as he tried to sleep. In the morning, his head throbbed. Early dawn light leaked around the shades and dimly illuminated the classroom. Cots were scattered about and they were filled with softly snoring shapes. The musky smell of ten unwashed college boys permeated the air. Coleman navigated a path among the cots and walked down the hall to the small restroom. He entered a classroom and found a bottle of aspirin in a desk and took two with a swig from the hall water fountain. He slid his back down the wall and sat, head between his knees.

"Am I doing the right thing?" He spoke quietly into the dim hall. "What now?"

He could feel the evil, the looming threat of the predator that stalked the streets outside.

Should I risk going back to the bus station? Try to make it to New Orleans?

Emily told him that some of the Freedom Riders had been arrested in Mississippi.

Is anybody going to make it to New Orleans?

Emily came walking down the hall. "I've been looking for you. I have an idea about how to get you out of Montgomery."

After a while, the group began to stir from the night's sleep. They spent the day in preparation for their departure from the capital city the next day.

Emily explained to Coleman that they were a group of anthropology and archeology students from colleges up north that came to Alabama to explore Indian mounds. One of their team was sick and was thus unable to make the trip.

Emily said, "You can take her place. The people in the town don't know the name of the person coming so it won't matter to them. The little town is called Jubilee."

A car was scheduled to pick up the researcher in Jubilee in one week. Coleman could start making his way out of Alabama then. He tried to not think about what would happen after he left Montgomery, what he would say to the people in the little town where he would be hiding, what he would do or even where he would go at the end of the week spent there.

Back to Washington? Somewhere else?

His mind turned back to a simpler past that seemed shrouded in the mists of distant time. He remembered summer days in the mountains of his childhood, grassy meadows, a gentle sun in a brilliant blue sky. He remembered Granny Mae and venturing to the creek to find an oasis of coolness in the hot summer, wading with bare feet in bracing water. Cold mornings in Washington, waking in his little cot, covered with warm blankets, rising to a simple day of service. Rosalee. Pangs of regret, words unsaid, touches not given.

Suitcases and notebooks, pillows and blankets, all the scholastic and personal belongings of the travelers were bundled and loaded into the panel van that would disperse the student researchers across the state.

Coleman felt out of place. He had been given some clothes along with some notebooks and a couple of textbooks to create his disguise. However, he was not an anthropology researcher, no matter how much information his new friends tried to hurriedly impart to him. After Emily told him the plan for his escape, Coleman attempted to simply stay out of everyone's way.

The next morning, the group was up early. After a quick breakfast and last minute packing, everyone except Emily and Coleman piled into the van, its engine idling at the curb. Emily stepped from the building and scanned the street and the buildings that lined it. She saw no one. Without taking her eyes off the street, she motioned behind her with a sweeping gesture and

Coleman quickly walked to the vehicle, taking a position in the middle of those sitting on the bench seat behind the driver.

There was no movement on the narrow lane. Emily took her place near the passenger door and the van pulled away.

Coleman wore sunglasses and pulled a dark hat low on his forehead. He peered through the corners of his eyes at the people on the sidewalk as the van made its way out of the city, careful not to make eye contact, not trusting the dark lenses to hide his identity. He did not see the killer. Soon, streets gave way to roads with increasingly sparse buildings and houses. He could almost sense a collective sigh when everyone realized they had made it out of Montgomery without incident.

They had been on the road for an hour and half when the driver pulled over to the side of a lonely paved road under the shade of an enormous oak tree. Coleman gazed out at the countryside that was visible through the woods while Emily studied an old road map.

"OK. I think we are on the right road now. If we are where I think we are, the turn-off to Jubilee should be just ahead."

The driver started the van again and eased back onto the road. Within five minutes, they saw a gravel road leading into thick woods on the right side of the paved road.

"That has to be it," Emily said. "There is a ridge right in front of us and that is probably this ridge right here on the map...Russell Ridge."

They started down the road. Though it was a dirt road, it had obviously been well kept as there were no large holes or ruts. They rode for about twenty minutes. Thick woods lined the left side of the road the entire way. On the right side, the rocky flank of Russell Ridge could be seen looming up toward the road and falling away again as they passed it. The slope of the ridge was anchored in a stand of trees that accompanied the road for several miles. The land opened up into a wide meadow that stretched away to a line of trees in the distance. It appeared as if the trees might border a river. Coleman reached for the map and confirmed that the Conchalochee River did in fact flow less than a mile south of Jubilee.

Within a couple of minutes after crossing the meadow, Coleman saw the first signs of civilization. At first, he thought he saw some rock outcroppings like those back on the ridge. However, he soon realized that they were foundations of buildings or houses that had long ago been destroyed, whether by neglect, fire, or some other calamity he could not tell. He counted what appeared to be four such structures and his eye was drawn to similar ruins farther away. The more distant old rocks and bricks marked the outline of what had probably been a massive house. It was at the end of a long dirt drive. The dirt drive emerged from a large circle of dirt and gravel. The road that the vehicle was traveling emptied into the same circle. As the driver guided the van into the circle, he slowed to a stop.

Emily turned in the seat to face Coleman.

She said, "Coleman, this is where our instructions say that we are to drop off our researcher." She turned back and pointed toward the opposite side of the circle.

She said, "You can see the street begins right there on the other side of this turn-around. Just walk straight up it. The town begins right over there."

As she pointed, Coleman saw the sides of some buildings about a hundred yards away. Emily gave a slight smile.

She said, "You will be safe here. No one knows that you have taken Paula's place. There is no way that anyone will find out that you're here."

Coleman put his hands on the back of the seat in front of him and silently nodded.

Emily patted his hand and said, "You'll be fine. Just remember what I've told you and they will never know. A driver will meet you at this spot at ten o'clock one week from today and will drive you all the way back to Washington or anywhere else you want to go. I just wish we had someone going sooner, but that was the arrangement we already made. Plus, nothing will appear out of the ordinary if we keep to the same schedule and thus it will be safer for you."

Coleman nodded again and climbed over another passenger and exited the van, taking a small duffle bag of donated clothes and toiletries along with his research materials. He gazed at the town's buildings and bent down to the car window.

"Listen, I really want to thank you, Emily," he said, "and all the rest of you."

Emily smiled and made a gesture to the driver. "Good luck, Coleman." The van pulled away.

He was alone.

CHAPTER 27

JUBILEE, ALABAMA

The car disappeared into a cloud of dust as Coleman turned to view his surroundings. The dirt and gravel circle in which he was standing was ringed by tall grass that extended past the stone foundations and stretched all the way to the river. The buzz of cicadas echoed from the distant line of trees in the opposite direction.

Holding his duffle bag, he turned and began to walk counterclockwise around the circle, the ruins in front of him.

Yes, that was probably one of those big old plantation houses, he thought.

As he continued walking, he saw a hillock layered with stone slabs and beyond that a paved street emerging from the dirt circle exactly opposite the entrance of the road. The street led for about a hundred yards until the first of the town's buildings started. As he walked, he could see that the town seemed to be comprised of only this one street, with a short row of closely set brick and stone buildings on each side. At the far end of the street, past the last of the buildings, a wooded hill rose. The street seemed to end in front of the hill. He could see a white marble monument or statue emerging from the grass at the opposite end of town.

As Coleman neared the town, his eye caught slight movement on the sidewalk. He squinted against the hazy light and saw that there were two men sitting there. Across the sunlit patch of ground between Coleman and the buildings drifted a raspy-throated tune. As he approached, he saw that an old black man lazily picked the strings of an ancient and heavily scarred guitar, an old white man sitting beside him and quietly humming a deep bass. The white man looked up and saw Coleman approaching across the empty space. As he reached over and tapped the forearm of the guitar player, he gestured with his chin toward Coleman and simultaneously pulled a harmonica out of the bib pocket of his worn overalls and gave a hard blow, emitting an off-key blast.

The black man looked up toward Coleman and kept on playing. The white man began to blow the harmonica very softly, every so often catching a note or two of the black man's song but mostly keeping his eyes on Coleman.

Though the early afternoon sun behind Coleman illuminated the old men's feet, their faces were made indistinct by the shadow of the building. As Coleman got nearer, the men's features became clearer. Still, the depth of age on their faces was hard to fathom. They could have been in their fifties or they could have been left-overs from prehistoric times, two old Creek spirit men formed out of river mud and guarding the gate to the underworld. The earthy sweet scent of tobacco hung about them.

The black man bent to spit into the coffee can spittoon between their chairs.

He said, "Hey there, stranger."

Coleman stopped.

"Hello, how are y'all?" Coleman said as he fidgeted with the duffle bag in his hand.

"I reckon we'll do," the black man said. He grinned at the white man beside him.

Coleman did not return the smile. He said, "I think I'm supposed to meet somebody."

The black man chuckled and said, "That's what my mama told me. She said, 'Roscoe, someday you're gonna meet somebody and law ain't that gonna be a glorious day! Somebody else will have to feed your sorry ass!'"

The white man guffawed at that, spitting out his plug of tobacco in the process. He retrieved it from the sidewalk, removed a piece of straw that had become stuck to the gooey mass, and carefully positioned the plug back in his mouth.

Coleman started to explain, "No, I mean that I think I'm supposed – '

"I know what you mean, son." The black man looked over his shoulder and the white man mimicked the motion. He turned back and said, "Somebody will be here in a jiffy. Sort of surprised she ain't already here."

The black man kicked the leg of the chair in which the other man was sitting and said, "Why don't you give one more blow on that harp."

The white man said, "No need."

The black man followed the white man's gaze as did Coleman. They saw a tall black woman in a trim professional dress suit walking toward them.

"You must be the researcher we've been hearing so much about. I'm Mayor Jefferson."

She spoke with a voice tinged with the soft twang of Alabama, an accent that brought to mind the taste of sweet tea on porch swings and the feel of a warm southern sun. The look in her eye was not so docile, reminding

Coleman of one of the big she-panthers that stalked the mountains of his childhood, a serious creature that stared long to decide if a person was prey or something she should allow to pass.

"Hello, Mayor. I'm Coleman Hightower." Coleman's mind churned with all of the things that Emily had told him. He managed to get out, "Thank you for having me."

The mayor said, "Our pleasure. Have Roscoe and Shot here been entertaining you? I guess you might call them our hospitality team."

Roscoe beamed and Shot chuckled.

The mayor said, "I should take you down to see the preacher. You're going to be staying with him and his wife. Come with me."

The mayor gestured with her open hand and started to walk down the sidewalk. Coleman followed. Roscoe and Shot grinned stupidly and tipped their chins as a farewell.

The street was devoid of people and noticeably clean. He saw someone peeking from behind a curtain and jerking back in response to his glance.

The mayor said, "I'm going to take you to the church. It's right past the grocery store. Pastor Henry should be there."

She turned to cross the street and Coleman hurried to follow. As they were about to reach the other sidewalk, Coleman saw a stern-looking middle-aged woman walking toward them. She intercepted them as they stepped onto the opposite sidewalk and said, "Is that him?"

The woman spoke to the mayor, though as she spoke she eyed Coleman from under a raised left eyebrow.

The mayor said, "Yes, Myrtle, this is Coleman – "

Myrtle said, "Why did you come here?"

Coleman stammered.

The mayor said, "Myrtle, Coleman is on his way to see the preacher. Now, we've got to be going. You have a good day!"

Mayor Jefferson took Coleman by the arm and led him away. They were followed by the squint-eyed stare of Myrtle.

"Don't mind her," the mayor said. " She's always grouchy."

The two of them passed under the cool shade of the green awning over the grocer's door and turned around the corner of the building. Coleman saw that the street ended in a circle of pavement at the base of the small hill that he had seen when he was walking into town. The hill was covered with trees and Coleman saw two single lane paved paths coming out of the circle of pavement and leading around the hill, one in one direction, one in the opposite.

Between the two paths and in front of the hill was a white marble column, about eight feet tall. On the top of the column was a depiction of a rising sun, a bronze half disc with long rays shooting to the sides and above the top of the column.

Coleman heard the sound of children on a playground coming from the left path.

"Jubliee School is down that way," said the mayor.

Coleman saw the unmistakable form of a church building to the right of the monument and down the paved path in that direction. The small church stood about fifty feet from the edge of the circle of pavement, was built of whitewashed wood siding, and was so well kept that the building seemed to gleam. There was a plain white steeple standing near the front of the gable of the church. There were a few steps that led up to an unadorned black front door. A small sign in front of the church read, *JUBILEE COMMUNITY CHURCH, REV. HENRY SMITHSON, PASTOR.* The mayor stepped up to the door and found it locked. She stepped back, looked at her watch, and glanced around.

She said, "He's usually here this time of day. We'll wait a few minutes and then walk toward his house if he's not here."

"Besides to the school and the church, where do the paths go?" Coleman asked.

Mayor Jefferson said, "Those are the roads that go back to the houses. That way," she said, pointing to the left path, "is North Community and the other way is South Community."

As Coleman attempted to get his bearings, a voice spoke up from behind them.

"Who is your friend, Mayor?"

Coleman turned to see a man, appearing to be in his early forties, walking from the South Community road and stepping onto the circle of pavement. He was a white man, clean-shaven and neatly dressed in plain brown trousers and a white shirt.

"This is Coleman Hightower." The mayor turned to Coleman and said, "This is Pastor Henry. You'll be staying with him while you're here."

"Coleman, Henry Smithson. Pleased to meet you." The pastor gave Coleman a firm handshake. "Welcome to Jubilee! We don't get too many visitors."

Coleman saw a glance pass between the mayor and the pastor, an unspoken question, a hesitation.

He returned the pastor's handshake and said, "Thank you. I appreciate your letting me stay at your house."

"Coleman, you are very welcome. My wife and I live in South Community, right down that road, and we have plenty of room. It's our pleasure." Pastor Henry motioned toward the path. "We'll go to the house and get you settled."

As Coleman and the pastor walked, a lone figure crouched unseen just beyond the crest of the wooded hill. He peered with luminous pale blue eyes down at the pair on the road. His slender fingers, tipped with nails blackened with layers of soil, reached into a worn leather pouch hanging from a strap slung around his shoulder and withdrew a gnarled root. He held it to his mouth. Wispy tendrils waved in his breath as he whispered long-forgotten words, an incantation. He broke the root and its smell assaulted his nostrils. As the pair disappeared from his sight, the figure bent and scratched a shallow hole. He pressed the two halves of the root into the rich soil and covered them, replacing the leaves. The figure rose and glided to the shade of a huge granite outcropping. He turned and gazed out, catching glimpses of distant hills through the thick trees. He closed his eyes and saw even farther, floating shapes, foggy creatures, as his own dark shape melted into the shadows, invisible to the daylight world.

CHAPTER 28

THE PARSONAGE

Coleman lay on the bed as a ceiling fan spun lazily above him, the small bedroom cool and dim. His hosts had been hospitable, the pastor and his wife Mary insisting that he eat his fill from a plate piled high with biscuits, thick bacon, honey, and fig preserves. Though his hunger was gone, anxiety remained.

How am I going to do this? Will I be able to fake it? What will happen if they find out?

He took a deep breath and rose. Good smells drew him to the kitchen. Mary was already working on dinner, slicing carrots and placing them into a roast pan beside a thick hunk of beef.

She said, "Hey, Coleman. How are you feeling?"

He thought, *Scared. Terrified that I will be found out. Confused about what to say and do.*

"Fine," Coleman said. "Where is the pastor?"

She said, "He went to the church. He'll be back in a little while." She motioned to a tall stool at the end of the kitchen counter. "Please have a seat. We can visit until he gets back."

Coleman awkwardly climbed onto the stool. He felt like some kind of bird sitting on a post.

Though he grew up in the country, he was uncomfortable, out of place in this house, in this town. The light was different, falling at an unfamiliar angle, no mountains around to intercept the sun's beams by mid afternoon. The people were different, not the tough hardy hillspeople who were guarded and generous at the same time. There was not the mistiness of prehistoric time laying about this place or at least not the same ancient wild patina of his mountain home. Here the atmosphere was more domesticated, speaking of centuries-old fields tended by dark hands rather than of deep hollows where the land only begrudgingly gave up sustenance and then to whomever – whether red or brown or white – could wrench it from the stony grasp of the mountains. The only whispers of home came from the fragrance of the roast and the smile of the hostess.

From his perch, Coleman said, "I saw the ruins of an old house when I first came into town."

Mary nodded and said, "That's the old Russell plantation house. It was burned down by the yankees way back in the war."

Coleman said, "What about the little hill with the stones on top of it?"

Mary turned in surprise and said, "That's the Indian mound. Henry told me that was why you came here. Is that right?"

Coleman's breath caught.

He nodded and said, "Yes, of course. That is why I am here. I just wanted to make sure that was the mound and that it was not somewhere else, you know, some other mound."

"No, that's the only mound we have." She turned back to her work. "There's a really big mound up close to Oxford, but that's the only one here in Jubilee."

Coleman's mind flew, searching for a new subject.

"The monument at this end of the street – what does the rising sun mean?" Coleman asked.

Mary said, "The street runs east to west and that hill is due east of town. So, the sun rises over the top of the hill every day. I guess it just made sense that the image of the rising sun would be popular here in Jubilee. Somebody made that monument a long time ago."

The spring on the screen door squealed and Pastor Henry walked in.

He said, "Coleman, I hope you have gotten a little bit of rest. I'm sure your travels tired you out." Coleman nodded.

The pastor said, "Do you know what you're going to do to start your research? I guess you saw the mound when you got to town."

The pastor's wife glanced at Coleman. He tried to will his blush away.

Coleman said, "Yes sir, I did see it. Mrs. Smithson and I were just talking about that."

"Please call me Mary."

Coleman forced a smile. He turned back to the pastor. "I'll go to the mound tomorrow morning."

Henry said, "Anywhere else you need to go or see?"

Coleman said, "Like what?"

Henry said, "Oh, I don't know, maybe the archives in the Town Hall. I'm not sure what's there, but it might help out."

Coleman willed the quaver out of his voice. "That's a good idea. Maybe after the mound."

Night came but sleep was elusive. The taste of roast beef lingered in his mouth. He had not eaten much or well during his travels and thus a home cooked meal was a comfort, but his mind was still in turmoil. He was afraid he would be found out, that his meager knowledge would not be enough to keep the ruse intact. However, the unrest had deeper roots than that.

What is all of this about? Why am I here?

His flight from the killer had created a blur on his path. He had felt certain that New Orleans would be the place for answers, that in the company of those with like minds to Rosalee's he would be able to see a way forward, a way to bring meaning.

What could possibly be important here?

CHAPTER 29

MAIN STREET

Coleman slipped out of the house to walk to the mound in the pre-dawn light without disturbing Henry or Mary. The breeze carried a wet earthy smell from the sunrise hill as he walked the gently arcing path toward town. The buildings came into view. He walked to the center of the circle of pavement that punctuated this end of Main Street and stopped. The tops of the two large granite buildings facing each other, almost twins but for the balcony of the Town Hall, were already edged with the gold of the morning sun. The matching circle of pavement was visible at the other end of town.

Coleman turned. The sky brightened behind the hill, a halo of light near the crest. His gaze came to rest on the monument. He walked closer to it. The base was an obelisk made of white marble with streaks of amber. Out of the front of the monument near the top extended a bronze rod and onto this rod was affixed the sunrise image. A half circle of heavily tarnished metal was at the bottom and rays extended horizontally on both sides with identical rays at regular intervals between the horizontal ones and the vertical one in the center. Coleman stepped closer and noticed that the bottom edge of the half circle was rough, as if it had been chiseled or otherwise cut. He noticed the same texture at the midway point of each of the rays and again at the tips. The remainder of the bronze was smooth, displaying the care and workmanship of a bygone age.

A crow flew over the hill, passing above Coleman's head, cawing and drawing Coleman's eyes away from the monument. The crow flew down the street. Coleman was startled to see a woman approaching him.

She said, "Why are you here stirring up trouble?"

It was Myrtle. Coleman forced a smile as she walked up to him and stopped, standing several inches too close. A stale scent wafted from her clothes.

"Ma'am, I'm not here to cause any trouble. I'm just here to study the Indian mound."

Myrtle snorted and ran her disapproving eyes over him.

She said, "We ain't had nothing but peace since it all happened and now here you are wanting to dig it all up again."

Coleman said, "What are you talking about?

She said, "Don't you go trying to trick me! Get you behind me! I know why you're here. And ain't nothing good gonna come from it. The Lord's fire is a winnowing fire! Ain't nothing cleanse a body like fire. Soap and water just pushes stuff around. Fire purifies, it sanctifies!"

Myrtle raised her hands toward heaven and shook them. When Coleman tried to respond, she waved him off and said, "I ain't got nothing more to say to you, you servant of the beast!"

She turned her head and marched down the North Community road, like a soldier retiring from the field of victory.

Coleman gave a bewildered frown and resumed his walk to the mound.

Shadows still pooled in the doorways of the stores. The windows were lifeless. He neared the end of the rows of buildings and saw Roscoe's and Shot's chairs, waiting for their daily occupants, the coffee can sitting between them. He continued down the paved street and reached the graveled circular road.

The mound stood to his left. It was at least ten feet tall and probably thirty feet in diameter. It was covered with grass that was punctuated with large slabs of white marble, the edges of which were marred with chips and scratches. There was no engraving on any of the slabs — he walked around the mound and confirmed this — and no plaque.

Coleman gazed toward the ruins of the house. The driveway led between huge old oak trees, their massive limbs stretching over the drive and creating an arbor. He started down the drive and felt like he was walking back in time. He could almost hear the clop of horse hooves that had paced this road, returning from Shiloh or Antietam almost a hundred years ago. Buggy-borne ghosts sped by him, bearing rose-cheeked daughters to cotillions. Gauzy half memories floated among the trees as he approached the house, vestiges of lives, happy and tragic, slave and free, still tied to this place by desire or duty or other purpose he could not fathom.

He faced the foundation of the house, standing where the steps no doubt had begun. He noticed chips of white rock on the ground and stooped to take one and pocketed it. He entered the boundary of the old house. Thin red dust covered the entire surface of the old foundation. No plants grew, not even a greenbrier vine or a ragweed. Chips of marble were scattered in the dust. He walked to where he imagined a wide soaring staircase had stood. He saw traces of twisted and scorched metal, likely the balusters. He continued to the rear of the foundation. He saw stone foundations of much smaller structures. Beyond these, the land gently sloped across a broad meadow down to the line of trees that denoted the river.

The sun had risen above the hill and shafts of light were cast toward Coleman. He went back up the drive and stopped once more at the mound, taking the chip of stone out of his pocket and stooping to compare it to the slab.

It's the same, he thought.

He shielded his eyes from the sun and looked toward town. He saw movement and realized it was Roscoe and Shot taking their customary posts. In the clear morning air, he saw Shot point toward him. Shot took out his harmonica and Coleman could make out a dissonant chord that reached his ears a second or two later.

Coleman thought, *What are they up to?*

He stooped once more to the marble slabs and when he stood again, he saw another figure standing with Roscoe and Shot, a man who was carrying something. With a chill, Coleman realized the man cradled a rifle in his arm. The man shifted and raised the weapon.

Coleman froze with terror when he saw the reflected light of a scope as the rifle was aimed at him.

CHAPTER 30

MAIN STREET

"How long has he been there?"

"I don't know, Galen. When me and Shot got here, Shot looked and there he was."

Galen lowered the rifle and turned the dial on the scope. He once again raised the rifle, resting his cheek on the stock. Through the scope, he found that he was eye to eye with Coleman. He lowered the rifle.

"He knows we're looking at him." Galen glanced at his watch. "I'm going to wake up Martelle."

The man slung the rifle on his shoulder and turned to walk back up the street. Roscoe and Shot took their seats, keeping their eyes toward Coleman. Galen crossed the street and entered the five-and-dime. He reached over the counter for the telephone, dialing the number and waiting longer than he cared to wait. At last, the receiver on the other end was raised with a click. He heard a sleepy "Hello?"

"This is Galen Whitmire. He's at the mound."

Martelle said, "What time is it?" A yawn.

Galen said, "Seven. Be here in fifteen minutes."

A pause.

"On my way."

CHAPTER 31

THE MOUND

The man with the rifle disappeared into one of the buildings. After seeing no one coming toward him and with his fear subsiding, Coleman surveyed the entire area. He saw no structures other than the mound and the demolished houses. Remnants of the night's fog lingered among the trees of the wooded area opposite the dirt and gravel circle. He saw the white flash of a tail as a large doe fled from his sweeping gaze. The smell of wet grass mixed in his nostrils with the aroma of rich pine wood.

He looked back down at the stones covering the mound. He thought of climbing to the top but decided against it.

There is nothing more for me to learn here.

He was about to turn to walk back to town when he saw a figure walking toward him.

The figure appeared to be a man, very thin and very dark. His worn plaid shirt and faded work pants were bunched up under a wide leather belt pulled taut, the end dangling loose. His head was covered with untrimmed black tufts mixed with gray. He walked with an economy of movement that was striking, no swinging of arms, legs moving smoothly, feet seeming to merely touch the earth for show, his body gliding along like a black swan on a still lake.

The man stopped in front of Coleman. Coleman felt like rubbing his eyes to check that he was not dreaming, to ascertain whether this creature was a figment. However, he could not take his eyes off the man. There was no expression on the man's face, just a blank stare. It was the man's eyes that transfixed Coleman.

The eyes were the palest of blue, almost white, the irises nearly blending with the sclera at their junction. The eyes stared directly into Coleman's and they were as uncommunicative as the rest of the face. It was not that the eyes had no depth, not like a reptile's eyes that were all mindless and soulless voracity. These eyes were just the opposite, with a depth so incomprehensible as to be unreadable, like the bottom of the Grand Canyon feels like a painting because it is so far away.

"What are you doing?" The man's voice broke the spell.

Coleman said, "I am, or I was, what I mean is that I was looking at the mound. Maybe you've heard that I'm here to do some research."

Blood rushed to Coleman's face and ears. He heard a roaring sound. He extended his hand.

"I'm Coleman."

The man gripped Coleman's hand with long fingers.

"I'm Martelle Fletcher."

The man still held Coleman's eyes with his. After a long moment, Martelle said, "Where are you from?"

Coleman pulled his hand from Martelle's grip and said, "I live in Washington."

Martelle said, "I don't think so. Before that – where are you from? I believe I know who you are."

Anxiety threatened to overwhelm Coleman. The man seemed to be looking not at him but into him or through him, like Coleman's very being was a telescope, a view into the past. Coleman's mouth went dry and he struggled to remain standing. He tried to compose himself before speaking.

Coleman said, "I grew up in the mountains but I live in Washington now. I've never been in Alabama before." Coleman gave a wary grin. "Maybe you're thinking I'm someone else."

Martelle stared at him.

"Maybe so." Martelle gestured down toward the old ruins. "Did you go down there too?"

Coleman turned. "Yeah. It looks like it was a big house. What about the other houses? What were they?"

"Slave cabins." Martelle snorted wetly and spat on the ground. "They didn't usually have'em so close to the owner's house but the river used to flood a lot."

Martelle stepped back and said, "You didn't have no relatives did a little spell-casting on the side, did you?"

The ground beneath Coleman's feet rocked and his vision swirled. It felt as if his heart would come out of his chest. His mind raced back to dark hollows, his nose remembering the smoke of laurel branches, his ears recalling the sound of ancient songs.

Coleman managed to regain control of his emotions and to utter a simple, "Yeah, I'm sure."

Coleman tried to divert the strange man's attention. He pointed toward a small dilapidated stone structure, the wooden slates and rafters of its roof caving in. He asked, "What is that?"

Martelle said, "That's the old springhouse. Spring dried up years ago."

Martelle continued to stare. He said, "D'you see anything else? I mean around this mound or the house?"

Coleman said, "Not really. I guess the Russells were pretty rich."

Martelle's eyebrows lowered. "Where'd you hear that name?"

Coleman's heart raced again.

He said, "From the pastor's wife. She told me that's who used to live there, the Russells."

Martelle said, "There was no need for her to talk about all of that." He stomped his foot and pointed a bony finger at Coleman. "All of that is in the past. No need to go digging into all of that."

Under his breath and to the ground, Martelle said, "Damn!"

He glared at Coleman and said, "It would be best for you to just go on back where you come from."

Martelle turned toward town. Roscoe and Shot were standing beside their chairs and the man who had raised the rifle stood with them. Martelle turned back and said, "Why don't you come on with me and leave this mound be?"

Coleman's mind screamed, warning him to not go with this man. The gilt-edged stones on the top of the mound, painted by the morning sun, beckoned.

Coleman said, "I think I'm going to stay here for a while."

Coleman knelt. Martelle looked toward the trio watching them and started his walk back to town. Coleman glanced at the thin man as he left and returned his attention to the mound. He did his best to push anxiety out of his mind, to calm himself, to decide his next step.

As his vision filled with the whiteness of the slab, the world around Coleman disappeared. Martelle, the old ruins behind him, the road, the watchers, they all faded away like the almost-forgotten memory of a faraway place and time.

The stones seemed to whisper to him, though he could not make out the words. All stones have stories and most of them are not the happy tales that woodland creatures and children of man seem to have in storybooks. The stories of stones start out as angry ones, molten fury spewing from the deep redness. Tales of unimaginable numbers of centuries, simmering under the weight of its fellows. The stones on this pile recall the grief-laden story of being cut out of their home and shaped not by the patient hands of wind and water but by the hasty and harsh iron claws of men. Grief and anger are enfolded in every stony mountain, every rocky hill, until time causes the rock to crumble and return to the elements from which they were formed, an un-heaven in which dissolution leads not to joy but to obliteration. All stones have secrets, untold events to which they have borne mute witness.

What secrets do you have?

Coleman leaned closer still. He saw minute veins of granite coursing through the bodies of the marble slabs. No blood flowed within but perhaps something else, some knowledge, some wisdom, the wisdom that keeps a mountain upright as fleeting things like civilizations and forests and oceans waxed and waned. Coleman stretched out a hand. The coolness of the stone invaded his hand. It was as if he could feel the pulse of the rock or of the mound within.

There are secrets here. I can know them if I search.

Just as surely, he knew other things.

Your secret will make all of this make sense. Washington, Dr. Browning, Rosalee, all of it. I am here because of Rosalee.

He lifted his hand. He looked around as if waking.

As he stood, his knees and thighs protested. He glanced toward town and saw that Martelle was just arriving at the trio of watchers.

He thought, *I really don't know what in the world this mound has to do with Rosalee.*

Another thought immediately rose to his mind – this one sure and immovable, like the stony pinnacle from which these slabs were cut.

I won't stop until I find out.

CHAPTER 32

TOWN HALL

By the time Coleman left the mound and walked back to town, Roscoe and Shot were not in their customary post. Coleman made his way to the Town Hall. Coleman's footfalls echoed down the tiled hallways as he crossed the lobby to a small office. The door was simply labeled CLERK. As Coleman entered, he heard a faint clicking sound.

A clock? No. The clicks were faster than that.

A small woman sat with her head down on the other side of a counter. A long multicolored knitted scarf flowed from the floor beside her and up over the front edge of the counter. Knitting needles flashed in her hands. Coleman cleared his throat and the woman said, "Good morning. You must be that boy coming to go through the papers. Pastor Henry told me you'd be coming. I'm Patsy." The clicking did not slow.

"Good morning Patsy. Yes, I'm Coleman Hightower. I came to look at some records."

"Sure thing."

Patsy's hands continued to work as she spoke. She gave the same impression as a juggler, able to carry on a conversation with the part of her brain controlling her speech independent from that controlling her unconsciously knitting fingers.

She said, "I pulled out some of the old newspapers and there's a box of other papers in the room down the hall."

Coleman said, "Anything about the history of the town would help." He had been rehearsing his lines since the night before, though his time at the mound this morning made the previous night seem like decades ago. "Especially anything about the mound."

The clerk fixed him in her gaze for a few seconds. The clicking continued unabated.

She said, "I don't think you're gonna find much. Let's go down the hall and I'll let you in."

Her fingers abruptly stopped and she placed her end of the knitting on the desk surface.

"That sure is a long scarf," Coleman said. "Must be a tall person."

Patsy looked at the mass of knitted yarn as if considering it for the first time.

"Oh that."

She picked up the loose end and shoved it over onto the desktop.

She said, "It's not a scarf. It's going to be a sweater for my cousin over in Meridian, a Christmas present. I'm going to make a bunch of these strips and knit the ends together and then knit all of the rings together to make a sweater." She looked over the counter top at the great pile of knitting on the desk. "I guess it must seem like a lot, but he weighed 600 pounds last Christmas and he ain't stopped eating since."

Patsy led Coleman down the hall and into a dim room that smelled of old musty paper. A mousetrap with a dried-up hunk of cheese sat in the corner. Spiders peered down from their webs, hundreds of unblinking eyes following the intruders to a table.

Patsy said, "I'll pull out the newspapers and bring them here for you. That box right there," she pointed to a large box on top of the shelf beside the table, "are the old minutes of the council meetings."

By the time Coleman had used the step stool to reach the box, pushing aside cobwebs and sneezing through a cloud of dust, the clerk was returning with a large cloth mailbag.

She said, "Here they are. All of this should keep you busy for a while. You're probably wasting your time."

Coleman settled in the chair and took a stack of yellowed papers out of the box. *Official Minutes of the Town Council of Jubilee, Alabama* was typed at the top of the first page of each stapled document. Under this heading was the date of each meeting. Coleman scanned through the minutes of the first set, from September 1945. There was a resolution to have a parade to honor a Marine returning from the war in the Pacific. There was discussion about buying some paint to refurbish the inside of the Town Hall and Sheriff's Office. There was a report from the sheriff that included telling of an incident in which one of the citizens was locked up overnight for public drunkenness.

Coleman laid the first document aside, careful to place it so that he would know that he had already examined at it. He pulled the next set of minutes out of the box. He noticed that this one was from 1950.

"Oh great. They're not in order," he said to himself.

Coleman spent the better part of the next hour stacking the minutes. As he examined the stacks, he found that there were minutes from every year from 1921 until 1954. There were no minutes from before or after that time.

Coleman walked back to the office.

"Excuse me, Patsy -"

The clicking continued.

Patsy said, "Yep. What d'ya need?"

He said, "I notice that there are no minutes from before 1921 and none after 1954 in this box."

Patsy nodded and said, "We keep the last seven year's worth of minutes in the safe upstairs. Every year, I bring the minutes from eight years ago and put it in that box."

"What about the ones from before 1921?" Coleman asked.

Patsy frowned. "Seems like what you got is enough to keep you busy. Anyways, I don't know where any more is at. I've been in this job for twelve years. Before that, Bertha Johnson was the clerk. She died two years ago. She might have known about some older minutes. But I can tell you that there ain't any other minutes in there now. I completely reorganized this entire office a few years ago. I took everything out into the hall and put it all back in a more organized way. It took me two and half weeks to do all of that!"

"The pastor's wife told me that the big house near the mound was burned down during the Civil War and so I thought that some older minutes might tell more about the mound," Coleman said. "Maybe there will be something in the newspapers about it."

"Maybe so," said Patsy. "Well, is there anything else?"

"No, thank you. I'm fine," said Coleman.

"OK," said Patsy. "Now, if you'll let me get back to my knitting. I'm about finished with one of the loops on my cousin's sweater. Only five more to go!"

Coleman thanked her and turned back to the papers. He started with the oldest stack of minutes and scanned each set. He saw mention of only routine matters, with no reference to the mound or any other significant event. His perusal of the other stacks yielded the same observations.

Coleman neatly stacked the minutes back in the box. *At least they'll be in order now*, he thought. *Not that Patsy seems to ever need to look at them.*

Coleman lifted the heavy bag of newspapers onto the table and upended the sack, dumping the papers out. He grabbed the top one from the pile and pushed the others back so that he would have some space to work. He saw the front page, which read *Jubilee Herald*. The date was April 19, 1935. The newspaper was only four pages long and mostly had human-interest type stories. There were some scattered advertisements – *Sale Tomorrow at Smith's Clothing Store* was one of them – as well as an obituary column telling of only one death and a wedding column telling of two weddings.

Coleman sorted the papers in the same fashion as he had the council meeting minutes. He soon had eight stacks. The latest paper he had was from only two months ago. The oldest was from 1921. He started with the oldest stack and examined each issue, searching for any mention of the mound. After two hours of scrutiny of the papers, he had only found evidence of small town news that most people would find at best quaint but more likely boring.

Just as Coleman was about to return the newspapers to the bag, he noticed a yellowed piece of news stock protruding from between the pages of the oldest stack. He carefully pulled the paper out and saw that it was a fragment of a front page. The only print that was visible was the title line *Russellton Gazette* and a partial date: *April 1, 1 – .* The tear of the page went through the last three numbers of the date. He turned the scrap over and found no printing on that side. He carefully examined the margins on the front and found no hint of any writing.

I wonder why I didn't see this before, he thought.

As he was examining the fragment, he heard a sound of movement. His eyes shot toward the mousetrap but it sat there undisturbed. He spun around and saw Mayor Jefferson standing in the door.

She said, "Hello, Coleman, how has your day gone? Finding what you need?" Her eyes flitted over the stacks of paper.

"Hello, Mayor. I've been sorting these minutes and newspapers. Haven't found much yet. Do you think you would have a little time to help me? To answer some questions?"

The mayor hesitated. At first Coleman thought she might say no, but she said, "All right. I suppose I have a few minutes."

The mayor took a chair adjacent to Coleman's chair and pulled a pair of reading glasses from her pocket.

Coleman said, "Mayor, I have looked through most of the minutes from the Town Council meetings that are in the box." He pointed to the box on the corner of the table.

The mayor said, "Didn't you find anything that caught your eye?"

As she asked this, she pulled closer to her one of the folded newspapers still lying on the table.

"Goodness!" she said. "There are some old editions in this bag!"

Coleman said, "I found some dating back to the mid-1920s. That was one of the strange things I noticed about both the newspapers and the sets of minutes. The oldest ones were from the twenties, none from before that. I know the town has been around for at least a hundred years. I was told that the big house was burned in the Civil War. Or was the town not here then, just the house?"

The mayor said, "There was a town here at the time of the Civil War. It was called Russellton and was named after the owners of the plantation, the

Russells. The town of Jubilee was built on the foundations of Russellton. As far as the newspapers, the Jubilee Herald began publication in 1921. Before that, there was another newspaper here in town. I guess the editions of that newspaper have all been lost."

Coleman slid the fragment of yellowed newspaper across the table to the mayor.

"Look at this," he said, carefully watching her face.

The mayor adjusted her reading glasses and read the words on the scrap. She cleared her throat and said, "Yes, this must be very old. This is from the newspaper printed back in the 1800s."

The mayor glanced over her shoulder as Patsy entered the room. "Patsy, did you see this?" the mayor said.

"Would you look at that?" Patsy declared. "We ought to put this in the display case upstairs!"

"Good idea," said the mayor. "Coleman, do you want to see the case upstairs. There are some interesting things in it."

Coleman checked the clock on the wall. "Yeah, that sounds good. I'm ready to stop work for the day anyway."

The mayor stood to lead the way upstairs. Coleman began to collect the newspapers to put them back in the bag. However, Patsy made a flapping motion with the back of her hands, as if she were shooing a flock of chickens.

She said, "Coleman, you just leave those papers right there! I'll put all of this away. Just take that piece of the old newspaper with you and go on up with the mayor." When Coleman did not immediately put the papers down, she playfully swatted his hand and added, "Now, git!"

The mayor opened the door and chuckled. She said, "Coleman, I learned a long time ago not to argue with Patsy. She always gets her way."

Coleman stepped into the echoing hallway and the mayor led the way up the stairs to the second floor. There, a landing stretched around the opening above the entrance hall floor below. The landing led to a large office door near the front of the building. On the glass door was painted in gold *Mayor J. Jefferson.* Just to the left of the door was a waist-high wooden case with a glass top. Coleman followed the mayor to the case. The mayor ran her hand along the edge of the case and stopped near the back of the left side of the case.

"Coleman, this is something that only I as the mayor and a few other people know. There is a secret latch on the side of this case."

As she said this, she pulled her finger back and Coleman heard a click. She carefully lifted up the hinged glass top of the case.

"Let's put the newspaper right here," she said as she carefully took the scrap from Coleman and laid it gently behind an old book and in front of a rusted cavalry saber.

Coleman examined the rest of the contents of the case. There was a piece of an old quilt in one corner. Propped against the quilt was a photograph of a parade through the street of the town. The remainder of the case was filled with some old tools and a parchment upon which could be seen the words *Diploma, Jubilee School.*

"These are just a few things the people of the town donated when we were sprucing up the Town Hall a few years back. That old sword was found out near the old plantation house," she said.

Coleman glanced at the closed door of the mayor's office.

Mayor Jefferson asked, "Would you like to see my office?" As she stepped to the door and opened it, she said, "Come on in."

Coleman stepped through the door and saw a large room with beautiful hardwood paneling on the walls. The far wall contained large French-style glass doors framed by large windows. Through the glass of the doors, he could see the stone balcony that overlooked Main Street. There was a huge desk that appeared to be made of walnut or some other dark wood. As he gazed around the room, he noticed paintings and framed old photographs hanging on the wall. On one wall, he noticed a faded rectangle on the paneling and a tarnished brass hook on the wall beside the empty space.

Coleman said, "This is a beautiful office. How old is this building?" He continued to gaze around the office as he spoke.

"It was built in the 1850s," the mayor answered. "So, it is over 100 years old."

"Mayor, do you know much about the sunrise monument at the end of the street?" Coleman asked.

The mayor said, "That statue was erected in the early 1900s. It shows the sun rising over the hill right behind that monument. That image, the sunrise, has become the unofficial symbol of Jubilee."

"That's what Mary said," Coleman said.

The mayor nodded. "The townspeople also use the symbol when they print flyers for events and such. It is such a beautiful image. It brings to mind the dawn of a new day, when everything becomes possible again," the mayor said. "Well, I guess it's about time to call it a day."

"Thanks for showing me your office," Coleman said. "I didn't mean to keep you here late."

On his walk back to the pastor's house, discomfort tugged at the back of Coleman's mind. Today had been a day of puzzles, unsolved riddles. Martelle's cryptic words. His thoughts at the foot of the mound. The fragment of newspaper. The missing town council documents. The looks he had seen, glances passed between people, between the pastor and his wife, between the pastor and the mayor. The mayor's reactions to some of his questions.

The mound was not the only secret-keeper.

That night, as he lay in bed and stared at the ceiling, his mind turned possibilities over and over until he slept and dreamed dark dreams full of murky shapes.

CHAPTER 33

THE DINER

Coleman spent the next morning poring again over old documents, boring accounts of mundane meetings, and so he was grateful that at nearly noon his stomach alerted him to the need for food and he decided to go to the diner. Stepping through the door of the diner, he immediately encountered twenty sets of eyes alighting upon him. Though many returned to their fried chicken plates and peach pie and sweet tea, Coleman could still feel eyes on him.

After tasking a seat and ordering, Coleman placed his elbows on the counter. He leaned forward and looked to his right. Two men sitting on that end stared at him wordlessly for a few seconds and went back to their quiet conversation.

Coleman turned to the left. There was a black man sitting on the stool beside him. The man said, "Friend, how are you today?"

His bass-toned voice fit his large frame. He had bright eyes and a wide smile. He leaned forward and said, "Don't mind them. Seems like some folks has forgot how to be neighborly."

Coleman said, "My name is Coleman Hightower."

The big man said, "I am Edward Jackson. Pleased to make your acquaintance." His large hand engulfed Coleman's.

Coleman said, "I'm here to do some research on –"

Edward waved away his words. "Everybody knows why you're here. You're here to look into the mound."

Coleman smiled and nodded. "I guess word gets around pretty quick."

A low chuckle came from deep in Edward's chest. "Yep, this here's a small town and everybody likes to talk."

Edward took a sip from his glass of iced tea. "Have you found out anything yet?"

"Not much." Coleman turned to the man. "What do people around here say about the mound? How long has it been there?"

Edward stared at the wall, collecting his thoughts. "I have to say that we don't really ever talk about it. We just know that it's an Indian mound and we leave it at that."

"Do you know what group of Indians lived around here?" Coleman pictured a book that Emily had slipped into his bag, a thin volume that listed the native American groups that had lived in the southeastern United States.

Edward said, "Don't know much about Indians. One's tribe's about the same as another to me. I seen John Wayne shoot up some Indians one time when I got to go to the picture show in Montgomery. But I don't think that's the same kind of Indians that was here."

The waitress placed a plate containing a thick hamburger and shoestring fries in front of Coleman. Coleman took a big bite.

Edward smiled. "They do make 'em good here."

Coleman grunted in agreement and after swallowing, asked, "How long have you lived here?"

"All my life. I was born in the house right across from where me and my wife live, in the house my mama lived in til she died in '58. Most of the people that live here have always been here."

Edward motioned to get the attention of a thin white woman sitting alone in a booth near the window. "Lois, come over here."

As the woman walked over to the counter. Edward said, "Coleman, this is Lois Green. She works in the drug store."

The woman offered a bony hand to Coleman. Coleman thought her hand felt like a bird, brittle bones with a fragility that threatened to collapse in Coleman's grip.

"Pleased to meet you." Her voice was low, her demeanor shy.

Edward said, "I was just telling Coleman that most everybody in Jubilee has been here all their lives. I have and I know you have. I was born in North Community and Lois here was born over in South Community. Ain't that right, Lois?"

Lois's smile was not much stronger than her grip. "Yes, I've been here forever."

Coleman said, "Maybe you know something about the mound. Do you remember anybody ever telling you who made it?"

Lois's eyes widened and mouth opened. She looked even paler than she had a moment before.

She said, "I don't know anything. Got to go." She turned toward the rear of the tiny restaurant but stopped when the front door opened.

"There you are! Should've known." A black man wearing a short white coat stood in the doorway. "I need you back at the store. I've got

139

prescriptions to fill and I can't do my job and yours too!"

Lois scurried out of the diner, slipping past the man. Edward said, "Ephraim, there ain't no reason to be that hard on that little woman. She's as good as gold to you and you can't even see it."

"Edward, you can just keep your opinions to yourself."

"It ain't an opinion if it's the God's truth," Edward said.

Ephraim eyed Coleman and stepped in, letting the door close behind him. "Who is your friend, Edward?"

"This here's Coleman. He's the one come to look at the mound." Coleman extended his hand. The man took it and gave a single shake.

Edward said, "Coleman, this is Ephraim Hopkins. He owns the drug store."

"My pleasure," said Coleman.

"Same." The man stared for a long moment. "I know that you're here to look into our mound. However, you'll soon find out that there is nothing much to it. It's just a mound that's been here a long time. And nobody's going to go digging it up. So, you might as well take your notes and then go on back up north."

A chemical odor drifted from the druggist's clothes, rubbing alcohol with a hint of lemony sourness. His lip quivered a little and stilled, retaining the hint of a sneer.

Edward stood up, his massive frame dwarfing Ephraim. "There ain't no reason to be rude. He's our guest."

The druggist stepped back and said, "You had best keep your nose out of our business." Ephraim turned and walked out.

Edward said, "Don't pay him no never mind. He's always snippety."

Coleman's eyes followed the druggist down the street until he was out of sight.

Coleman asked, "Why was he so angry? What's the big deal with the mound?"

Edward pulled his body back to its perch on the stool and chuckled, a rumbling sound coming from deep within.

He said, "Some people make a big deal out of everything. Ephraim's one of them."

Coleman took another bite of his burger. The door of the diner opened behind him. Conversation hushed. Edward turned on his stool and stared. Coleman turned to his right toward the door but saw no one. He felt a hand on his shoulder and a familiar voice in his left ear.

"Hey Coleman."

"Rosalee!"

CHAPTER 34

THE TOWN HALL

Moments after her arrival, Rosalee was in Coleman's makeshift office. He had ushered her away from the diner and out of public view as quickly as he could.

"How did you get here? How did you know where I was? I haven't been able to get in touch with you." Coleman rubbed his eyes, still not knowing if he should trust them.

She said, "I took a bus, same as you. I went to the college in Montgomery and I talked to somebody who was there when you were. After he was sure that I really knew you and wasn't trying to hurt you, he told me what had happened and that you came to this little town. He even helped me find a ride here in a produce truck."

Coleman said, "You didn't see –"

"No." Rosalee shook her head. "No sign of the shooter – at least I don't think so. I didn't get a good look at him that night and Montgomery is a crazy place right now. About anybody could hide there with all of the soldiers running everybody here and there. I was too busy watching out for myself. But, as far as I know, I didn't see him and he didn't see me. He's probably long gone."

Coleman saw color in Rosalee's cheeks and brightness in her eyes. She appeared stronger than he had seen her since before the shooting.

"Now that I know how you got here," Coleman leaned closer and said, "I need to know why."

Rosalee sat back, seeming to be running over a script in her mind. She shoved the script aside and said, "I couldn't let you be down here doing *my* work, doing what I set out to do long before I met you. So, I snuck out of the hospital after I talked to you. I found out I was better healed than I thought I was."

Coleman said, "Was there anything else? The things we talked about in the cemetery that night? I told you, promised you, that I would stay by your side."

Rosalee said, "Like I said, Coleman, all of that was a mistake. I didn't come here for you, not in that way. I came here for the cause. I came here because someone working for the cause, working for the cause on my behalf, might be in trouble. Don't try to make it more than that."

Coleman crossed his arms and said, "Well, I'm not in trouble."

Rosalee frowned and started to rise. "O.K. I guess I can go then."

Coleman said, "Why do you hate me? What happened?"

Rosalee settled back into the chair and said, "I don't hate you. If anything, I hate myself. I let my guard down. The stuff that happened to me with my parents and everything since then taught me to depend on myself. There in the cemetery, for just a little while, I took my eye off that. Look what happened. We both got shot and that policeman got killed. I should've never let you in. It only led to pain, pain for you and pain for me."

Coleman said, "I don't see how you can think that. How did opening your heart to me cause that man to shoot us? How could it have made any difference?"

Rosalee pointed at her chest. "It brought weakness into here. Animals like that man can sense weakness. They are drawn to weakness the way a wolf is drawn to a hurt baby deer."

Rosalee again started to rise. "If you don't need me here, I'm going to find a way to New Orleans or at least as far as I can get. Lots of the riders have been arrested as soon as they get into Mississippi."

Coleman said, "Please don't leave."

Rosalee said, "I don't know why I should stay. You said you didn't need me."

"That's not what I said. I said I wasn't in trouble." Coleman listened for any movement in the hall and said, "I need your help trying to figure out this place."

"What do you mean 'figure it out'?"

Coleman said, "This place is different. There's something going on. They're keeping secrets."

She said, "What kind of secrets?"

He said, "One thing is that there are white people and black people living together and getting along."

"That happens in plenty of places. Back in Washington, white people and black people live together and mostly leave each other alone," Rosalee said.

Coleman said, "That's not what happens here. They don't leave other alone. They live and work side-by-side. Besides that, the mayor's black — and a woman."

Rosalee said, "Really? A black woman mayor in a town in Alabama? That *is* a little strange. What do they say about it?"

He said, "Mostly something like 'That's the way we were raised.'"

Rosalee said, "Maybe that's true."

Coleman said, "I think there's more than that. There's something about the mound at the end of town that people aren't telling me. I don't know what it is, but they seem to not want me to find out the truth buried in the mound."

"What's so special about a big pile of of dirt?" she said.

Coleman said, "I don't know but it seems like it is connected to how people get along. I know it sounds crazy, but I think that something about the mound explains why this place is different."

Rosalee said, "Let's go dig it up."

"We can't do that! It's probably a burial site. Anyway, there's no telling what the people would do if they saw us digging." Coleman said. "We have to figure out how to find out more about this town and the mound without people getting too suspicious. Will you help me?"

The cool dim room seemed to shrink. The two of them sat in silence, both of them waiting for the answer to come. Coleman could see possibilities drift behind Rosalee's eyes. She finally spoke.

"I'll stay but not for long. No more than a couple of days."

Coleman nodded. "I leave on Monday anyway."

Rosalee closed her eyes for a moment. "O.K. I can stay until then."

Coleman said, "We'll have to tell the people that you came to help with the research. The first thing we need to do is go and talk to Pastor Henry. I'm staying with him and his wife. They have another room and so I think you can stay there too. We have to make sure he knows why you're here so that he can explain it to other people who ask."

Coleman said, "Another thing – we can't give any hint that we might be a couple."

Rosalee stood. "I got no problem with that."

"No problem at all."

CHAPTER 35

THE PARSONAGE

Pastor Henry stared at Coleman and Rosalee as they stood on the porch. A slight breeze stirred the hot air around. Silence stretched.

Rosalee thought, *What do I need to say?*

Finally, the preacher said, "So, why did you not come with the group at the beginning?"

Rosalee said, "I was too sick to travel at first. Then, I got better and here I am."

There was just enough of a ring of truth to be believable, especially with the traces of weakness that remained in Rosalee's eyes. When Pastor Henry's hard look finally softened, Rosalee gave an internal sigh.

Pastor Henry leaned back. "Very well. I'm glad that you're here. Of course, you may stay in our extra bedroom." The pastor turned toward Coleman and said, "Coleman, how has your research gone so far? How do you plan for Rosalee to help you?" Henry raised a glass of iced tea.

"To be honest," Coleman said, "I was just telling Rosalee that it seems like nobody wants to talk about the truth. Nobody wants me to find out anything about the mound."

Henry said, "What makes you say that?"

Coleman said, "There have been a couple things. First, even though this is a very small town, nobody seems to know much about its history. The other thing is that everyone seems to get along very well here. Colored people and white people. You even have a colored woman as your mayor. When I ask about this, all I get is something along the lines of, 'We're too busy living to hate each other' and 'It's always been this way here'."

Henry said, "It is true that people here are more interested in living a peaceful productive life than in looking at the differences between all of us. I think that also explains why we aren't as interested in the history of the town as we are in the present. We really are too busy living." Coleman remained silent.

Henry said, "The feeling that people aren't opening up much may be coming from a lack of trust." Coleman eyes shot up at Henry.

Henry said, "I'm not saying you're not trustworthy. I'm just saying that you can't expect people to tell you everything the first time you meet them. You have to give them a little more time to get to know you."

The fire in Coleman's eyes subsided. "I guess you're right," Coleman said. "Pastor Henry, there are millions of people in America right now whose lives are being ruined because of hatred. I'm talking about the Americans who just happened to have been born with dark skin."

Rosalee said, "My own father was shot and killed mostly because he was a black man."

Coleman said, "Our colored neighbors and friends are losing their homes and their places of worship and even their lives all because of hatred. But, I'm also talking about the people with white skin who can't see that the hatred is killing them from the inside. The hatred is turning them into tyrants and arsonists and killers. Rosalee and I see it every day in Washington."

Coleman absent-mindedly reached over and touched Rosalee's hand. Pastor Henry glanced toward the movement and Rosalee drew her hand away from Coleman's.

Coleman said, "Here in Jubilee, you have something special. It's like you are immune to the hatred. Those people out there need what you have. If there is anything we can do to bring what you have to them, we have to do it."

Rosalee saw again the compassion in Coleman's face. She felt his drive to protect. She remembered the thoughts she had in Arlington. She realized that the pastor was watching her.

Henry said, "I have to ask this. There has already been some talk in town. Are the two of you more than simply partners in your research? You seem to be awfully close."

Redness rushed to Coleman's face. He said, "No, of course not. Sure, we're friends but nothing more than that."

Rosalee frowned and said, "What if we are? Why does that matter?"

Henry held up his palms. "Don't get me wrong. I'm O.K. with that, but some people around here aren't. I just don't want you to have any trouble."

Anger burned just under the surface. Rosalee expected to face prejudice on her journey, just not from a preacher.

I should've expected it.

She thought of Mrs. Rucker and the way she almost worshiped her own pastor.

Just because they say they got the love of God in them, it don't mean they're different from anybody else. Just look at Dr. Browning.

Rosalee said to Henry, "I don't know why we should have any trouble. This is a free country."

Henry turned to Coleman and said, "I thought you said y'all weren't a couple."

Coleman shot a glance at Rosalee. "We're not." Coleman pushed his elbow into Rosalee's side. "Rosalee's just trying to make a point that people are free to love and partner with whoever they want."

Henry leaned back. "Actually, people aren't free to be with just anybody in Alabama or lots of other states. There is a law here that marriage between the races is not allowed. Not just marriage but " – he paused for a second – " any kind of physical relation. And it's not just southern states. Arizona, Indiana, Delaware, and a lot of other states have the same kind of law. I know a pastor in Missouri who was asked to marry a mixed race couple and he had to tell them no."

Rosalee said, "That's just crazy."

Henry said, "Maybe so, but that's the law."

Coleman moved down the steps toward the street and tried to pull Rosalee away with a look. Anger flared in her eyes.

Coleman said, "We're going to go and decide the next steps to take. Come on Rosalee."

Rosalee moved toward the steps.

The pastor said, "Coleman, before you go." Coleman stopped and turned.

Pastor Henry said, "Please be careful."

CHAPTER 36

MAIN STREET

Coleman led Rosalee past the sunrise monument, steering her toward the mound.

She said, "I saw that mound from the car. I didn't pay too much attention to it at the time, didn't know it was so important."

Coleman said, "It is important, at least to the people in this town. I don't know why."

Rosalee said, "Maybe we'll see something that will help it make sense."

The sun was high and hot. Sweat already ran down their backs. The glare meant that Coleman did not see Edward Jackson until he was almost right in front of them.

"Howdy Coleman. You ran out of the diner so fast that I didn't get to meet your friend," Edward said. He turned toward Rosalee. "Young lady, I hear you are here to help Coleman with his work." He stretched a moist hand toward her. "Edward Jackson's the name."

Rosalee let Edward's hand engulf hers. "Rosalee. Good to meet you."

Edward scanned the street from under a hand held up to his forehead. "Where y'all headed on such a hot day? You'd be better off sittin inside. In fact, why don't we go over to the shade where it might be a little cooler?"

Edward led them to the sidewalk. He offered a seat on an old green bench to Rosalee and she sat. Coleman waved off the offer and Edward sat, the bench slats groaning beneath him.

Coleman said, "I was taking Rosalee down to the mound to let her get a look at what we're researching."

Coleman followed Edward's gaze. There was no one else in sight.

The big man's voice became quiet.

He said, "Coleman, I think you might ought to be done with looking into the mound. Lots of people not real happy that somebody's here snooping around that old pile of dirt. Can't you just take what you got so far and call it a week?"

Coleman frowned and said, "Mr. Jackson, I don't know why this is such a big deal."

Edward said, "Well, I don't know what to tell you, but it is. And I got another thing to say. You might not like it."

Coleman's eyebrows went up. "What is it?"

Edward's gaze shifted to Rosalee and back to Coleman.

Edward said, "I don't think ya'll should be walking around together like you been doing. Folks be gettin the wrong idea."

Rosalee cleared her throat. "And what idea is that?"

Edward's voice got even quieter. "That y'all are a couple, you know, sweethearts or something."

Rosalee sprang from the bench. "I don't see how that's anybody's business but our own!"

Coleman said, "Mr. Jackson, we're not a couple, not sweethearts. We're just friends and coworkers on this project. Will you pass that around to the people?"

Edward nodded. "I can try but they probably won't believe me. It'd be better if y'all stayed apart and maybe just decided to go on home. I know that ain't a neighborly thing to say but I shore don't want y'all getting hurt or anything."

Coleman said, "We'll be fine. Nothing's going to happen to us here."

Coleman and Rosalee gestured goodbye to Edward and turned to walk.

Rosalee said, "I'm getting kind of tired having to say there ain't nothing wrong with us being together and knowing that we ain't really together."

Coleman remained silent.

Rosalee squinted into the copper-colored haze. "My God, it's hotter'n blue blazes out here!"

Coleman wiped his forehead with his arm. "Yeah, it's too hot to go to the mound right now. Let's go to the Town Hall."

As they crossed the street, Coleman saw Galen Whitmire staring at them from his store window. Coleman raised a hand and waved. Rosalee looked just in time to see Galen give a scowl and retreat to the interior of the store. Coleman chuckled.

Coleman's little room in the Town Hall felt like heaven after the hellish heat outside. Rosalee collapsed into a chair and leaned back, letting the cool dimness revive her.

While Rosalee rested, Coleman sifted through the papers on the table. The words on them blurred. His mind went blank and he saw Martelle's eyes, frosted orbs showing no detail, casting back only fear and confusion. Those eyes had looked into his very memory, dredging up things that had long been buried.

Coleman's mind flew. Images formed and dissolved. He saw a patch of white. Black scribbles appeared. The image became clearer.

The newspaper.

Coleman said, "Rosalee, we need to go upstairs."

Rosalee groaned. "We just got here. Let's cool off."

Coleman was already headed to the door. He said, "There might be a clue."

They climbed the stairs and saw no one else. Coleman's hand probed for the secret latch on the display case. Wood and metal moved beneath his fingers and he heard a click. He raised the glass lid and surveyed the contents. A small card leaned against the quilt, a detail he had not noticed before. The card gave a date – *1911* – and a name – *Esther Washington, Hero of Jubilee*. There was no other clue about the meaning of the card.

Coleman withdrew the scrap of newspaper. He said, "I found this downstairs. It's from an old newspaper, maybe the eighteen hundreds."

The fragile paper threatened to disintegrate in his hand. He held it up and saw only the title and the incomplete date. There was no other print, no other mark. He looked at the other items in the box. He replaced the newspaper and reached for the old sword that rested at the back.

As he removed the blade, its metal scabbard hit the rear wall of the display case and a wooden panel fell down, revealing a small compartment. Coleman replaced the sword and reached into the compartment. A folded paper met his touch and he retrieved and unfolded it. The paper was very old, though not as fragile as the newspaper. He closed the case and spread the paper on top.

Rosalee bent forward. "What is that?"

Coleman said, "It's a map."

Coleman immediately recognized the layout of Jubilee. The buildings of the town were just as he knew, the large bank building and its twin, the Town Hall. The same number of smaller structures. There was the hill and a symbol that denoted the monument, though the symbol on the map was not a sunrise but the entire sun, a complete disc with rays extending out all the way around.

"Look at this." Coleman pointed to the bottom of the map, to a drawing of a large mansion. Tall ionic columns graced its front. A wide wrap-around porch encircled the ground level and a broad veranda was visible on the second floor. The drawing was within a circle and the circle was connected by a line to the foundation of the old Russell mansion. Coleman searched for a date on the map.

"Here it says that this map was drawn in 1915." He pointed to the date in the right lower corner of the old paper. He said, "That's strange. The pastor's wife told me that the house was burned in the Civil War."

Rosalee said, "That would have been in the eighteen sixties, fifty years before this map was made."

Coleman's finger traced the line of the river on the right edge of the map. He counted four small cabins between the house and river.

He said, "Martelle said that these little houses were slave cabins before the end of the war."

Coleman's eye went to the top of the map and he saw two clusters of houses. These would be the North and South Communities. However, as he looked more closely, he saw different labels on these places.

He said, "Look at this. South Community is called Russell Village on the map and North Village is called Picaninny."

Rosalee said, "Maybe they just changed the names between 1915 and now."

Coleman's eye followed the small roads and they seemed to be the same as the ones at present. There was the circular drive in front of the monument and Main Street. He continued down through town to the other circular drive. He gasped.

"What?" Rosalee said as she leaned closer.

He said, "Where the mound is supposed to be, there's a church." Coleman turned the map. "That is clearly the hill and that is clearly the old house."

He repositioned the map as he first had it and leaned in. The church was labeled Russellton Methodist Church.

"What does it mean?" Rosalee said.

Coleman said, "It means we have to close this case and get back downstairs before anyone sees us."

Coleman folded the map. He pulled up his shirt and tucked the map into his pants. He reached back to the compartment inside the case, repositioned the false panel covering the compartment, and closed the case. He and Rosalee quickly retreated to the little room downstairs. As soon as the door was shut, Rosalee spun around.

She said, "What the hell is going on in this place? I'm beginning to see what you're talking about. We got to find out what they're hiding. This place is all mixed up. On the one hand, you got all this secrecy about a mound. On the other hand, you got people going crazy over two people walking down the street together just because one's white and one's black. On the other hand, you got black people having the same chance at getting ahead as white people."

Coleman smiled. "That's three hands."

Rosalee said, "We got four between us, don't we. All I'm saying is that it don't seem to add up. Why do they keep some big dark secret and frown on us being together but at the same time get along so well and let black folk have an opportunity to succeed?"

Coleman said, "People have an opportunity to succeed most

everywhere, whether they're white or black, if they work hard enough."

Rosalee fixed him in a cold stare and said, "Is that what you really think? That hard work is all you need?"

Coleman said, "Of course not. Luck is part of it and the talents you are born with. Hard work is a big part of it, though."

Rosalee said, "You are white. You can dream about things like having an important place in the world, living in a nice neighborhood, having a really good job and, because you are white, you have a pretty good chance of making it happen if you work hard or are lucky." She stood up a little straighter. "I am black, my people are black. No matter how much we dream about those things, not many of us will ever get them, no matter how hard we work. That makes us discouraged. And, after long enough, it makes us angry."

Her words pierced Coleman. He knew he had crossed a line, had stumbled into a blind-spot. He tried to gently guide the discussion back.

Coleman said, "Don't you think that it is different in Jubilee? That black people here are more – "

"Respected?" Rosalee said with raised eyebrows.

Coleman said, "Yes, respected. And valued."

Rosalee slowly nodded. "I guess you could say that."

Coleman pulled the map from under his shirt and said, "Why do you think it's like that here?"

Rosalee said, "I don't know." Her eyes scanned over the papers on the table and the map that Coleman had spread.

She looked Coleman in the eye. "I'm staying here to help you find out."

CHAPTER 37

THE PARSONAGE, THE NEXT MORNING

The distant rumble of thunder nudged Coleman from the depths of his sleep. Though not yet fully awake, his mind swam toward the surface of consciousness. He opened his eyes and saw the bedroom dimly lit for a second by lightning. Through the open window, Coleman could smell the ozone-infused rain.

Coleman was shaken as his heart slowed from its racing of a moment before. It was not the storm that had led to the panicked feeling. Instead, it was the dream that he had just experienced.

In his dream, Coleman stood in the dirt circle where the van had first left him days before. It was dark. He looked to his right and saw the white stones on the mound, glowing white in the shadows. In the waking dream he had days before at the base of the mound, the stones had been messengers, couriers of inspiration bringing him the courage he needed to go on. In this dream, however, the stones were the teeth of some ancient monster rising up out of the earth. He began to run down the street. He could hear the creature behind him, its hot breath on his back. As he came to the buildings, he could hear the sound of whispered cries coming out of darkened doorways and the black holes of windows. He ran as fast as he could, with his eyes fixed on the sunrise statue. However, the harder he tried, the slower he ran. He heard a scream behind him, a familiar scream, and he turned just in time to see Rosalee being attacked by the monster, her body crushed by those gleaming white teeth. The sound of her bones grinding jolted him awake.

His eyes grew accustomed to the dark. There was another dim flash of lightning, followed many seconds later by a deep pitched rumble of thunder. Coleman glanced at the clock ticking on the nightstand. Ten minutes after four. The storm receded, uttering diminishing murmurs over its billowing shoulders while it went. As the storm departed, however, it was not peace that was left in its wake, at least not in the heart and mind of Coleman. He felt confusion and turmoil.

He pivoted his legs out of bed and slipped into his clothes. He crept into the hall, paused at Rosalee's door, and heard soft snoring within. He moved quietly to the front door and went outside.

The sky was dark, faint stars visible in the rain-washed sky. The air was the coolest he had felt since arriving in Jubilee.

As he walked on the road around the base of the sunrise hill, facts, half-truths, and outright deception muddled in his mind. He remembered a B movie he had seen in which a town's inhabitants had been replaced with Martians and he thought that the film could have been set in Jubilee. It was becoming clear to Coleman that there were untold truths here.

Lots of them.

The piercing gaze of Martelle Fletcher snapped into view in his mind's eye. His stomach flipped. He closed his eyes and stood in the middle of the road.

How could he know? Coleman could feel Martelle peering into his memory like he was flipping through pages of a book. Coleman tried to forget about their meeting at the mound.

Gradually, the road and the hill dissolved into gray hulking shapes in the dimness. The gray became infused with wisps of green, tendrils that grew in length and breadth and wrapped around the foundations of his consciousness. Shafts of light shot through. His new view was infused with scents, the pungent smell of collards on the stove, elemental scents of earth and rock, the sickly sweet smell of tobacco. The scene came into focus. He was sitting in his grandmother's kitchen. Granny Mae knelt beside a girl seated in a tall ladder-backed chair. The girl was a little older than Coleman, probably eight or nine. Her hair was braided in pigtails. A cotton dress came to her dirty knees. She wore no shoes and the soles of her feet were thickly calloused. Granny Mae was examining the girl's hand.

"This here wart ain't too far along," Granny Mae said to the girl's mother who stood by the kitchen door. "I reckon we can try and see if we can get shed of it. Did you bring a rag?"

The mother handed Granny Mae a bit of worn cloth. The old woman stood and turned the girl's chair toward her. Granny Mae put a hand on the girl's forehead and placed the rag on the wart. The old woman began to chant, a low rumble coming from her chest. She blew in the girl's face and started whispering unheard words. At the same time, she rubbed the rag on the wart. The girl's eyes became glassy and she began to rock back and forth very slightly in the chair as Granny Mae continued to whisper. Granny Mae blew again and the girl's eyes blinked. The little girl looked around, confusion on her face. She saw her mother and rose and ran to her arms.

Granny Mae smiled and carried the rag to the mother. Granny Mae said, "Go and bury this somewhere good where nobody knows. That wart'll be gone in a couple of days."

The mother nodded her thanks and handed three large sweet potatoes to Granny Mae. Granny Mae turned and said to Coleman, "Run out to the spring house and fetch the butter while I put these on to boil."

She patted Coleman's head and the green hollow of memory evaporated and the gray road rematerialized.

They called her a conjurer. People came to her for healing from different ailments, bringing for payment something from their garden or sometimes, if the healing was particularly significant, a chicken or a hunk of salted pork. Granny Mae had started training Coleman to walk in her footsteps, but it soon became clear that Coleman's destiny lay elsewhere. Coleman was not interested in the healing arts and never entertained that he carried any of her healing proclivities in his being.

Before going off to college, Coleman's father had said, "I always reckoned you'd do what Granny Mae does, you know conjurin. I figured that's what your mama woulda done if she hadn't passed."

"Papa, that's not what I wanna do."

His father said, "Well, mostly life ain't about the wannas – it's about the haftas."

Coleman knew that being a conjurer in the isolated valley where he had been born was not his path.

What could Martelle have sensed in him? Was it some paranormal footprint, some vestige of ability that he had inherited from his grandmother?

More likely that Martelle's just crazy.

As he walked down the empty street, uncertainty swirled around Coleman's mind just like the moths that fluttered around the bare light bulb burning in the wall beside the five and dime door.

Maybe we should just go on, leave for New Orleans without telling anyone, maybe get arrested in Mississippi along with everyone else.

However, he wondered if Rosalee would travel with him. He doubted that she would.

Maybe it's time for me to move on, by myself. She sure doesn't seem to want me around.

Images scrolled inside his mind, scenes of dry dusty Western towns, sagebrush and cactus, towering rocky crags, images all done up in orange and purple and red and gold.

I could get lost out there, start over.

He knew deep down that running away was not an option. Martelle had seen inside him, just like Granny Mae could see beyond the physical world. Though Coleman was not a healer, he knew there were forces that were drawn to him and that drew him to them. He could never completely hide. God's will or destiny or spirits from another realm – he did not know what to call it or what others might call it, but he knew it was real.

He also knew there was a fight coming. He did not know how it would happen. Maybe it would be a fight for the truth. Maybe it would be a fight for his life. Or someone else's life.

Whatever it was, he must stay here, in this strange place steeped in dark mystery, and fight. He turned back for the house as the eastern sky brightened.

I've got to tell Rosalee.

CHAPTER 38

TOWN HALL

"Did Galen see you come in?" the mayor asked. She moved to the window. The sun was well up over the hill, making the buildings glow. She saw no movement in the street or the window of the five and dime.

"Nobody knows I'm here except Patsy." The pastor sat in a chair in front of the mayor's desk. He wiped a hand across his brow. "Thanks for letting me come talk to you."

"Have they found out something?" The mayor asked as she moved back to her desk. The old chair creaked as she sat.

"No, it's nothing like that." Henry leaned back and said, "I think we need to help Coleman."

"What are you saying?" She looked at him over her reading glasses. "We're trying to keep the secret and make all of this go away."

The pastor leaned forward, rubbed his hands, gathered his thoughts. He said, "I know. But maybe that's not the right thing to do."

The mayor said, "I don't know what you mean. I made a promise to the people of this town to protect them and to make this threat go away quietly. In my mind, it's working. He hasn't found anything yet, has he?"

Henry said, "No, not yet, but he is suspicious. He told me yesterday that he knew that people were keeping some kind of secret about the mound."

"Shit!" She looked up at the pastor. "Sorry."

The pastor held up a hand.

The mayor said, "Patsy told me that she saw Martelle Fletcher walking back from the direction of the mound not long before Coleman came to the Town Hall. I wonder if Martelle talked to Coleman."

Henry said, "There's no telling what Martelle might have said to him."

The pastor and mayor sat in silence. Pastor Henry broke the stillness. He said, "You know, people are talking about them, the two of them,

156

Coleman and Rosalee. Talking about them being a couple."

The mayor gave a slight nod and turned her face toward the ceiling, closing her eyes.

Pastor Henry said, "What do you say about that?"

"What do you want me to say?"

He said, "I don't know. I thought it might help you decide what to do?"

The mayor opened her eyes and faced the pastor.

She looks tired, he thought.

The mayor rubbed her face and said, "I don't think that it makes any difference. Back then, what we had just wasn't meant to be, not if we planned on staying here. We knew it. For the good of the town, for the good of these people here, we set it aside."

The pastor stared at the hazy sky through the window and said, "Maybe the times have changed. Maybe we should give Coleman and Rosalee a chance."

"Henry, this is not our fight. First off, we don't even know if they are together like that. Even if they are, my responsibility is to the people here. I'm not some kind of activist."

Henry said, "I know that but maybe the best thing you can do for the people of this town is to help them open their minds and hearts."

"Pastor, I think that's your job."

Henry said, "You're right but I can't do it alone. Not in this case."

The mayor said, "O.K. What is it that you want me to do? Just how am I supposed to protect the town from two outsiders and get the people of the town to accept them as they are at the same time?"

Henry said, "I think we should tell them."

The mayor said, "You don't mean tell them the truth?"

Henry nodded. "That's exactly what I mean. Tell Coleman and Rosalee the whole truth. Everything in the book."

The mayor stood and placed her palms on the desk.

She said, "Absolutely not! That's what I promised not to do."

Henry said, "What you promised is to make this end quickly and quietly. If we tell Coleman and Rosalee, I think they will be fine with the explanation and then they will move on. If we don't tell them, they will keep searching until they find out the truth anyway. Or until someone does something stupid and gets them hurt. Or worse."

"You really think Galen would go that far?" she said.

"You're the mayor and you know him better than I do, but I think Galen would be willing to do anything to keep the secret. Of course, he's probably the one with the most to lose if the truth gets into the wrong hands."

The mayor said, "It would be bad for everyone."

She collapsed into the protesting old chair, her head back, facing the ceiling.

She said, "I'd be worried that telling them will just make Galen act sooner rather than later. I don't think that telling Coleman and the girl is the thing to do. We just need to keep on watching them and making sure they don't go any further."

The pastor stood. "Whatever you say. Like I said, you're the mayor."

She said, "Yes, I'm the mayor, and I hope I'm doing the right thing."

CHAPTER 39

MONTGOMERY, ALABAMA

When he first arrived in the city, he thought he might have an easier time finding somewhere to sleep and enough to eat. He had always thought of the weather down here as mild, a place where sandy beaches were washed with warm ocean breezes and where food left behind by hospitable southern ladies was plentiful.

However, Montgomery was much different that he had expected. Stern-faced soldiers patrolled the street, helmets perched on their heads, rifles held at the ready. Almost daily, one of the soldiers yelled at him. "Hey, you! You're going to have to move along. Can't sleep there."

He was relegated to the dirty forgotten backstreets of the city, places patrolled not by soldiers but by roving bands of feral dogs that were fierce competitors for the meager scraps of food found in impromptu dumps that hid in the alleys. It was not long before he realized that he could not stay here.

He knew that he would have to make the telephone call.

He scrounged enough change to make the call, not trusting that a collect call would be accepted, in fact knowing for a certainty that it would not. The phone rang only a couple of times before he heard the familiar clipped voice.

"Hello, this is Dr. Browning."

"Hey." He waited, half expecting the line to click and suddenly go dead. There was silence on the other end. "Know who this is?"

"Of course." Dr. Browning's voice remained even. "It seems that our former arrangement did not proceed as agreed."

The killer said, "I didn't mean to shoot them. I was running and was trying to catch up to give'em a real scare. I was going to shoot up in the air.

But the gun went off too soon and then I had to shoot my way out of there with that policeman showing up and all."

Dr. Browning said, "I suppose it is just as well. The desired outcome was accomplished. That boy will not reflect poorly on the church. Where are you now? And why are you calling me? I thought I made it clear that this arrangement ended our dealings. Did you not get the money?"

The killer said, "I had to run. Nobody saw me or anything and the gun's at the bottom of the river but I couldn't take no chances. I come south."

"And the money?"

"That's why I'm calling you. The money's run out."

"That is not my problem."

The killer chuckled. "I'm making it your problem. The money's run out because I had to run. It cost money to get down here."

"And, again, just where are you?"

"Montgomery, Alabama. There's a Western Union at the bus depot where you can wire me some money."

"As I have said, our dealings have ended."

"Is that so?" The killer's sneer came across the phone line. He said, "Even if I tell you I know where that boy is? The one you hired me to scare? And more than that – he ain't alone. The nigger girl's with him." There was a pause on the line. "Hey, you still there?"

"I'm here."

"The boy hitched a ride to some little town a ways from here and then the nigger girl come a few days later and went there too. I can wrap up this business, but only if you wire me some money, same amount as before."

Dr. Browning said, "That is too much."

The killer said, "O.K. Fine. I'll just call the newspaper and tell'em everything I know. It'll be a big story. *Preacher Hires Hit Man.* That'll look real good on the front page. They'd probably pay me." He held the receiver away from him as if he was about to hang up. "I think I'll just forget about you and call them right now."

"No," Dr. Browning said. "I suppose it is reasonable to send you more money. I'll wire it to you today, same name and amount as the last time."

"That's real good."

Dr. Browning said, "Listen to me. You must clear this up. I do not want that fellow, Coleman, or his Negro companion to cause any more trouble. Do you understand me?"

"I understand you just fine. This'll probably be the last time you ever talk to me."

"That is my intention."

"Yeah, that's fine with me too." The killer gave another little chuckle. He said, "When Mama told me that my daddy was some high-falutin preacher, I didn't believe her. After she died and I hunted you down, I was glad. Glad that I had somewhere to get some spendin money from time to time. But now I know. You're just a goddamn son-of-a-bitch and I'm real happy to get shed of you." He quickly added. "After you wire me that money."

From the receiver, the killer heard, "It will be there shortly" and then a click.

The killer smiled as he hung up the payphone.

"Thanks, Daddy."

CHAPTER 40

MAIN STREET

Saturday's sun went to work as soon as it cleared the hill, spreading a suffocating haziness over the town. Coleman returned from his early morning walk and woke Rosalee. They walked in silence through the shimmering heat, headed toward the Town Hall.

Humidity pressed in on them from all sides, the mugginess seeming to liquefy in their throats. Crows sat on the edges of rooftops, their mouths open and their bodies sluggish. It was the kind of day that drove early into the minds of every son and daughter of the South the absolute truth that hell was hot and that heaven was a cool comfortable place that offered up sensations akin to sitting on a smooth rock with your feet dangling in a mountain stream.

As they walked, a dog loped from the sunny street into the shade of the store awnings on the other side of the street and collapsed, panting until it rose and ambled off to find water. Edward Jackson exited the diner and walked toward them.

"It's already a hot one. Gonna get hotter." When the big man got closer, he said, "I sure was hoping y'all'd be gone by now. No offense."

Coleman said, "Seems like there's some unfinished business here for us."

Edward said, "I passed around the tale that y'all ain't sweethearts and that you're just here doing some harmless work and won't nothing bad come of it. Some folk took it and some folk didn't. Ain't nothing more I can do."

Rosalee crossed her arms in front of her and remained silent.

Coleman said, "I appreciate you trying. We won't be here much longer. The car's coming for us on Monday and we'll be gone."

Edward said, "I just hope everybody'll leave you alone until then."

"Mr. Jackson, I wanted to ask you something," Coleman said and paused when he saw movement. Ephraim Hopkins was standing at the large plate glass window of his drug store, staring at the trio, a scowl on his face. The druggist abruptly turned and picked up a telephone receiver.

Edward did not notice Ephraim. He said, "What is it?"

Coleman cleared his throat and said, "I just wondered if you know of any bad things that happen here in Jubilee. Like robberies or murders or anything."

The big man gave a squinted-eyed glance at Coleman and Rosalee.

He said, "I guess it seems a little quiet around here to someone from a big city like Washington, but y'all'd probably be surprised at the problems we have from time to time. It's family things rather than stealing or killing or such."

Rosalee said, "What kinds of family things?"

Edward wiped his brow with the back of his hand. The growing heat had deposited great patches of sweat under his arms.

He said, "Young lady, it's mostly fights between husbands and wives. The sheriff'll get a call from a neighbor that 'so-and-so is fighting again'. He'll go around there and try to settle things down. Every once in a while, somebody won't listen to reason and will get locked up. A few years ago, we had a man who actually beat his wife. He's in prison down in Atmore. We also have a few men and even a couple of women who drink too much sometimes and they got to be brought in to let'em dry out."

Coleman asked, "How about problems between colored people and white people? Do you ever have to face that?"

Edward said, "You know, I have to be honest, I do wonder sometimes whether some white people around here have a feeling down deep in their hearts that they's better'n me. But, even when one of my white neighbors is mad at me about something, they don't ever bring up the color of my skin." He gave a deep chuckle. "Now, I have had somebody suggest that my mother was a dog." He smiled. "But he didn't call me a *black* son-of-a-bitch or something worse than that."

Rosalee asked, "Why do you think it's like this in Jubilee when it's not in other places?"

Edward said, "I think it is just the way we was raised. Our mamas and our papas taught us that the color of a person's skin was not the important thing. We all live together in this tiny little town. Our families have all lived here for generations. If we didn't get along with each other, the town wouldn't be here."

Across the street, Ephraim Hopkins exited the drug store and walked to the five and dime. Again, the big man did not notice the druggist.

Edward said, "I'd better get back to work. I'll keep on telling everybody what y'all want them to think." He patted Coleman on the shoulder and walked away.

As he and Rosalee were turning to go to the Town Hall, Coleman again saw movement in the drug store window. Lois Green had come to the window and peered out. Her eyes met his and he saw concern, maybe tinged with fear. He pointed at his chest. She gave a single nod and retreated into the interior of the store.

Coleman glanced toward the five and dime and saw no activity. He gently pulled Rosalee's hand and they crossed the street and entered the drug store. Lois was at the back counter. Her head swiveled up as the door opened and closed.

Coleman said, "Lois, did you want to talk to us?"

Lois whispered, "I don't know when he's coming back."

Coleman said, "We didn't see any sign of him just now. He went in Mr. Whitmire's store. What is it?"

She said, "You need to stop asking about things. Especially the mound."

Coleman shot a glance at Rosalee and said, "That's what we've been told."

Rosalee said, "What do you know about the mound?"

Lois said, "Enough to know that y'all should leave it alone. Mr. Hopkins is out to get y'all if you keep snooping." She held her hands to her chin as if praying. "Just leave it alone and get out of Jubilee as quick as you can."

Coleman said, "I just can't believe the mound could be anything that bad." He looked at her eyes and saw fear. "Why won't someone tell us something?"

Lois said, "I've already said more than I should. You got to leave before Mr. Hopkins gets back." She scurried to the storeroom in the back.

Coleman motioned to Rosalee. They walked to the door and peeked outside. There was no one in view.

They stepped onto the street. A furnace blast breeze blew into their faces. They hurried to the Town Hall and retreated to the little room where they collapsed into chairs. Sweat soaked their clothes as they leaned back and waited for the dimness to give back the vision that the sun had stolen.

Rosalee said, "So what now? We know something's going on. How are we going to find out what it is?"

Coleman said, "I don't know yet, but I have a feeling that whatever is going on here is big and important, like it could help other people too."

Rosalee frowned. "What do you mean, help other people?"

He said, "Look at the town. It's different here, both of us can see that. What if there is some secret that can help black people and white people everywhere get along? Shouldn't we at least try to find out?"

Rosalee said, "You heard Edward. It's just because this is a little town and everybody's always known each other. There's not any deep dark secret about that."

Coleman said, "What about the mound? It's obvious there's something about it that people don't want us to know."

Rosalee nodded. "Yeah, but that don't mean that it has anything to do with blacks and whites getting along." She sat back and gazed at Coleman for a moment. "I know you want to find out about this place. I want to know the truth too, but in the end it just ain't that important. I'm fine staying here another couple of days, but then I'm moving on to what I really came down here to do. I'm heading toward New Orleans."

Coleman's face was impassive. "You might be going on without me. I know the plan is to leave on Monday, but I don't know that I'll be ready to go then."

Rosalee held up her hands. "Fine by me. You and me, we can go along together for a while or we can split up. It don't matter to me."

Coleman said, "Another thing. I got a feeling that things might get rough, that there might be some kind of fight."

Rosalee said, "What do you mean, you got a feeling? I can tell the people here don't like us very much."

"It's more than that." Coleman said. Hazy memories flitted through his mind. "Sometimes, I get a feeling that I can see things before they happen."

Rosalee said, "Do you mean fortune telling?"

Coleman said, "No, nothing like that. Just I get a feeling or even a vision of things that haven't happened yet." Granny Mae floated in front of his mind's eye. He heard her chant, felt her healing hands on his shoulders. "I think it might run in my family. My grandma was a healer."

Rosalee chuckled. "Like one of those people who do like this –" she put her palm on her forehead and jerked her head back, "– and say 'Be healed'?"

Coleman crossed his arms. "No, not like that. She would just help people with different problems, like warts and burns and colds and stuff like that."

Rosalee said, "What did she do?"

"For a burn, she would draw the fire out. She would put some kind of a cloth on the burn and say some words. She said that you had to stop the fire from getting to the bone or the person might die."

"That sounds crazy."

Coleman said, "It might sound crazy, but it worked. I saw people get better real fast after she treated them."

Rosalee said, "What does that have to do with seeing the future?"

"Sometimes, people would ask Granny Mae to help them make decisions. They thought she could see how things would turn out."

"Could she?"

"I don't know. She never told me."

Rosalee said, "Are you a healer? Can you see the future?"

Coleman said. "I know I'm not a healer. Granny Mae started to teach me but I never really liked it."

Rosalee said, "How about the other?"

Coleman stared into the dark corner of the room. "I don't know. Sometimes, I think I can see the future or at least get a hint about it."

Rosalee sat for a few moments and then started to rise. She said, "Like I said before, that sounds crazy."

She moved toward the door.

"Where are you going?" Coleman asked.

Rosalee said, "Outside. I've got some things to think about."

CHAPTER 41

THE MOUND

She barely noticed the heat as she shuffled down the covered sidewalk. Disparate thoughts flashed before her, bidding her to leave or urging her to stay.

What does all of this craziness mean?

She had never given much thought to premonitions or intuition or to anything that she could not touch or see.

There's too much in the here and now to go worrying about stuff that might not even happen. But, what if he's right? What if there is something here?

The sidewalk ended and she stepped into the bright sunlight. The heat pressed on her. She lifted her eyes and saw the mound and her feet carried her in that direction. She saw a patch of shaded grass at the wood line near the old springhouse and moved toward its relative comfort. A log lay at the edge of the grass. She sat.

The mound crouched in front of her, its stones almost blindingly white. *What's in there?*

The memory of her father strolled into her consciousness. It had been a hot day like this one. As he walked toward her, she sat on the sidewalk, looking at a big black beetle, its lifeless hulk squatting on the sidewalk. Half of its shell was gone. A swarm of little red ants was milling around the dead beetle. A steady red stream filed inside and reemerged, carrying off unseen bits of insect flesh. She picked up the beetle and felt how delicate it was. She shook the ants out and as she did, the beetle turned to powder between her fingers.

Her father said, "Better not let your mama see you touchin that bug. She'll tan your hide. She thinks bugs carry diseases."

"Do they?" She squinted into the sun.

"Some do, probably. Not that one, though." He sat down beside her.

167

"Daddy, why do bugs die?"

He said, "Everything dies."

"Rocks don't die." She looked around. "Mailboxes don't die."

"They're not alive. You have to be alive to die."

She turned back to the dust that had been the beetle. "Do bugs know they're alive?"

On that hot Baltimore day, her father did not have an answer. In the years since, the question reappeared in Rosalee's mind from time to time, like the nagging ache of a seldom-used muscle that makes it hard to fall asleep.

What does a bug know about its life? What do any of us know?

I know I'm alive, but what does that mean? Does it help me know what to do?

The pull of the Freedom Riders was strong. She had planned to be a part of that group. If she had been, if she had not fallen to the shooter, she might have faced the flames of Anniston or the beatings of Birmingham and Montgomery or the jail cells of Jackson. She felt the weight of duty but, if she was honest with herself, she also sensed the thrill of importance, the heft of history that came with the actions of her C.O.R.E. colleagues. She wanted to be there, in the thick of battle.

Maybe the opportunity has passed. Maybe my place isn't there but here.

As soon as she thought it, she tried to reject it. She had given Coleman access to her dreams before, there in the cemetery. She knew it must have been a mistake.

The mound's stones summoned her vision. What was it? Movement? At the periphery of the mound, toward the old house's ruins, shadows coalesced and rose. The shimmering heat obscured details. A dark shape gathered form and began to move toward her. Rosalee shifted on the log, preparing to flee. The shadowy shape morphed into a figure, a man, but unlike anyone she had ever seen. He was remarkably thin and seemed to float instead of walk. Even from a distance, she could see his piercing blue eyes.

He said, "What you doing out here?"

The high-pitched voice caused Rosalee to come out of her trance and realize that this specter was actually flesh and blood.

"Just sittin." She willed herself to remain calm.

Martelle wiped his forehead. "Ain't nobody just sittin on a day like this one. Why you out here by the mound?"

Rosalee swallowed the tiny amount of saliva in her mouth.

She said, "I was walking and just ended up here."

He said, "Hmm. I know that you and that boy been asking around about the mound and other stuff. Like I told him, y'all best be keeping out of our business and gettin on back to wherever it is y'all from."

Rosalee's fear started to dissolve, being replaced with the first sprouts of indignation.

She said, "I don't see why everybody's so worried about us asking about this pile of dirt."

Martelle looked over his shoulder at the mound. "I guess we figure that it's *our* pile of dirt and nobody else should go poking around in it."

Rosalee said, "It's not like we're digging up anything. We're just asking questions."

Martelle said, "Why is it any of your business?"

Rosalee's voice rose. "Cause it is. Coleman's here cause he has to be."

Martelle's eyebrows went up. "What about you?"

Rosalee said, "I'm here to help him."

Martelle turned toward the town and moved to leave.

He said, "If y'all know what's good for you, you'll just drop it and go on home."

Rosalee said, "Is that a threat?"

Martelle chuckled and said over his shoulder, "No, I don't make threats. I just tell it like it is."

Rosalee's mind was clear, even if the heat still spread haziness over the town. She looked at the mound for another moment and began to walk back to the town, back to Coleman.

CHAPTER 42

THE PARSONAGE

Coleman lay in bed. The ceiling fan was stingy with its comfort, merely pushing warm air around the room. As Coleman stared up, a conversation with Rosalee ran though his mind. Just before bed, she had told him about her walk, whom she had encountered. The mound came back to Coleman, its green turf, tooth-like stones scattered about. Then he saw the eyes of Martelle Fletcher, eyes that peered deep inside him.

His grandmother's eyes had been brown, nothing like the milky blueness of Martelle's. But they shared a certain piercing nature, an ability to see past the externals, to look deep inside at the essence.

"I can see you're gonna turn out different 'n your daddy."

She sat across the kitchen table from Coleman, watching him while he ate biscuits dipped in sourwood honey. Golden gooiness escaped the biscuits and ran onto his fingers. She pushed a dishtowel and a glass of buttermilk across the table. He licked his fingers and wiped them on the towel.

"Now wash it down." He took a big gulp.

"What do you mean, Granny Mae?"

He did not want to be different. He wanted to be big and strong and to drive a pick-up truck and to have a rough face that prickled his son's face when he kissed him.

She smiled, took the towel, and wiped the buttermilk from his lips.

She said, "You're gonna be a kind man. You're gonna help people. You might even be a conjurer, I don't know. But, I know for sure that you're gonna give your life to truth, not to scrabbling in the dirt for money."

As he lay there, his mind thumbed through the pages of his memory, flashes of gold-sunlit childhood summers, the missing mound on the map, the feel of Rosalee's lips touching his, the taste of coffee in the

Lamb of God rectory. He tumbled through visions and emotions. There was no firm present on which to stand, only the fluid past that floated and reordered itself and drifted up to meet him and glided away. The little bed disintegrated and he was on an ocean of time. Waves rose and fell. At the crest, he could make sense of the flow of images. In the troughs, he was borne away from reality.

He opened his eyes. The sweat had evaporated. He shivered. A feeling of failure and futility cloaked him.

At dinner, Pastor Henry had pressed for details of their plans, had questioned them about their progress, had asked about the reason for Coleman's melancholy. Coleman remained quiet and Rosalee followed his lead.

In the dark, Coleman struggled over the same question he had faced in quiet moments for days. He felt the need to be honest with the pastor. The kind clergyman had encouraged him and seemed protective. Coleman felt a kinship. He felt he could no longer lie to him. Somehow, Coleman knew he could trust the pastor with the truth.

He rose from bed and crept down the hall. He stopped at Henry and Mary's room and tapped on the door. "Pastor Henry," he whispered.

A sleepy voice answered. "Coleman, what's wrong?"

Coleman said, "I need to talk to you and it can't wait until the morning."

Henry ushered Coleman to the den and clicked on a little lamp.

"What do you need to tell me?" Henry said as he sat in his chair.

Coleman said, "The truth."

The pastor sat back, his hands in his lap. "Very well. What truth are we talking about?"

Coleman said, "The reason I am here and about Rosalee."

Coleman told the pastor everything – the inauguration, the attack, his meeting Rosalee, C.O.R.E., the shooting, his coming south on the bus, his running from the killer, Rosalee's coming to Jubilee.

After his revelation, Coleman said, "I really think that whatever there is in this town, it might help people in other places."

Pastor Henry said, "You might be right."

Coleman said, "I also think that whatever is in the mound might be related."

Pastor Henry said, "What have you found so far?"

Coleman said, "I haven't found anything about who actually built the mound. But, I did learn a little about the history of the town and how it used to have a different name. Russellton."

"Yes, that is correct," Henry said in an even voice. "The Russells owned the big plantation house that was burned in the war. The old town was named after them."

Coleman said, "That's part of the problem. I found a map that showed the plantation house before it was burned. The map was dated 1915, fifty years *after* the Civil War ended. That doesn't make sense. And on the map, the mound isn't there. A church is there instead."

Henry's face was blank. If not for the dimness of the room, Coleman would have seen the color of that face drain away. Henry was quiet for a long moment.

"I see," he said. "And where did you find this map?"

"In the Town Hall."

"Have you told anybody else about this map?" Henry asked.

"No. I wasn't sure what it meant and didn't want to cause trouble." Coleman said. "It seems like a lot people are concerned about that mound. They don't want me to find out much about it."

"Has Galen Whitmire talked to you?"

Coleman leaned back. He said, "I think I've already said too much. Never mind. I'll be leaving after tomorrow and everything will be fine."

Henry said, "No, Coleman. I need to know if Galen has threatened you. That is not right and I need to say something about."

Coleman held up his palms. "No, no, it's nothing like that. Everyone's been nice. Or, at least, they have not threatened me."

Henry sat in silence, waiting.

Coleman said, "Martelle Fletcher came out to talk to me when I was at the mound. He did the same to Rosalee today."

Henry nodded. "Listen Coleman, I need to tell you about Martelle. You've probably never met anyone like him."

Coleman said, "Actually, I have." Henry's eyebrows went up. "My grandmother was what they call a conjurer. People would come to her for healing and other things, like help with making decisions."

Henry said, "That's very interesting. And you're right, Martelle Fletcher is that kind of person, someone who can do things that other people can't – or at least that's what he tells them." Henry leaned forward. "But Martelle is not like your grandmother. He doesn't do it to help people. Martelle is a root doctor."

"A root doctor?"

"Yes. Some people around here believe Martelle can cast spells and make bad things happen to people. They believe he can make them sick or even die." Coleman's eyes widened. "Those people pay Martelle and he then digs up a root and says some kind of magic words to it before burying it. A lot of people around here believe in that sort of thing."

Henry watched Coleman's face. Fear was in those young eyes.

"Of course," the pastor said, "I don't believe all of that. I know that the spiritual world exists. But, I don't believe that the unseen forces we read about in the Bible can be controlled by people like root doctors and witches and such."

172

Coleman breathed deeply. "What do you know about the mound? Strange that it is not there on that map."

Henry said, "Coleman, you have to understand. There are people here who do not trust outsiders. I believe it's just best to lay the mound aside."

"What if someone wanted to come and dig into the mound?"

Henry's eyes widened.

"Are you saying that is what you want to do?"

Coleman said, "No, not us. I'm just asking what if someone else wanted to do that?"

Henry said, "Of course, that would not be possible. That mound could be a sacred site. It wouldn't be right to dig it up. We couldn't allow that."

Coleman sat back. "What do you mean, it might be a sacred site? Don't you know what it is?"

Henry said, "Since you have been honest with me, I'll tell you what I can about the mound." Coleman leaned forward. "You are correct that the mound has not been there that long. As your map says, it was after 1915. The mound was made during a difficult time in our town's history and no one here wants to talk about it, especially not with outsiders. I'm very sorry Coleman, I can't tell you more than that. I don't have any direct memory of that time and I doubt that anyone who does would be willing to talk to you."

Coleman's face fell. "So that's it? There's nothing more you can tell me?"

Henry held up his hands. "I'm afraid not. I'm sorry."

Coleman said, "We're going to keep looking tomorrow."

Henry sat back. "Coleman, like I told you, no one who knows anything is going to talk to you." The pastor leaned forward and placed a hand on Coleman's knee. "I don't want you to get yourself in trouble. You've got Rosalee to think about also."

Coleman shifted his leg away from Henry's touch.

"To be such a peaceful place, there sure are a lot of threats coming our way."

Henry said, "Coleman, you know that I would never threaten you. I'm only giving you some advice as a friend."

Coleman stared and said nothing.

Henry glanced at the clock. "I'd better get ready for bed. Sunday morning comes early for me."

He turned back to Coleman and said, "Think about what I said. Think about Rosalee and what is best for her."

CHAPTER 43

JUBILEE COMMUNITY CHURCH

Coleman and Rosalee went to church on Sunday morning with the pastor and Mary. The musty smell of the church building brought to Coleman's mind memories of Sunday mornings with Granny Mae, walking hand-in-hand with her down the aisle to take their place in her accustomed pew. Feelings of terror at the thought of hell-fire, the taste of peppermint sticks Granny Mae would pull out of her purse to keep him quiet, the recollection of the warmth radiating off the pot-belly stove in the corner of the sanctuary, all of these flooded his mind as they entered the vestibule of the little Jubilee Community Church.

At the same moment that his eyes were drawn to a portrait hanging on the wall, he heard Mary saying, "John, this is Coleman. He's been staying with us this week. This is his friend Rosalee." Coleman and Rosalee shook the man's hand. After several more greetings, Mary moved to enter the door to the sanctuary of the church while Coleman took a slight detour to examine the portrait.

The faded photograph was in an ornate gilded frame. The face belonged to an old black woman, probably in her seventies or eighties. Her dress was of dark cloth with a bit of lace on the collar. The face was not smiling but seemed serene. Her bright intelligent eyes stared straight into Coleman's. A tarnished brass plaque under the portrait read: *"Auntie" Esther Washington, 1845-1921.*

"Who is it?" Rosalee whispered.

Coleman said, "The woman on the card in the display cabinet."

Mary said, "Coleman, come on. The service is about to start."

Mary led them to a pew about halfway down the aisle. The piano started playing as they neared the empty seats.

"All hail the power of Jesus' name, let angels prostrate fall…"

The words came out loud and strong from the standing congregants as Coleman, Rosalee, and Mary slid to their seats. Mary fished the hymnal out of the holder on the back of the pew in front of them. A little girl standing in front of them turned and smiled up at Rosalee. She returned the smile. Several singing faces turned and nodded.

The congregation was asked to sit. After some announcements and a passing of the offering plate – Mary waved off Coleman's attempt to place a dollar in the plate with a whispered "You're our guest" – Henry rose to the podium to deliver his sermon. As Henry began to speak, Coleman thumbed absently through the hymnal. The words written inside the front cover caught his eye – *Presented to the Jubilee Community Church by the Esther Washington Sunday School class.* He wondered what made Esther Washington so important.

The pastor's speaking his name interrupted his thoughts. "Coleman Hightower," the pastor said while motioning his outstretched hand in Coleman's direction "has been staying with us for the past week and his coworker Rosalee joined us a couple of days ago. They, unfortunately, are going to have to leave us tomorrow. Thank y'all for making them feel welcome this week and, Coleman, thank you for choosing our town for your research. I hope we have lived up to the trust you have placed in us."

Trust. Coleman's eyes drifted to the cross hanging on the wall behind the pastor, a crude cross fashioned from pine boards, old iron nails visible in its joint. It was a much different cross from the majestic one hanging in the Lamb of God.

What does trust even mean?

Coleman had trusted Dr. Browning, had placed his life and his future in the hands of a man who had said he had Coleman's best interests at heart. He glanced around the church, considering the profiles of those he saw, looking away when they felt his eyes on them and started to turn toward him.

Is there anyone here who I can trust? Even the pastor has secrets he is keeping.

After the service, as they passed through the vestibule, Coleman looked over his shoulder at the portrait. The placid eyes stared at him, seemed to follow him. It was almost as if the mouth was about to move, to utter words that would make all clear, that would lift the confusion.

Mary said, "Let's go on home and get y'all some dinner."

He kept looking until they exited. The bright sun broke the spell, bringing him back through the mists of the past to a stark present.

After lunch, Rosalee stood up and started to help Mary with the dishes. Mary said, "No ma'am. I'm not going to let a guest of mine do the dishes. Y'all get on out of here and I'll clean up."

"O.K. I'm going to walk up to the sunrise monument then, let my lunch settle," Rosalee said.

Coleman said, "I'll meet you up there in just a little while."

Rosalee said, "See you there." The screen door squealed shut behind her.

Coleman went to his room and changed clothes. A blanket of depression fell over him. He slipped on his shoes and walked outside.

Coleman walked back up the road to the circle at the end of Main Street. He stood before the sunrise statue. His mind wandered back to his conversations of the previous week, the things he had learned, the things he had felt. His emotions swirled.

He could not make sense of everything. He was ready to climb in the car with Rosalee tomorrow and leave this place. He knew that she planned to go on, to join the Freedom Riders, in New Orleans or in prison, she did not seem to care which.

Where do I want to go?

A few months ago, he planned to remain at Rosalee's side. Now, it was clear that she did not want him there.

If I go with her, will I just being stringing myself along, making it harder than it has to be? Maybe I should just leave her now?

Where would he go? That was still the question.

Back to Washington?

That was out of the question. Dr. Browning would soon find out that he was back and Coleman had clearly seen the ruthlessness of his former mentor. He knew that Dr. Browning would stop at nothing to protect himself. Coleman would never be safe in Washington again.

He imagined the reception he would have if he returned to his father's house, the smirk that would paint his father's face. He anticipated his father's words.

Son, I told you this is a rough old world, even off in the big city. Ain't no place for you and me but here, in the mud.

Coleman could not face that.

The sense of failure that plagued him intensified.

He turned and looked down the street. Though the afternoon sun was hot, it was not quite as oppressive as the day before. Billowy clouds occasionally blotted out the sun, giving a little reprieve from its radiating heat. He did not see anyone on the street.

Where did Rosalee go?

He began to walk. As he neared the other end of the street, he glimpsed the mound. Again, he did not see anyone.

He turned and walked back, thinking that Rosalee may have walked down the North Community street instead. Movement in the edge of his vision caught his attention. Lois Greene was in the drug store. She tried to scurry out of his view when he turned her way. Coleman stopped. Still seeing no one, he walked to the store. The door was locked.

"Hey Lois. I saw you. Come out here and let me ask you something."

After a long moment, the woman slunk to the front window.

Coleman said, "Have you seen Rosalee?"

Lois kept her eyes on the floor. She shook her head.

He said, "She was supposed to be here, at the sunrise monument. Did you see her?"

Without looking up, Lois said, "She's gone."

Alarm leapt inside Coleman's chest. "Gone?"

Lois nodded, her face still down. "She got in a car and rode off."

Coleman stepped back and said, "That can't be. The car is not supposed to come until tomorrow and I'm supposed to go with her."

"Guess it came early."

It did not make sense. Coleman's mind scrambled for reason.

Could she have left me here without saying a word?

He turned back to Lois.

"Who was driving?"

Lois's head jerked up, a confused expression on her face. She parroted, "Who was driving?"

Coleman said, "Yeah, who was driving? Was it a man or a woman?"

Lois stammered. "I don't know. I think it was a man. Yeah, it was a man."

Coleman said, "What color was the car?"

"What? Oh, the color of the car. It was…"

He said, "What color was it?"

She said, "It was blue. I think it was blue."

Coleman said, "You don't know what color it was? Was it blue or another color, like red?"

Lois started to wring her hands. She said, "Yeah, it might have been red. I don't know."

Coleman knocked on the glass door. He said, "Lois, open this door. You're coming with me to the pastor's house."

"Why? I didn't do anything!"

"You're not telling me the truth."

"Yes, I am. She's gone!"

"I can see she's not here, but I don't think she just got in a car and rode off." Coleman knocked on the glass again and said, "Now open this door!"

Lois slowly walked to the door and turned the latch. Coleman jerked the door open, grabbed Lois's wrist, and dragged her to Pastor Henry's house.

After repeating again and again to Coleman and Pastor Henry that Rosalee left in a car, Lois began to cry.

Pastor Henry put a hand on her shoulder.

"Lois, I know it's hard, but if you know something you're not telling us, you've got to say so."

Lois nodded. "O.K.," she said in a soft tear-distorted voice.

Henry said, "Do you have something you're not telling us?"

She nodded.

Henry said, "Did somebody take Rosalee somewhere?"

Lois nodded again.

Henry said, "Was it Galen?"

Lois began to sob. She nodded.

Coleman erupted. "Where is she! Where did he take her?"

Still sobbing, Lois wailed, "I don't know!"

Coleman jabbed a finger toward Lois's face and said, "If anything happens to her, it will be on your head!"

Lois lurched toward Coleman, anger now coloring her face.

She said, "What about your head? I told you to quit prying but you didn't. And then that colored girl showed up. I know more than one person told you two to stop traipsing around but you didn't. Ain't a lot of this on your own head?"

Coleman started to move toward Lois. Henry stepped between them.

The pastor said, "O.K. Let's calm down. This isn't helping get Rosalee back." He turned toward Lois. "Did you hear anything about where Galen was taking Rosalee?"

Lois turned toward Henry, her face softening. She said, "Ephraim was helping him. That's all I know. Ephraim told me to tell the boy that the colored girl left town. I don't know anything else. I didn't see them take her."

Henry turned to Coleman. "We've got to get together a search party. I'll go over to North Community. I'll get Mary to go with you and gather everyone in South Community. That is, everyone who is not already with Galen."

CHAPTER 44

MAIN STREET

They spread out through the streets of the residential areas. About half of the houses were vacant. Most of the residents of the occupied houses agreed to help in the search.

By the time the group was assembled in the circle in front of the sunrise monument, the sun had begun to set and the early evening was made even darker by gathering storm clouds. Henry made a mental tally of those who were not here and who were thus assumed to be with Galen's crew.

His heart ached. Those people with Galen were his neighbors, members of his church, some close friends that he thought he knew, people that he had believed would have been unable to take part in the kidnapping of an innocent girl.

Is Jubilee really any different? We might not have riots and bombings and lynchings, but maybe we are just the same as places that do.

In a flood of emotion, he again felt the pain and despair that had tormented him all those years ago, anguish at being kept apart from the woman he loved, from the woman he still loved.

He turned to the crowd. He divided them into groups and sent them in different directions with instructions to return here in no more than two hours and to send a runner sooner if any sign of Rosalee was found.

Henry saw Coleman over the heads of the dispersing group and said, "Coleman, why don't you come with me? I'm going with the first group but I'm coming back here soon to see if there is word from any of the other groups."

Coleman said, "I've got to go on my own. Can't be with anybody right now. I want to be able to move fast."

Henry said, "Son, don't worry. We're going to find her."

Coleman turned and started down the street at a trot.

179

CHAPTER 45

THE MOUND

Coleman approached the mound and turned to run toward the woods that were opposite the old plantation house. A whistle from the direction of the ruins made him turn his head. Martelle Fletcher was walking down the drive. Coleman turned and charged toward the thin man.

"Where is she? Where have you taken her?" he yelled as he ran directly at Martelle, his fists clenched and face scarlet. "God help me, but I will kill you if you don't take me to her."

Martelle held up his thin hands. "Hold on a minute here. I ain't taken nobody nowhere. I heard there was trouble and I come to see how I can help out."

Coleman reached Martelle and grabbed the front of the thin man's shirt.

He said, "Don't try to play games with me! I know you work with Galen Whitmire and so you got to know where he's taken her!"

Martelle pushed his way out of Coleman's grip and straightened his shirt.

Martelle said, "It's true that Galen and me have done business before, but I ain't had nothing to do with anything he's done about your girl."

Coleman started to calm down. He saw no sign of anyone else and said, "Why are you wanting to help?"

Martelle did not answer the question. He peered into Coleman's eyes for a moment.

Martelle said, "When we was here at the mound before, I asked you if you had any kin that had the gift. You lied and told me that you didn't. Why?"

Coleman's mouth fell open. He said, "What does that have to do with anything? I've got to find Rosalee!"

Martelle said, "Just answer my question. I need to know why."

Coleman said, "I don't know. I just don't talk about that. My grandmother lived a much different life than me. I really don't know much about it."

Martelle stared, seeming to peer inside Coleman. Coleman shifted and was about to reach out and grab the strange man and try to shake some sense into him when Martelle said, "What I saw in your eyes the other day I've never seen around here before. I saw a white light and heard a woman's voice saying that this is a good 'un. I ain't been able to get it outta my mind since then."

Coleman did not know what to say. After a long moment, he said, "Are you going to help me?"

"I don't know," Martelle said as if to himself. "If I do, they're really gonna be pissed."

Martelle mumbled to himself. Coleman could not make out what he was saying.

Coleman said, "I don't know what you saw in my eyes the other day." Martelle blinked as if just waking from a deep sleep. "To be honest, I don't think you really heard my grandmother. I think you heard your own conscience, telling you that it is not right to hurt other people just to protect some long-kept secret, no matter what the secret is."

Martelle remained silent.

Coleman said, "And I don't know if I'm good or not. I just know that you will never be at peace if you help them hurt Rosalee."

Martelle was motionless, like he had been turned to stone by Coleman's words, some medusa-like power in his speech. Martelle blinked his eyes.

He said, "I didn't have nothing to do with this, but I do got an idea about where they got her. You stay around here until I get back."

Like some kind of dark spirit, he was gone.

CHAPTER 46

THE DEER CAMP

"Go tie her up in the slaughterhouse. I'm going behind the bunkhouse to take a leak. Be there in a minute."

Behind her blindfold, Rosalee prayed. She had never been a religious person, had received any faith in a higher power secondhand, first from her mother and then from Mrs. Rucker.

When Galen and Ephraim grabbed her from behind as she gazed at the sunrise monument and blindfolded her, she fought to the limit of her strength. At one point, she felt a fist slam into her face and she saw stars appear in the darkness created by the blindfold. After that, her arms and legs would not work and she was dragged quickly through what smelled like a pine forest. All through her journey, she struggled to remember prayers that her mother prayed.

Dear Jesus, help me in my turmoil, deliver me from my captors, remember me in my distress.

Rosalee heard a door being opened. She was pulled inside some kind of structure. She felt hands at the back of her head and the blindfold fell. She gasped.

She was inside a small wooden barn-like building. Two ropes dangled down from rusted iron pulleys that hung from a crossbeam. The ropes were caked with dried blood and flecked with bits of hair. As she was pulled across the single room of the structure, her feet stumbled over deer hooves, bits of bone, and broken antlers that were scattered on the dirt floor. Rough hands spun her around and pressed her back to a thick support post worn smooth by years of use while her nose was assaulted by the smell of blood and decay. As she was tied to the post, the beat of her heart matched the gallop of the ghosts of hundreds of deer, slain creatures that still haunted the site of their dismemberment.

The figure of Galen was silhouetted in the open door. He completed the closing of his pants zipper and said, "So, what is Lois going to say?"

From behind her came the voice of Ephraim. "That she saw the girl ride off in a car."

"Do you think they'll believe her?"

Ephraim finished tying the knot with a final jerk of the rope, stood, and walked toward Galen. "I told Lois she had to make them believe. Lois does what she is told."

Galen spat into the dirt. "I hope you're right. If they believe Lois, that boy will leave town searching for her. Right now, we gotta get rid of her."

Ephraim kicked at a piece of bone. "What if he comes looking for her?"

"We'll just have to get rid of both of them."

Rosalee was falling down a dark hole. She felt coils of panic start to entwine her heart and mind. She willed the fear away.

She said, "Why are you going to kill me? What did I do to you, to anybody here?"

The two men turned toward her with bewilderment on their faces, like the last thing they expected was for her to talk.

Galen said, "We told you to keep out of our business and to stop asking questions." He waved his hand toward Rosalee's bonds. "This is all your fault. Whatever happens is all on you and that boy."

Rosalee said, "But still, that don't mean you have to kill me, does it?"

Galen said, "We have to protect our town, our people. I don't want to have to do it, but you left us no choice."

Galen turned toward Ephraim and pulled a gun out of his belt. He opened the cylinder and spun it, showing Ephraim that there were six bullets in the pistol.

"Like I told you, Ephraim, right at the top of the neck. Use all of them just to be sure. Down by the river, below the flood line. Take some of the others outside to help dig. Shovels are right over there."

Ephraim glanced at the shovels leaning against the wall as he tucked the pistol under his belt. Galen tapped a finger on Ephraim's chest.

Galen said, "Not until dark. Don't want nobody seeing y'all."

Galen and Ephraim turned and walked out of the shed, closing the door behind them and leaving Rosalee without another word.

After a minute or two of silence, Rosalee saw that no one was coming to the shed to guard her. She began to twist her hands, flex her legs, anything to try to loosen the ropes that bound her hands and pinned her to the post. After several minutes of struggle, she had accomplished nothing except scraping her wrists and straining the muscles in her legs.

I been a fighter all my life. Ain't gonna stop now.

She saw a piece of bone near her feet and managed to scoot it closer to her. She thought that she might be able to use the sharp edge of the bone to cut the rope if she could get it into her hand. After an hour or more of trying, she was unable to move the bone very far and realized she would never accomplish the feat before nightfall.

She turned her mind to devising another plan. However, she found her mind wandering. She was back on the sidewalk in Baltimore with her piece of chalk. She was sitting on Mrs. Rucker's porch eating cobbler. She was immersed in impossible greenness and holding Coleman's hand.

Each time she discovered that she was not working on a plan, she urged her mind back to work. Finally, her mind revolted entirely and she drifted to sleep.

Rosalee woke with a start to the low rumble of thunder. She opened her eyes and saw that both the angle of the sunrays slipping between the boards of the barn and the intensity of the light was appreciably lower.

How many hours until dark? Three or four probably.

She had been fighter all of her life. However, now, sitting in the dirt floor of a slaughterhouse, she wondered why.

I fight against everything. Some things are right to fight against – injustice, hate, ignorance. But I fight against love and peace and happiness.

Peace. That was what she wanted. More than anything, she wanted to be at peace. At peace with the world, at peace with God, at peace with other people.

I want peace inside me, peace with myself, no more fighting against myself.

She had spent her whole life – or at least her life since the death of her mother – fighting against settling for anything less than perfection. Perfection in justice, perfection in law and order, perfection in herself and those around her.

No more fighting. I want peace.

She felt weight dropping from her, had a sensation that she was shrinking and expanding at the same time. She felt the ropes fade away, the shed degenerate. However, she did not feel free of her bindings but one with them. She felt no boundary between her wrists and the rope, between her body and the air, between the ground and herself. She felt that she was a part of the earth beneath her. She felt no separation between her blood and flesh and brain and bone and the earth's grass and soil and rock and water. The tips of her fingers, resting on the dirt floor of the shed, extended through the crusty and rocky sphere and touched all other beings.

I want peace with love.

She knew that God and His creation had been offering her love for years. Mrs. Rucker's motherly love, the love of friends, love offered by men – including Coleman – all of this love she had rejected to at least some degree. Rosalee realized she had been at war with love, the one force in the universe that had in its power the ability to provide the peace that she wanted. She surrendered.

I want peace.

There in the barn, hours or even minutes from her death, she smiled in the dirt and waited for Ephraim and his gun.

CHAPTER 47

THE MOUND

Coleman paced around the mound, stopping every few steps to attempt to detect any sound – sounds of triumphant searchers returning with Rosalee, sounds of Galen's men creeping up to attack him, sounds of Martelle returning from wherever he went.

Coleman's tenuous trust of Martelle was fading as the time since the strange man left dragged on.

How could I think that he was going to help? He's been against me from the start!

Coleman struggled to decide what to do. Strike out on his own? But where? To the woods? To the river? He did not know the area and would be searching blindly in the dark night.

He decided to go back to the church. Pastor Henry said that he would return to town shortly to receive information from any returning searchers. Coleman felt sure he would find the pastor at the church. He turned toward the town and felt his way through the blackness.

Dark buildings towered over Coleman as he walked slowly up the street. A thunderstorm rumbled, coming near the town.

As he went, dread collected in the pit of Coleman's heart, like dark rainwater poured out of a night storm.

Will I ever see her again? Why did I let her go to town alone?

Coleman reached the sunrise monument and turned toward the church. He found Pastor Henry standing in front of the building, the open church door behind him.

"Hey Coleman. I just got here. Did you see anything?"

Coleman shook his head and said, "Has anyone else?"

Henry said, "Not that I've heard."

Coleman's head dropped. He raised his hand to his eyes.

Henry placed a hand on the young man's shoulder and said, "Coleman,

186

we've got to have faith that Rosalee will be found and that she won't be hurt."

Coleman said, "Is that enough? Faith?"

Henry squeezed Coleman's shoulder and said, "Son, it's all we've got right now." Henry glanced inside the door. "Let's go inside. I want to pray for Rosalee and to pray for you."

Coleman stepped inside the door and Henry followed, closing the door behind him. Henry stopped.

"Shh."

Coleman said, "What?"

"Shh. I hear something," the pastor whispered.

Henry turned around. Coleman strained his ears but heard nothing.

"Come over here to the corner," Henry said.

Coleman moved to his side.

When he was still and standing in the corner, Coleman heard a tiny shuffling, quieter than the tread of a mouse.

The shuffling was coming from outside, on the stoop of the church.

CHAPTER 48

THE DEER CAMP

Rosalee watched as night came. It was like darkness welled up from the earthen floor of the barn and completely occupied it and then poured out to fill the entire world with an inky gloom. She waited for the sound of footsteps outside the door.

Instead, she heard another rumble of thunder, a little louder and closer than before. A much fainter sound came under the thunder, a faint scratching behind her. The scratching intensified. A rat? A possum? She twisted her body around and looked at the back wall of the shed. As she watched, one of the boards twitched. She saw a shadow between the barn's boards. The board twitched again and then pivoted inward. A head appeared in the space under the board.

"Shh. Don't say anything," the head whispered.

Rosalee could see the dark skin of the man. She caught a glimpse of pale blue eyes, lighter than a robin's egg.

Martelle.

Rosalee remained silent. She saw no shadows or movement at the door. She looked back at Martelle, who was now lying on his back, head thrust through the gap in the wall created when he removed the board.

Rosalee whispered, "What are you doing?"

Martelle lay quietly for a moment, listening.

He said, "I'm here to help you. Just saw your man and told him I'd bring you to him. Spect he's at the church by now."

Rosalee said, "I thought you sided with Galen."

Martelle wriggled through the gap in the boards and said, "Never can tell."

Martelle untied the ropes and pulled Rosalee to her feet. He listened again for anyone outside the door and then pushed Rosalee toward the hole in the back of the shed. She squeezed through and Martelle followed her outside.

The thin man put his mouth close to Rosalee's ear. "You grab onto my belt. We're gonna run pretty fast through these woods. Don't want you to get lost."

He moved toward the edge of the woods and turned back to Rosalee. "Be real quiet."

He crouched, like he was a night creature about to pounce. He turned again to Rosalee.

"Don't fall."

They sprang into the dark woods. Martelle's footfalls sounded like branches blowing in the wind or even the low scampering sounds of tiny animals, nothing to arouse suspicion in the scanning ears of Galen's men. Rosalee was not quite as skillful in disguising her footfalls but her petite frame made the sound of her steps low enough to avoid detection.

Shortly, the woods gave way to a broad grassy area and the dark shadows of the town's buildings soon became silhouetted against the clouds that were occasionally lit from within by lightning. Martelle led Rosalee through the town. Ahead, the church building became visible, its whitewashed walls glowing dully in the night.

Martelle stopped at the stoop of the church. Rosalee could hear sniffing sounds as Martelle turned his head from side to side. He crept up to the door and turned the knob and pulled the door open.

Inside was a velvet blackness, a complete lack of any light. Martelle eased inside. Rosalee followed, still gripping Martelle's belt tightly. Martelle froze.

"Pastor?" he whispered into the darkness. "I got the girl."

Rosalee jumped when arms grabbed her from behind. For a split-second, she prepared again to fight. However, the arms spun her around and embraced her in a warm, gentle hug. She smelled a familiar smell.

Coleman.

"I'm so happy you're safe," Coleman said.

Rosalee said, "Me too." She kissed him on the cheek.

Pastor Henry grasped Martelle's hand. "I can't thank you enough for helping rescue this innocent girl. Come on into the church. It's about to storm and y'all can stay in here."

"No, I'd better get outta here. Galen don't know I'm helping y'all." Martelle looked out at the growing storm. "I'll let you know if trouble is coming."

"How will you send word?"

"I'll come back." Martelle turned and disappeared into the night.

Henry led Coleman and Rosalee inside and flipped the light switch on the wall, but there was no response from the fixture overhead.

"Power's out," Henry said. "Just a minute."

Henry opened the drawer of the small table against the wall and struck a match. He lit a candle perched in the holder on the table. He turned to Rosalee.

"Are you hurt?"

Rosalee rubbed her wrists. "No, nothing more than a little rope burn."

"Good." Henry smiled. "Let's go up front."

Coleman and Rosalee followed Henry as the wavering flame of the candle cast crazily dancing shadows on the walls and ceiling of the sanctuary. Another flash of lightning and then a much louder boom of thunder came.

Henry motioned for the two to sit in chairs in the pulpit area. Henry pulled another chair closer.

"What I am about to tell y'all is the thing that no one around here talks about. No one who doesn't live here even knows about it. We don't talk about it because we all swore an oath to keep the secret."

Henry's eyes crept to the cross hanging on back wall. Coleman could see a tear roll down Henry's upturned face. Henry sniffed, wiped his cheek with his sleeve, and turned his head back to face the young people.

"It's time to trust someone with this secret," the pastor said.

Henry walked to the podium at the edge of the altar area. He opened a small door at the base of the podium, invisible until Henry released the catch and opened it. He lifted out a dusty book and returned to his seat. He placed the book in his lap, put both of his hands on top of the book, and faced Coleman and Rosalee.

Henry said, "Have you seen the portrait of Auntie Esther in the vestibule?" Coleman and Rosalee nodded.

Henry said, "The story of Jubilee is really her story. She is the reason that Jubilee exists. This book, one of the most sacred things in our little town, is Auntie Esther's diary and I'm going to read the whole thing for you right now. This book tells the story of her last days and the story of our town before."

"Before what?" Coleman asked.

Henry said, "Before April 15, 1921."

CHAPTER 49

THE DIARY OF AUNTIE ESTER

This here is written by Junebug. Auntie Ester says that I am her best pupil. On the night that Auntie Ester Washington was put in the jail, she told me to write down everything that she told me and everything that happened to her. She said that her eyes were too bad and the arthritis in her hands hurt her too much to write in the dark cold cell. She told me to write down what she said because this might be her last night on this earth but I told her that wasn't so and that she would be here tomorrow and the day after and the day after that. Anyway, this is what she said:

April 14, 1921 – Junebug, I want you to tell everybody that I ain't a bit sorry for what I did or for what I said to Mr. Russell. I figured that it was about time that someone did something. I didn't foresee what would come of it, that's for sure. But still, I ain't a bit sorry.

I guess I had better tell folks what I'm talking about so they will know when they read these words years from now. Now that I think on it, I had better tell them all the way from the beginning.

I was born 80 years ago this fall in a cabin behind Mr. Russell's big old house. I was a slave, owned by Mr. Russell's granddaddy, just like my mama and papa and my brothers and sisters. My papa was sold off when I was just a baby, to a man in Mobile I was told. When I was 8 years old, my mama died. I was all alone in the world. But I knew even then that I couldn't give up. As I turned into a woman, everybody could tell I wasn't going to be no beauty. Some of them even called me homely. By the time I was 18 or 19, I already knew that I wouldn't never have any children of my own, not that those young bucks on the plantation didn't try. I knew that since I wasn't able to make more slave children for the master and that I wasn't pretty enough for him to make me a house slave, I might be the kind of girl that the foreman took off in the woods with the shotgun and come back later without her. So, I knew I had to work for my very life. I become the hardest worker you ever seen. I worked as hard in the fields as a man. Shoot, I worked harder than any two of some of them field hands. After the war, most of us colored people stayed on at the plantation cause we didn't have nowhere else to go. Even though we weren't exactly owned by the Russells, it was still almost the same as before the war except that the times were hard and we didn't have much to eat. The Russells didn't have much more their own selves, though not as bad as us. Still, I made it through all of that and me an unmarried young colored woman.

I started teaching a couple of children when I was about 25 years old. I taught myself to read and write after one of the old house slaves give me a little book and taught me how to make out the letters and what sounds they made. Pretty soon, I was teaching all of the young children on the plantation, them that was too young to work in the fields or in the house. The parents of them children would give me food, some collards or sometimes even a chicken, for teaching them. With that and the little garden I planted outside my window, I made a living. It kept me out of the fields and kept my body from wearing out too soon. My friends who were close to my age wore they selves out scratchin out a living from the land. I watched most of them die young and that was hard. Pretty soon, I was the only one left that had been alive before the war.

To tell you the whole story, I need to tell you about Mr. Russell and to tell you about him I got to tell you some about his family. Like I said, Granddaddy Russell owned the house before the war and it was him that built the town. Granddaddy Russell had been a sailing ship captain and had made a whole heap of money doing it. So, he decided to take that money and buy all the land around these parts and have his very own plantation. I remember him always being real stern back in the plantation days. They say that Master Russell ran the plantation the same way he ran his ship. In fact, some of the same men that were in the crew of his ship come to help him run his place here. Besides that, Mr. Russell put things here and there in the town to remind him of the sea. The tavern there on the corner is called the Ship's Wheel Tavern and it was named that by Granddaddy Russell hisself. He had one of his house servants ring a bell inside the house every hour, just like they did on his old ship.

By the end of his life, Granddaddy Russell seemed to lose his sternness. He became kindly soft toward most of us colored folk. He even gave some of us Christmas presents and such. When Granddaddy Russell died somewheres around 1890, his son, Mr. Russell's daddy, took over the house. Nobody ever did see him too much. Everybody said that he drank hisself to death. I don't know about that, but I do know he died somewheres around 1905. That was when our Mr. Russell took over the running of the house and the town.

Now, Junebug, you know our Mr. Russell. His sternness makes his old granddaddy look downright neighborly. Thing is, he's always been that way ever since he was a little boy. Course, I remember him when he was growing up. He was one of them little boys who was always crying about something or always beating up somebody over something. All the white people was afraid to do anything about it seeing as how the Russells owned most everything in the town. So, they just put up with him. Course, us colored folk sure couldn't say anything either.

When our Mr. Russell took over, he seemed to start thinking he was a king and that this whole town was his kingdom. Well, that ain't exactly so. It was more like he was a sailing captain and this whole town was his ship. He talked about his old granddaddy like he was Solomon, like old Grandaddy Russell was the wisest man who ever drew breath. Our Mr. Russell even put up a monument in his granddaddy's honor, you know the one, Junebug, the brass ship's wheel on that rock pillar right down at the end of town. Mr. Russell told everybody that they had to show him abeyance, just like them ship's hands used to do on his granddaddy's ship. Everybody, white or colored, has to stop, put their right pointer finger knuckle up on their forehead, and wait until Mr. Russell passes by when they happen upon him on the street. And woe be to the person who don't do that!

And it ain't only saluting him that he makes everybody do. Course, he owns most every building in town. All these white people who run the stores in town got to pay Mr. Russell fore they pay anybody else. Not too long ago, Mr. Peterson, you know the man who runs the grocer store, he didn't have enough money to pay his rent cause he had a bunch of fruit that went rotten and he couldn't sell them. I was standing there in the store when that mean old son of Mr. Russell, Billy, came by to collect. I reckon Billy couldn't see me cause I was over on the opposite side of the store but I could see him and Mr. Peterson just fine. Mr. Peterson was out on the sidewalk setting up a crate of onions when Billy starting yelling at him from across the street.

"So, Pete, where's that money you owe my daddy?"

Mr. Peterson closed his eyes and raised his head up from his onions and turned around real slow. "Billy, you remember I told you the other day that I am a little behind because of that shipment of fruit that went bad. I'm almost caught up and should be able to give you the money by this Friday."

"Pete, when is the rent due every month?" Billy looked at Mr. Peterson like he was a little child in school that had been caught passing lovey notes, even though Billy had just turned twenty and Mr. Peterson was almost forty.

"Billy, like I told you, I will get you the money when I have it." Mr. Peterson spread his hands apart while he said it.

And then, that Billy did something that would've been hard to believe if it hadn't happened here and if I hadn't seen it with my own two eyes. Billy stomped across the street and hit poor Mr. Peterson right across the face with the back of his hand. Mr. Peterson staggered back and put his hand up to his lip that was now bleeding. Billy rared his hand back like he was going to hit him again and Mr. Peterson held his hands up and said, "Yessir, yessir, Mr. Russell! I'll go get the money right now!" Mr. Peterson then bowed down a little and backed his way into the store. He came back a minute later with a handful of money. "This is all I have. It is the full amount of the rent but I won't have enough to pay for the shipment of produce that is coming in tomorrow. So, I probably won't have enough for the rent next month." When Mr. Peterson said that, Billy hit him again and made him drop the money.

"Why you brainless little shop-keep! Don't you sass me! I don't care if you're so stupid you can't run your store good enough to make your rent. And I don't need to hear no excuses. Now, pick up all of this money. And none of it better be dirty!"

Billy made poor Mr. Peterson get down like he was a dog and pick up every last bit of that money. Billy just stood there and held out his hand until Mr. Peterson put the money in it. I could see people peeking out the windows on the other side of the street, watching the whole thing. "I'll see you in exactly 3 weeks to get next month's rent. And if you're late again, you'll have more than a fat lip. It might be hard to stock your shelves with two broke arms." Billy gave a real mean-looking smile, sort of like a smile that a snake might give if he was able to smile, and then turned around. I seen all them people peeking out the windows on the other side of the street close the curtains real quick when Billy turned around.

Mr. Russell and Billy treat all the rest of the white people in town about the same way. Most of the time, the white folk are too scared not to pay him on time or to do anything else the Russells say for fear that them or their families will get hurt. A long time ago, there was a blacksmith in town that used to joke around when Mr. Russell was still a boy. This blacksmith was a big burly man and Mr. Russell was a little on the scrawny side when he was growing up. This blacksmith would say things like, "When you going to start getting some whiskers on your face?" and "Ain't you getting no muscles yet?" When Mr. Russell growed up and took over the house, this blacksmith still said things like that. Everybody knew he was only joshing and trying to be friendly. But one day, that blacksmith just up and disappeared. Nobody was sure what happened, but everybody whispered that Mr. Russell and the men from his house went in the middle of the night, took the blacksmith out in the woods, shot him dead, and buried him out there. If anybody had any doubts fore that, they knew never to say anything that wasn't very respectful to Mr. Russell or to his family.

Mr. Russell has a big motorcar, a long Lincoln. He likes to drive it hisself. Every morning, he drives real slow up the street from his house, turns around in the circle beside his granddaddy's monument, and then parks in his own space right in front of the town hall where his office is. Anybody who is on the sidewalk has to stop with their hand up at their forehead until he passes by. Most folk know to just stay inside until they see that Mr. Russell's car is in its spot.

Now, let me tell you how I came to be in this here jail cell. It all started yesterday. I happened to be out early cause I needed to drop off an old dress at Mr. Gibson's store cause Mrs. Gibson was going to fix a place where the hem was frayed. My eyes are too dim and my hands too shaky to do that kind of work any more. I needed the dress to wear to Brother Chandler's funeral. Since I wasn't sure whether Mr. Russell had come by in his motorcar yet, I came up by the alley between the town hall and Mr. Gibson's store. That was when I heard Mr. Russell pulling into his space. I froze right then and there. In that instant, I heard Billy Russell walk out of the town hall and start to talk to his daddy. "Hey Daddy. I was just inside looking to see who was on my list for today. I'm going around to collect our piece from the sharecroppers today. I'm doing half of them today and the other half next week."

I couldn't see either one of them and I was sure glad they couldn't see me. If they had of knowed that anybody was listening in on them, I don't like to think what they would've done. Even though I couldn't see him, I could tell Mr. Russell didn't care too much about Billy's plans for the day, cause he said, "What's going on up at the nigger church?"

Billy said, "Oh that. That old nigger, name of Chandler, died and they're doing that stupid sitting up with the dead thing. They think that evil spirits will come and get him if there ain't somebody with him all the time until he is buried."

Mr. Russell said, "Well, the best time of every day for me is when I drive my Lincoln up the street. I like to look at the town that our family built and then admire the monument to my grandfather. On many mornings, the rays of the rising sun are shining up behind the hill and they seem to be a halo around the monument. I'm able to bask in the glory of our family's name. After all that our family has done for the people of this town, you would think it wouldn't be too much to ask to have this time each morning to be undisturbed. This morning, though, I was gazing at the monument when I caught some movement out of the corner of my eye. It was a little nigger boy coming out of the front door of that dump of a building they use as a church. Why my dear old granddaddy let them build that church so close to town and where it can be seen from the street, I don't know. I swear that someday I'm going to get rid of it. Anyway, that little nigger boy came out the door and then looked up and saw me. I believe he was going to run away without showing proper respect but then he stopped and saluted. Still, I could've done without having to see him."

Billy said, "They'll be burying him today, so you shouldn't have to put up with it again."

Mr. Russell said, "I shouldn't have to put up with it anytime. Surely the people in this town, of all people, should know the proper order of things. Some of us are just born to be leaders. God gave us the brains to know what is best and the means to make it happen. Other people are meant to be the managers under these leaders. Their purpose in life is to take what the leaders say and make it happen. The storekeepers in Russellton are this kind of person. And then, there are those under them, the manual laborers and niggers. They are supposed to do what they are told and not talk back. The good book says so. 'Thou shalt be obedient to thy master, pleasing them in all things, and not talking back.' That's what it says."

Billy said, "Yep, you're right. There are some people in this town that get kindly uppity, both white and nigger. Like that brainless grocer."

Mr. Russell said, "So, how is that little grandson of mine. Is he sleeping all night yet?"

Billy had married a girl who is from clear the other side of Montgomery and they had set up house in one of the outbuildings around the big Russell house. Billy's wife, Miss Peggy, just had a baby boy two weeks ago. Billy said, "How would I know? I've been sleeping in my old room in the big house. Peggy can take care of all that baby stuff herself. I've got to have my sleep."

Mr. Russell huffed and said, "Why, you ain't nothing but a piss-ant! You get back to your own house tonight! Stuff cotton in your ears if you need to! It ain't right to leave your wife all alone."

Billy said, "Yessir, Daddy. I'll go back tonight." I could hear Mr. Russell walking toward the door of the town hall. I took a little step back cause I was afraid he might see me.

Mr. Russell said, "Anything else we need to talk about? If not, I'll see you later today after you have collected the sharecroppers' money."

Billy said, "I'll talk to you later today, Daddy."

Thank the good Lord Billy walked the other way down the street or he might've seen me. After they had both left, I snuck around the corner of the building and took my old dress into the store.

While I was walking home from the store to get ready for teaching my class of children, I kept on thinking about what Mr. Russell had said. He was saying that the Bible said that the way things was in Russellton was right. But, it just didn't seem to be right. I kept on thinking and remembered the preacher saying that we was all one in God's eyes, that there ain't no Jew or gentile, no free or slave, even no man or woman, not in God's eyes. We is all the same. Well, if that's true, how can what Mr.

Russell said be true, too? Them thoughts kept on lingering in the back of my mind, like a pot of collards you put on the back of the stove while you're frying the chicken. They stewed back in the back of my mind while I was teaching the children yesterday. You remember, Juney. You asked me what I was thinking about. Well, that was it. It just kept going through my mind what Mr. Russell had said and how he said it was from the Bible.

Yesterday, after teaching, I decided to take a walk down the street and then back home. I needed to clear my mind. Of course, I was careful like always to stop and nod to any white people I met on the way and then let them pass before I started up again. Like you know, there's lots of trouble that comes any colored person's way if Mr. Russell or any of his people catch them not showing respect to white folk. I think most of the white people are kindly embarrassed by the way we are supposed to treat them. Some of them will say something like, "Auntie Ester! So good to see you doing so well on this fine day!", treating me like I was white like them. Others of them will look around real sly-like and then give me a little smile or a nod of the head if they don't see any Russells around. I didn't see many people on the street. It was right at noontime and so most of them were probably either at home having dinner or eating in their stores. Mr. Russell always drives back to the big house for his dinner. Since I knew he would be at home, I dared to look up at the second floor of the town hall building and could see through the big old picture windows right into his office. There was the back of his huge desk. I could see the painting of his granddaddy's sailing ship on the wall. Hanging under the painting, I could see his granddaddy's cat o' nine tails. Do you know what that is, Junebug? That's a whip that's got nine cords coming out of one handle. Granddaddy Russell used it to whip the sailors what done something bad.

After peeking up at the window, I kept on walking all the way to the other end of town. Most of the stores were pretty quiet. I could hear some talking coming out of the Ship's Wheel Tavern as I walked by. Why anybody would want to go in there and drink the devil's drink in the middle of the day, I don't know. I crossed the street before I got to the tavern so that I wouldn't happen to run into anyone if they was coming out. I looked on down past the tavern and could see the big Russell house in the distance. Course, the pretty Russellton Church was between the house and me. I thought about how different that church was from our own. It is different on the inside and the outside, I believe. On the outside, the Russellton church is gleaming white. Sometimes, when the sun is shining just right, it is so bright it will hurt your eyes. It has a tall pretty steeple and stained glass windows. I've been down there at night when the church is lit up inside and them windows look as pretty as an meadow in springtime, with colors so bright they put you in a trance. Our church is the exact opposite. It was white at one time and the little specks of paint that stick to the old wood are still dingy white. There ain't no steeple, though somebody did put a cross made out of rough sawn wood up under the eaves at the peak of the roof. Over the door is a big black "N". Our Mr. Russell had that painted there to show this was the nigger church. Our church was built at the opposite end of the town from the white people's church. Granddaddy Russell had it built in his later years so that us colored folk would have our own place to worship the Lord and not have to stand outside the white church, just listening to the singing and preaching.

But the biggest difference, I believe, is on the inside. From what I could tell about the white people's church, the songs seemed all high and mighty. I couldn't even make out what some of the words was. And the preaching, it was right dull and boring. There was lots of flowery talking but not a lot of love that I heard in them services. Our church, though, we is all about love. Our pastor, Brother Joshua, is one of the kindest men I know. He always begins the service praying for anybody in need and then asking the Lord to help all of us treat each other with kindness. Even when I see him pushing his broom in his other job as a janitor at the town hall, he always has a smile on his face and a nice word for anyone who passes by.

After looking at that church building for a few minutes, I started back down the street toward home. Course, as you know Juney, I live where all the other colored folk live down in Pickaninny. I spent yesterday afternoon just piddling around my little shack, getting some weeds out of my little patch of beans and putting some jars up on my kitchen shelf. It being Wednesday, I got ready to go to prayer meeting at the church.

I always enjoy prayer meeting. It seems a bit more relaxed than Sunday morning. Brother Joshua starts it out by asking for prayer requests and then he preaches a little short sermon. Then, we pray for all of the people we just put on the list. Anybody who wants to pray out loud can do it. It was last night's prayer meeting that really put all of the things that happened today in motion. Sister Sylvia had done her usual thing of listing all of her kinfolk who had this ailment or that and then a few other people had told about some others who needed to be on the prayer list. And then, Brother Joshua lit into his sermon. He started preaching about Shadrack, Meshach, and Abednego. They was three little Hebrew fellows what had been taken from their home in Jerusalem to live in a foreign land. And then, on top of that, they had been told they had to bow down and worship a big old gold statue. They was supposed to stop whatever they was doing and bow down to that statue whenever they heard any kind of music. The thing was, though, they wouldn't do it cause they knowed it was a sin cause they would've been worshipping an idol.

Well, Brother Joshua was just preaching up a storm about them Hebrew boys and how they would rather be chunked in the fiery furnace fore they would bow down to that idol. As for me, I was just sitting there, fanning myself and saying my amens along with everybody else, when a little thought crept into the back of my mind. I didn't notice the little thought at first. It was the same way you can be in your house working on something and not hear the little mouse scurrying about over by the wall. And then, you first notice the scratching of them little feet and wonder, *How long has that little mouse been in here? Didn't I hear him before?* Well, I don't know how long that little thought had been in the back of my mind but it was right at the end of Brother Joshua's sermon that I first took notice of it. And I got to be honest Junebug, when I first noticed it, it like to scared me to death. I says to myself, *I can't do that! I'm an old woman!* But the more I thought about it, the more I knowed it was what I had to do.

I went home from the prayer meeting and I stayed up all night thinking and praying. I went back and forth, back and forth. Even though at the beginning I was kindly scared, after a while it weren't that that made me so uncertain. My real worry was whether it would do any good. I kept saying to myself, *Why throw away everything if it ain't going to do no good?* But what I kept on coming back to is that nothing can't happen unless you try. So by morning time, God had me all ready to do what I had to do.

I put on my flowperedy dress and my bonnet and I walked up to the church. I saw that pitiful building with the peeling paint and the big old N painted up there over the door. I thought it was the prettiest sight I had seen in a while. The sky starting to get pink over behind the hill. I knew the appointment that God had made for me was drawing nigh. So I walked up to the side of the street and waited.

In just a little while, I heard it. It was way down at the other end of town. It was kindly foggy so I couldn't see it yet. Pretty soon, though, I could make out the shape. It was coming real slow up the street. It was making a sound like low rumbling thunder. The sound got louder and then I could see him. He was sitting behind the wheel, looking up at the sky. At first, I thought he might just go on by. For an instant there, I wished that's what he would do. But then, he happened to look down and he turned his head real slow over my way. He seemed a little bit surprised to see me. But then, he stopped the car and seemed to be waiting. He looked me straight in the eye and I looked right back in his. And then, I gave him a smile and a nod. It was like I had just kicked him in the guts. That calmness on his face turned into shock and he got to looking real mad. He turned off the motor. With all the noise gone, I said, "Good morning! Ain't it a pretty one?"

It was like I had just thrown scalding hot water on his head. He got all red in the face and he said in a deep mean voice, "Old woman, can't you see who I am? Or has your vision gone? Can't you at least hear my motorcar and know who I am?"

I said, "Son, I know who you is. You is one of God's children, just like I am. And I want to wish you a blessed day on this beautiful morning."

Mr. Russell jumped out of that car like they was a hornet's nest under the seat. He started pacing to and fro beside his car, turning his head to look at me every time he passed by. It was like he was trying to figure out what to do with me but his rage couldn't let him think. About that time, I heard his son Billy yelling from down the street. I could see that Billy was walking from down at the town hall. "What's a matter, Daddy? Your motorcar broke down?"

Mr. Russell started yelling like a man escaped from the insane asylum. "What's the matter? You're asking me what's the matter? Can't you see what's the matter? This old thing has not given me my proper respect. She stood there, knowing who I was, and didn't show her respect. And she spoke to me in a most familiar way!"

Mr. Russell started pacing back and forth again. Billy looked over at me, kindly confused. It was the first time I had ever seen Billy not knowing what to do. After a minute, Mr. Russell stopped and said, "Billy, I want you to take this thing to the jail while I decide what I'm going to do."

Billy looked at this daddy for just a second and said, "Yessir. But, Daddy, what..."

Before Billy could get anymore out of his mouth, Mr. Russell whipped around and said, "You're not going to start sassing me too, are you?"

Billy come over to me. He grabbed my arm and tugged at me to come with him. As we was walking away, Billy whispered, "I sure wish you hadn't done this, you old nigger woman. There's going to be hell to pay and it ain't going to be just you. I ain't never seen my daddy this mad 'bout anything." Billy yanked my arm and made me walk a little faster with him over toward the jail. Once we got there, he took me back to the cell in the back of the building and closed me inside them iron bars. And that's where I waited until somewheres around noontime. Billy come back and says to me, in a real low mean-like voice, "Get up and come with me. Daddy wants to see you."

Me and him, we walked up to Mr. Russell's office, on the second floor of the town hall. When we walked in, Mr. Russell was sitting in that big old chair of his and he was staring out the window. Billy stopped, with his hand still grabbing my arm, and we stood there waiting for Mr. Russell to notice us. After a minute or two, Mr. Russell turned around and said, "I just want to know what came over you to think that you could ignore the tradition of respect that we have in this town?"

At first, I didn't rightly know if he's was just saying that or if he was really asking me a question. But I seen that he raised his eyebrows up like he was waiting for me to say something, so I said, "I wasn't meaning no disrespect. In fact, I was right friendly to you. I just wanted to wish you a blessed day. There wasn't nobody else around and I didn't figure that there was any need to act like we didn't know each other. Shoot, I been knowing you since you come into this world. And I know you seen me often enough."

Mr. Russell looked at me with a kind of slack-jawed look on his face. I reckon he's never had a colored person talk to him like that, like he was just another person. Probably never had a white person talk to him like that neither.

Mr. Russell sat up a little straighter and cleared his throat before he said, "You know fully well that this town is built on a foundation of a tradition of respect. And there is no other thing in this town more worthy of respect than the family of my dear grandfather. If he wasn't for him, Russellton would not exist. And none of you would have a home here. In fact, most of you niggers would have been dead or scattered all over the country. My granddaddy provided a place of refuge for you and your people after the war that sheltered you from all of the horrible things that were happening elsewhere. And how do you repay that kindness? By spitting and trampling on the memory of my grandfather. You can't even show a simple, common gesture of respect to him and his descendants."

I drew up some courage and said, "Mr. Russell, I knowed your granddaddy as well as any other colored person. And you're right, he treated us right nice at the end of his life. I remember him sending me at Christmastime a little bag that had some ribbon in it, ribbon that I used for a dress. The little bit I knowed about your daddy, he was a right fine fellow as well. There ain't nobody doubting that your family's done a lot of good, both for itself and for this here town. But, everybody walking around scared of you just ain't right. Everybody, white and colored, is scared to say or do anything for fear that you will come down on them. And this making everybody salute you, that seems a lot like worshipping. We was reading the story of Shadrack, Meshach, and Abednego in the prayer meeting last night..." Before I could finish what I was saying, Mr. Russell started bellowing like an old bull.

"That's it! That's it! The whole fabric of respect on which our town is built is coming unraveled! First, we have storeowners thinking they can take my money anytime they want and not pay it back until it is convenient for them. And now, we have niggers thinking they can walk around like they own the place and no one can say anything about it. And now I see. It is all related to that eyesore that you niggers call a church. I now see it for what it is. It is a hotbed of radicalism. And the filth flowing from inside it is polluting not only the feeble minds of the niggers, if you have a mind, but it is spreading to the white people as well." While he said this, Mr. Russell had started pacing back and forth again, like he had done out by the motorcar. "Billy, take this smart-mouthed old thing back down to the jail. And then, go around and tell everybody to gather in the street in front of the town hall at exactly one o'clock. I will not tolerate anyone's not being there. Have the white people stand right here close to the town hall and the niggers farther back." After he said that, Mr. Russell turned around.

Billy took me back down to this cell and locked me back up. I sat right on this here bench until he come back to get me. By that time, all the people had gathered together in front of the town hall. I seen them when Billy took me out the front door of the jail. He pulled me by the arm back up to Mr. Russell's office. When we walked in, Mr. Russell was standing on that stone balcony outside them big old windows. He said over his shoulder, "Billy, bring her out here." Billy pushed me out to the balcony and had me stand just behind Mr. Russell. Mr. Russell looked back at me for a second and turned back to the people on the street.

Mr. Russell said, "Citizens of Russellton, please listen. I have something important to tell you. Recently, there have been attacks on our very way of life. There have been some people who have refused to pay their rent on time. Instead of you people cheerfully meeting me on the streets of our little town, I now notice y'all avoiding me or even worse, scurrying off the street so that you won't have to see me. But worst of all, this morning the most egregious thing that I have ever witnessed occurred. This nigger woman standing right here trampled underfoot all that we care about. Since God has appointed me and my family to be the leaders of this town, it is my duty to do something about these attacks on our heritage. God himself told us to submit to every ordinance. I cannot in good conscience stand by while the more radical members of our society try to push their views on us. Though I would rather have peace in our town, peace between you and me, I see that I must now rule with a rod of iron."

While Mr. Russell was saying all of this, I was looking out at the people of the town. Most of the colored people were just staring down at their feet. Every once in a while, one of them would look up to try to catch my eye and I would give them a wink, trying to let them know that I was all right. It didn't seem to help, cause they kept on looking real worried for me. Most of the white folk seem to be staring at the stone wall up over our heads. I reckon they didn't want Mr. Russell to think they wasn't listening but at the same time didn't want to catch his eye or mine by accident.

Mr. Russell went on, "And so, I have decided to take action. For far too long, I have indulged everyone in this town, allowing your indiscretions, but no longer." Mr. Russell's voice was getting louder and louder and my, was his face getting red! "You are an evil and adulterous generation that seeketh after a sign! We'll, I'm going to give you a sign and that's for sure! Tomorrow morning, I will be bringing back a taste of the discipline that my dear grandfather used back in the prime of this community. Granddaddy passed down to me the instrument of God's own correction that he used so effectively on the deep blue ocean and in the fields of his plantation as well. And tomorrow morning at precisely nine o'clock, my son will use that instrument, the cat o' nine tails, to impart discipline to this nigger woman here. Don't think that this is a cruel punishment. It is intended to be exactly the opposite. By this brief application of the whip to this solitary nigger woman, I hope to spare the rest of you from much more severe acts of God's own justice."

Standing up there on the balcony, I could hear some gasps coming up from the crowd. I looked down at the white people and several of the women were standing there with their mouths opened up, like they couldn't believe what they had just heard. Some of the colored people at the back of the crowd were crying. I could see the tears coming down they faces though I couldn't hear any sobbing. I had been thinking about what Mr. Russell might do to me, ever since he had chunked me in the jail. I thought he might do anything from having me drug down the street by a mule, to hanging me, to just having me shot. So, I wadn't too surprised when he said he was going to whip me.

But, Mr. Russell wasn't finished. He went on, "So, this will be the correction for this one nigger's disrespect. However, there is another matter and this one is a much deeper cause for concern. There is one institution in this town that seems to be the primary source for the evil thoughts that many people have been having. Within this building, there are dangerous teachings that would have all of you throwing away the traditions of this town that are the main reason for our community's success. And again, as the leader of Russellton, I am duty-bound to take action. Therefore, I have ordered my son and the men in my employment to burn down tomorrow night that rubbish pile that has marred the beauty of own town for years. Of course, I am referring to the nigger church."

At that, I heard a couple of wails come up out of the colored people. Real quick, though, the men folk standing beside the wailing women hushed them up so that Mr. Russell wouldn't see who had done it. Most of the white people just looked down at the ground. I felt like I had just been punched in the belly. I didn't have no idea that what I done might cause Mr. Russell to burn down the church. I looked over at the back of his head, thinking that any second he would tell everybody that he really didn't mean it. But he didn't say anything of the sort. In fact, he just finished up his speech.

"I expect all of you to gather here tomorrow morning at nine o'clock. I want you to witness the discipline being dispensed. Tomorrow night after sunset, I want everyone to be in your homes, praying to God for forgiveness while my son takes care of erasing the blight of the nigger church from our fair town. On Saturday morning, we can all wake to a bright new day in Russellton, where God's system of justice and leadership has been put back to right. And now, go to your homes and places of business and prepare your hearts for tomorrow."

The people had just started shuffling away out of the street when Billy jerked me back inside and Mr. Russell came in behind us. "Get her back down to the jail. Nobody is to see her. I don't want any trouble between now and tomorrow morning." Mr. Russell walked over to the painting of his graddaddy's ship and let his eyes fall down to the whip. He bowed his head down like he was praying. Without another word, Billy drug me by the arm back down to the jail.

I spent the next few hours feeling like I had fallen down a well. I was thinking, What have I done? Why is God allowing this to happen? After a while, though, I remembered that nothing can't happen without God letting it happen. I knowed that what I done was what God wanted me to do. So, I just had to turn everything over to Him. He is going to take care of our church.

And so, here I am, an old woman, sitting near the end of my life and looking back. What if I hadn't done what I did today? What would've happened? I would still be dead not so long from now. But now, I can go and meet God at the end of my life knowing that I didn't bow down to somebody who is holding hisself up like a god. I don't know if this whipping will kill me or not. But, whatever happens I got to think that God is going to use what happens here for good. It says in the Bible that God, He makes all things work for the good of them that love Him and do what He wants 'em to do.

And now, Junebug, I got to go to bed. I sure am glad that Billy let you in here to bring me some supper and to talk to me. I reckon he wouldn't like it if he knowed that you was writing all of this down, but you don't have to tell him. Just carry that book back out in the basket you brung the food in, he won't never notice it. I'm an old woman and I got to get my sleep, even if it is in an old jail cell. So, good night, Junebug. You know I love you.

I, Junebug, managed to sneak this book past dumb old Billy. In fact, he had already dosed off by the time I was leaving. After I left Auntie Esther in that cold jail, I went home and started to pray. I was so worried about her. I laid in my bed that night, I asked the Lord to deliver her. I knew He could, but I didn't know if He would. I fell asleep but had all kind of scary dreams about a wolf chasing me in the night.

The next day, the sun was bright but the air was cold. Everybody in the whole town started to come out of their houses and walking down toward the street to the ship's wheel monument. Without having to be told, all of the white people gathered close to the monument and all of us black people farther back with Mr. Russell's men standing in the middle. They was all holding shotguns and giving mean looks at the people on both sides of them. I shivered in my thin sweater and wished that I had put on my thicker sweater when all of a sudden I forgot all about the cold. Billy come walking down the street with Auntie Ester with Mr. Russell walking right behind them.

She walked slowly, with Billy sort of pulling her along. She didn't look scared, though. She looked up at the sky and then at the crowd. I saw her give a little smile to several people. She blinked both of her eyes and smiled at me like she was saying, "It's going to be all right, child," like I had heard her say a thousand times before.

Billy turned her around and pushed her over toward the ship's wheel. He pulled two pieces of rope out from under his belt. He looked at Mr. Russell and asked him, "Do you want me to strip her down?"

Mr. Russell was holding that whip in his hand and he hit his hand with the handle of it while he looked around at the crowd for a second and said, "No, leave her top on. We'll just whip her through it." Billy pulled Auntie Esther's arms and tied one of them to one side of the wheel and the other to the other side. He backed up and Mr. Russell handed him the whip. Mr. Russell turned around to all of us standing there.

"I have asked y'all to be here this morning to witness the cleansing of this town. Yes, this is a cleansing. Whosoever is not with me is against me and he, or she, that gathereth not with me scattereth abroad." He was standing there beside Auntie Esther. He turned his head from side to side as he talked. "I have wanted to gather you, the people of this town that my grandfather built out of the wilderness, like a mother hen gathers her chicks to herself. But, you are an obstinate people. And so, a cleansing must come. I wish it were not so."

Mr. Russell gave a nod to Billy. Mr. Russell stepped to the side.

Billy cracked the whip once and that made me jump. He stopped and stared at Auntie Esther's back, like he was judging the distance. He reared back and swung the whip. The tip went so fast I couldn't see it. Auntie Esther jerked just a little but she didn't make a sound. Like it was magic, a long tear appeared in Auntie Esther's blouse. A thin line of red was on the strip of skin that was now showing. I heard some little gasps from the people behind me. Billy hit her again. Another little jerk. And then I heard it. Auntie Esther was singing.

"I got joy like a river. I got joy like a river. I got joy like a river in my soul." I could just barely hear her from where I was standing. Auntie Esther never had been much of a singer. She sang loud at church but her voice reminded me more of a bullfrog than a nightingale. That day, though, she sang as it had been the voice of an angel.

When she started with her song, it only seemed to make Billy hit harder and faster, like he wanted to get it over with or make her stop singing. But she didn't stop.

"I got peace like an ocean. I got peace like an ocean. I got peace like an ocean in my heart."

Billy was grunting with every strike and taking big deep breaths in between. I could now hear women, both white and black, crying real soft. Some of the white men in front of me put their hands up over their faces for a second and then put them back down before Mr. Russell saw them. But nobody didn't do nothing. We all just stood there, waiting for it to be over.

Mr. Russell was mostly standing and looking back and forth at the crowd. He would every once in a while glance over at Auntie Esther. I saw his lips moving and figured out that he was silently counting. Twenty. Twenty-one. Twenty-two. I didn't know how long this was going to last. Mr. Russell didn't say. When Billy had hit her thirty times, he looked over at Mr. Russell. Mr. Russell gave him a mean look and so Billy started up again. Mr. Russell stared back out at the crowd. Thirty-one. Thirty-two.

I noticed that Auntie Esther had stopped singing. The only thing I heard now was people sniffling and the sound of the whip. The back of Auntie Esther's blouse was gone. All I could see was red meat on her back.

When Mr. Russell had mouthed out thirty-nine, he held up his hand to Billy. Billy was already in mid-swing, but he stopped the whip before it hit Auntie Esther again. Mr. Russell said to Billy, "Check her."

Billy handed the whip to Mr. Russell and walked over to Auntie Esther. He walked behind the monument and stooped down a little to look her in the face. I saw his hand come up to her face, like he was opening her eyes. He stood up and said to Mr. Russell, "She's dead."

There were some gasps from the crowd and a few low mournful wails that came out of the women. They all stopped when Mr. Russell gave them a mean look. He turned to Billy and said, "Cut her down."

Mr. Russell turned to us and said, "Now, y'all look at this. This is what happens when you break the law. The wages of sin is death. What this nigger woman did was wrong." His voice began to rise with the color in his cheeks. "I saw some of y'all crying for her, both black and white. Well, I don't want to see it. She brought it on herself. Just like a dog that won't mind its master, she had to be taught a lesson. If the dog can't learn the lesson, it just has to be put down. That's what happened here today. "

Billy cut one of the ropes and Auntie Esther's body twirled around, facing us but with one of her arms still tied up. Her eyes was open but I could see there wasn't no life in them. They was all glazed over. Billy cut the other rope and Auntie Esther fell over face down in the dirt. Mr. Russell pointed a finger at her and started shaking. He was trying to say something but was having a hard time getting the words to come up. Finally, he looked out at all of us and yelled, "That is not a human. That is an animal. I am going to have it thrown out into the woods just like I would any other dead animal that is found in the street." He slowly walked back and forth and got a lot quieter, sounding real mean. "And just to make myself clear, I better not hear anything about a funeral or any other such ridiculous thing." With his finger still pointed toward the body in the dirt, he said "I don't want to hear this dog's name ever spoken again in this town."

Mr. Russell looked at Billy and said, "I am going home for a while to get ready for the bonfire tonight."

Billy and the rest of Mr. Russell's men took Auntie Esther's body off in a wagon and we never knew where they took her. After a while, everyone went back home like Mr. Russell said. Later on, though, when Billy and the men were long gone, a lot of people started coming to the church. Since this was the last day we would have it, everybody wanted to come to the old church and pray here one last time. When I went in there, Brother Joshua was sitting on the front row. He was staring at the altar. When he saw me, he stood up and walked over to me and said, "Are you all right Junebug? Auntie Esther meant a lot to all of us but I expect she meant more to you than anybody else."

He could probably tell I had been crying. I said, "I'm all right, Brother Joshua. I believe that the Lord sent an angel to watch over Auntie Esther. She didn't seem to suffer but just sang her way to heaven." He nodded and gave me a little hug and we sat down together on a pew. I said, "But still, it's hard to think that she won't be here no more. And to have to watch her get beaten like that was terrible."

Brother Joshua said, "Junebug, you and all of the other children in this town have had to see a lot more than you should have to see at your age. Shoot, it's a lot more than any of us should have to see."

I said, "Well, I know that Auntie Esther is at peace now. She told me that she was ready to die. She was only trying to treat Mr. Russell like a real person and to have him treat her like one."

Brother Joshua said, "She was very brave." He looked down at the old wooden floor of the church. I saw his eyes getting all teary. "I just wished I could have been brave like her. Maybe I could have stopped it."

I patted him on the knee. "Things will get better someday," I told him.

"I don't know." He looked back down at the floor.

I said, "I just wish that we could sit up with Auntie Esther tonight. That's the least we could have done for someone who did such a brave thing."

Brother Joshua slapped his knee and said, "That's just what we should do." He nodded his head. "Yes."

I said, "But, Brother Joshua, we can't cause we don't have no body. What's we going to sit up with?"

"We don't need a body. We have her in our hearts and our memories. Junebug, you go around and tell everybody that we're going to meet here just before nightfall. Tell everybody to come. If they're too scared to come, that's all right. Just tell them to stay at home and pray for all of us who do."

I said, "But Brother Joshua, Mr. Russell said that him and his men are going to burn down the church tonight."

"Junebug, we have to be brave like Auntie Esther." He said, "Now run on. Make sure you tell all the black folk to come."

I went around and talked to almost everybody. Some folks seemed scared but they still said they would come. By the time I got back to the church, there was lots of people standing outside. Brother Joshua was standing close to the door, shaking people's hands and hugging people. As the sun started setting, he said, "All right everybody. Come on in to the church and let's begin our service."

When everyone was sitting in the pews, Brother Joshua went up to the pulpit. He looked over the congregation as everybody got real quiet. Then he began to speak.

"What we saw today was the worst thing that any of us has ever saw. None of us went off to the Great War, but if we had of, I don't think anything over there would have been as bad as that."

Everybody shook their heads, some of the men grunted, some of women said "Naw", lots of the people said "Amen".

"What we saw our dear sister do today was as brave as anything ever done. She stretched out her arms and died for us, just like our Lord did!" By now, he had big old tears coming down his face. "And now, it's our time to be brave!"

Some of the people said, "Yes, Lord" and the rest nodded their heads.

"Mr. Russell is coming here tonight to burn down this house of God, this place that Auntie Esther loved so much. Well, I don't know if we can stop him, but I aim to be here to try!"

"Me too," some of the people said. It looked like everybody planned on staying. I wondered if any of them would up and run when Mr. Russell showed up.

Brother Joshua said, "We may not have Auntie Ester with us so that we can show the proper respect by sitting up with her tonight, but we can still sit up with our memories of her. Sister Anabelle, would you come up and lead us in singing? I think it would then be fitting for those who are so led to come up and share some words about what Auntie Esther meant to them."

Sister Anabelle came up and told us to open up the hymnals and she had us sing.

Didn't my Lord deliver Daniel
Deliver Daniel, deliver Daniel
Didn't my Lord deliver Daniel
And why not every man?

While Anabelle was up there singing, I saw her eyes get real big. She looked toward the back of the church. When I turned around, I saw torchlight coming through the little windows in the door. Everybody started turning around and some of them started getting scared and crying out. Brother Joshua walked toward the door and he turned around and held up his hands.

"Now remember Auntie Ester and how she didn't show fear. Anabelle, you stay up there. All of y'all keep singing and I'll go and check outside." He turned around, walked to the door, and opened it. Before he closed it behind him, I slipped out and stood beside him.

We saw four torches, bouncing in the dark, getting closer to the church. After a few seconds, we could see four men but we couldn't see their faces. They kept walking.

Sister Anabelle kept the people singing behind us.

He delivered Daniel from the Lion's den,
Jonah from the belly of the whale,
And the Hebrew children from the fiery furnace,
And why not every man?

I reached up and grabbed Brother Joshua's hand. He didn't even look down at me but he gave my hand a little squeeze. I could feel that his hands was sweating. His voice was kind of shaky when he said "Now listen here! We are here to honor the memory of a dear friend of ours. We don't mean harm, but we ain't coming out."

Those four men stopped walking when Joshua started talking. The one in the middle walked right up to the door.

"Joshua, we ain't here to hurt you. We came to pay our respects to Auntie Ester and to make sure that nobody bothered y'all's service. So, y'all can go on back inside. We'll keep watch out here."

It was Mr. Peterson, the man that owned the grocer store. He turned and told the three other men to walk around the church and to keep their eyes open for trouble. Brother Joshua grabbed Mr. Peterson's hand with both of his hands and shook it. Mr. Peterson then reached around Brother Joshua's shoulders and gave him a hug.

Me and Brother Joshua was about to go back inside the church when I heard some horses coming up the street. Brother Joshua pushed me behind him and said, "Go on back inside, Junebug."

But I didn't.

Mr. Peterson and his men with torches came walking around to the front of the church. They was standing in front of me and Brother Joshua. We all looked out to the street and saw Mr. Russell and Billy come riding up. Three more men were on horses behind them.

Mr. Russell said, "Well, Billy. Looks like they're some people who don't know how to follow directions."

Mr. Russell looked like some kind of boogerman, with the torches making shadows dance all over his face. He sat up on his horse, with his hands crossed on the saddle, looking back and forth at all of us standing there. "Tell me, Billy, didn't I say that everybody should stay in their houses tonight?"

"Yessir, that's what I heard," Billy said before spitting on the ground beside his horse. Mr. Russell swung his leg around and got down off his horse. Billy and the other men did the same thing, with all of them just dropping the reins.

About that time, we all heard the people in the church begin another song. I heard Anabelle singing out loud,

I've got joy like a river
I've got joy like a river
I've got joy like a river in my soul...

Mr. Russell said, "What's going on in there?"

Before the four men with torches said anything, Brother Joshua walked right up to Mr. Russell. He said, "Mr. Russell, we're sitting up with Auntie Ester."

Mr. Russell jerked backwards like he had been hit in the face. He turned around and said to Billy, "Didn't we take care of the disobedience in this town earlier today?"

Billy nodded and started to say something but Mr. Russell beat him to it. "Didn't I say that there would be no funeral for that woman? Didn't I say that the name of that dog shall not be spoken in my town again?" He was getting louder and louder. "Well, I see we got some more cleaning up to do, Billy. We might as well take care of all of it at once." He pointed his big old finger at Brother Joshua and said, "You go on back in there with all the rest of the niggers and then we'll just burn this dump down on top of you. Boys, if he don't go back inside, kill him and throw him in with the rest of them."

Brother Joshua didn't turn around. He just stood there. He took in a deep breath and was about to say something when Mr. Peterson walked up and put his hand on Brother Joshua's shoulder. Mr. Peterson stepped in between Brother Joshua and Mr. Russell. The other men with torches came up to stand in a line with Mr. Peterson in the middle.

Mr. Peterson looked at Mr. Russell and said, "I don't think it's going to happen that way, Mr. Russell."

Mr. Russell looked at him and said, "Who do you think you're talking to, you mealy-mouthed little store clerk?"

Mr. Peterson gave it right back to him. He didn't sound scared at all, but I bet he was down inside. Mr. Peterson said, "I'm talking to you and I'm telling you and your men to drop your guns."

Mr. Russell threw back that big old head of his and gave a laugh. He laughed and laughed, like the old men who sit in the benches on a Saturday laugh at each other's jokes. Billy started laughing too. Mr. Russell's other men just smiled. After he got over his laughing fit, Mr. Russell looked at Mr. Peterson again and said, "Well, what if I tell you that I don't take orders from a little nothing that bags up radishes for the women of the town."

Mr. Peterson just looked right back at him. "I think you'll listen to them."

Mr. Peterson looked behind Mr. Russell into the shadows toward the street. I looked too. Out of the darkness, I saw men moving into the light of the torches. Lots of men. White men and colored men. I looked around. They were everywhere, all around the church. They had rifles, shotguns, pistols, all pointing at Mr. Russell and Billy and his men. The eyes of Mr. Russell's men got real big. They all held up their hands. A few of the men came from the shadows, took the pistols Mr. Russell's men had tucked in their belts, and led them away toward the buildings of the town.

Mr. Peterson said, "Mr. Russell and Billy, I need you to put your hands up too." Mr. Russell slowly put his hands up in the air and then Billy did. Some of the men came up and got Mr. Russell's and Billy's guns. While they did, Mr. Russell was staring real mean at Mr. Peterson.

"Grocer man, you're going to be sorry about this night, if you live long enough to be sorry." Mr. Russell sounded like a big old dog growling when he said that.

Mr. Peterson said, "Brother Joshua, go on back inside and lead your congregation. We'll take care of all of this." Mr. Peterson said, "Galen, take these two down where the others are."

All of the men walked off, leaving Brother Joshua and me just standing there.

Brother Joshua looked down at me, grabbed my hand, and almost ran into the church, pulling me behind him. When we got inside, all of the people stopped singing and turned around. Brother Joshua went right up to the pulpit. I sat in the front row.

He said, "Brothers and sisters, a miracle has happened. A miracle of God. I do believe that Auntie Esther is celebrating in heaven with us that this town has gotten just a little bit of the courage that she had."

All the people were looking around at each other, not knowing what had happened. "I'll tell y'all what happened outside in just a little while. Right now, though, I want us to sing praises to the Lord. Sister Anabelle, will you lead us in singing Down By The Riverside?"

Sister Anabelle started us up.

I'm gonna lay down my burden
Down by the riverside.
Going to lay down my burden
Down by the riverside.
Gonna study war no more.

Brother Joshua stayed up front. I never did see him so happy. He was dancing and clapping his hands and singing so loud. Everybody else figured out by the way that he was acting that everything was going to be all right

211

and they started dancing and clapping too.

We sang a whole bunch of songs that night. Brother Joshua told everybody what had happened with Mr. Russell and his men and how all the people of the town come out to protect us and our church. People was shouting Hallelujah and Thank you Jesus while he was telling them all that happened. After a while, some of the people that hadn't come to the service before came in. They said they had heard all the singing and shouting and come to see what was happening. A little while after that, some more people came in carrying food all wrapped up in kitchen cloths and jugs of spring water and cider. Even though we usually don't eat inside the church on account of it being a sin and all, tonight was special. We all got some food and sat in the pews or on the floor and had ourselves a party! It felt like Christmas, decoration Sunday, and somebody's birthday all done up together! After we ate, we sang some more and some people went up to the pulpit and talked about Auntie Esther. I didn't get a bit sleepy all night.

The windows started getting lighter and the people started to get up, a few at a time, and head home. Brother Joshua and me walked out of the door and looked up at the brightening sky. "Junebug, I guess you never stayed up all night before, have you?"

"One time, me and Sally stayed up all night 'cause we wanted to see if we could. She fell asleep while it was still dark, but I made it until I just saw the sun peeking over the hill. But other than that, I ain't never stayed up the whole night." I said. Then I saw saw smoke rising up from the other end of town. "Look, Brother Joshua!" I pointed toward the smoke.

"Let's go see what's happening," Brother Joshua said. We walked to the street and I saw the ship's wheel. We walked over and stood in front of it. The bottom half of the wheel was broke off and the spokes on the top half were broke off the outside of the wheel. All that was left was the half circle at the bottom with rays going up, looking like the sun with rays of light shooting up. Just as I was thinking that, the sun rose over the hill and shined on my and Brother Joshua's faces. We smiled at each other. We turned around and started down the street. Neither one of us could hardly believe what we was seeing.

There was people all up and down the street, black folks and white folks working together. We saw some men hauling a big sign up and fixing it so that it covered up "Russellton" on the town hall. The sign said "Jubilee". Brother Joshua called up to one of the men.

"What's that mean, Thomas? What's Jubilee?"

Mr. Thomas looked down and smiled at us. He said, "Good morning, Joshua. And good day to you, too, Miss Junebug! Jubilee is the new name of our town! No more Russellton!"

On the other end of the street, I saw that the sign at the tavern was being tore down and everything that said "Russellton" was being taken down or painted over or covered up.

Brother Joshua said, "Where is Mr. Russell?" The men on the ladders looked at each other.

Thomas said, "Down at the end of the street," jerking his chin in the direction past the diner. Brother Joshua thanked them and nodded and took my hand and we started walking.

Everybody along the way seemed so happy. Some was whistling and some was singing. I saw Mr. Booker, one of the deacons in our church, patting the back of Mr. Daniel, one of the white men in town. They was both laughing and talking. Brother Joshua and me smiled and shook our heads.

We came around the corner at the end of the street and what I saw was hard to believe. It was like a hill had risen up in the night just beside the drive to the old house, like God had decided there wasn't enough hills or mountains around here and so He decided to make one more. The day before, the Russellton Church was there. Now there was a big pile of fresh dirt.

There was a bunch of men patting down the dirt with shovels and putting big slabs of white rock on the sides and top of the mound. As we walked around to the other side of the hill – it was so big I couldn't see over the top of it – we saw a line of men carrying more of the white rock down the driveway. That's when I saw that the house was gone.

All that was left of the big house was the burnt nubs of the tall columns that had been on the front porch. Behind the nubs was just a big pile of smoking black boards. The white rock had been the pretty white marble floor inside the house. I seen it one time when we went to sing Christmas carols for the Russells and Mrs. Russell had brought out cookies for us. One of the men carrying the marble was Mr. Galen Whitmire. He saw me and Brother Joshua and he come over to us after he dropped his marble on the dirt mound.

Brother Joshua shook his hand and said, "Mr. Galen, I don't think I'll ever be able to say thank you enough."

Mr. Galen said, "Joshua, you can call me just Galen, no mister needed. And I should be the one thanking you. You and Auntie Esther, God rest her soul. Y'all were the ones who gave us all what we needed, a shot of courage."

Brother Joshua said, "If it hadn't been for you and Mr. Peterson and the other men, Mr. Russell would have had our church burned down and us in it. So, where is Mr. Russell?"

Mr. Galen said, "Well, we did what we had to do."

Brother Joshua stepped back and said kind of quietly, "Galen, what did y'all do?"

Galen said, "The kind of hatred and evil that the Russells had is the kind that has to be dealt with drastically. It's like a boil that has to be lanced or it keeps festering."

"Where is he? Where is Mr. Russell?" Brother Joshua asked him. He asked him firm, like he was tired of getting no answer.

Mr. Galen pointed at the dirt mound. "That's them," he said.

Brother Joshua didn't know what he meant and neither did I for a few seconds. Then Brother Joshua let out a little sound, almost like a little bitty cough.

Brother Joshua said, "Under that dirt?" Mr. Galen nodded.

"All of them?" Brother Joshua said. Mr. Galen nodded again.

That's when I knew. All the Russells was dead.

Mr. Galen said, "Every last one of them. The only way to rid this town of the evil of that family was to wipe out every last sign of them."

"But Galen, that just ain't right! That's no better than them! Good people can't just bury somebody alive and think that God won't punish them." Joshua kept shaking his head. He looked like he was going to cry.

"Oh no, we didn't bury them alive." Mr. Galen pointed over our heads at one of the big old oak trees in front of the smoking ruins of the house. We hadn't seen it before, but there was a whole bunch of ropes with nooses at the ends of them hanging from the big fat bottom limbs of the tree. Under each rope was a dining room chair from the house, all of the chairs turned over.

"We had a trial right there on the front porch of the house. We had a jury, three white people and three black people. We gave every one of the Russells a chance to plead their case. But, in the end, they were all found guilty and the sentence was carried out. I kicked over every last chair and hanged 'em myself. Then, we burned down the house."

Brother Joshua was still slowly shaking his head. "I don't know, Galen. It seems awful fast."

"Yessir, Joshua. That it was and that was what it took."

About that time, two men come walking up. One of them said, "Galen, look at who we found."

The two men each had the arm of a skinny white woman and she was walking between them. She was carrying a tiny little baby, all wrapped up in a light blue blanket. The woman was dirty and I could see that she was shivering. When the men stopped her in front of Mr. Galen, she just held the baby tighter. I had only seen this woman once or twice but I knew who she was. It was Billy Russell's wife. And that was his baby boy.

Mr. Galen said, "Where'd you find her?" he asked the two men.

"Down by the river, trying to make it downstream," one of them said. "What're we going to do with her?"

Before Mr. Galen could say anything, the woman spoke up. She had a shaky voice, like she was real scared or cold or both.

"Misters, I know this family was evil. I'm glad you done rid this world of them. If you hadn't of done it, I was going to run away as soon as my baby boy was strong enough to make the trip."

One of the men holding her looked over at the oak tree. "We can't just let her go, Galen. What if she goes and tells everybody what has happened here?"

The woman saw where he was looking and she started crying. Big tears started coming down her face. She held her baby even tighter and said to Mr. Galen, "Mister, please! I'm begging for mercy for me and Baby Hank!"

Brother Joshua put his hand on Mr. Galen's arm and said, "Galen, she ain't a Russell. She hates them as much as we do. You can let her go and she won't tell nobody. Besides, you can't go and kill an innocent little baby! God will not let an evil like that stand!"

Mr. Galen looked at the woman and then the tree and then the mound and then back at Brother Joshua. "I just don't know."

The woman fell down to her knees. "Please mister! I know that you have a heart! I know you're not like them godless Russells! I am begging you for the life of my baby!"

Mr. Galen stood for a long time, looking at the woman on the ground, weeping and still clutching her baby. Finally Mr. Galen said, "Well, it is true that you haven't been here long enough to become like one of them. And though your baby boy is a Russell, it don't seem right to make him pay for the sin of his fathers. You can go. But, I'm telling you. You walk and you keep walking and don't you ever come back. And if you ever tell anybody about this…"

The men standing around kicked the dirt with their feet.

Mr. Galen said, "If you ever tell anyone about this, you'll wish you hadn't."

The woman started sobbing. She grabbed Mr. Galen around the knees and kissed his leg and said, "Thank you, mister, thank you."

Mr. Galen wiggled loose from her and the two men helped her up. I saw them walk her and the baby over to the road coming into town. One of them helped her wrap up the baby again and the other pointed down the road. She started walking. I saw her look back once before she turned the corner and walked out of sight.

This here is the end of Auntie Esther's diary.

She's in heaven.

CHAPTER 50

JUBILEE COMMUNITY CHURCH

Coleman and Rosalee sat looking at Pastor Henry as the sun peeked through the windows of the church. Pastor Henry closed the book.

"So, what happened after that?" Coleman asked him.

Henry said, "It wasn't easy to build a town on such a terrible foundation as Russellton. However, the people – black and white – realized they had to work together. They decided who would be the best at the different jobs in town. It didn't matter what color the person's skin was. They had some arguments, to be sure. But it was arguments between people who knew that they were no better in God's eyes than the other person."

Rosalee said, "Didn't anyone wonder what happened to the Russells?"

Henry said, "The Russells didn't deal with anyone outside of Russellton very much. The only living relative was a cousin who lived out west. The people in the town sent a letter or two to him, but they found out he died before any of this happened."

Coleman said, "Did the mother and the baby live? The one that Galen let go? Did she ever tell?"

Henry said, "She never told." Henry stood up. "Let me show you something."

He walked into a small room just off the sanctuary, rummaged in a drawer, and came back holding an old scrapbook. He opened it to the first page and pointed at a yellowing photo.

Henry said, "That is the woman. And here on the other page is something else."

Coleman read aloud, "Henry Smithson Russell, Birthdate January 31, 1921, Birthplace Russellton, Alabama."

Henry said, "That woman in the photo, the one Galen let go, was my mother. The baby was me. After my mother carried me down that dirt road out of Russellton, we went to Montgomery and lived with relatives for a while until she could manage on her own. She raised me using her maiden name, Smithson. She told me that my father had been killed in an accident. It was only on her deathbed, when she was dying of consumption, that she told the story I just told you. Well, she told the part that she knew. I learned the rest after I came here myself. My mother never told another living soul." Henry ran his finger over the old photo. "She was a brave woman," he said.

Coleman sat back in his chair and looked toward the ceiling. "So all of the Russell family is out there under that mound?"

Henry nodded. "Everyone except me."

Coleman said, "Oh yeah. All except Baby Hank." Coleman closed his eyes. "There has never been any question about them, no investigation, nothing?" Henry nodded.

Coleman said, "Don't you think that is wrong? This was murder."

Henry said, "It wasn't murder. It was a sentence. There was a legal process, the only process the people of the town had available at the time. There was a trial, a verdict, and a sentence."

Rosalee nodded. "It was justice."

Coleman said, "It was vigilante justice!"

Henry said, "Coleman, generations of people had been oppressed by the Russell family. If they had delayed what they did, the Russells might've brought people from outside to interfere and who knows what would've happened. They might've killed everyone in town. They did what they had to do and it was the just thing. The people who were the jury are all gone, all passed away. Of course, Galen is still here."

Coleman said, "Why does Galen hate us? Why does he want to have us killed?"

Henry said, "Galen is afraid. He is afraid that people outside Jubilee will find out that he was the hangman for the Russells. He is afraid of things he can't control. It does seem like he hates. But hate is just fear in another form."

Coleman touched Rosalee's hand. Rosalee smiled.

"I've been told that before," Coleman said. "What would happen if people outside Jubilee knew what happened here in 1921? Would something be done?"

"The younger people in Jubilee don't know what happened back then. It's not something that we talk about. We choose to leave it in the past. If there was some kind of investigation by the state police or the Alabama attorney general, it wouldn't be a good thing for our little town," Henry said. "Are you thinking about telling someone, Coleman?"

Before Coleman could say anything, the door burst open, letting in cool morning air. Martelle entered the church and said, "Galen and a bunch of men are coming down the street." He pointed at Coleman and Rosalee. He said, "They're coming to kill them."

CHAPTER 51

JUBILEE COMMUNITY CHURCH

Henry stood and said, "Let's hide y'all in the back."

Coleman said, "No, we need to face them."

"They'll be here any second," Martelle said. "Better decide in a hurry."

Pastor Henry stood and started toward the door of the church, Coleman and Rosalee right behind him.

The morning had dawned clear, though mist still floated through the town. Henry, Coleman, and Rosalee planted their feet on the church stoop and faced the street, waiting for the mob.

The mayor appeared from behind the church, leading a group of searchers just returned from the woods.

"Galen's coming," she said, "and he's not alone."

Henry said, "We know. Martelle's already told us."

She said, "Martelle's helping us?" Henry shrugged and nodded.

Galen appeared at the corner, leading a cluster of men.

The mayor stepped up beside Henry on the church stoop. Henry motioned Coleman and Rosalee back but they did not budge.

Galen approached the stoop and stopped, his gang behind him. He said, "Pastor and Mayor, we don't want to have to do anything to you so step aside." Galen stood with his arms crossed on his chest, a holstered pistol hanging from his belt. The other men had pistols and long guns in their hands. "This has gone far enough. That boy has snooped too much and we have to do something about it."

Coleman jabbed a finger toward Galen. "Why did you try to hurt Rosalee if you were trying to get at me?"

Galen looked at Coleman with disgust, ignoring the question. He looked back at Pastor Henry and said, "I figured if we took her, we could force the boy to leave, but it didn't work. We come here to finish the job."

The mayor took a half step forward and said, "Can't let y'all do that."

Galen smiled. "Madam Mayor, I don't think you got much of a choice." He motioned over his shoulder. "Looks like I outman and outgun y'all." The men behind him shifted and tightened their grips on pistols, rifles, and shotguns. Their faces were hard, their eyes cold.

Galen chuckled and said to the mayor, "I guess I shoulda known that you and the pastor would be O.K. with these two being a couple. I seemed to recall y'all wanting to do the same thing. I say that it ain't right. But that don't matter cause it ain't just me. The state of Alabama says it ain't lawful."

The mayor said, "These two don't live in Alabama and they haven't done anything here that's against the law."

Galen glared at Rosalee. "I see how them two look at each other. I can guarantee they been doing unlawful things when nobody's around."

Coleman's face flushed crimson. He said, "Listen here, mister! You can't stand there and talk that way about this woman. She is one of the finest people I know, a lot better'n you!"

Henry put a hand on Coleman's chest and pushed him gently back. "Coleman, just let it go," he said quietly.

Coleman did not let it go. He said, "We haven't done anything to be ashamed of. If you say anything more about her, I'm gonna come over there and make you sorry you did."

"Boys," Galen said over his shoulder, "if he takes a step this way, shoot 'em both where they stand."

Henry held up his hands and said, "Galen, let's take this down a few notches." Henry whispered to the mayor, "Get Rosalee inside."

The mayor motioned for one of the men standing near her to take Rosalee inside the church and guard her. The man shepherded her into the dim church interior.

Galen said, "Pastor, I need you to send the boy over here. Do that and we'll leave y'all alone."

Pastor Henry said, "You know that I can't do that, Galen."

The mayor said, "Galen, I know you think that what you're doing is right, but it's not." She motioned toward Coleman. "He is not a threat to you."

Galen put his hand on the pistol butt and said, "I'm not worried about a threat to me. I am worried about what you should be worried about, Mayor, the threat to this town." He gestured to the men assembled with him. "None of us thought that this boy should've been invited to stick his nose into our business in the first place. Now he knows a little of what happened here and that might be enough for him to bring more people here, maybe even the law."

Pastor Henry said, "Actually, Coleman knows everything."

Galen's eyebrows shot up.

The pastor said, "I read Auntie Esther's diary to him."

Galen said, "Pastor! You had no right!"

Henry said, "Galen, it's you that don't have a right. No right to hurt these innocent young people."

Galen said, "Damn it, Pastor! If the boy had just left town looking for the girl like we figured he would, we could've let her go and everything would've been all hunky dory. But that stupid boy had to come searching for his girlfriend and mess everything up."

Coleman said, "It wasn't me. I didn't come get Rosalee."

Galen sneered and said, "Well, she didn't just untie them ropes herself and bust out the back of the shed."

A high voice drifted from the side of the church building. "I broke her out."

Dozens of eyes pivoted to see a dark figure rise up from the ground where he had been sitting, previously hidden by the men standing in front of him.

Martelle glided up to the stoop and said, "I done a little bit more than that too. Things is about to get kind of crazy around here pretty soon."

Galen's said, "Martelle! What are you talking about?"

A crocodile smile stretched across Martelle's face. He said, "You'll find out pretty soon."

Galen said, "You're just a crazy idiot!"

Martelle said, "Galen, tell these men to leave the boy alone." Martelle's eyes gleamed in the light of day, pearlescent orbs from another world.

Galen laughed. "Martelle, you know very well what has to be done. You've agreed with me all along."

Martelle said, "I changed my mind." He motioned toward Coleman. "That boy ain't going to do no harm to nobody. I could see it with my own two eyes." He glanced around at the group of men. "You don't have to have the gift to know that he ain't a threat."

Martelle fixed Galen with a cold gaze, his milky blue eyes piercing the man. He said, "Anyways, Galen, you ain't worried about this town. You ain't worried about nobody but your own self."

A woman's scream erupted from within the church building.

Some of the mayor's men leveled shotguns at Galen and his gang, weapons they had kept hidden until now. Galen stepped back.

The rest of the mayor's men – along with the pastor, the mayor, and Coleman – ran into the church.

The guard was rising from the floor.

"He came in the side door and jumped us! He slashed at me with a knife and then ran." Blood streamed down from a long gash on his face.

The guard said, "He's got the girl!"

CHAPTER 52

ALABAMA STATE POLICE HEADQUARTERS

"Damn!" The colonel read the phone log once again and ran his finger down the duty roster.

"Damn!"

The weekend had been a good one. The grandkids had come over and the barbequed chicken tasted better than ever.

Now I'm coming back to this shit.

Only one year and three months until he would leave all of this behind, living off his pension, playing with the grandkids any time he wanted.

The colonel leaned over and pressed the intercom button.

He said, "Sally, ask Trooper Howard to come in here."

In a few minutes, a tall uniformed man strode into the office and said, "Sir?"

"Have a seat, Virgil."

"What's up?"

"Take a seat, trooper, and I'll tell you."

The colonel leaned back in his seat and said, "I've got a job for you. Just came in."

"Sure thing, sir. What is it?"

The colonel remained silent. He stared at the patrolman seated in front of him, squinting, thinking.

Trooper Howard said, "Sir, what's a matter? Am I in trouble or something?"

The colonel leaned forward, putting his forearms on the desk. He said, "Not yet."

"What does that mean?"

"It means I want you to not go berserk over what I'm about to ask you to do. I don't want you to get yourself in trouble."

"Sir, you know me well enough to know that ain't gonna happen."

"I hope that's true." The colonel lifted a paper from the desk and said, "We got a call this morning about a possible murder a long time ago, with some possible evidence that needs to be investigated. It sounded crazy and I wouldn't have thought much about it except the weekend officer-in-charge had a report about the same place."

The trooper said, "Where is it?"

"I'm getting to that."

The colonel looked down at the report again and said, "A call came in yesterday that a cleaning lady over at Alabama State said that some strange man's been poking around and asking a bunch of questions about some researchers. Well, really he was only asking about one of them, a man that left town a week ago to look into an old Indian mound. The stranger asking questions matches the description of somebody who's wanted for armed robbery in Montgomery. It's possible that he wants to settle some old score with this researcher, based on what he said to the cleaning lady."

The trooper frowned and said, "O.K. sir, but what does one have to do with the other?"

The colonel said, "The call this morning said that the evidence of the old murder was buried in that Indian mound."

"Must've been a real old murder. Weren't those mounds made a thousand years ago?"

"Maybe. The researcher I mentioned has spent the last week looking into the mound. If there is any evidence of an old murder, he will know by now." The colonel referred to the paper. "Coleman Hightower is the researcher's name."

"Fine, sir, but why am I in danger of getting in trouble?"

The colonel gazed at the patrolman again and said, "Virgil, if I had anybody else to send, I'd do it, but there just ain't nobody else. Blythe's on vacation and Brock ain't ready to go out on his own, not on a call like this one."

"Colonel, just give it to me straight. You ain't making a lot of sense."

The colonel said, "The mound is up in Jubilee."

The trooper's face became steely, his jaw muscles flexed. He nodded and said, "O.K. sir. I can do it."

"Virgil, there's something else. The man on the phone, the one that said the evidence was in the mound, said that Galen Whitmire was the murderer."

"Why that son-of-a-bitch."

The colonel stood up and walked around the desk. He placed a hand on the trooper's shoulder and said, "Now listen, Virgil. We just got past all of that. I don't want it all stirred up again. The judge said it was an accident and that's all there is to it. I'd send somebody else if I could, but you're the only one."

The patrolman remained quiet for a moment and said, "Sir, I can handle it."

The colonel said, "I want you to go up there. If this stranger is there and causing problems, bring him in. If that researcher is finished looking into the mound, take what he's found as the gospel. If he's found signs of a crime, we'll follow the evidence where it takes us, if to Galen Whitmire, then fine. But if that researcher says there wasn't no crime, then the case is closed. You hear me? You understand?"

"Understood, sir."

CHAPTER 53

THE SPRINGHOUSE

The sun crept over the horizon as he dragged her from the church toward the mound. They entered the adjacent woods and birds sleeping in the thickets exploded into the air like fireworks. The world swirled like a kaleidoscope in Rosalee's terrified mind.

The man pushed Rosalee into the corner of the old springhouse. He moved behind her and tied the end of the rope to a post. He said, "Listen, don't try to get out of this rope."

The killer ducked under a collapsed rafter and moved to the opening and checked to see they were not followed. He turned back to Rosalee.

He said, "You probably won't believe me, but I really don't want to hurt you." He sat facing her. "Tell me. What's in this mound I keep hearing people around here talking about?"

Rosalee's mind spun. She felt like he was in some strange world where all of her fears came together. When he grabbed her, she had immediately known who he was, would never forget the cruel eyes.

How can this man, the man who shot me, who almost killed me, how can this monster be here tormenting me?

She said, "What are you doing here? How did you find me?"

The killer said, "A nigger cleaning woman at that school told me y'all was coming here." He pointed a finger at Rosalee. "There's gold in that mound, ain't there? I heard that Indians used to bury gold with their dead chiefs."

The killer waited for Rosalee to speak. She sat silent, bewildered.

He said, "You help me get that gold and I'll leave you alone." He leaned back and spoke into the dim structure. "If I had the gold, it wouldn't matter that y'all knew who I was. I wouldn't have no reason to kill you. I would have enough money to leave the country, to go to Cuba or maybe South

225

America. People say you can live like a king there if you got a little money. I know I gotta get outta here. Started out as the son of a whore and there ain't nothing but trouble been followin me all the days of my life."

Rosalee's heart felt as if it would beat out of her chest. She managed to say, "I swear to you that there is no gold in there. At least not that I know of."

The killer's voice now sounded pleading.

He said, "I'll let you go if you just tell me where to dig. I ain't got long." Rosalee said nothing.

The killer said, "If you don't know or ain't gonna to tell me, you ain't no use to me and I might as well kill you now."

He slid a long evil blade from a sheath on his belt. The rusty knife was dull in the low light, like a long claw extending from the killer's dirty hand.

A rustling sound floated from outside into the springhouse. The killer jerked toward it and froze. He sniffed the air.

In a harsh whisper, he said, "Going to go check this out. You better be quiet as a mouse. And you better tell me something when I get back or your guts are going to be spilling in this here dirt."

He disappeared.

Rosalee struggled against the ropes while listening for the killer to return. The knot was tight, but it began to loosen. Her muscles became taut, her breathing rapid. She imagined the blade entering her, slicing through her intestines, the tip exiting through the skin of her back.

The rope fell away and she sprang up. She paused at the doorway and did not see or hear him.

She ran.

CHAPTER 54

THE MOUND

Coleman hurried out of the side door of the church and saw a faint trail left by recent footsteps through the tall grass behind the buildings. Martelle joined him. They began to run.

Henry yelled, "Everyone else spread out. Let's make sure whoever has her doesn't double back."

At Coleman's side, Martelle said, "Don't rightly know who it could be. Everybody was right there at the front of the church."

Coleman scanned the field and woodline ahead and said, "He ain't from here."

Martelle glanced at Coleman and said, "You know who it is?"

Coleman said, "Got a pretty good idea. Tried to kill us both in Washington and he followed me down here."

Martelle glanced at Coleman again. He said, "I don't know who you are exactly, but you shore got a lot of people that want you dead."

Coleman said, "Just lucky, I guess."

As the Coleman and Martelle cleared the ends of the buildings, they had a clear view – the mound to their left and the town to their right with the broad field in between. On the street emerging from the town was a group of men, Galen Whitmire in front.

Coleman's eyes swept the field and he saw her.

Rosalee was standing just to the right of the mound, her hand held to her brow, trying to identify the crowd coming down the street.

Coleman pushed Martelle toward the town and said, "Go and stop Galen from doing anything to her."

Martelle raced toward the group of men.

Coleman sprinted toward Rosalee. He was a few yards from her when he called, "Rosalee!"

Rosalee pulled her eyes away from the town. Her face broke into a broad smile. She started toward Coleman and suddenly stopped and yelled, "Coleman! Watch out!"

The killer sprang from the side of the mound where he had dug a small hole. Coleman was knocked to the ground.

The killer picked him up from the ground, his arm around Coleman's neck and the knife held in his other hand, pointing toward Coleman's chest. Coleman struggled to free himself, but the killer's grip tightened until Coleman's vision faded and he almost passed out.

"I'm getting kindly tired of all this," the killer said. "It's 'bout time to end this here thing."

The killer saw men coming from town, a thin black man out in front.

The killer shot a glance at Rosalee and said, "Nigger girl, you better stay back or I'm going to stick him, just like a hog."

Rosalee raised her hands. Martelle ran up beside her and stopped, the rest of the men fanning out behind them.

The killer held Coleman in front of him and faced the group. He said, "If y'all don't want to watch this boy die, y'all are going to do what I say."

Edward Jackson moved to the front of the group. His deep bass boomed out in the early morning. "Son, don't go doing something you'll be sorry about the rest of your life. Just let Coleman go."

The killer said, "Can't do that. This one and that one there," he motioned with his head toward Rosalee, "got some stuff on me that I can't let stand."

Edward said, "We can work something out."

The killer nodded and grinned. He said, "You got that right. We shore enough going to work something out. What y'all going to do is start digging in this old mound and give me the gold and then I'm going to get on outta here and y'all are going to let me go."

Edward said, "Son, there ain't no gold in this mound. I can guarantee it."

The killer yelled, "How the hell you going to guarantee anything to me, you stupid nigger?" His eyes flicked around the crowd. "What you waitin on? Ain't none of y'all going to dig to save this boy's life? Y'all going to just stand there and let me finish the job I started back in the cemetery?"

Coleman knew that no one could reach him to help before the killer stabbed him. Time slowed. Ribbons of color twirled in the sky, bringing visions. Coleman saw his father plowing. He saw Granny Mae churning butter, a big spoonful of snuff bulging behind her lower lip.

Rosalee looked at him, rays of golden light spilling over the hill and framing her face, a face so beautiful that Coleman ached even now. Her eyes met his. Across the yards, she gave him strength. He remembered a promise.

I will never leave you. I will never forsake you.

His hands fell to his sides. As his right hand brushed by his pants pocket, he felt the shape of an object there. He put his hands inside his pockets.

From far down the road, the roar of engines appeared. Everyone's heads jerked toward the sound.

An Alabama Highway Patrol car sped toward the town.

"Damn it!" the killer yelled. "I ain't gonna let you tell them pigs what I done."

The killer shifted his grip on the knife to get a better angle. Coleman felt the killer's hold on him loosen and he pushed himself away, spinning around to face the killer. The sun shone from behind Coleman and into the killer's eyes. The killer lunged with the knife extended in his right hand. The tip of the blade plunged toward Coleman's neck. Coleman took a half step to the left as his right arm came up under the killer's arm, deflecting the knife. In Coleman's right hand was a silver pen with a tiny dent in its side. The pen sank deep into the killer's chest, between two ribs, and punctured his heart. The killer's heart pumped, pushed all of its blood out around the pen, and with dwindling strength, stopped. The wretched body crumpled to the ground at Coleman's feet.

Rosalee rushed to Coleman's side and embraced him. He said to her as if in a dream, "You got away from him."

She said, "Yeah. I don't need you to save me." She patted his chest. "But, I'm glad you tried."

The crowd gathered around the couple. Galen pushed his way forward.

"What are they doing here?" he asked as he pointed at the approaching police cars.

Martelle said, "I called 'em. Thought we might need 'em before all was said and done."

Galen said, "Martelle, what were you thinking? This is going to ruin everything!"

Martelle said, "Maybe, maybe not. We'll have to wait and see."

A tall officer with cropped hair crouched beside his black car and shouted, "Hands up, everyone! I mean it! I want to be able to see your hands!"

The officer's pistol was pulled and pointed in the space above the heads of the crowd. Two other cars skidded to a stop behind his and two more state patrolmen exited, their Sam Browne belts shining in the morning sun, guns drawn.

Mayor Jefferson arrived and stepped forward, her hands high in the air. She said, "Patrolman, I am so relieved you're here."

Behind her, Galen whispered, "That's the one!"

Ephraim said, "You mean the trooper?"

"Yeah, the one whose partner died in my wreck. He's been out to get me since the trial, since the judge said it wasn't my fault. Said that he better not ever catch me alone. Hell's bells, I'm a dead man."

Edward Jackson said, "Just shut up and stay still!"

The highway patrolman remained in the cover of his car door and kept his gun raised. He squinted in the direction of the mayor and said, "Who are you?"

She said, "I am the town mayor, Mayor Jefferson. A terrible thing has happened and we need your help. This man," she nodded toward the body, "tried to kill this young man." She motioned toward Coleman.

The patrolman glanced at the dead body crumpled on the ground between him and the crowd.

Keeping his gun pointing forward, he glanced over his shoulder and shouted, "Patrolman Brock! Come up here! Arvil, you cover him."

One of the other officers sprinted to the side of the first patrolman and crouched beside him.

The tall officer said, "Now, Mayor, I want you and the boy to come over here real slow with your hands up. Patrolman Brock and Patrolman Bryant back there are going to make sure everyone else stays where they are. Do you understand?"

"Yes, officer." The mayor said over her shoulder, "Everyone stay very still. We'll get this sorted out in a few minutes."

Coleman looked behind him. Galen caught him in a reptilian stare and said, "You better watch what you say, boy."

The mayor said, "Coleman, let's go."

The two of them began to walk very slowly toward the policemen, their arms stretched skyward. They stopped a few feet from the patrol car.

The patrolman contemplated them for a long moment. He said, "Mayor, I'm Trooper Howard. Now, tell me what happened."

The mayor and Coleman waited, neither of them knowing what the other might say.

"Trooper Howard," the mayor said, "the man on the ground tried to kidnap the friend of Coleman here. Coleman managed to fight him off and the man ended up dying. I've never seen the man before."

Coleman said, "I've seen him before. He shot me and Rosalee."

The faces of the officer and the mayor pivoted toward Coleman.

Trooper Howard said, "Do you know his name?" Coleman slowly shook his head.

Trooper Howard yelled behind him, "Bryant, come up here and see if there is any identification on the body."

Trooper Bryant holstered his pistol and trotted to the side of the motionless figure.

Trooper Howard said, "Mayor, I'll tell you what brought us here in the first place. Headquarters got a strange call yesterday, said a man was hanging out around Alabama State College asking questions about a young man who had come up here to Jubilee." He looked at Coleman. "The person matched the description of a vagrant we had been trying to find. The vagrant was wanted for armed robbery." The patrolman turned back to the mayor. "We were already planning to come up here to check this out when we got the call this morning."

The mayor said, "What call would that be, officer?"

Trooper Howard said, "We got a call that there was a murder here a ways back and that the evidence is buried in this mound."

The mayor stood wordless. The patrolman waited.

Coleman could feel the weight of decades bearing down. The mound was like a dam holding back a vast lake of guilt. If its secret broke now, the guilt would be a torrent that would sweep away the town.

The patrolman pulled out a small notebook and flipped it open. He said, "The good thing, we found out early this morning, is that a researcher came to Jubilee to look into the mound."

The patrolman looked up from his book. He scanned the crowd standing near the mound. His eyes locked on Galen Whitmire.

Galen melted back into the group.

Trooper Howard turned back to Coleman and said, "Are you Coleman Hightower, the researcher?"

Coleman said, "Yessir, I'm Coleman Hightower."

The patrolman said, "All right. What did you find? Was there any evidence of a crime?"

Inside his chest, Coleman's heart raced. His mind flew. He recognized this moment as a juncture between his former life and a future life or the end of life. A yawning chasm opened on all sides of him. The threat from the killer was gone, that nameless shadow that had chased him the past weeks and months, but danger still lurked. Even now, he could feel Galen's eyes burning into his back, a gaze fueled by suspicion and distrust.

Coleman slowly turned his eyes toward the mound. He now knew the secret, the evil that was covered by good earth, malevolence held down by slabs of marble. He thought of the bravery of the people, ordinary townsfolk who had risen up to confront injustice, who had not let a travesty pass without speaking and acting against it.

People like Galen.

He remembered words Rosalee had said. "Everybody's got fear down inside them. That fear can turn hateful. What you got to do is get it out in the light. Then the fear goes away and all that's left is love."

Coleman saw the crowd, the sun rising over the buildings in the distance.

I've never been in a place like this. This place was built on fear. But now, it is filled with love. I can see it. I can feel it oozing out of the very bricks of the buildings. Yes, they've got room to grow but they care about each other and I know that whatever they do comes out of that care.

"Son, did you hear me?" The officer squinted into Coleman's face.

"Yessir, I heard you." Coleman looked at the mayor. She met his gaze. He turned back to the patrolman and said, "Officer, I found that this is an Indian mound. There was no sign of a crime."

Trooper Howard stared at Coleman for a long moment. He looked back at the crowd, searching for Galen, not finding him. He said, "Are you sure? Is that the statement you're standing on?"

Coleman nodded. "Yes."

Trooper Howard said, "O.K. You're the expert."

Patrolman Brock approached and said, "Hey, I just called it in and this is our man. Wanted for armed robbery. They found out the boys in Charlotte were looking for him for the same thing."

Coleman said, "And he was the one who shot me and Rosalee Dawkins and killed a police officer in Arlington, Virginia in March. I was a witness."

The first patrolman gave Coleman another long stare. He said, "O.K. Brock. Call that in too." He flipped his notebook closed. "And tell 'em we didn't find any sign of an old murder."

The patrolman turned to the mayor. He said, "Tell your citizens over there not to go anywhere 'cause we're going to need to question them." His eyes searched Coleman's face for a few seconds and he said, "But it looks clear to me that this was self-defense."

As the patrolmen went to assess the scene and make arrangements for the coroner's car to come and take the body away, the mayor and Coleman walked back to the group.

The mayor said, "Everybody please stay here and talk to the officers about what we saw with that man and Coleman."

Galen was ashen. The fire of a few minutes before had extinguished. In a trembling voice, he said, "What did you tell them?"

Coleman said, "I told them that I didn't find any sign of a crime in the mound."

Martelle stepped forward. "That's good enough for me." He turned his eyes on the other men. "How 'bout y'all?"

They all nodded, even Ephraim Hopkins.

Martelle said, "Galen, if you lay hands on this boy or this girl, I will make sure that the state police know exactly what you did here in 21."

Galen hung his head, completely defeated.

The rest of Galen's men dispersed, embarrassed looks on their faces, as they mixed with the others and waited to talk to the patrolmen. Coleman walked over to Martelle who was standing apart from the crowd.

Coleman said, "Thank you for saving Rosalee's life."

Coleman took Martelle's hand in his. The man's chalky gaze lit on Coleman, attempting to read something deep inside and then relenting, before he said, "I was only trying to do the right thing."

Martelle turned his head and said, as if to himself, "I don't always do the right thing, but this time…"

Coleman released the hand and Martelle drifted away.

CHAPTER 55

THE MOUND

She spread her arms wide. The warmth of the southern sun permeated her, seeped into her heart.

She held out her hand and smiled as he took it and simply gazed at her. She said, "You know love ain't easy, like a lot of people think it is." As she spoke, she pulled him close. "Love is a little bit like a battle."

She closed her eyes, the sun saturating her with its strength. When she opened them, he was looking at her face, searching her eyes.

She smiled and said, "What I mean is that you give your love to something or someone and right away, other things are already crowding in, trying to steal the love, trying to take your attention."

He squeezed her hand and said, "You don't have to worry about that with me. I made a promise. I'll keep it."

She said, "I ain't talking about you."

He stepped back and said, "Is there someone else?"

She laughed. "Nothing like that." She grasped his other hand. "My parents and their parents before them and almost everybody I knew growing up was heading on the same path. They were on the path because they didn't know they had a choice, that the way they went through life was something you can change and not just something that happened to you. The thing is, if you're heading down the wrong path, jumping from one stone to another but going in the wrong direction, you have to change your path in order to change your destination. You stay on one path too long and pretty soon, it's been a year. Every year is a stepping-stone. In fact, every life can be thought of as a stepping-stone. If you simply do what your parents or your friends do without thinking, you will just stay on the same path they were on. I ain't going toward a destination that wasn't meant for me. I've done that before."

Coleman said, "Fine. I'll go on the path with you."

Rosalee said, "What I was meaning about love is that something else will be fighting for my love, for the love that I give to you. It's the thing that I have set my path toward, the thing that I won't give up on."

Coleman stared, waiting.

Rosalee squeezed his hands and said, "Coleman, it's justice."

She turned to the sun.

She said, "My path is laid toward justice. Nothing is going to take me off it."

She turned back to Coleman and said, "Back in the shed, when I thought Galen was going to kill me, I came to a place of peace. I realized that the only way for true peace to come to me is to stop fighting, but that doesn't mean to stop going down the path to justice. It means to stop fighting those who try to take me off the path I've chosen. I prayed for peace and I got it. I'm going to keep on praying for peace and working for justice."

Pastor Henry walked up and said, "Coleman, we have to get y'all back to the house. Your and Rosalee's ride will be here in a couple of hours."

Coleman said, "Pastor, I need to ask you and the mayor something. Rosalee, I'll be right back."

Rosalee watched as Coleman pulled the pastor and Mayor Jefferson into a huddle by the mound. Beyond them, the state patrolmen questioned the townspeople. Some of the people were drifting back to their homes, their statements already given.

People from both sides, Galen's men and the ones who had helped the pastor and mayor, mingled and talked and laughed. Some of them hugged. Reconciliation floated in the air.

Coleman returned.

He said, "Rosalee, I've been talking to the pastor and mayor and now I'm going to ask you something."

Rosalee waited. Pastor Henry approached and then stopped several yards away. The mayor was well behind him and looked down when Rosalee's head turned that way. The townspeople who had been walking stopped and turned toward the couple, seeming to sense significance.

Coleman took her hand.

He said, "Rosalee, I have heard you speak of your path in life, your search for justice. Like I told you in the cemetery, I want to be at your side. I am satisfied with the love you choose to give me. If your love has to be split between me and justice, my love for you will more than make up the difference."

Rosalee stood, her mouth open. She had not expected this, had thought he would fade away just like others, small men who could not stand in the shadow of her first love.

With a start, she realized that Coleman would not stand in anything's shadow, that he would cast his own shadow, that he was choosing his own path. His path was to *her* just as her path was to justice. His first love was her and he would save a little love for justice because that was what she most desired.

"Rosalee, I want to be your companion on the path, I want to be your husband. Will you be my wife?"

"Yes."

She heard herself say the word even as she thought it.

Coleman smiled. "Will you marry me now?"

She said, "Now?"

Coleman motioned toward the pastor and the mayor.

He said, "The mayor has the authority to issue marriage licenses and the pastor says that the church is not reserved this morning." He grinned. "We can get married right now."

Rosalee turned toward the rising sun, again feeling its rays shine into her, through her.

"Yes."

CHAPTER 56

JUBILEE, ALABAMA

Coleman and Rosalee Hightower walked hand-in-hand down the street. Some of the men had already carried the couple's meager belongings down to the mound to await the car.

When they reached the Town Hall, the mayor walked out to meet them. She wordlessly took Coleman's hand and walked with them.

The trio reached the mound and stopped. Pastor Henry joined them.

The stones were lustrous in the sun but quiet. No tales were left. Everyone who needed to know the mound's secret knew. The stones would remain mute, taking their cold hard knowledge to eternity or at least until time's gentle hand had reduced them to dust and their secret dissolved into the music of the earth.

The car arrived at the circle in front of the mound at precisely ten o'clock. Coleman stowed their bags in the trunk and turned to shake Pastor Henry's hand. Henry ignored his hand and gave him a warm hug.

"Coleman and Rosalee, I wish y'all the best," Henry said. "I believe that time will show that your coming here will lead to real healing in our town."

The mayor nodded. "We clearly have some old wounds. You have helped us get on the road to recovery."

Coleman smiled.

He said, "Jubilee has been a refuge for us. Thank you both."

Coleman opened the door for his wife. Rosalee turned and embraced the mayor. Pastor Henry gave her a hug.

"Where are you going?" Henry said.

Rosalee looked at Coleman and said, "New Orleans."

Coleman nodded and climbed into the seat beside Rosalee. The car drove around the circle, gravel crunching under its tires, and left a plume of dust in its wake as it sped back toward the main road.

Pastor Henry kept his eyes on the diminishing car and said, "That could've been us, a long time ago."

The mayor nodded.

She said, "It wasn't time, though. Twenty years too early."

Pastor Henry said, "I guess so." He turned to the mayor and said, "What's going to happen now?"

The mayor said, "Jubilee will never be the same. We've already seen change. Galen was sitting there in the church for the wedding. Lois Greene and Ephraim were there too."

She turned and looked up the street, toward the sunrise monument.

She said, "Back in 21, a cleansing with death was needed. The evil in some people of the town was too much to be allowed to live on."

The pastor said, "There was almost killing again."

The mayor nodded. "But, it didn't come to that. Galen couldn't see it, couldn't see what was needed, that the tool used back then was not needed this time."

Pastor Henry said, "What was the tool?"

The mayor said, "Last time, back in 21, the tool was death. This time, the tool was love. Jubilee was cleansed with love."

Henry turned. His eyes swept over the mound, down the road. The car was gone, the only trace being lingering dust floating down toward the river.

The pastor said, "Coleman said that what we have here is special, that it might help other places, that all of the riots and church burnings might go away if they had what we have."

The mayor said, "After what happened here last night, I don't know. Do you really think that there is anything here that can help? Do you think they can take something good from here and make it spread?"

The pastor turned and placed his hand on the mayor's arm.

"I don't know, Junebug. But those two are going to try."

CHAPTER 57

ATLANTA, GEORGIA, AUGUST, 2014

Coleman took a seat at the kitchen table to read the paper with his coffee, something he did every day before turning on the morning news programs.

He skimmed over the first few pages of the paper and his heart caught even before he fully recognized the name. A little story about a little place in the right lower corner of page three. No picture. Only a title – *LAKE TO COVER SMALL TOWN* – and a dateline – *JUBILEE, AL, AUG 8*.

He took a deep breath before reading the article. The floor seemed to rock a little, like he was standing on the deck of a ship in a light swell. He returned to the fine print.

Jubilee, Alabama's long history is coming to a close. The little town that rose around a plantation house will soon be at the bottom of a new reservoir that will serve the thirsty residents of Montgomery.

He looked away. His heart pounded. He tried to will himself to relax, to fight off the emotion he felt rising in his chest. His eyes went back to the paper.

Mayor Henry Smithson, Jr. says that all of the residents were paid a fair amount for their property. "We are happy that the state plans to name the reservoir Lake Jubilee. We feel that is a proper way to remember our little town."

Coleman gazed out of the window. Forms and faces from the past rose in the distance. A promise kept, a secret untold for all these years. A letter a few years before told him that Pastor Henry had died. Former Mayor Jefferson followed him to the grave a year later.

A protest by a group from the Tunica-Biloxi Native American Tribe threatened to derail the construction of the lake. The protesters were concerned about the desecration of an ancient mound that was in Jubilee. However, after a private ceremony and an undisclosed settlement, the group announced that they would drop their plans for a lawsuit.

Officials state that the reservoir is expected to be fully operational within a year.

From a kitchen drawer, Coleman retrieved a pair of scissors and a thick red-bound scrapbook. He carefully cut out the article. Opening the scrapbook, he encountered another newspaper article, a decades-old account of a defrocked senior Presbyterian pastor who had died in prison after being convicted of embezzling from the charity he headed.

He flipped past photos of great men – King, Jackson, Lewis, others – many of them standing with Rosalee, smiling up from the pages, shining through the years.

On a page near the end of the scrapbook, a newspaper headline stretched over the photo of a smiling black man, the first African-American president.

She was so proud of that. Said it was the dawning of a new era.

On the next page was her obituary, 2013. He ran his finger over her portrait, a black and white photo from a time before the cancer had changed her, had depleted her.

On the opposite page, he taped the article.

She got what she prayed for – peace.

Everybody at New Hope Baptist Church said that Rosalee had the peace of the Lord inside her. When she died, there were not enough seats for all of the people who came to honor her.

Coleman closed the book and put it back in the drawer. He walked to his big easy chair and pointed the remote at the television before plopping down. Immediately, yellow and orange flames flickered on the walls of the small den, reaching through the screen all the way from Ferguson to give their hellish color to his home.

He watched for several minutes and muted the TV.

I'm glad she didn't live to see this.

He thought of the workers, the dreamers, the people who hoped like his Rosalee had. They hoped for a world where people would get along with the business of living and not have time or strength for hate.

For a while there at the end, Rosalee thought they had made it. A world where a black man can be president was a different kind of world. That was what she thought and it made her last days happier.

He sat back and closed his eyes.

Was it all a lie? Or were we just fooling ourselves?

A single tear leaked out of the corner of his eye and ran down his face. He spoke her name to the empty room.

"Rosalee."

ABOUT THE AUTHOR

Timothy J. Garrett lives with his wife Cynthia near Athens, Georgia. He is a physician, a healthcare executive, and an amateur bass player. Visit his website at www.timothyjgarrett.com and follow him on Twitter at @drtimjgarrett.

Made in the USA
Columbia, SC
28 January 2020